Glory
Bishop

DEBORAH L. KING

Glory Bishop
Red Adept Publishing, LLC
104 Bugenfield Court
Garner, NC 27529
https://RedAdeptPublishing.com/

This is a work of fiction. Names, characters, places, and incidents either are the product of the author's imagination or are used fictitiously, and any resemblance to locales, events, business establishments, or actual persons—living or dead—is entirely coincidental.

Dedicated to my biggest fans: June Sevier Riley, Perry Riley,
Deborah Davis, and Richard Espy

Chapter 1

June 1983

"All right... all right... all right. Y'all don't hafta go home, but you hafta get the hell outta here." The old man shook his head. "Dammit... ya made me cuss in church! Y'all go on now. I got things to do. Can't be in here foolin' with y'all gals all night. I'm lockin' that gate in five minutes. I mean it for real this time!"

The group of teenaged girls giggled as they gathered their Bibles and purses. They always laughed at Mr. Nick, the church custodian. Every Thursday night, without fail, he'd threaten to lock them in the church if they didn't finish their Bible study by eight o'clock. Of course, they were always done with the Bible part by seven thirty, but the girl talk lasted until he kicked them out. They talked about all the things girls talked about. They talked about school and mean teachers and nice teachers and cute teachers. They talked about clear nail polish on their fingers and bright red on their toes—about soaps that smelled like perfume and perfume that smelled like candy and wearing real perfume only on their hands so they could wash it off before they got home. They talked about putting on makeup on the bus and using Wet-Naps to wash it off after school and about hiding shorts under their skirts and using tampons at school and leaving the top two buttons of their blouses undone.

And they talked about boys—the boys at school who they could never have and the boys at church they could never want. Gary Hayes, the cutest boy at church, was dumber than a box of rocks, and

1

Johnny Turner was a mama's boy who everybody pretended wasn't gay. Willie Clayton always snuck out of service before collection, and Andre Bradley thought he could sing but really couldn't. They talked about Kevin Flowers, the nicest boy in the church—he was smart and funny and short and ugly—and Rick Parker, whose voice made them all tingle, except he was fat and smelled funny. Malcolm Porter, the preacher's son, was much too old to be called a boy and always spoke in Bible verses because he knew the Bible by heart, and JT Jackson, the devil's son, had gotten arrested and had a girlfriend with a baby and always wore gym shoes to church. They talked about hiding notes and holding hands and sneaking kisses that made them melt. They dreamed about running away to college and seeing the world and falling in love and never having kids and wearing pants and dancing and smoking and drinking wine... and... and... and...

Their whispers, giggles, and squeals continued through the maze of rooms in the giant storefront church, moving down the aisles and out the front door. A few of the girls stopped to hug the grumpy old man shooing them out into the hot summer night.

Glory Bishop said goodbye to the girls at the bus stop and turned to walk the three blocks to her job at Herschel's Salon, one of Chicago's late-night beauty parlors. Its last customers came in at nine p.m., and Glory's shift started whenever she arrived. Herschel, the owner, worked the late nights, and Thursday nights were always busy with his extra-special customers getting ready for the weekend. Thursday nights at Herschel's was the best *girly* party on the South Side. Glory's mother would definitely not approve... if she knew about it. Glory mostly just did the laundry, cleaned up, and tried to avoid the party.

Seventy-Fifth Street was alive as always. The old-time Chicago neighborhood was full of new people, and sixteen-year-old Glory loved it all—the blinking light bulbs and pulsing neon, the closed stores with black metal gates and huge padlocks, and the big green buses and checkered taxis crawling through double-parked cars. Loud, laughing men in front of the liquor stores called her Church Girl and offered her free beer. The women in front of the beauty shops drank and laughed much louder than ladies should. Independent businessmen in fancy jogging suits discreetly hawked their wares. Independent businesswomen in fancy red dresses loudly hawked theirs. She loved the crowd inside and outside of Harold's Chicken, waiting as long as it took for the best food in town, the teenagers at the game room cheering and groaning as high scores were made and lost, and the taverns with the thumping music and smoke spilling out every time the door opened.

Glory loved the noise, the smoke, the music, the crowds—all of it. She dreamed of the day when she'd have her own apartment overlooking Seventy-Fifth Street. By day, she'd be a bright young college student, just like in the magazines. In the evenings, she'd work at the salon and then walk home to a third-floor apartment, spending nights up on the roof, looking down on the street lights or looking up at the stars.

Throbbing bass vibrated the doorknob Glory held as she waited to be buzzed into the salon. The music, flashing lights, and ribbon curtains covering the windows only hinted at the loud, colorful world inside.

"Good evening, Glory-Glory!" Herschel's deep voice boomed over the music. "Come on in! We're partying like it's 1999! Oo Oo!"

His heavy footsteps shook the floor as he danced among the occupied chairs, his clients in various stages of curling, waxing, plucking, and shaving, all cheering and bouncing along to the music. Glory laughed and clapped as the six-foot man in purple satin palazzo pants twirled around the room, his sheer, iridescent work smock glittering in the reflected light of the disco ball hanging from the shop ceiling. His great Jheri-curl wig, pinned up at the sides, created a giant shiny black mohawk cascading down his back. "We're Prince-ing, darling! It's just like drinking but with no hangovers! Oo Oo!"

"Hey, Glory-Glory!" the men in the chairs sang as Glory walked by them to the back rooms of the shop.

Past the purple beaded curtain and through the door marked Employees Only, Glory settled into her sanctuary. The first room—Herschel's combined office, kitchen, and storage room—smelled of the exotic herbs and spices he used to create his special lotions, perfumes, and hair tonics. That day's scent was vanilla, musk, and something woody. The second room—the lounge and laundry area—had deep, soft couches from the '70s, artwork from the '60s, tables from the '50s, and carpet from who knew when.

The giant washer and two dryers let her finish all the real work in about an hour, and then she'd spend the rest of her time reading from the collection of books she would never tell anybody she'd read. While the girls at church giggled over the dirty parts in the Old Testament, Glory read *Forever* by Judy Blume and learned about *The Best Part of a Man* from Xaviera Hollander. Whenever Herschel caught her reading, he'd say, "Shame on you, Glory-Glory. Your dear mother would not approve of you reading such things. Put it right back where you found it... as soon as you finish reading."

In the privacy of the stuffy lounge, Glory shrugged out of her long-sleeved blouse and peeled off her thick pantyhose. Then she twisted her skirt around and tightened the pins that held it up on the sides. Most of her clothes hung too loose on her slender five-foot-six-inch frame because her mother believed she'd grow into them. But Glory hadn't grown in two years. The scratchy, hot outfits always left ashy gray spots on her light-brown skin. Though she'd never tell the girls at church, she didn't hide shorts under her skirt, and her toe-nails weren't polished. Pulling the three cloth bands that bound her thick brown hair into a long fat ponytail, she used her fingers to fluff her hair out so she looked like the poster picture of Diana Ross. She laid her blouse and pantyhose over the back of a chair and grabbed an orange pop from the fridge. Twirling in her skirt and undershirt, Glory sang gospel songs and scrubbed and mopped to the beat of the worldly music, the ungodly words muffled by the closed door. The pounding rhythms and shouts from the party in the shop always made her laugh—they sounded exactly like church service.

Glory danced around the rooms, moving mounds of damp towels and greasy smocks that always managed to land too close to the clean towels. The day's lunch dishes were piled on the coffee and end tables. She'd never understand how people passing through the kitchen to get out to the shop didn't think to take their dishes with them. The trash overflowed with empty wine-cooler bottles, and the TV screen sizzled from a tape left playing in the VCR. Where most people would be irritated, Glory was elated. This was her time, her space, her peace.

She was standing at a softly rumbling dryer, folding "mountain fresh" scented towels, when she heard the door opening behind her.

"Hello, Miss Glory."

She continued folding, pretending not to hear.

"I said, *hello, Miss Glory.*"

She would not give that devil's son the satisfaction of responding.

The door closed, and she hoped he'd gone, but then he was behind her... his arms around her waist... his lips touching her shoulder. "Remember the first time you let me kiss you? You said you'd be my wife."

Glory shrugged off the kiss and tried to ignore him—tried not to notice his scent or relax in his arms. She tried not to respond to his voice... tried not to care.

His lips touched the back of her neck. "Remember the second time you let me kiss you? You said you'd be my girl."

Glory deliberately brushed his kiss from her neck and moved to the washing machine, careful to keep her back to him.

"Oh... so it's like that now, huh? No problem. I'll just sit down and watch you work. I've got all night. And you know, I always did appreciate you from behind, too."

Glory growled under her breath, taking her annoyance out on the wet towels she pulled from the washer. She heard him sigh loudly as he settled down on the old couch. She whispered a prayer for patience and strength.

"Know what?" he asked. "I feel like singing."

Glory continued her work and tried to ignore him as he flubbed his way through "Ribbon in the Sky" and "Isn't She Lovely," but when he started singing "Brick House," she threw down the towel she was folding and gripped the edge of the table.

"Josiah Jackson, you leave me alone. Right now!"

"Oh... so you're talking to me now, huh? I win big. I get to hear your pretty voice and look at your fine a—"

"No!" Glory turned to face him, arms folded, seething, channeling every bit of hurt and anger into a glare that she wished would burn him to cinders. "No. I'm not talking to *you*. I'm asking the devil to leave me alone! I'm asking Satan himself to leave me alone and never speak to me again."

"Well," he said, standing and moving toward her. "Your prayer is gonna be answered. I'm leaving for the navy tomorrow."

He smiled. He actually smiled. That no-good lying two-timing devil smiled his smug smile—that *I'm the finest boy in the world, and I know you agree* smile. That *I win* smile.

Glory hated that smile. And she loved that smile. And all she could do was squeeze her eyes shut to keep the tears from spilling out.

"How could you do that to me, JT?" she whispered. "How?"

"I'm sorry, Miss Glory." He tried to take her hand, but she pushed him away. "I'm leaving in the morning, and I need to make things right with you. Please, just listen to me. You don't hafta talk to me. You don't hafta forgive me. Just listen. Then if you still hate me, I swear I'll never bother you again."

Glory opened her eyes. The smug smile was gone—no mocking, no joking, only the slightest hint of a plea in his voice and in his eyes—the force of will that always made her trust him... or used to make her trust him.

Glory sat away from him on the couch, arms still folded, not looking at him. She listened to his tale of a weekend with his cousins and wine and reefa and the twenty-two-year-old next door and his not really remembering it until his aunt called his mother about a baby that looked like him. She tried to stay angry and to push him away when he knelt in front of her, begging forgiveness. She tried not to see the tears in his eyes.

"Why didn't you tell me?" Glory asked. "Why didn't you tell me when it happened? Why did I hafta hear it whispered in church... from those stupid gossips who think you're the devil?"

"I was scared. I didn't want to hurt you. I knew you'd be mad, and I couldn't fix it. I didn't have a do-over for this." He dropped his head and laughed a little. "I was outta Barbie shoes." JT laid his head on her lap, and despite herself, Glory began stroking his hair.

"Why haven't you been back to church? It's been months. Your mother brings the baby with her. Why don't you come? Are you ashamed?"

"No," JT said, a bit of anger in his voice. "I just don't believe in their God no more. I made mistakes—I always make mistakes, but my God forgives me. That church don't. You said it yourself: they think I'm the devil. They want me to stand up there and apologize for having a son. Not happening. The only people I need to apologize to are my mama, you, and maybe my son. Everything else is between me and God."

"I hate when you talk like that. How can you question God, Josiah?" Glory stood up, pushing him away.

"I'm not questioning God. I think I'm actually understanding God." He followed her to a dryer, helping move the warm towels to the folding table. "Think about it. God made this big, beautiful world, and that church tells you that loving the life God gave you, or anything God made, is evil. I think that's dissin' everything God does right now—"

"What's her name?" She would pray for him, but she couldn't stand there and listen to him blaspheme. "The mother. What's her name?"

"Um... it's Michelle." His voice wavered slightly when he spoke the name of his baby's mother. He was all confident, challenging God, but not when he talked about his own sin. *Good. He should be ashamed of himself.*

"You could marry her. Give your son a proper fam—"

"Girl, are you crazy? God, no! She already got three kids. She don't want no part of this baby, and... well... just no." Before Glory could pick up another towel, JT pulled her into his arms, mischief shining in his eyes. "And besides... I'm already married, remember, *Mrs.* Glory?"

"Well, actually," Glory said to that self-satisfied smiling face she loved and hated, "my daddy said that since you didn't ask him first, and you didn't have a job, we're not really married."

"But you let me kiss you, so we are." He kissed her lightly on the lips. She didn't pull away.

"But you tricked me, and we were five. So, we're not."

AFTER THE KITCHEN AND lounge were cleaned and the laundry done, the party out in the salon was still going strong. The music had changed to something soft and romantic. Slow dancing with JT, Glory found herself dangerously caught up in the moment.

"We should stop." Glory pulled herself from his arms, reluctantly breaking the kiss that threatened to go too far. "Want a drink?" she asked, moving toward the kitchen. She grabbed two orange pops and a bowl of grapes from the fridge. Herschel always kept grapes in the fridge. She paused for a minute to enjoy a cool blast of air from the freezer.

Stopping in the doorway to watch JT load a tape into the VCR, Glory noticed that he seemed to have grown bigger in the two months since she'd last seen him. His gray jogging shorts with the thin white stripe showed off well-defined leg muscles. The matching jacket was unzipped to the waist, and by the light of the glowing TV, the dark skin on his bare chest looked like steel. His shoulders were broader, too—his arms stretched the sleeves of the gray jacket.

"You've been working out?" Glory asked, handing him the orange pop.

"Yeah. Hafta be ready for Uncle Sam." He accepted the cold can from her. They sat on the couch in silence as the opening credits of *The Ten Commandments* silently flashed on the TV screen.

"How long you gonna be gone?"

"Three years."

"Three years?" Until two months ago, Glory had rarely gone three days without seeing him. She took a deep breath and forced back tears. "Your son's not gonna know you when you get back."

"I know, but he'll get to know me again. Hell, I might not know me when I get back. I'm gonna talk to him every week. Mom is taping my pictures to the wall around his crib."

"Who's gonna take care of him? His mother?" Glory hoped she didn't sound jealous.

"Nah… I told you, she don't want him. My mother's gonna keep him. My dad's gonna give her back child support every month to take care of him. She's still mad at him for suggesting I join the army. It's a good idea, but I decided to go for the navy. Not trying to wind up in Vietnam or someplace like my dad was."

"Bad things happen in the navy, too."

"Yeah, but not up close."

"What're you gonna do there, in the navy?" Glory tried to picture JT as the sailor in *An Officer and a Gentleman*. The image made her heart ache.

"Well, first I'm goin' up to Great Lakes for boot camp, then probably down south for more training and school. I'm gonna work on airplanes. Probably on an aircraft carrier."

"Is that safe?" Glory felt like her questions were stupid, but she wanted to keep him talking.

"Hmph… the boat's bigger than a cruise ship with big guns and an airport. We could hit a target from two hundred miles away. Nobody could hit us without a bigger, badder boat, and we're the biggest and baddest. So yeah, I'm pretty safe." He took another swallow, draining the can.

"I don't want you to go," Glory finally said. Her words came through a choked sob. She didn't care that he saw her cry. She didn't care that she sounded like a baby. She didn't care when he took the can from her hand and placed it on the table and took her in his arms as she cried on his shoulder. "Why do you hafta go right now?"

"I get a bonus if I sign up now. I get to pick the job and school I want. I even get to pick where I live when I'm not on the boat, and—"

Glory interrupted him with a long kiss.

"I thought we needed to stop," he said, catching his breath.

"We do." Glory lay back and pulled him down on top of her. They probably had two hours left, and then he would be gone. She drew him closer, kissed him harder, tried to devour him in that kiss. Lying beneath him on that old couch by the light of the silent TV—her mouth locked to his, her body pressed to his, her heart beating with his—Glory held on to him for dear life.

"Glory," JT panted into her ear, "this is too—"

Glory pulled him closer, kissing, sucking, inhaling him, needing to touch every part of him. She moved her hands under his open jacket and around his back. His muscles were tight, almost trembling, his skin moist with sweat...

"Oh, God, Glory—"

She moved her hands down his back, moving herself against his growing hardness.

"Girl... slow down..." he whispered. "Remember... we hafta... stop—"

"I don't wanna stop," she whispered back. Their lips touched again. Glory wanted... *needed* more of him than his kiss. She needed all of him. She needed to hold him... absorb him... consume him... pull him into the very core of herself... commit his whole being to memory.

JT pulled back from her, peeled off his jacket, and tossed it to the floor. "Wait." He paused, his breathing heavy, sweat beading at his brow. "This isn't right—not here, not like this."

Glory reached up and pulled his face to hers so their foreheads were touching, their lips inches apart. "Josiah Jackson, you're leaving me. I need you, and you're leaving me."

"Are you sure?" He lifted himself slightly. "Really sure, Miss Glory?"

She felt his hand tremble against her belly as he reached between them, fumbling with the drawstring in his waistband.

She kissed him again, this time softly, slowly, shifting her body to allow him to settle comfortably between her legs. "Yes."

As JT moved inside her, Glory closed her eyes and prayed through the pain, prayed he could feel how much she loved him, prayed she was doing it right. She prayed not to the angry God who would condemn her for surrendering her virginity to the devil on a couch in the back room of a salon but to JT's loving God who would forgive her impatience and honor her love and bring him back to her.

PEEING BURNED A LITTLE. When Glory thought about what she'd just done—what they'd just done—her stomach quivered, and she smiled. When she wiped, she saw only the slightest tinge of pink on the tissue. No proof of her former virginity. No bloody sheet. No visible evidence of sin. *So maybe it wasn't sin?* Glory laughed at her own joke as she finished up and left the bathroom.

Herschel stood waiting for her, blocking the hallway, freezing Glory in place with his folded arms and serious look. "Well, Glory-Glory. Is all of your work done back there?"

"Um... yes, si—" Glory always felt awkward answering the man in shimmering purple. *Sir* was definitely not right, and *ma'am* just felt wrong. "Yes, Herschel. I'm all done."

"Took a little longer than usual, didn't you?"

"Um... well... JT... we talked a lot... but it's still early—"

Before she could finish her sentence, Glory found herself enveloped in big, muscular arms, crushed against Herschel's huge padded bosom.

"Oh, Glory-Glory, relax, darling. I'm just messing with you." He rocked back and forth, stroking Glory's hair. "I just wanna make sure you're okay." He placed his hands on Glory's shoulders, holding her at arm's length, looking deeply into her eyes. "You are okay, right, darling?"

Glory dropped her eyes, willing the blush not to rise in her face, suddenly understanding that Herschel knew.

"Oh, please, darling, no need to blush here. I have much better things to do than spy on teenagers in heat, but, sweetie, you walkin' like you threw your hip out. You cain't go home walkin' like Two-Dollar Tootie. C'mon. Hands on your hips... that's right, darling. Roll 'em around... work it on out!"

Glory couldn't help but giggle as she and Herschel stood in the narrow hallway, shaking their butts like floozies, Herschel's padded hips bouncing off the walls on either side.

"C'mon, Glory-Glory... can you go down low... all the way to the flo'!" Hips rolling, butts bouncing, they tumbled to the floor in a laughing heap. Herschel, coughing and fanning himself, patted Glory's knee. "Sit with me for a second, darling. I've got a present for you."

Sitting on the floor beside Herschel, Glory wondered, not for the first time, how such a tall man could fold himself to sit so gracefully in the smallest spaces. She looked at the two strips of pills in Herschel's outstretched hand.

"You take five tonight and five more twelve hours later."

"What are they for?" Glory asked, although she thought she knew the answer.

"Make sure you get your period." Herschel forced the sharp foil strips into Glory's hand.

Glory closed her hand around the pills. Having a baby hadn't crossed her mind. *God's punishment for Eve's sin. Painful childbirth because she disobeyed God and tempted Adam.* Maybe the devil had held back her blood so she would think *doing it* with JT wasn't bad.

Herschel closed his hand over Glory's. "The timing is very important, Glory-Glory. You hafta take 'em twelve hours apart. Not too soon and not too late. You'll probably get a bad tummy ache, but don't throw 'em up. Take 'em with food or something, but not milk—just crackers and a bit of water."

Grunting, Herschel stood up and pulled Glory to her feet. "You didn't do nothin' wrong... but you need to take care of yourself. You come see me tomorrow, and we'll get you set up so you don't hafta take *emergency* pills. And grab some of those rubbers back there." He patted Glory's head and danced his way back to the party that was still going strong in the salon. "Try the purple ones. They're grape and delicious... ooo, ooo!"

Glory returned to the back rooms. Everything was silent and dark except for the hum and flicker of the TV. JT sat at the edge of the couch, his clothes back in place, jacket zipped up to the collar. He placed a wine-cooler bottle on the table a little too hard, beside another empty one. Glory paused in the doorway, not wanting to startle him. His shoulders slumped, his head bowed. He looked sad... broken.

"Remember when I tricked you when we were little?" JT asked softly, wistfully, staring into the flickering darkness. "You kicked my *ass*, and I still wouldn't take it back. My dad said it wasn't cool to make a girl marry you, especially if she could kick your ass." He took another swallow from the bottle. "You know I was the only boy in fifth grade with Barbie dolls in my backpack?" He looked up.

She nodded.

"My mother found 'em and called my dad. He wasn't surprised that it was you again. He said *you* were lucky to have such a good *friend*. Told my mother not to mess with those dolls." JT took another long swallow.

Glory smiled at the memory. The Saturday after her father died, when she was nine years old, her mother had made her throw out all her "worldly" toys. She'd cried all weekend after she carried the big pink Barbie case down to the dumpster. Monday morning, on the playground before school, Josiah Jackson became her superhero when he'd pulled a brown paper bag with her dolls from his backpack. She kept them at school during the week, and he took them home to his house every weekend. He'd called it joint custody. Whenever she was sad, he managed to produce a Barbie shoe to make her smile.

"That day in church, when your mother slapped you and busted your lip? I wanted to kill her. I even asked my dad if he had a gun. He guessed it was about you. He told me I couldn't go around killing everybody who hurt you." He took another swallow. "Reminded me I couldn't protect you from jail." He placed the empty bottle on the table.

Glory sat down on the couch beside him. Rubbing his back, she watched his shoulders tremble.

He turned to face her with tears falling. "I messed up, Miss Glory. You were supposed to be first. When I think about my first time, it's supposed to be you. My baby's mama ain't supposed to be some drunk ho I don't even remember. It's supposed to be you." He pressed his fists against his forehead. "It's always been you, my whole life... you... everything is you... you... you..."

Glory tried to hold him, but he quickly stood up, wiping his tears with his fists. He straightened up, stretching, moving his shoulders, looking tough. She stood in front of him and wrapped her arms around his waist. She didn't loosen her grip until she felt his arms around her.

"I messed up so bad, Miss Glory. I literally fucked up." He squeezed her, and she felt his lips press against the top of her head. "I'll never forgive myself for hurting you."

"It's okay, JT," Glory said, holding back her own tears. "I forgive you, and your God forgives you."

THE RADIO CLOCK SHOWED eleven thirty at night when JT pulled his car up to the curb in front of a shuttered storefront. A dim light shone in the entry hall that led to the upstairs apartments where Glory lived with her mother. A few mailboxes hung open, and a small wastebasket sat overflowing with junk mail. Glory laid her forehead against the car window, not wanting to move, not wanting to get out, staring at her building's heavy wood-and-glass door, knowing that when she walked through it, JT would be gone.

She leaned back in the seat and looked at him. He hadn't said a word the whole ride. The nighttime mist had turned to drizzle, and the shadows from the raindrops on the window became dark tears sliding down the reflectoin of his face. He still looked like the little boy who told her to close her eyes and say "I do" and then kissed her. Since it had happened in church, it meant they were married, he'd said. She punched him until a teenager stopped her, but he wouldn't take it back. He'd started calling her *Mrs.* Glory because that was what you called married ladies.

"Are you sure you're okay, Miss Glory? I swear, I didn't plan that." His whispered question sounded just like the ten-year-old boy who'd rescued her Barbie dolls from the dumpster—the boy who could light up her day with Barbie shoes.

"I'm fine. It only hurt a little. I know you didn't plan it. I wanted *you*. I don't regret anything," Glory said, though that was a lie. She regretted waiting and being angry at him for two months. She regretted not being able to go with him.

"Are you gonna wait for me, Miss Glory?" His voice was low and unsteady, almost like the thirteen-year-old boy who'd wiped blood from her split lip her after mother had slapped her. He'd put his arm around her and asked her to be his girlfriend. When she said yes, he'd kissed her, split lip and all.

She slid closer to him, took his hand from the steering wheel, and pulled his arm around her. She slid her arm under his jacket and around his waist, basking in his warmth. "Yes. I'll be right here when you come back." Glory wished that were true. She prayed that would be true. She desperately needed that to be true as much as she needed him not to go.

"I hafta do it," he said in answer to her unspoken plea. "I can't be a good father now. I'm seventeen. All I know how to do is play basketball and *Ms. Pac-Man*. I cain't do nothin' for my son. I cain't do nothin' for you." He held her tighter, trembling, like he'd done an hour earlier when they made love again for real... just like when they'd lain down together... when they touched... when they gasped... when they kissed and they trembled together.

She kissed him again. She tried to reassure him and to thank him in that kiss. She tried to pour herself into his soul in that kiss. Then she laid her head on his shoulder, and they listened to the growing storm as the blue light of the radio clock rolled over to midnight.

Chapter 2

"**M**iss Glory, wake up!"

"Hmmm." Glory sighed. "I don't wanna go in yet... did the rain stop?" She squeezed her eyes shut tighter because lying against JT was exactly where she wanted to be.

"Glory, wake up. It's morning!" JT shook her, and it took a moment for Glory to understand.

"Wha... what?" Glory looked around. The water drops on the windshield sparkled in the sunrise. As Louis Armstrong sang the last notes of "Wonderful World," the radio clock showed 5:37 a.m.

In the space of a few seconds, Glory went from bliss to confusion—from sadness to resignation to quiet terror. It was sunrise, and their last night was over. It was sunrise, and she'd spent the night in the car with Josiah. It was sunrise, and her mother always said only whores let the sunrise catch them.

Glory laid her head back against the seat. JT unlocked the doors, opened and closed the driver's side, opened the passenger side to help her out of the car, and closed the door behind her. Each *thunk* matched her heartbeat and sounded so final. That sound meant their time was running out.

Standing at the door to her building, looking up at JT with the morning sun behind him, Glory imagined herself the heroine of a novel sending her lover to freedom while she stayed behind. She would be brave and not let him see her cry. "You need to get home," Glory said. "What time are you getting picked up?"

"Six thirty." JT pulled her into his arms. "But I don't wanna let you go yet."

"I don't want you to let me go." Glory pulled away. "But I'm in enough trouble as it is. I hafta go in now."

"Miss Glory, will you marry me for real? I mean for your eighteenth birthday. We don't hafta wait three years. I'll come home to visit. It'll be me and you and JJ. I'll get us a house, or we could live someplace warm or overseas—anywhere you want. Will you?"

Glory stopped holding back her tears. "Yes," she whispered. "I wish I could go with you now."

"I wish I had a ring for you." JT wiped her tears with his thumb then dug his wallet out of his jacket pocket. "I know it's not a ring, but I started keeping these for emergencies. Never know when a man might need one." He held up a neon-orange Barbie shoe.

Miserable as she was, Glory couldn't help but smile.

THEIR APARTMENT WAS mostly dark. All the windows were covered by black plastic bags and heavy curtains, closed to prying eyes and the evils of the world and sunshine and light. In the immaculate apartment Glory shared with her mother, the only music came from the few gospel albums she'd been allowed to keep after her father died. The TV had been long silenced, its severed cord still coiled on top, and even the telephone was gone, all to keep out the evils of the world.

The first thing Glory noticed, above the faint scent of pine cleaner, was the strong smell of sage and burnt paper. Having quit smoking a long time ago, Mary Bishop refused to ever again surrender to tobacco. Instead, she took deep, heavy drags on tightly rolled scraps of brown paper. She wouldn't drink coffee, either, saying it was just as bad as getting hooked on cigarettes. Instead, she would put two or three spoonfuls of sage into a cup of boiling water and sip her *tea*.

The only lights burning were over the stove in the kitchen and in the Sacred Heart of Jesus candle that hadn't been lit since Glory's father had died.

In the semidarkness, she could make out her mother's sleeping form beside the plastic-covered couch. She had fallen asleep kneeling on a pillow, her face on a prayer cloth, her right hand resting on the huge family Bible.

Glory moved quietly to her bedroom and quickly shed her clothes. She slipped into her bathrobe, dropping the foil strips of pills into her robe pocket. She always showered after work. The exotic scents of evenings at the salon lingered on her, and godly women didn't walk around smelling like that. Joy, sadness, and guilt roiled inside her. She'd been with JT. They'd made love, and she'd spent the night beside him. He was leaving for three years, and she'd hardly kissed him goodbye. And her mother had been worried enough to light the Jesus candle.

Standing under the warm spray, Glory touched the hickey just below her collarbone, smiling at the memory of how JT had touched her. She moved her hands over her body, exploring the familiar places yet feeling brand-new. It was no longer a girl's body but a woman's. Moving her hands lower, she felt that new tingle, the one she'd felt with JT on the couch... the one that made her tremble...

"Satan! You will not have this child!"

Glory barely had time to react when her mother ripped the shower curtain from the rod. A moment later, the lash of an extension cord burned against her bare back. She staggered, managing to turn off the hot water as she fell to her knees at the bottom of the tub.

"I bind you in the name of Jesus!" Her mother's voice was the angry growl of a determined warrior.

In the fetal position, Glory crouched, shivering under the spray of the cold water.

"Demon of lies! I bind you in the name of Jesus!"

Even as the rough cord raised stinging welts across her back, the cold water cooled them.

"Demon of dark! I bind you in the name of Jesus!"

The lashes kept coming... harder, sharper, burning deeper.

"Demon of dishonor! I bind you in the name of Jesus!"

Soon, even the cold water gave no relief, and the lashes kept coming.

"Demon of rebellion! I bind you in the name of Jesus!"

Finally, Glory cried real tears.

"Demon of disobedience! I bind you in the name of Jesus!"

Glory cried because of the burning, unrelenting pain.

"Demon of sin! I bind you in the name of Jesus!"

She cried because her only savior was leaving, and she would endure a lot more before he came back.

"That's right, baby. Cry it out. Call on the Lord. Fight the demons! Jesus!"

She called on Jesus because that was what her mother wanted to hear and because demons didn't call on Jesus. Glory always tried to keep count, but she never could. Jesus had gotten thirty-nine lashes—her mother never stopped before forty. When it finally ended—the casting out of demons, the purging—her mother calmly left the bathroom, closing the door behind her. Glory stayed curled on the tub floor, watching pink-tinged water wind its way to the drain, shivering until the water ran clear.

MARY BISHOP LEANED against the padlocked door that led to the back porch, its plywood-covered window decorated with faded flowered curtains and a framed picture of Jesus. "Where you been?" she asked when Glory, still shivering in her beige bathrobe, sat down at the kitchen table.

Glory sipped the steaming cup of tea her mother placed in front of her, her mind still on the ten tiny pills she'd just washed down the drain. The bitterness of the sage could not be hidden, even by honey and lime.

"Look at me, girl. Where you been?"

Glory looked at her mother's swollen face. Her eyes were red and puffy, bloodshot from crying.

"Look. In. My. Eyes. Where. You. Been?"

Glory would look into her mother's eyes, and she would tell the truth... because her mother believed a demon couldn't lie if it looked you in the eye. "I was out front in the car. We fell asleep talking... waiting for the rain to stop."

"'We' who?"

"Me and Josiah." Glory didn't break eye contact, and she silently prayed there was nothing throwable within her mother's reach. "He's going to the navy today, and he wanted to say goodbye," she added quickly. "He showed up at the shop... and we just drove home and talked in the car."

"That's all? In the car all night—all y'all did was talk?"

"No, ma'am," Glory answered. "When we woke up and it was morning..." Her mother raised an eyebrow. "I kissed him goodbye."

"Um-hmph," her mother grunted, the edge of suspicion in her voice barely hiding her relief.

"He's gonna be gone for three years. He might not even come back." Glory dropped her eyes, hoping she could keep from crying.

"Well, baby, you just hafta pray for him to be safe." Her mother kissed the top of her head as she walked past Glory and out of the kitchen, apparently satisfied. "Maybe while he's gone, God'll touch his heart and drive all the evil outta him."

Glory sipped the bitter sweet-and-sour tea and didn't answer.

"Malcolm Porter came by yesterday," her mother called from the living room. "He brought me some choir stuff, and he asked after you. He such a nice young man. He gon' be pastor one day, too, you know. C'mon. Lock this door."

"Yes, ma'am," Glory answered, careful to offer no encouragement. Her mother stood waiting for her at the door.

"Ya know, baby, he's at the age where he's lookin' for a good, godly woman. He's gon' make somebody a fine husband. Bein' first lady of a church like ours ain't nothin' to sneeze at."

"Please, Mama, don't make me see Malcolm. I'm too young to think about stuff like that."

"You never too young to be a godly woman, and you never too young to think about your future."

Glory kissed her mother's cheek and locked the door behind her. Looking around the living room, she saw the extent of her mother's worry: the ashtray overflowing with butts of burnt brown paper, the Bible opened to the book of Job, and the pictures. They lay side by side in front of the still-burning Jesus candle—her brothers and sisters. Five small children—four chubby faces smiling at her from black-and-white photos in gold metal frames and one peaceful little angel dressed in white, sleeping in a bronze frame—a lock of curly black hair in the corner—mounted on a stand with a pair of tiny bronzed shoes. These were children she'd never met, children who had died twenty-five years before Glory was born.

This time, Glory's tears were only of guilt and shame. She'd been letting Satan cloud her mind with lust, lead her astray, and cause her to sin, while her mother had been terrified, reliving her worst nightmares, praying that her last child wasn't dead.

Chapter 3

"I heard he left 'cause he got somebody else pregnant."

"Uh-huh. He had a court date, and he was goin' to jail."

"That's what he get for hangin' out on the West Side with all them low-life heathens."

"Well, you know, that's where his daddy is from."

"Yeah. Like father, like son."

Glory ignored the talk. Every Sunday during service, the church prayed for his safety and deliverance, and every Sunday after service, the church gossiped about why JT Jackson had really left. In five weeks, the stories had grown ridiculous: pregnant girls, drug deals, robberies, murders. And every Sunday, Glory pretended not to hear them. It had been five weeks since their night. Five weeks since they said goodbye. Five weeks since she washed the pills down the drain. Five weeks... and not a word from him.

Her periods never came regularly, but Glory was sure it had been much too long since the last one. She had a few cramps, and she never got cramps—the books said minor cramping was normal. She walked carefully from the church to the salon, stepping lightly, holding her breath when she passed smokers, staying close to the buildings to avoid too much sun and the fumes from the passing cars.

On Seventy-Fifth Street, the only differences between day and night were the sunlight and the ages of the people. The old men outside of the liquor stores offered her free beer. Through the propped-open doors of the taverns, she could hear old men playing pool and old women laughing loudly. The bored CTA supervisor would trade a few bus transfers for a bit of conversation. The arcades were mostly empty except for the two or three dropouts and the old lady behind the counter. The salesmen on the street corners offered newspapers and bags of fruit, the old Mexican guy pushed a hot tamale cart, and every second storefront had somebody outside selling snow cones or popsicles or ice cups.

Weekday afternoons, the salon would fill with old ladies—some hairdressers, some customers, and some just visitors trying to get out of the summer heat. They laughed too loudly at the women walking by, told dirty jokes about the men walking by, cussed at all the kids running by, and constantly yelled at the TV because Asa Buchanan was doing dirt on *One Life to Live*. Glory would tiptoe quietly by them to the back rooms, always careful not to draw their attention.

Heading into the salon's back room on a hot July day, she was hit by the overpowering smell of roses as she opened the door.

"Good afternoon, Glory-Glory!" Herschel called out, making himself heard over the music and the drone of six electric fans. "Happy rose day!" He stood at the stove in front of a large pot, not wearing a wig that day—just a flowered bandana tied over cornrows, matching the bright-yellow lab coat and yellow-trimmed safety goggles. He looked like a big, sunshiny mad scientist. Even with the back door open and a fan in every window, the room smelled strongly of roses. "Grab some gloves, and finish pulling the petals off the ones in the sink, please. And how are you this beautiful day?"

"Fine, and you, Herschel?" Glory pulled on green gardening gloves and set to work on the mound of roses in the double sink. Many were wilted, but a few were big, full blossoms at the peak of their midsummer beauty. Glory tried not to feel like a murderer, ripping their heads off and plunging them into the sink full of ice water. "How many did you get?"

"I'm awesome today, darling! One hundred fifty pounds of assorted roses. Careful with the hips... any word yet?" Herschel turned down the music, eyes rolling at the screaming laughter of the women out in the shop.

"No, not yet. I know he's busy... getting used to navy life and stuff. His mother only got that one phone call and one letter." Glory sighed. "Okay. I'm not worried or anything like that," she added quickly. "He's probably just... you know... *ouch!*"

"Watch out for the thorns. No protection is perfect, darling. Sleeping Beauty was your age when a single prick changed her whole life."

Glory moved away from the sink, glad that the thorn let her change the subject, wondering if Herschel's intense stare was concern or suspicion. "I think the evil witch changed Sleeping Beauty's life when she was a baby. The spindle just—"

"Nooo, darling," Herschel interrupted slowly, deliberately. "She knew the dangers... and she could have avoided it. She could have protected herself, but she chose to take the chance, and she got priiicked... and changed her whole life. Whatever she wanted to be, whatever she wanted to do with her life, changed... all... because... of... a... prick."

Glory moved back to the sink, carefully avoiding eye contact with Herschel. "How do you know?" she asked, holding the thorny stems more carefully this time, slowly peeling the petals and leaves.

"Somebody's been moving the books around on the third shelf, and you left a bus transfer for a bookmark. You're the only one here who takes that bus."

Glory hung her head, embarrassed at her own carelessness. The books on the third shelf were women's health books. Medical stuff, nutritional stuff... maternity stuff. The day after she washed the emergency pills down the drain, she started studying all she could about being pregnant.

"Don't hang your head. Look at me, Glory-Glory. Did you take the pills like I told you?"

Glory turned to face Herschel. The disappointment in the tall man's face felt almost as bad as the righteous fury of her mother and God. "No, Herschel. I threw 'em out."

"I see." Herschel lowered his goggles. "Why, pray tell, did you do that?"

"I don't know," Glory sighed. "I was mad, I guess." She turned around and continued pulling the rose petals. "I just want him to come home and—"

"And you think being pregnant is gonna do that?"

"Well... no, but..."

"But what? Oooh, waaait a minute. You don't really trust him to come home *to you*, do you? You're tryin' to trap him?"

Glory didn't know what to say. She wouldn't turn to face Herschel. She couldn't face him, suddenly feeling very stupid. "No, that's not it. I just... just... I was mad, for real. We fell asleep in the car, and my mother thought I was dead, and I got in a lot of trouble, and I was gonna take 'em, but... but—"

"But what?" Herschel said in the deep male voice he only used when he didn't believe her.

"I shoulda been JJ's mother," Glory whispered. "JT even said so. Me, not some tramp who doesn't want him. If he doesn't come back... if he gets killed or something... I won't have anything."

Glory felt a heavy hand gently squeeze her shoulder. "Darling, I know you miss him, and three years seems like forever... but it's not. Having a baby at seventeen, though—that *is* forever. Everything would change. Your whole life would hafta revolve around a baby, and babies don't stay babies long. You wouldn't have time to *get yo'self together*, because babies don't wait for you to finish growing up. They grow up right with you." Herschel moved to the sink and started packing red rose petals into another giant pot. "The problem is, Glory-Glory, by the time a teenager learns how to teach a child, it's too late. The child is already a teenager."

"But I'm not like that," Glory said, still peeling rose petals and carefully avoiding the thorns. "There's nothin' I want to do more than be the good wife and mother. The Bible says—"

"Hmph. I know exactly what the Bible says about *the good wife*. Her value is above rubies. She runs the house and tends her family and makes money and is educated and works twenty-four hours a day." Herschel carried the pot over to the stove and set it down with a loud *thunk*. "But that good wife had servants, and she definitely was a wife *before* she was a mother."

"But—"

Herschel slammed a bowl of ice down on top of the pot. "Y'all be killing me with this *Bible says I need a man to save me* madness. The Bible was written *by men* at a time when women were property. Women have come too far to still be trapped in that mess."

"How would you know?" Glory mumbled a little too loudly. "You're not even a real woman."

"Little. Girl." Herschel slowly turned to face her. "*You* are not a real woman, either. *You* are a seventeen-year-old *girl* who could one day be a great woman."

Glory fought back tears as she ripped the heads from the roses, ignoring the thorns poking through her gloves. Having a baby would prove that she belonged with Josiah. She wouldn't need to stand up and apologize to the church for sin because in her heart, they were already married. She would have the baby and finish school and work at the shop and go to college... and when Josiah came home...

Tears flowing again, Glory felt Herschel's strong arms hugging her from behind.

"Listen to me, Glory-Glory," Herschel said, "I don't mean to lecture you, but you are too smart for this. A real woman—the good wife—would have a lot more than a baby for her man to come home to. While JT's gone, you'll finish school and build a life for yourself and make sure you can be the good wife when he comes home."

Glory wiped her tears with the back of her damp glove. It seemed like everything made her cry lately. She smiled a little. Maybe it was hormones. "Well, it's been a long time since my period, so..."

"How long?" Herschel went to the sink and gathered yellow rose petals into a colander. "Move those stems to that box over there. I hafta take 'em up north when we're done with 'em."

Glory moved a bunch of stems to a big cardboard box near the open window. Through the fan, she caught a glimpse of a teenager jumping rope. The girl was about her age, with a pregnant belly bouncing well below her short T-shirt. She seemed to be having fun until a toddler wandered into the ropes, causing her to miss. The girl snatched the child up by the front of her shirt, yelling her frustration. The toddler kicked and screamed until the teenager put her down.

"I said, how late are you?" Herschel followed Glory's gaze. "Oh, that's Shay. She act like she don't know how to *not* get pregnant. Stupid heffa. Already got two, and she about to drop another one. Her mother always in here sayin', 'Please pray for my new grandbaby.' I'm prayin' for her to get some sense." Herschel turned back to his work, tossing the petals in the colander. "Did you take a test?"

"She's a terrible mother," Glory said, silently praying for the toddler and the unborn baby. "And no, I didn't take a test yet. I don't know how late I am. They only come every few months, anyway. Last one was around Easter."

"Easter? And y'all did it a month ago?"

"Five weeks." Glory couldn't take her eyes off the frustrated pregnant teenager. She winced when the girl roughly shoved a bottle into the crying toddler's mouth. How would that baby grow up to honor her mother if her mother wasn't honorable? Glory went back to moving the rose stems. "Five weeks and four days."

"So"—Herschel stuffed the yellow rose petals into a food processor—"you don't know if you're late. This could be your normal schedule?"

"Well, yeah. But it's not. I just feel different. I had cramps for a while, and a little soreness up top, too. And the book said—"

"Hold up." Herschel pulsed the food processor a few times, adding two or three drops of oil between pulses. Then he let it run for twenty seconds until the petals were a dark-mustard-colored goop. "Okay, first we need to see what's going on. Look in that cabinet over my desk in the box that says Daisy. Grab one of the kits in there."

Glory took off her work gloves and went to the old metal teacher's desk where Herschel handled salon and women's business. It sat as a small divider between the two rooms. In the white metal cabinet above the desk, Glory found a cardboard box marked Daisy in green crayon. She reached in and pulled out a white plastic bag stamped "hCG."

"The white bags?" Glory called, trying to be heard over the whir of the food processor.

"Yeah. Open it and get out the little cup. Wash your hands and go pee in the cup, then bring it back and set it on the desk." Herschel went back to pureeing rose petals.

Glory's hands shook as she opened the bag. She caught a vial just before it crashed to the floor. Minutes later, she watched as Herschel mixed the test liquid with three drops of pee and set the vial in the holder.

"Now," Herschel said, heading back to the stove to check the simmering rose petals, "we wait two hours." Glory stayed at the desk, staring at the mirror in the bottom of the test holder. If she saw a brown circle, she and Josiah would be parents. "C'mon now, Glory-Glory. We still have plenty to do! I set the timer. Staring at it won't make it go any faster."

Glory pulled herself away from the pregnancy test and went back to the sink full of roses. Sorting the petals wasn't hard work. Dark red from light red. Light red from pink. Yellow from gold. White from off-white. When her mind wandered, Glory would hear Herschel clear his throat. She'd look and see the white with red trim mixed with the white with pink trim. The pink roses made her smile. The baby's room would be pink for a perfect little girl. Josie Rose Jackson or Rose Barbie Jackson—Glory couldn't decide. Rose for her older sister who died and Josie after JT, of course. Or Barbie because she was a gift from JT and because it would be cruel to name her Josie Barbie-Shoes Jackson. Glory couldn't help but giggle.

When the stove timer buzzed, Glory took a deep breath. She removed her gloves and laid them side by side on the table, palms down, thumbs just touching. Perfect. She dried her hands on her apron, took another deep breath, and said a silent prayer.

"Girl, will you please quit stalling and go check the thing already?"

"I'm going." Glory sighed. Herschel was ruining the solemnity of the moment. She tried to count each step and remember how she felt so she could share all the details with JT. Leaning over the desk, she looked at the tiny mirror.

"Hmmm, that's odd."

Glory jumped at the sound of Herschel's voice. She hadn't heard him approach. "What's odd? It's a brown circle." Glory held her breath for Herschel's confirmation, but she could see it right there in the mirror. A brown circle. She pressed a hand to her belly and a hand to her heart.

"That's a brown spot, not a brown ring. It's not supposed to be a spot."

"So what's the brown spot mean?"

"It means you need to take another test." He held up a hand. "Not right now. Wait a week, and don't pee the morning before you take it."

"Okay." Glory smoothed her apron, only lightly touching her stomach. "Me and Barbie Shoes can wait another week."

"Barbie Shoes?"

"Yes. Barbie Shoes." Glory tried to be serious, but she couldn't stop smiling. "It's gonna be her nickname."

"Well, Glory-Glory"—Herschel headed back to check the roses on the stove—"I truly hope you're not pregnant. 'Cause if you name that baby Barbie Shoes, I'm reporting you for child abuse."

TWO DAYS LATER, GLORY got her period. Three days after that, she got out of bed and tried to act like her heart wasn't broken, only because her mother hinted that she might need to be purged of demons of sloth.

Chapter 4

Sunlight streamed through the jewel-painted windows of the old Lake Shore Bank and Trust building that housed the brand-new Lakeshore Christian Fellowship Church. In the grand lobby, where bank tellers had once worked, stood rows of stainless-steel chairs with legs padded to protect the ancient marble floors. Along the sides of the room ran plush burgundy carpet lined with heavy mahogany pews with deep burgundy cushions. Spiral staircases led to the balcony encircling the sanctuary, where there were more chairs, and doors led off to the church offices and Sunday-school rooms.

Every seat in the house was filled, and all the office windows and doors were open to hold the overflowing crowd. All five choirs were packed into the loft, decked out in their burgundy robes, along with the musicians in their black pants, burgundy ties, and white shirts that would be gray with sweat by day's end.

Seated in the third row with the other girls of the Mary and Martha Young Ladies' Circle, Glory tried to concentrate on the service. The choir kept the church bouncing, and Elder Riley Porter was on fire this second Sunday in August. Always a godly man, he was even more spirit-filled on Youth Revival Sunday, his voice rising and falling, controlling the energy in the room and feeding on it. The saints gathered to ask God's blessings and protection for the young people heading back to school in hopes that they would continue their godly ways and avoid the worldly temptations of sin and damnation. But try as she might, Glory could only think of JT.

After Elder Porter's prayer for the babies, the children's choir sang of their "Promise," and Glory thought of the baby she *knew* she'd been carrying, even if only for a couple of weeks—the little girl she imagined having her eyes and JT's hair and smile. When the young children stood up, a boy in light blue and a girl in white with pink flowers gave their well-rehearsed testimonies and asked for prayers of protection from mean people and bad grades. Glory could just see Barbie Shoes trying to be brave, giving her speech. The older kids did a skit and ended with a nervous boy struggling to sing "Pass It On," with the cracking voice that came with being twelve years old. Glory smiled. Her daughter would have sung that song perfectly.

When Elder Porter called the Young Davids to come forward, yielding the pulpit and taking his seat on the dais, mothers all over the sanctuary nudged their sons to stand up. The teenaged boys made their way to the front of the church, and Glory and the other girls seated in the third row tried not to laugh when Willie Clayton made a beeline for a side door. Glory sighed. JT should have been there. In her heart, she knew he wouldn't have stood up, but still, he belonged there.

Malcolm Porter rose from his seat at the right hand of his father and approached the pulpit. He looked around the church and then down at the boys standing in front of him and began to recite.

"If a man have a stubborn and rebellious son, which will not obey the voice of his father, or the voice of his mother, and that, when they have chastened him, will not hearken unto them." Malcolm lowered his voice to a calm, matter-of-fact tone. "Then shall his father and his mother lay hold on him and bring him out unto the elders of his city and unto the gate of his place. And they shall say unto the elders of his city, this our son is stubborn and rebellious. He will not obey our voice. He is a glutton and a drunkard." Malcolm shrugged as if the problem were simple. "And all the men of his city shall stone. Him. With. Stones. That. He. Die!"

The whole congregation jumped. A few shouted in agreement. Elder Porter beamed with pride.

Malcolm lowered his voice to nearly a whisper. "So shalt thou put evil away from among you, and all Israel shall hear and fear."

Some of the boys at the front of the church kept their heads bowed and tried to look reverent, while others looked bored, annoyed, or oblivious. Young women in the congregation sat up straighter and pushed their chests out.

"Then said David to the Philistine: 'Thou comest to me with a sword and with a spear and with a shield, but I come to thee in the name of the *Lord* of hosts, the God of the armies of Israel, whom thou hast defied."

The mature women tightened their hat pins and fanned themselves a little harder. Some of the old women stood with hands raised, preparing to shout.

"So David prevailed over the Philistine with a sling and with a stone and smote the Philistine and slew him, but there was no sword in the hand of David.'"

It was always this way when Malcolm spoke—him quoting the Bible from memory, the congregation going wild, mothers nudging their single daughters and pinching their wayward sons, teenagers quietly mocking him, and Glory wondering why nobody noticed that he only spoke in mismatched King James Bible verses... Biblical gibberish.

"Let no man despise thy youth, but be thou an example of the believers, in word, in conversation, in charity, in spirit, in faith, in purity."

Malcolm ended his message to the shouts of adoration from the congregation. The boys at the front fidgeted nervously, and Andre Bradley reached for the mic to give his testimony. Glory sighed. Everybody knew what was coming. He'd been humming the same tune all day.

"Giving honor to God, who is the king of my life," Andre began in his most preacherly voice. He'd been humming "I Won't Complain" all morning, and Glory braced herself for what would surely be an over-the-top spectacle.

Andre worked the song. He rearranged high notes and low notes, talked through a verse, then sang it twice. The congregation clapped in all the right places while his mother sat in the front pew, flailing and crying. Glory heard the other girls whispering that his mother was crying from embarrassment. Glory didn't disagree. It took him almost a full minute to end the last note, and when he finally did, he pulled out a black satin hanky to wipe his brow.

Rick Parker took the mic and made a show of cleaning it off. "I guess I'm not as good a man as you," he said to Andre. "Because I do complain. I complain and moan and ask God, 'Why me?' But I also pray. Know what I pray for, Andre?"

Behind her, Glory heard a whisper: "Ooo, I smell a pissing contest." She covered her face to hide her laughter.

"I pray for wisdom and enlightenment. I pray 'Faaather... o-pen our eeeyes...'" His voice went soft like Luther Vandross and low like Barry White. He even growled a little like Teddy Pendergrass, and by the time he finished, the full choir had joined in on the chorus, and nearly every woman and girl in the church was on her feet.

Glory kept her seat and swayed to the music. That song always made her cry. As great as Rick's version was, it didn't hold a candle to the way her daddy used to sing it to her.

Next, Kevin Flowers took the mic and started a song. "I... know I cain't sing!" The congregation laughed. "But, um, yeah... I'd like to thank everyone for their prayers as I head off to basic training Tuesday. And"—he looked out at the congregation and met Glory's eyes—"I ask that everybody remember my friend, JT Jackson, while he's struggling in navy boot camp. I know he misses everybody and needs *all* of our prayers."

Glory lowered her eyes. Whatever Kevin meant couldn't have been for her. She hadn't heard from Josiah in two months. Her seventeenth birthday had come and gone without a word, but he'd obviously been in touch with Kevin. She was relieved to know that he was okay. Maybe he'd called Kevin instead of writing. Maybe he didn't have time to write. Deciding to ask after church, Glory relaxed and tried to listen to the rest of the boys' testimonies, pinching herself whenever her mind wandered to thoughts of JT.

Dressed in all white with only earrings and maybe a headband, Glory and the other Mary-Martha girls waiting at the front of the church had all agreed to be dignified, decent, and in order—none of the wild theatrics of the boys or the cuteness of the younger kids. They listened to Malcolm's random verses about purity and submission with solemn faces, keeping their eyes down so as not to accidentally roll them.

Kelly Foster testified about her gymnastics scholarship and asked prayers for patience and good judgment. Lisa Bell spoke about trouble with classes and asked forgiveness for disobeying her parents. While the other girls spoke about ACT and SAT tests and college applications, Glory realized that she'd given no thought to life after high school without JT. Without him, she had no future. She tried not to cry and hoped the tears that slipped out looked like very intense praying.

"Before we pray for these future mothers and wives of our church family, is there another young lady who would like to share a word?" Malcolm's question brought Glory's attention back to the service. Before she could reach for the mic, she saw Trina Toliver and her grandparents approaching the front. The Mary and Martha Young Ladies' Circle's plan for proper decorum was out the window.

Trina's outfit was nothing like what she usually wore when it took her two hours to return from *running back home to find her Bible right quick* every Thursday night. Her disappearances were an ongoing joke, with the girls guessing what she'd be wearing when she came back. Once she came back with her dress inside out, and nobody but Glory would tell her. But this time, she wore a long, high-collared black dress and flat shoes. A gold cross pendant rested on her usually exposed chest, and she even had on a black pillbox hat with a veil. *A veil?* With her grandparents beside her, her testimony could only be one thing.

"Giving honor to God who is truly the king and love of my life," Trina began, "I come to you today because I have sinned. I disobeyed my grandparents, who have always only wanted what was best for me ever since they took me in as a baby. Two months ago, very late at night, instead of saying my prayers and going to sleep like I was told, I stayed up late reading the Bible. If I had not disobeyed, I wouldn'ta heard the knock on my window.

"It was a boy from church, and I let him in because he said he wanted to pray with me. I didn't know how drunk he was, and after I prayed with him, he covered my mouth and held me down and raped me. I think my granddad heard the struggle, 'cause he came down, and the boy ran out the basement door before Granddad could stop him.

"We didn't call the police 'cause I was scared and ashamed and the boy was troubled and leaving town the next day. I just wanted to pray for God to touch his heart and take the devil outta him. But I know God is good, and even out of this horrible thing came something good. Even though I sinned by disobeying my grandparents, and God punished me with rape, God has blessed me with a baby, and I'm gonna raise this child with the love and fear of God. And when Josiah Jackson comes home, he's gonna confess to what he did to me the night before he left town and—"

"Liar! Liar! Liar! Liar!"

It took Glory a moment to realize that her thoughts hadn't actually escaped her lips—the screams she heard were somebody else's.

"You a lowdown dirty liar from the pit of hell!"

"I'm sorry, Mrs. Jackson. It's true!" Trina cried, coughing and choking. Her grandfather placed a protective arm around her.

"No!" JT's mother tried to push past the ushers blocking her path. Someone took her crying grandson from her arms. "I know *exactly* where my son was the night before he left, and ain't enough liquor in the world to make him touch a nasty *ho* like you!"

In the midst of Trina's sobs and Mrs. Jackson's angry yelling, crying babies, and the buzz of a congregation more shocked by Mrs. Jackson's outburst than by Trina's testimony, Glory locked eyes with her mother. The only thing she could hear was her own heartbeat. She didn't intend to be defiant, and she prayed to JT's God that her mother would understand. When order was restored and Elder Porter asked again if there was another testimony, Mary Bishop nodded once. Glory reached for the mic.

"Good afternoon, everybody. I thank God for another day and for my mother who loves and protects me and has forgiven me. Um... a couple of months ago, I stayed out all night."

The congregation gasped. Glory dropped her eyes. If she was going to get through her testimony, she couldn't bear the shocked and disappointed looks of the congregation. Even the other Mary-Martha girls drew away from her.

"Josiah Jackson drove me home from work, and we sat in the car talking, and it was storming so we listened to music and waited for the rain to stop... and... um... we fell asleep, and it was sunrise when we woke up."

The tsking and grumbling of the congregation grew louder. She looked up, and her mother nodded again.

"Josiah Jackson slept in the front seat of his car next to me all night, the night before he left for the navy."

Her mother nodded again. Glory looked to the back of the church, but JT's mother and his best friend, Kevin, had already left.

Trembling, Glory tried to replace the mic in the stand. Her mother had allowed her to sacrifice her good name to expose an evil lie, and still, she hadn't told the whole truth. Trina had tried to cover her sin with a lie, and Glory had hidden her sin with the truth. *Is my sin any less than Trina's? Is protecting JT, especially after he abandoned me, worth lying in church... in front of God?*

A man said something about fast-tailed girls. A mother in a side pew yelled something about the spirit of Jezebel infecting the church. Trina's howls of protest turned to cries of pain when her grandparents started hitting her. Elder Porter pounded on the pulpit, demanding order and respect in God's house, and the organist played the theme from *The Young and the Restless*.

Glory couldn't stop shaking. *Was JT's loving God just a trick of the devil? Am I truly possessed by the spirit of Jezebel?*

"He that is without sin among you, let him first cast a stone."

She felt one firm, reassuring hand on her shoulder and another taking the mic from her trembling hand. Glory looked up to see Malcolm Porter taking the mic and moving to stand in front of her.

"And the tongue is a fire, a world of iniquity: so is the tongue among our members, that it defileth the whole body and setteth on fire the course of nature, and it is set on fire of hell. He that is without sin among you, let him cast a stone!" Malcolm leaned over and whispered to Glory, "Fret not thyself against evildoers or workers of iniquity."

Stepping forward, blocking Glory's view, Malcolm chided and challenged the shocked congregation. "These six things doth the Lord hate. Yea, seven are an abomination unto him. A proud look, a lying tongue, and hands that shed innocent blood, a heart that deviseth wicked imaginations, feet that be swift in running to mischief, a false witness that speaketh lies, and he that soweth discord among brethren."

The crowd's grumbling decreased, and a few people clapped.

"Thou shalt not raise a false report. Put not thine hand with the wicked to be an unrighteous witness. Keep thee far from a false matter, and the innocent and righteous slay thou not, for I will not justify the wicked. Do they not err that devise evil? But mercy and truth shall be to them that devise good." He gestured at the crowd. "Trina and Miss Bishop have given testimony and asked God's mercy. Hypocrites! Who among us has never been tempted by or reached for the forbidden fruit?" He glanced at Trina. "Or even enjoyed it... in our youth?"

The congregation clapped and shouted agreement. Trina wailed again. Glory prayed that Malcolm would stop talking and just let this be over. By the time he finished speaking, the congregation was on its feet. There were prayers for more protection of the young women, blessings on the honest, and redemption of the fallen.

———————— ❧ ————————

IN THE ROBINSON ROOM for after-service refreshments, Glory found herself crushed in a throng of girls demanding the real story of her night with JT. They were genuinely disappointed that Glory and JT had only slept in the car. A few old women still tsked, earning glares from some of the younger women. Trina and her grandparents were nowhere in sight.

"Hello, Miss Bishop."

The crowd surrounding Glory giggled and dispersed, leaving her standing alone with Malcolm Porter.

"Um, hi, Malcolm." She shifted from one foot to the other. He was only a head taller than her and not really imposing, but after his eloquent rescue, Glory didn't know what to say.

"Glory, did you thank Malcolm for speaking up for you?" Mary Bishop appeared at Glory's side, giving her daughter the hint and cover she needed.

"Oh, I'm sorry," Glory said quickly. "Thank you, Malcolm. That was really nice of you."

"Please, Miss Bishop, thank you for your courage." He turned to Mary. "People forget what it's like to be young. They act like they never overslept. Mother Bishop, what your daughter did was more than just brave—it was noble. She sacrificed herself to save a sinner. She is truly a testament to your motherhood."

Glory watched her mother frown. A sensible and righteous woman, Mary Bishop was not vain, and compliments made her uncomfortable. "I do the best I can. The Lord does the rest. But I do want to thank you properly. Come for dinner today. Glory is a great cook."

Glory tried to keep a straight face. *Please say no, please say no, please say no...*

Malcolm took Mary's outstretched hand. "I would love to, Mother Bishop—honest, I would. I can't today." He smiled at Glory. "But I promise I will accept your offer one day soon."

GLORY USUALLY WALKED home alone from church, but that day, her mother insisted they make the Sunday afternoon walk together. They stopped at a corner store for drinks, a Coca-Cola for her mother and a Sunkist Orange for Glory. Mary Bishop not only thanked the cashier, but she told him to have a blessed day as well. Glory sighed. Her mother was happy. This would be a long walk.

"Lovely service, wasn't it, baby? The little ones did so nice."

"Yes, ma'am. They were really cute." Glory knew her mother didn't particularly like the kiddie shows but wasn't going to point that out while her mother was practically skipping down the block.

"One day, I'll have a grandbaby up there singin' her little heart out in a pretty pink-and-white dress."

Glory hid her gasp behind the cough and long swallow from her can.

"And those boys—oh, my. They cut the fool sometimes!" Mary laughed. "Lord, who keeps lettin' that Andre have the mic? And his poor mama up there, rollin' around. I think she be dyin' from embarrassment."

Glory laughed with her mother. "Yeah, Mama, that's what we said."

"But that Trina!" Mary lowered her voice. "Lord forgive me for sounding a gossip, but really? A boy knockin' on her bedroom window in the middle of the night to pray. Prolly 'cause she had a red light shining."

"Mama! That's not nice."

"I know, baby, I know. But did she really think anybody would believe that mess? And her po' grandaddy lookin' like an old fool. Shoulda took a hand to that girl a long time ago." Mary shook her head. "I just don't know. Hazel knew that girl's mama went bad. Gave that child everything—spoiled her rotten—and she went bad. So what do they do? Let the baby run wild, too, talkin' 'bout 'God don't need no help.' God gave them a responsibility. God gave them a second chance." Mary fanned herself with her Mahalia Jackson fan and pressed the Coke can to her forehead before draining it and dropping it into a trash can near a bus stop, disturbing a swarm of flies on a fallen donut. "Well, it ain't my place to question. Maybe God is giving them a third chance."

As they walked on in silence, Glory noticed the mannequins with new school clothes that she'd never wear—the Jordache jeans and sweatshirts with no collars. She pointed out a light-blue pleated skirt and matching wool sweater that her mother approved of. It was the closest thing to normal clothes she'd be allowed. At some stores, Glory carefully averted her eyes lest her mother see her looking at the Michael Jackson posters or sinful red-sequined dresses and high-heeled shoes. She was surprised to feel her mother taking her hand.

"You know, baby," Mary began, "I was really pleased with you today." Glory's mother would never say she was proud. *Pride goeth before a fall.* "I didn't feel your sin was worth confessin' to the whole church, but that boy, no matter how bad he was in the past, was always a good friend to you. You did right by him today. That's what a godly woman does."

Glory blinked back tears. Her speaking up might have also damaged her mother's reputation. Only Malcolm's speech turned the congregation and distinguished her from Trina. Her half-truth made her no better than Trina.

"Um, Mama?"

"Yes, baby?"

Glory returned her mother's reassuring hand squeeze. "That morning, when I kissed Josiah, he asked me to be his girlfriend and to wait for him till he gets back." *Demon of lies and deceit!*

"I see. And I guess, since you're nervous about tellin' me, you said yes."

Glory took a deep breath. "Yes, ma'am. I did." To her surprise, she felt her mother squeeze her hand again.

"You know, baby, when I was your age, maybe a little younger, there was this boy. Ooo wee, he was somethin'. My mama and daddy had plans for me. Marry a good man—a famous preacher, actually—and be first lady of the big church. But this boy... Lord, this boy." Mary fanned herself harder. "The letters he wrote would set me afire. Promised to take me outta the woods, outta the South, show me the lights. Wrote me letters about making all my dreams come true."

Glory had heard variations of this story all her life. Her mother's first husband had been an ungodly smoker, drinker, gambler, and cheat, the king of all seducers and sinners.

"Now, I didn't wanna marry that old preacher, and when that boy said he'd take me away, I was ready to go."

"Mm-hmm." Glory nodded.

"I guess having a boyfriend so far away for—how many years is he gon' be gone?"

"Three."

"Ooh. Three. That's a lotta writin' for a long time, too. Maybe God is giving y'all time and space to grow. Mighta saved me some tears if I hada done right. Don't let his fancy letters stir up demons of lust and disobedience in your heart or cloud your mind. You know, that boy took me to Harlem. All sin and high livin'. *Harlem Renaissance*, they call it now. More like Sodom and Gomorrah. Nuttin' but drinkin' and reefa and jazz and whorin'. Ya hear me? His letters may sound pretty, and he may even promise godly things, but you know what's right."

To Glory's surprise, the anger she heard in her mother's voice was at Mary's own past life, not at Glory's admission. "So you're not mad at me, Mama?"

"No, baby, I'm not mad. I was young once, too. A stormy night and a boy goin' off to war. I'm surprised he waited till dawn for a kiss. You get a lot of letters?"

Glory sighed. She would *not* cry. Not here on the street on this beautiful August day. Not in front of her mother. "No, ma'am. Not really."

"Oh?" Mary pushed open the door to their building. "How many?"

"None," Glory whispered.

"I see," Mary said, stepping into their apartment.

In the cool darkness, Glory turned on lights while her mother checked the dinner Glory had prepared. Mary put a Walter Hawkins album on the stereo while Glory set plates on the kitchen table.

"So..." Mary picked up their conversation. "You're here waiting for him, and you haven't heard from him at all, not once?"

"No, ma'am." Glory took her seat at the table. *No, I will not cry.*

"Well, baby, he's young. He's learning a new life right now. People change."

"I know..." Glory concentrated on her food. Her mother's words hurt.

"But you did right by him. You stood up there when you didn't have to. Maybe he'll write soon."

She watched her mother savoring the pot roast and brightened a little. Glory had learned to cook it from her dad when she was nine—cut meat up in big hunks, add onion-soup mix and mushroom-soup mix, and chop the vegetables kind of big. The time they'd had a snow day last year and she let JT in after her mother left for work, he'd liked it, too.

"Malcolm Porter shielded you like Mary Magdalene today. Naw, don't look all uppity like that. You know what I mean. All those snooty folks so ready to condemn, I'm surprised they could see you for the beams in they own eyes. He spoke so well... moved the whole church."

Glory laughed a little. "Yeah, especially Cheryl. Did you see her floppin' around like that?"

"Back in the old days, she'da throwed her panties on the stage. Ah ha ha ha!"

"Mama!" Glory's eyes went wide. Her godly mother's slightly dirty jokes always shocked her.

"Baby, after service, I thought she was gonna bust outta that dress right there in the Robinson Room. And all Malcolm did was look for you."

Glory blushed. She'd fallen into her mother's trap, talking about Malcolm Porter. "Well, Mama, I don't think his speech was all for me. I think Malcolm Porter just likes to hear Malcolm Porter speak."

"Well, baby, no matter. You wait for that *boy* all you want, but that *man* stood up for you today, so you gon' make him one of these here delicious pot roasts as soon as he say the word."

Glory sighed. "Yes, ma'am."

Chapter 5

"Hey! Miss Bishop!"

Glory picked up her pace.

The footsteps behind her grew closer and faster.

"Miss Bishop, it's me, Malcolm!"

Glory sighed and slowed down. She looked back to see a tall young man in a gray suit and tie, almost jogging to catch up to her.

One of the men standing outside the liquor store stopped talking and looked in Malcolm's direction. "You okay with him, Church Girl? Some boys don't know a lady when they see one."

"Yes, sir." Glory sighed. "I know 'im. He's okay." She'd managed to avoid Malcolm Porter for almost two weeks. Every time he rang the bell at their apartment building, Glory had peeled up the corner of the window cover and watched for him to leave.

When he'd stopped by the church nursery, she'd excused herself to the ladies' room, and now, almost two weeks later, he hadn't given up. Malcolm wasn't a bad person, and Glory did feel a bit guilty hiding from him after he'd saved her from practically being stoned and crucified in church, but he reminded her of that new English teacher at school who was trying to be cool and still be a teacher. Everybody laughed at him. Malcolm tried to hang out, and he even played basketball with the boys at church. Sometimes they went easy on him and only made jokes about the ball bouncing off his fluffy afro. Other times, they called him "preacher boy" and dunked in his face.

Glory took a few steps toward Malcolm and away from the front of the store. The last thing she needed was gossip about her talking to men at the liquor store. With the Jezebel spirit loose in the church, the Mary and Martha Young Ladies' Circle stayed under close supervision. Bible study now ended promptly at seven thirty in the evening, and with the church mothers always watching, girl talk was limited to a few minutes in the bathrooms, showing off polished toenails and giggling about secrets. There were still questions about her night with JT, and Glory always told the "truth": they'd slept in the car and listened to worldly music. Outwardly, Glory laughed at the girls' disappointed sighs. Inside, she prayed that JT hadn't forgotten *everything* they'd done and planned.

Glory waited while Malcolm caught up and straightened his jacket. The shine of his church shoes, the same shade of gray as his suit, was the only thing that kept him from blending in with the sidewalk. He always wore dress clothes. Even his casual clothes were plaid dress shirts and jeans with starched creases. Glory couldn't quite find the right words to describe Malcolm Porter, the preacher's son. He was taller and thinner than JT, with thin, delicate hands. He wasn't bad looking or good looking. Light-brown skin, dark-brown hair, brown lips, brown eyes—even in his neat gray suit, he was just brown.

"Hello, Miss Bishop." Malcolm smiled. His gums were brownish, too.

"Hi, Malcolm." Glory squinted up at him, shielding her eyes from the late-Sunday-afternoon sun.

"It's pretty hot out. Can I drive you home?"

"Well, I usually walk. It's not too far. I like the exercise."

Malcolm placed a hand on her shoulder. "Well, how 'bout I walk with you? This ain't the best neighborhood for a lady to walk by herself."

Glory looked up and down Seventy-Fifth Street. Walking the five blocks with Malcolm meant no chance to stop at the salon and strip off her hot pantyhose and sweater. Five blocks, walking slowly, making small talk in ninety-degree weather in pantyhose and a sweater, with Malcolm Porter, or five minutes in an air-conditioned car... with Malcolm Porter...

"Okay," Glory said. "You can drive."

With Malcolm's hand still on her shoulder, Glory allowed him to guide her across Seventy-Fifth Street. He held one hand out to the side to ward off traffic. Glory knew somebody somewhere on the block was watching with amusement, and she would likely hear about it at church on Wednesday. When they stopped at a brown Cadillac, Glory couldn't help but smile.

"Nice, huh? It's a '69—not quite antique, but it's classic. Got it when I was fifteen. Still almost in mint condition." He held the passenger door for her.

When the door closed behind her, Glory looked around. Where JT's car had been dark gray and junky inside, this one had light wood and white leather. It was spotless and smelled of window cleaner and cherry air freshener.

Malcolm opened the driver's door, reached in, and started the car, turning on the air conditioner. "This should keep you comfortable for a bit. I gotta grab something. Be right back."

"Oh? Okay," she said to the closing door. Glory laid her head back against the seat. The last time she'd been in a car was with JT, and she needed not to think about him. School started next week, and she would be a senior. She needed to focus on that and not on the boy who'd left her. But the last time she'd been in a car, he'd cried, and she'd promised to marry him, and then after nearly three months, she'd gotten no response to her letters. Other people had heard from him. Just not her.

Glory heard the trunk open and close, then Malcolm got into the driver's seat beside her.

"Sorry to keep you waiting, Miss Bishop. I hope it wasn't too bad."

"No, Malcolm, it was fine." Glory looked around the car again. "It's nice in here."

"Thanks," Malcolm said, pulling the car into the light afternoon traffic. "Mind if we take a short ride?"

"Um, well...?"

"Just up the street to Jeffrey Park? It's too nice to go in."

"But—"

"I promise I'll clear it up with your mother later." Malcolm winked at her. "I hear she thinks I'm cool."

Glory sighed and nodded, positive that her mother already knew about and approved of this ride.

Sitting in the park under the hot afternoon sun, Glory felt ridiculous with three napkins stuffed down the front of her blouse. Looking across the picnic table at Malcolm's passionate gestures with a chicken bone, she couldn't hold back a chuckle.

"What so funny?" he asked. "Never seen a man enjoy a wing?"

"No, not that." Glory laughed again. "You've got a mild-sauce mustache, you're wearing a napkin bib, and you're holding that wing like it's tryin' to escape."

"Well, you, Miss Bishop, are pretending to eat like a delicate lady, but you're wearing mild-sauce lipstick and manicure."

"Well, it's Harold's," Glory said. "It would be disrespectful to do anything less." She waved a fly away and took a sip from the can of ginger ale. Though she would have preferred orange or grape, the dry beverage was cold and refreshing in the heat.

When not in preacher mode, Malcolm Porter could be funny and intelligent. He saw some of the same quirks in church people that she did, and even though he was almost thirty, he didn't seem that old.

"Malcolm, can I ask you a question?"

"O-kaaay..."

"Why don't you call me by my first name? In front of the whole church, you said 'Trina and Miss Bishop.' You don't call any of the other girls 'Miss.' People notice."

"Does it bother you?"

Glory thought for a minute. "Not really. People just think you're weird."

Malcolm smirked a little. "Yeah, Jesus was weird, too." He took a swallow of his drink. "I call you Miss Bishop because you're a lady. You're different from those other girls. Silly, mean, sneaky, thinking they're getting away with stuff, reading dirty novels in church. I never see you do that. They probably do all sorts of things when nobody's around." He took another sip.

"Well, actually, Malcolm, everybody does. Nobody's perfect."

"I know that, but there's a difference between imperfect and defiant." Malcolm leaned in close to Glory, a playful grin on his face. "Forgetting your Bible: imperfection. Forgetting your Bible and coming back two hours later with your dress inside out: defiance. Laughing behind her back: mean, sneaky. Ministering to her private-ly: you." He winked at her, leaned back, and took a long swallow, draining the can.

Glory's eyes went wide. "You knew about the dress thing?"

"Yes, Miss Bishop. I heard all about it."

Glory just sighed. The other girls were just too stupid to under-stand that if Trina got caught, more adults would start coming to Bible study—which was exactly what happened.

"My turn." Malcolm opened another can. "Why did you do it?"

"Do what?" Glory knew what he meant, but she played the odds that it might not be the same question she'd avoided answering for two weeks.

"Why did you stand up in church and sacrifice yourself? Nobody believed he raped Trina. She let a drunk boy in to pray in the middle of the night? And she's way more than two months pregnant. He's not in town, and nobody would've cared in a week." Malcolm took a bite of another wing and chewed for a second. "Why did you say anything?"

Because if I'm not having his baby, there's no way that tramp is gonna get to say she is. Glory went through all the half answers she'd given over the weeks and finally decided on the truth. Not her truth—JT's truth.

"Because I want him to come back to church. The reason he stopped coming is because he doesn't believe in our God anymore, and..." Glory took a deep breath. "I understand why."

Malcolm's smile faded. "Go on."

"The Bible says Jesus died for our sins and that God forgives. We confess to God and ask forgiveness and have a clean slate."

"Okay," Malcolm agreed, but his expression didn't change.

"But our church doesn't forgive. We still hold JT's sin against him and want to keep punishing him for it. His sin is between him and God. Why should he apologize to the church? He didn't sin against the church. He apologized to his mother and to his son and to... his God. It's not your—our business..." Glory took a deep breath.

"Go on."

She noticed a slight smile on Malcolm's face. *Does he actually get it?* "And letting that lie stand would've hurt JT's mother and his best friend. Being quiet would've made me a liar, too. He would've done the same thing for me. And I believe in JT's God, too." *There, I said it.* "Even when I do sin, and even if the church wants to stone me, my God forgives me."

Saying those words freed something in Glory. She couldn't imagine the demon of blasphemy her mother would beat out of her if she'd heard them, but Malcolm's face told her this secret rebellion was safe.

"Woman, woman, woman…" He reached across the table and rested his hand on hers. "You have some interesting ideas."

THE UNDERGROUND FOOD court at the River Oaks Shopping Center offered a welcome retreat from the early-September heat. Glory's irritation at yet another *unscheduled* outing with Malcolm was somewhat diminished when he let her talk him into buying himself a cool studded black-leather belt, but no matter how much he insisted, she would accept nothing from him other than a snack.

"So, I talked to my dad about what you said." Malcolm pushed a cheese-covered tortilla chip into his mouth.

"What did I say?" Glory asked. *Why are nachos so delicious and messy?*

"About the church being unforgiving—"

"What?" Glory's eyes went wide. "Malcolm! I didn't mean for you to—"

"Calm down. I took all the credit." He winked at her.

Glory didn't know if that made her feel any better.

"Anyway, he agreed that we might be driving young people away with public shaming. The original intent was, you know, 'Look, don't be like so-and-so.' But it's not working, is it? No, it's not." Malcolm shook his chip for emphasis, sending drips of cheese sauce all over the tiny table. "It didn't stop Trina, and JT didn't leave God—he just left his church."

"Okay. So what did Pastor say?" Glory wiped up the spilled sauce.

"Well, next summer, we're having an old-fashioned homecoming, a sort of family reunion. Not a revival or anything like that—just calling everybody back home like nothing ever happened. We're gonna do a series on forgiveness—"

"And 'God Don't Need No Help'?"

"Oo woman, the mouth on you." Malcolm laughed, shaking his head. "Always interrupting. Yeah, something like that. Basically, letting everybody know all is forgiven and they can come back home."

Glory reached into the basket and took another nacho, avoiding Malcolm's gaze. She knew he wouldn't like her response.

"Okay. What?" He was obviously disappointed at her lack of enthusiasm.

"I think the homecoming is a great idea." She ate the chip and took a swallow of her Orange Julius. Maybe if she filled her mouth and stalled long enough, he'd let it go. She ate more.

"But...?" He leaned back in his seat and folded his arms.

Of course, he won't let it go. "How about instead of forgiving people for their sins against God and themselves, maybe ask their forgiveness for the church's sins against *them*?"

Malcolm raised an eyebrow.

Glory lowered her head and let the words come out in a rush. "You know... humiliating them and driving them away? They have God's forgiveness for their sins. Why do they need yours? Like I said, God don't need no help." She looked up.

Malcolm's face was inscrutable.

"Well?" Glory asked.

"So you want me to tell the righteous that they need to apologize to the sinners?"

"'All our righteousnesses are as filthy rags.' Isaiah 64:6." Glory grabbed another chip then saw it fly from her hand and felt her arm immobilized and her wrist locked in Malcolm's grip, her elbow pressed hard against the table. A moment later, Malcolm released her wrist and wiped up the spilled cheese, a playful grin back on his face. She had barely seen him move.

"Don't quote Bible verses at me. I know the whole book by heart."

"Well, I'm glad you took all the credit for the idea." Glory rubbed her wrist, took another drink, and smiled.

Their church discussions often went like this. His mood darkened a bit when she disagreed, but his smile always returned when he'd made his point. Glory found it easier to steer the subject back to him than to argue. Sometimes, she felt guilty for being so manipulative—speaking her mind just because she knew he would let her, letting him think she agreed with him, encouraging the older man's attention just because he made her feel special. It had taken five or six outings before Glory accepted the fact that she really liked Malcolm Porter, the preacher's son. He wasn't as *preachery* as the other girls thought, at least not when she and he were together.

He was so different from JT. Where JT had liked to talk about his future, Malcolm talked about the present. At twenty-seven, he was just finishing Bible college, living his future. JT's dream of basketball stardom had ended when he joined the navy. Malcolm's real plans for a life of godly service had begun when he became youth pastor at Lakeshore Church. JT knew all about the neighborhood and dreamed of seeing the world. Malcolm knew the world and planned to save the neighborhood. While JT could be flexible when it came to God, Malcolm was passionate. He stood firm and put his foot down. Glory could easily sway or silence JT, but Malcolm was on fire for the Lord.

Out in the world, Glory found herself enjoying Malcolm's protective hand on her back or shoulder, guiding her, but at church, he stayed distant and respectful, careful to maintain proper decorum. The only thing the girls at church ever said was "He musta got some, 'cause he isn't so uptight anymore." Glory giggled along with the crowd because nothing could be further from the truth.

———— ❧ ————

GLORY STOOD IN THE foyer with her face pressed against the glass and counted eight seconds between the lightning and the thunder. Normally, a CTA bus would arrive outside her apartment building at 5:58 and again at 6:07, but on this stormy late-September morning, both buses could get there at six fifteen and have standing room only because all the seats were full of water. Glory checked the clasps on her yellow raincoat, pulled open the heavy door, and stepped from the safety of the foyer into the early-morning storm. She opened her umbrella and barely had time to say goodbye before a gust of wind turned it inside out, ripped it from her hand, and carried it up into the trees. She forgot to count the seconds between the lightning and thunder, but she was sure it was fewer than eight seconds.

"Good morning, Miss Bishop. Need a ride?"

Glory jumped and looked around. Malcolm stood beside his car, holding a giant bright-green umbrella. The brown Cadillac had never looked so beautiful. Trudging through the stream of debris and fallen leaves, she made her way to the curb.

"Hi, Malcolm." Glory smiled up at him. "I'm soaked. I don't wanna mess up your seats."

"I'll put your coat on the floor after you get in. It'll be fine. Hold this." Malcolm handed her the umbrella and reached for the clasp at her collar.

"Oh, okay. That makes sense. I can do it."

Malcolm brushed her hand away. "You're too slow. Now, hold this like I said."

Glory took the umbrella and stood still while Malcolm quickly unclipped and peeled off her raincoat and backpack. He brushed a leaf from her hair. "Okay, get in."

Glory climbed into the passenger seat while Malcolm tossed her belongings onto the floor in the back. She wondered why he was there, but another thunderclap reminded her that on an ugly day like this, it didn't really matter.

"Hey," Malcolm said, climbing into the driver's seat. "Where to?"

"Sixty-Third and Ashland. Wolcott." Glory looked at him and couldn't help smiling. "Why are you out this early and in this rain?"

Malcolm smiled back. "The storm woke me up, and you told me you leave at five forty-five or something like that. I woulda rung your bell, but I figured you'd be out eventually, and I didn't wanna bother your mother. I don't like you riding the bus on a day like this." He reached across the seat and placed a hand on hers.

Staring out at the rain, Glory found herself frowning. She knew Malcolm liked her, and it made her feel good. But he was a grown man. He had to know they could only be friends. He was twenty-seven and treating her like a girlfriend—a grown woman—but he was driving her to *high school*. Was this that Jezebel spirit? Was she tempting him... leading him on? But how could a kid lead a grown man on?

"You're quiet. What's on your mind?"

Glory jumped.

"Didn't mean to startle you." Malcolm chuckled, patting her hand.

"I was just thinking that I'm gonna get to school too early. My first class is at seven fifty—"

"So we'll stop for breakfast. I know just the place. I hope you're hungry."

The thirty-minute drive was much shorter than her usual hour-long bus ride, and Glory was pleasantly surprised when Malcolm stopped the car beside the Red Apple restaurant. He kept a hand on Glory's shoulder as they shared the umbrella walking in.

A waitress in a pink uniform waved a hand around the empty dining room. "Sit anywhere. Be right with you. Coffee?"

"Yeah!" Malcolm called back. "Decaf for the lady. This place has great coffee," he said to Glory, ushering her into a booth by a window. "I used to come here a lot with the night ministry."

"I've always wanted to come here," Glory said, looking around at all the stainless steel and bright-red plastic. The vinyl seat squeaked when she slid across it.

The waitress placed two steaming white coffee cups on the table. Malcolm blocked Glory's hand before she could reach for her cup. "Decaf?"

"Oops." The waitress picked up the cup. "Be right back."

Glory watched Malcolm scowl at the retreating waitress and then turn his attention back to her. He could be *so* grumpy if he didn't get his way immediately. "How did you know it wasn't decaf?"

"They use brown coasters for decaf." Malcolm looked at his watch. "So we've got an hour. School's a couple of blocks over, right?"

"Yeah. Malcolm, why do you know this neighborhood? Englewood is pretty far from South Shore."

Malcolm laughed a little. "Well, back in my wild times, I went pretty much everywhere. I know a lot about a lotta neighborhoods. Then, when the Lord delivered me, I came back here to help try to clean up some of this mess." He nodded when the waitress set a brown coaster and a fresh cup of coffee in front of Glory.

"Thank you," Glory said to the waitress, even though she would have preferred tea. Malcolm always ordered decaf coffee for her. She loaded it up with cream and poured in sugar until he took the container from her hand.

"That's too much. You're sweet enough as it is." He smiled but moved the sugar out of her reach.

Glory stirred her coffee while Malcolm ordered. Since their first picnic, Malcolm had always done the ordering. He sometimes asked what she liked, but he always made the final decision. She frowned a little. He could be so bossy, treating her like a kid one minute but the next minute calling her "woman." Glory thought of all the real grown-up women at church who would love to be babysat by Malcolm Porter. Herschel said it was disrespectful of Malcolm to treat her like that, but her mother said it was ungrateful of her to not appreciate a godly man like Malcolm.

"So now..." Malcolm said, sipping his coffee, drawing Glory back to the moment. "You never did tell me the truth about what was on your mind."

Glory sighed and pushed her coffee cup away. "I'm wondering why you're here. Why me?"

Malcolm put down his cup and leaned forward in his seat. "I didn't want you on the bus in this weather. I think I said that already."

"Malcolm, you know what I mean. I'm serious. I feel like I'm being bad."

Malcolm reached across the table and took her hand. "Okay, Miss Bishop... Glory... what you just said is why I'm here. Because you're the kind of woman who worries about how an innocent breakfast looks. You're such a good girl—"

"No, that's not what I mean. I mean, there are lots of women at church your age. I'm too young for you. Why me?" She saw a flash of anger as Malcolm let go of her hand. Glory lowered her eyes. She hadn't meant to upset him. "I mean, I'm in high school, and I work at a salon. There are older women at church who have careers and lives. They're glamorous. I'm just... a... a... girl with old lady clothes... and ugly hair..."

Malcolm reached across the table and took her hand again. "'Who can find a virtuous woman? For her price is far above rubies. In like manner also, that women adorn themselves in modest apparel, with shamefacedness and sobriety, not with broided hair or gold or pearls or costly array. But—which becometh women professing godliness—with good works. Favor is deceitful, and beauty is vain, but a woman that feareth the Lord, she shall be praised.'"

Glory sighed in relief when the waitress interrupted Malcolm's sermon. He always turned to the Bible when he wanted to make a deep point. She knew he was sincere, saying she was perfect the way she was, but his Bible talk sounded kind of silly.

Their waitress carried platters of pancakes and French toast in her right hand and several more plates balanced on her left arm. She quickly dealt the dishes and pulled ketchup and napkins from her pockets. Glory looked at the spread and sighed. Malcolm always ordered some of everything. He never seemed to notice that she didn't touch much of it. She bowed her head while he blessed the food and waited while he chose what he wanted. She contented herself with French toast, bacon, and fruit, grateful that the food gave them something different to talk about.

AT 7:40, MALCOLM SLOWED the car in front of sixty-five-year-old gray-marble Wolcott Technical High School. "I'll be out here at three o'clock."

"Well, I can't leave in the middle of a class period, so I'll leave at around 2:40, after ninth period. I'll be waiting in the bookstore, right over there." Glory pointed to the tiny run-down brick building on the corner across the street from the school. The little store sold school supplies and had the best burgers and fries in the neighborhood.

Malcolm looked at the building and shook his head. "Nah. It's probably okay when it's crowded at lunchtime but not after school. Wait in the school. I'll be out here whenever you get out."

"So you're gonna get here at three o'clock and wait till I come out at 3:20—after tenth period—instead of me leaving after ninth period and waiting for maybe twenty minutes in the bookstore?"

Malcolm double-parked the car. "Yes. I know a lot more about this neighborhood than you."

"Well"—Glory lifted her backpack to her lap and reached for the door handle—"I think you're being silly. I've been just fine in this neighborhood for three years... *ow*!" She looked at Malcolm's hand clamped on her wrist.

He pulled her away from the door. "You always talking without thinking. Maybe I know something that you don't." He let go of her wrist and stroked her cheek with his finger. "I know that store. I know the man behind the school-supply counter. He likes young girls. I don't want you in there with him by yourself." Malcolm opened the driver's-side door and grabbed the umbrella. "Sit tight. I'll walk you to the door."

Glory rubbed her wrist and hoped there wouldn't be a bruise again. But she acknowledged Malcolm might be right. She had heard stories of Mr. Harris offering hugs and back rubs to girls. Some of the fast girls actually got free stuff from him. Glory never asked how, but there was no way the dirty old man would ever look at a girl like her, anyway.

Malcolm kept his hand on her shoulder, guiding her up the stairs at the front of the school building to the doors she hadn't used since the first day of freshman year.

"I NOTICED YOU DIDN'T take the PSAT last year, and you haven't signed up for any college entrance tests yet. Why is that, Glory?" The guidance counselor flipped through the manila folder in front of her.

"Um, well, I sort of forgot," Glory lied. Her mother didn't think it was necessary to pay money to take a test just for more school.

"So, have you decided which colleges you'll apply to? You have excellent grades, and your other scores are great. You can go pretty much anywhere."

"Um, no, ma'am. Not yet."

"I don't see your college-planning form here either, Glory." Mrs. Rochelle looked over her glasses at Glory.

Glory avoided her eyes. "I thought I turned it in. I'll look for it at home."

The guidance counselor stared at Glory for a full minute. "Mm-hmm. See that you do. I'll be requesting a parent conference if I don't get some answers by next week."

Glory left the counselor's office and headed for her locker. Going away to school was something she'd read about in the magazines and books at the salon, and the whole month of August, the talk there was about low-maintenance hair for living in dorms. A couple of girls even volunteered at the shop just so they could watch and get ideas for doing hair and making money at school. Glory had only broached the subject of college once with her mother. Mary, of course, said no, telling her that it was just an opportunity for devilment and worldly temptation. Glory's place was at home and church, in godly service, and now, since Malcolm Porter wanted her, there was no need for college, anyway.

"BOO!"

Glory didn't flinch. She dug a novel and an *X-Men* comic out of her book bag and placed them on the top shelf of her locker. "Hi,

Quentin." She grabbed her gym clothes and stuffed them into her book bag.

"Nothing scares you, does it?" the gangly red-haired teenaged boy asked, leaning against the lockers much closer than Glory liked.

"Yes, Quentin. I'm scared of balloons and demons." Glory didn't lie, but she knew Quentin wouldn't believe her.

"Ha. Okay. So, whatcha reading?" He reached over her head and grabbed the comic book. "*X-Men*?" He looked down at her and smiled. "You read this?" He grabbed the novel. "Wait. *The Hitchhiker's Guide*? This too?" He reached for another book.

Glory leaned forward, burying her head in her locker. "Please stop." She spoke to the back wall because the boy reaching over her head, riffling through her books, was completely ignoring her. "No. Don't. Put that down," she deadpanned. Glory sighed and waited. When he got quiet, she pulled her head out and looked up. He stared down at the pile of books in his arms—the books she'd borrowed from the school library and planned to return one day. "Okay. What?"

"Um... um..."

Glory grabbed the books and started placing them back on the shelf. "I wish you'd ask before going through my locker."

"Oh. Uh... sorry. It's just that now, I don't know if I should be scared of you or in love with you."

Glory slammed the locker. "Scared. You should be scared." She checked her book bag again for anything worldly. A corner of the latest issue of the *New Expression* newspaper poked out from inside her math book. Glory sighed and opened her locker again. "Quentin, isn't there a normal girl somewhere you should be in love with?" She flipped through the pages of two more books.

"But, Glory..." He flopped an arm around her shoulder and pulled her close. "That's the beauty of it. I'm weird. You're weird. We could make beautiful weird music together. Like a totally awesome gospel-punk fusion."

Glory tried to pull away. He pulled her closer, apparently caught up in his vision of their imaginary relationship. "Think of it. You, me... our wedding at, like, the museum or something. Maybe your top God guy could do the ceremony."

Glory pulled back from him with exaggerated sadness. "I'm sorry, but I'm already taken. I've had an arranged marriage since childhood." She dramatically turned to walk away, slamming the locker door one final time.

Quentin fell to his knees. "Nooo!" He kept his anguished scream lowered to a harsh whisper so as not to attract the hall monitors. "As soon as I finish at MIT, I will challenge him for your hand!"

Glory failed to suppress a giggle and hoped nobody was watching this performance.

"Seriously, though." Quentin rose to his feet, dusting off his knees. "You're reading *The Hitchhiker's Guide* and *X-Men*. Are girls even allowed to do that?"

"Goodbye, Quentin." Glory fake sobbed as she walked away, shaking her head at the friend she'd had since freshman year. His jokes made her feel like a normal girl. She hoped she'd done it right—acted like a normal girl. She was never sure whether she was being too harsh or too friendly. Sometimes she suspected Quentin might not be completely joking. The last thing Glory wanted was another boy liking her.

It wasn't even one o'clock, and her school day was basically over. Extra classes and summer school for three years had left her with very little to do her senior year. She'd wanted to take college courses, but her mother had nixed that.

She'd had lunch. Next came study hall and then admin, which was just sitting at the desk in the office and "helping." She could skip all of those and just leave—maybe put in some hours at the salon and visit with Herschel. It was apple season, and the salon would smell wonderful. She could be home every day by two o'clock if she wanted to. But she couldn't leave that day—Malcolm was picking her up at 3:20—so Glory made her way up to the second floor to find a comfortable spot in the library for the rest of the day.

This would have been a perfect afternoon to spend with JT. Like the time when she was fourteen, and she'd let him in for an hour after school. They played cards and ate pizza puffs and drank orange pops. Then they kissed and lay down on the living room floor and kissed some more. And after he moved on top of her, and they kissed even more and pressed real hard, he'd jumped up and said he had to go. She didn't see him for two days after that.

Or when they were fifteen, and they'd gone to the museum. They rode the dinosaur ride and had ice cream at Finnegan's and stuck their faces in the clown heads and kissed in the circus. Or the time they went to Rainbow Beach and played in the waves—but then, in the middle of the night, Glory had gotten a whoopin' because her mother found sand in her pocket.

Had it really been just four months since he left? It was starting to feel like forever, but she still waited for him. With Malcolm, when he let her talk and made her laugh and called her "woman," she felt like she was growing up and her life was moving on. At church, when people talked of the letters from far-off students and even prisoners, she knew that she wasn't on JT's mind at all. He still hadn't written to her, not once. At work, listening to the ladies at the salon talk of cheating soldiers and low-life men, Glory knew that he'd forgotten her. But at night, alone in her bed, when she touched herself and felt the tingle, and it was all she could do to keep from calling out his name, Glory still waited for JT.

Chapter 6

Dusk was Glory's second-favorite time of day, and in late October, it came early. At five o'clock, she watched and waited for the first visible stars, those bright enough to shine through all the lights of Seventy-Fifth Street. Thanks to the time change, it would be dark soon. As the bus passed the brightly lit convenience store, Glory pulled the buzzer then got off two stops early. Her only Halloween indulgence would be an Affy Tapple taffy apple, a treat her daddy had taught her to love.

In a couple of days, the unseasonably warm weather would have the streets full of costumed kids celebrating the devil's holiday, begging for candy. Glory had only trick-or-treated once when she was five, and her father had been home for Halloween. She'd been terrified of demons, but he'd assured her that no devil could get through him, and she'd ended the night with an overflowing bag of candy. The day her dad went back on the road, her mother threw out all the candy Glory had left and whipped the demons of gluttony out of her for crying.

The few offices near her building were closing, and evening traffic was picking up. She would have just enough time to drop off her backpack and maybe change her blouse before Malcolm picked her up at six. He was, no doubt, parked nearby, waiting for her. The thought made her smile and pick up her pace. With her sweater tied around her waist and her backpack over one shoulder, Glory enjoyed her treat and watched the stars come out on her walk home.

The entry to her building was almost in sight when she tripped. She tried to regain her balance when she hit the wall and felt her backpack slip from her shoulder. *No!* With her face and shoulder scraping the wall and a callused hand covering her mouth, Glory felt herself being pulled into darkness.

Please, no! Struggling to escape, she realized she was in the gangway half a block from her building, a place she'd played hide-and-seek as a child.

Oh, God! No! Clawing at the hand pulling her over debris and deeper into the shadows, she sank her fingernails into gritty skin. The monster growled and loosened his grip. Glory managed to scream before the hand closed around her throat, slamming her head against the brick wall, cutting off her air, silencing her scream. She thought she heard someone call her name, but all sound was drowned out by the sudden screeching of tires and the crunch of cars colliding on the street.

"Yeah, it's just me and you. Cain't nobody out there hear nothin' back here." Pinning her to the wall, he smelled of sour smoke and the stench of the urine-soaked gangway. "I like me some schoolgirls." With his free hand, he pushed her skirt and slip above her waist and then lifted and turned her left leg so hard her hip popped.

Glory fought to pry his fingers from her neck and reached out to scratch his grease-slicked face. Clutching her by her neck so that her right foot barely touched the ground, holding her against the building with his body, he pounded her head against the wall until her vision clouded.

Jesus... Daddy... help me...

The monster's moist, hard flesh pushed against her, and his gritty hand ripped aside her underwear. Ragged nails scraped her thighs as his fingers probed and dug into her body "Imma smash this cherry. Maybe leave a baby in you..."

Pass me not, oh gentle savior... Glory closed her eyes and waited for the violation, grateful that the honor of first was not being stolen by this demon. She imagined she heard God calling to her.

"... then choke you out and turn you over and bust yo'..."

Hear my humble cry... Maybe she would see her daddy soon.

"Gloooryyy!"

The monster's hand left her body, and his grip on her neck loosened. Glory opened her eyes to see a shadow... an angel of the Lord bringing his sword down on the demon.

"Touch not mine anointed, and do my prophets no harm!"

The monster staggered and tried to run, slowed by his falling pants. The angel brought the sword down again.

"There shall not a hand touch her, but whether it be beast or man, it shall not live!"

Sinking to the ground, Glory shook her head. The words, the rage, the angel sent by God was Malcolm. He brought the sword—no, the steering-wheel lock—down again. The monster fell to his knees, howling, bleeding from a deep gash in his head.

"Behold, I will smite with the rod that is in mine hand upon the demon, and it shall be turned to blood!"

"Malcolm! Stop!" Glory screamed.

"I saw the Lord standing upon the altar, and he said, smite and cut them in the head, all of them!"

Malcolm brought the weapon down again and again. The monster's howls turned to whimpers. And then silence.

"And I will slay the last of them with the sword. He that fleeth of them shall not flee away, and he that escapeth of them shall not be delivered!"

Climbing over the bleeding man, Glory reached Malcolm. "Please Malcolm, don't kill," she begged. "Please, don't kill. Please, don't kill." She wrapped her arms around him and squeezed—his body a wall of trembling rage, his heart pounding, his panting deep and guttural—until she felt his tension ease, and he lowered the weapon and wrapped his arms around her.

Then Glory's knees buckled, and she sobbed. God had answered her prayers and sent Malcolm to save her. And Malcolm picked her up and carried her out of the darkness.

"GOOD EVENING, HERSCHEL'S. How can I help you today?"

"Herschel?" Glory held the phone receiver in a trembling hand.

"Yes. This is Herschel. Who's calling, please?"

"It's Glory."

"Well, hello, Glory-Glory! Change your mind about working this evening?"

"Um, no. I'm at the hospital. I didn't know who else to call. The police took Malcolm—"

"What? Where are you? Did Malcolm hurt—"

"No... um... there was this man... and he grabbed me... and Malcolm... he..." Glory's voice broke as she choked on the sob that threatened to escape again. This was the third time she'd tried to call, and the first time she'd actually gotten Herschel. The nurse took the phone gently from her hand.

"Hello? This is Alice. I'm a nurse here at South Shore Hospital. Gloria has some injuries... yes, I'm sorry, Glory. We can't reach her mother. You're related how? Her uncle Herschel, I see. Okay. I'll tell her. Thank you, sir. Come to the emergency room and ask for her. Yes. Oh, she'll be just fine. I'll be with her until you get here."

Nurse Alice hung up the phone and bent down to Glory's level. "I'm gonna wheel you back to the room, and we'll wait for your uncle."

Glory just nodded. Thinking was hard, speaking was hard, her head ached, and the pain medicine wasn't working. She shouldn't have stopped for the taffy apple. *Demon of gluttony!* She should have gone straight home like she was supposed to. *Demon of disobedience!* She shouldn't have walked so slow. *Demon of sloth!* Tying her sweater like that probably made her blouse look tight. Were her socks rolled down with her legs showing? *Filthy Jezebel!*

Back at the room, a policewoman stood waiting outside the door. The young officer helped Glory onto the gurney, while the nurse let up the sides and adjusted the pillow. Glory lay on her right side, facing the wall, resting on her gloved hands, careful of the bandages on the back of her head and the right side of her face. She tried to stay perfectly still, but she couldn't stop shaking, and the shaking made everything hurt.

The old nurse sat in a chair beside the gurney, keeping a hand lightly on Glory's shoulder, softly singing gospel songs. Glory wished she would stop.

Was God punishing me for that night with JT? For lying? For keeping the secret? But God had sent Malcolm. When she'd given up and stopped fighting, God had sent Malcolm. *Why couldn't they find my mother? Why did the police take Malcolm? What's taking Herschel so long?* The panic rose again, and she tried to take slow, deep breaths like the nurse told her to. It hurt her head and her throat.

Glory heard the door open and close behind her. She could hear commotion outside the room. Maybe her mother was out there, calling down the wrath of God. Glory tried to move, but nurse Alice's hand pressed her shoulder.

"Rest, sweetie," Alice said. "That's some police business. The police lady just went out to check. Nothing for you to worry about. Nothin's gon' hurt you here."

Closing her eyes, Glory saw only darkness and the bricks, so she stared at the off-white wall and its outlets and dangling cords. She counted the cords and followed the length of them with her eyes and then followed them again. Anything to keep her eyes from closing.

The door opened again, and Glory felt Nurse Alice get up from her seat. When the door closed, the scent of flowers, wood, and vanilla reached her nose, and Glory breathed a sigh of relief.

"Hi. I'm Herschel Cole," whispered a softened deep voice. "How is she?"

"Hello, Mr. Cole. Thanks for coming."

"What happened? Was she in an accident?"

The old nurse sighed. "I'm sorry, no. She was assaulted."

Glory heard hushed whispers, and she heard Herschel gasp, take a few steps, and clear his throat.

Nurse Alice patted Glory's leg. "She's been waiting for you. She needs a bit of moral support."

Glory felt them moving around the room, the nurse at her back and Herschel moving around to stand in front of her. Glory tried to turn to face him.

"Don't move, darling. I'm coming to you."

A pair of starched, pleated khakis came into her field of view, and as Herschel came down on one knee to Glory's eye level, Glory looked into the face of a man whose heart was breaking. His shaking hand reached out to her bruised and bandaged face, hovered, and drew back. He brought a trembling hand to his chest, then brought his fist to his mouth, to his forehead, and back to his mouth. Glory's own heart ached watching giant tears slide down her friend's face.

Nurse Alice appeared at his side with a tissue.

"It wasn't Malcolm?" Herschel asked in a raspy whisper. It was more a statement than a question.

"No, Herschel." Glory closed her eyes without fear for the first time in hours. "Malcolm saved me. I prayed, and Malcolm came—"

"Did Malcolm kill that muthafucka?"

Glory opened her eyes, shocked by the sharp, angry growl.

Herschel, head bowed and eyes closed, trembled and clenched his fists at his forehead. "Did he kill him? Did he *make him die*?"

"I don't know," Glory whispered. "The police took him, and they won't let me talk to him, and my mother isn't home, and I think Malcolm hurt him really bad, but I begged him not to kill, but I was so scared..." The words came out in a rush, and Glory cried for the first time since Malcolm had let go of her hand in the ambulance. Deep, heavy sobs erupted from a part of herself she hadn't known existed—a place of fear and guilt that not even beatings could touch. "I was disobedient. I got off the bus before my stop. I was greedy. I wasn't dressed right... I coulda got away, but I wasn't careful... and Malcolm might go to jail..." A sudden throbbing in her head took her breath away. She coughed, choked, then brought her hands to her face, causing herself more pain when she touched the bruises there.

"No!" Herschel said sharply, taking Glory's hand. "Absolutely not. That evil son of a bitch *attacked you* because he wanted to. You didn't cause this. And you are gonna be okay, and Malcolm is gonna be just fine. His daddy'll see to it. C'mon, darling, breathe with me. Slow and steady. That's right... deep... relax..."

Glory watched Herschel's tear-streaked face as she took deep breaths. "I'm glad you came dressed as a man."

Herschel paused. "Oh, really?"

"Yeah." Glory managed a small, painful grin. "Otherwise, your makeup would be a mess right now."

GLORY SAT PROPPED UP in the hospital bed, staring out the window, with Herschel in a nearby recliner, reading a magazine, waiting for her to sleep. She was sleepy, but closing her eyes was not an option. Behind her eyelids, she could see only the dingy brick wall of the gangway. Sleeping with evil thoughts would open the way for demons to enter her.

And the demon had almost entered her. He'd been right there at her gate. He'd slid up against her—damp, thick, and hard... he'd almost gotten in. With her eyes closed, Glory could see the brick wall behind him, smell the sour stench of the smoke and filth of the gangway. She could feel his hand on her neck and his beard on her cheek, his bulk crushing her against the wall, his fingers kneading her openings, and the Jezebel spirit in her body betraying her like a starving whore, eager for demon seed.

But Malcolm had come, and maybe he killed the demon. He was probably going to jail for defending a gate that was already opened, a garden already raided, a cherry already smashed—and probably forgotten by the boy who'd smashed it.

Glory opened her eyes and felt bile rising in her throat. She'd dozed off. The pain medicine had made her sleepy, but she wouldn't, couldn't, let it take her. The wall clock showed nearly eleven. She'd only been asleep for a few minutes. It had seemed like hours... hours looking up at windows, hoping and praying somebody would look down into the gangway and see. Hours staring into a dripping, foul mouth full of jagged teeth, promising to take her unnaturally and make her the mother of demon spawn. But Malcolm had come and bludgeoned the demon with the wrath of God, fighting for purity that she'd left months ago on the couch with JT in the back room of Herschel's salon.

Glory opened her eyes again. Herschel was gone, and she could hear sirens outside, probably bringing in new patients. *Was there a car accident?* Maybe sirens had drowned out the warnings to keep her sweater on and her socks rolled up like a proper, godly young lady. Maybe they'd masked the sound of her head hitting the brick wall or the sound of her ripping clothes and muted the sounds of her struggle, drowning out her screams.

But Malcolm had come and struck down the demon like an avenging angel of the Lord... a good, godly man led to crush, kill, and destroy in the name of her fake innocence.

Something—sounds, whispers, footsteps—made Glory opened her eyes. The pain in her head made it hard to focus, and it hurt to move her neck. The curtain moved, and in the dimmed light, she looked into her mother's anxious face.

"Hi, Mama," Glory said, surprised that she couldn't cry. She thought she should be crying with her mother, since she'd cried with Herschel. *What kind of daughter am I?* "How was church?"

"Um, church was fine, baby." Mary's brow wrinkled. "We, ah, got back late. So, baby, how are you?"

"I'm fine. I had a kind of rough day, though."

"Oh, Jesus." Mary Bishop broke down, pulling Glory into her arms, jarring her, rocking and sobbing. "Please, Lord, let her be all right. She's all I got left."

"Mama, I'm okay. I'll be fine."

More people appeared. Somebody moved to help Mary, Herschel pressed Glory back into her pillow, and somebody turned on the overhead lights. Shielding her eyes from the sudden glare, Glory made out the faces of her mother, Ms. Washington from church, Elder Porter, and Malcolm.

"Mama, please stop. I'm okay."

"But... you sound like... like... your mind ain't right. You all bandaged up, talkin' 'bout a rough day. Lord, I thought your mind was gone."

"I'm sorry, Mama." Glory sighed. "I was trying not to worry you. Can somebody please turn down the lights?"

Herschel pressed a hand to Glory's shoulder. "You rest now. I'll get the lights on my way out, now that your mama's here. Mrs. Bishop, it was delightful to meet you, even under these circumstances."

Mary Bishop dabbed at her tears. "It was good to meet you too, Herschel. Please call me Mary." She pulled the tall man into a motherly hug. "Thank you so much for sitting with her. You've truly been a blessing tonight. Truly a blessing."

"You're very welcome, Ms. Mary. It's the least I could do. Glory is such a blessing at the salon."

"Before you go," Elder Porter spoke up, "let's pause for a word of thanks for God's mercy in the rescue and healing of this child."

The small group spread out and joined hands, with Herschel gently holding Glory's right hand and her mother firmly gripping her left. As Elder Porter began speaking, Glory tried to close her eyes, but the image of the brick wall forced them open. She kept her head bowed and tried to follow the prayer, but with her eyes open and her head aching, it was impossible. Her own lust and fornication and disobedience had opened a way for demons, and now she couldn't pray.

Glory raised her head and found herself looking into Malcolm's eyes. Like hers, they were wide open. He nodded and blinked slowly. Glory stared. His eyes looked hard, his jaw tight, and his expression cold. She wondered if he saw something bad when he closed his eyes, too. *What if Malcolm can't pray, either?*

After the prayer ended, while Herschel dimmed the lights and shook hands, Glory watched Malcolm move to the far corner of the room. He leaned against the wall and stared out of the window. His folded arms seemed to strain the sleeves of his white dress shirt. Even in the low light, the thin fabric couldn't hide the fuzzy mark of his past, tattooed on his shoulder. *Is that why he always wears jackets or plaid dress shirts?* He had always seemed so easy and mild. Now he looked hard, tough. *How come I never noticed that?*

Promising to visit church soon, Herschel said his goodbyes, reminding Glory of the doctor's instructions to rest and not tax her brain by stressing or thinking too hard. Glory turned her head to hide a smile when Ms. Washington slipped her arm through Herschel's to walk with him to the elevator and hear more about how he'd come to own a beauty salon.

Mary moved around the room, smoothing covers and fluffing pillows. "The police said he grabbed you a block from home. Why was you a block from home? The bus stop is right outside our door."

"I was at the store."

"So you got off the bus and walked all the way back to the store? For what?"

"No, ma'am. I got off at the store to get a taffy apple." Glory hung her head. *Here it comes.*

"You what? For a what? Lord Jesus." Mary collapsed into a chair. Elder Porter moved to pour her a cup of water. "You disobedient, greedy... and this is what happens!"

"Now, Mary, please—" Elder Porter began.

"See. What I tell you?" Mary pushed the offered cup aside and rose, advancing on her daughter. "You follow your own mind, you let demons of greed and rebellion rule you, and God punished you. You was probably just a struttin' down the street, and God sent—"

"Mother Bishop!" Malcolm's voice cut through Mary's tirade. Glory looked up. He was still facing the window. "With all due respect, Mother Bishop," Malcolm said slowly, "our God does not punish his children with rape. God protects and comforts. God does not send demons to punish. 'I sent them not, neither have I commanded them, neither spake unto them. They prophesy unto you a false vision and divination and a thing of nought!'"

"But I know my child, and I know she got the demons of—"

"No!" Malcolm turned to face Mary. Glory saw rage in his face—he was far angrier than she'd ever seen him. "Mother Bishop, we almost lost your daughter today. Are you suggesting I disrupted God's plan?"

"Well... all I'm saying," Mary persisted, "is she coulda been killed, and it wouldn'ta happened if—"

"Are you suggesting that for the sin of being young and impulsive, the God of love and patience and virtue would punish your daughter by having her beaten and stripped, spread open, raped, and murdered in a dark, nasty, piss-soaked gangway half a block from her home, where nobody would've noticed her rotting body for days? Is that really the God you believe in?"

Malcolm turned to Elder Porter. "Dad, is this what we're teaching our members?"

"Malcolm, stop! Please!" Glory cried.

"That... that... thing drug her back there to *beat her* and to *fuck her* and to *kill*—"

"*Boy*, that's enough!" Elder Porter moved to stand in front of his son. "You're going too far. That's a mother scared for her child. Have some compassion!"

Malcolm folded his arms, going quiet at his father's orders, his anger still hanging in the air. Glory watched Malcolm's ugly words stab at her mother's worst fears. Mary's face contorted in agony.

"He wasn't gonna kill me, Mama," Glory whispered. "He said he was gonna leave a baby in me, so he wasn't gonna kill me. You wouldn'ta lost me, Mama. I'm okay."

"Jesus!" Mary exclaimed, throwing her arms around Glory, squeezing a little too tight, breathing deeply. "Baby, did he... did that monster...?"

"No, ma'am, he didn't. I'm fine." Glory looked over her mother's shoulder at Malcolm. His eyes still simmered with a barely contained rage that frightened her. "Malcolm stopped him before he could touch me. I prayed. I called on Jesus, and Malcolm came." She watched the anger in Malcolm's face turn to... what, relief? *Was he about to cry? Was he afraid, too?* Then it dawned on Glory: Malcolm thought he'd been too late. He'd thought he'd failed to protect her.

Ms. Washington placed a hand on Mary's shoulder. "Mary, Herschel said we shouldn't stress her. With a concussion, she needs rest. Lemme take you back to my house tonight. We'll come back in the morning—bring her some fresh clothes and stuff."

"Yeah, you right," Mary said, not letting go of her daughter.

Glory let her mother lay her back and fluff the pillow. She accepted another sip of water and watched her mother smooth and fuss about until Elder Porter called for a word of prayer before parting. With all heads bowed and eyes closed, Glory again raised her head and looked into Malcolm's eyes.

———— ⚮ ————

GLORY BOUNCED UP AND down on her toes. She couldn't help it. The pile of candy was so big, and her daddy was going so slow. *Can't I have just one?* She reached out and slid a silver-wrapped piece from the edge of the table. Turning her back, she carefully peeled the flag and opened the foil then placed the whole piece of chocolate into her mouth. It tasted foul, and racked with guilt, she turned around to face her daddy, but he was gone. Glory watched in horror as her mother stomped on his dead body while demons of gluttony ate all of her candy. Then JT took her gently in his arms and kissed her and laid her down on the couch while Herschel stood in the corner, laughing. And when JT lay on top of her, pain exploded in her brain because the monster slammed her head against the brick wall, and her mother stomped on JT's mangled dead body while demons of lust touched her down there and set her on fire... but Malcolm came with his sword and killed the demons and struck down her mother...

Glory opened her eyes. It took her a moment to remember that she was still in the hospital. The sun was rising, and Malcolm sat beside the bed, arms folded, legs outstretched, chin on his chest, sleeping in the chair. Lying on her side, Glory took a good look at him. His complexion had lightened since the summer. He wasn't really just plain brown but more like pale not-really-brown. His thin arms were more muscular than she'd thought, and the top button of his shirt was open. She wondered if he was hiding another tattoo somewhere. He looked a lot stronger than she expected. She imagined him built not solid like a basketball player but lithe like a runner. When she'd held him, he'd felt so powerful. Malcolm Porter—the preacher's son, demon slayer, and rescuer of pretend virgins—was very soothing to look at. *Why didn't I ever really look at him before?*

Malcolm opened his eyes and peered deeply into hers for a minute before speaking. "Hi, Glory."

"Hi, Malcolm."

"How are you?"

"I've felt better."

"Okay. How's your heart, your spirit? How do you feel?"

"I'm okay. Really. What happened at the police station?"

Malcolm laughed a little. "Nothing much. Just a lotta paperwork and waiting. They asked some questions, and then after a while, a sergeant comes through and says it's a good thing I didn't kill 'im." Malcolm sounded bitter. "They towed my car, and I got a reckless-driving ticket for blocking traffic. Said if I'd parked first, there wouldn't be anything to talk about. No other charge, because they 'can't find a weapon, wink, wink.' Said 'Glory must be a real tough girl to whip the guy's ass like that, wink, wink. Say hi to your old man for me.'" Malcolm sighed. "My dad brought me some clean clothes and got my car out. Back bumper is dented, but that's it."

"I thought I heard an accident. How did your car get hit?"

"When I didn't see a place to park, I just stopped the car and got out. The guy behind me didn't like it. Tried to move a '69 Caddy with an '83 Chevette. If I hadn't been busy, it woulda been funny."

"Malcolm?"

"Yeah, Glory?"

"How did you know? How did you find me?"

Malcolm sighed. "I saw you walking." He shook his head and laughed a little. "I thought you looked like a kid with those ponytails and your sweater like that. Then I looked again and didn't see you. I thought you went in a store, but I saw your backpack on the sidewalk, and something in my spirit just felt wrong. I looked around for a parking spot, but then the Lord said, 'Go,' so I just stopped the car, grabbed the steering wheel lock, and took off."

Glory let a tear escape. "And you saved me."

Malcolm leaned forward in the chair, wiping his face with his hands. "Glory, in that gangway, you saved me."

"I don't get it."

"For the enemy hath persecuted my soul. He hath smitten my life down to the ground. He hath made me to dwell in darkness—"

"Malcolm, please," Glory said. "I'm sorry. I can't understand that right now."

"No, I'm sorry." Malcolm sighed. "Sometimes, it's hard for me to have the right words in plain English. Lemme see if I can do this better." He steepled his fingers, and his brow furrowed in concentration. "I used to have temper tantrums when I was little, so bad the housekeeper would strap me down to keep me from hurting myself. Mother said there was a hellion in me that I needed to tame."

Glory nodded, but she couldn't imagine her mother encouraging her to tame demons.

"But I didn't tame it," Malcolm continued. "I locked it up and just let it out when I got bored. I let this dark hellion out to play and destroy until I got tired, then I'd lock it back up till next time. I'm ashamed to admit now... I loved letting it out. In my wild days, I looked for reasons to cut loose any time I could." Malcolm wiped a tear from his cheek. "But then the Lord delivered me. I locked the hellion up and threw away the key, and my whole life changed."

Glory understood. *Didn't I read forbidden books and taste wine coolers and lie with JT? Didn't I give in to the demons and enjoy it?*

"Then today, when I saw... that thing... that monster... with its hand on your neck... its pants down and his... his... I thought he... I thought... he was... I ripped open the cage. I let the hellion out, and it felt good. Oh, God, it felt so good. It's like I freed the monster and let it feed, and I loved it. I wanted to kill him. I needed to kill him."

He wiped another tear and smoothed his hair. "But then you put your arms around me. Your touch, your voice, your light was something more powerful than my darkness. You chained the hellion that I had set free. I was trying to kill that... that... and if I had killed, I don't know if I coulda came back from that. You helped me to not kill." He reached out and touched Glory's cheek, wiping her tear. "'There ariseth light in the darkness: she is gracious, and full of compassion, and righteous.' Thank you for saving me, Miss Bishop."

Glory pushed away thoughts of Malcolm's dark side. "Do I look bad? I haven't seen a mirror. I don't mean to be vain, but I'm scared." She tried to stretch, but her whole body hurt. She shifted in the bed, pulling herself up some but staying on her side.

Malcolm leaned back in the chair and folded his arms again. He smiled a little. "Glory Bishop, you're the most beautiful woman in the world. Herschel said you'll be back to normal in a few days. The cut on your lip might take a week, but no scars."

Glory blushed. She never felt beautiful, and she couldn't imagine what Malcolm saw in her, especially now. She tried closing her eyes again, but the brick wall was still there. The counselor had said to expect nightmares for a while.

"Malcolm?"

"Yes?"

"What do you see when you close your eyes?"

Malcolm ran a hand through his hair. "Nothing good. You don't wanna know."

"I think I have an idea," Glory said. "I keep seeing the brick wall in the gangway. I can't close my eyes to pray anymore."

"I'm not gonna tell you what I see. You don't need that."

"You're probably right." Glory shuddered. "I guess I don't. How will you pray?"

"Time. It'll take some time. I'll watch TV or read a book until I see new things in my mind. God won't let this keep you away too long. Um... your boss is kinda interesting, isn't he?"

The question caught Glory off guard. She'd never told Malcolm much about Herschel, and now she wasn't sure what to say. "What do you mean?"

"You know what I mean. He's kinda *funny*. I'm glad he was here for you, though. When I called, and they said somebody was with you, I thought it was your mother, but Dad said she was at the soup kitchen. We all got here and met up with Herschel. He really cares about you. What does he do?"

"Um, he's the owner of the salon I work at. He used to work in New York and California, but his family is here. He makes natural hair and skin stuff." There was no way she could tell Malcolm all that Herschel did for her—no way Malcolm would understand. "I didn't know where else to call. My mother was off work, you were busy, and there was no answer at the church. I didn't even know who would answer at the salon." When Glory could pray again, she would apologize for the lie. She'd called the shop three times, praying for Herschel to answer.

"Glory?"

"Yeah, Malcolm?"

"Be my lady."

"What?"

"I think you heard me."

Glory closed her eyes and faced the brick wall. "I don't know if I can..." The weight of the monster pressed against her. She opened her eyes again.

"What don't you know?"

"Malcolm... I'm not... clean..." Glory tried to get the words out without crying. She'd said them to the nurse and the policewoman and the counselor, but she hadn't been able to say them to her mother. And now she had to tell Malcolm because he had unleashed his own personal demon to save her.

"What do you mean 'not clean'?"

"He put his... fingers in me," Glory whispered. She felt bile rising in her throat, just as it had when she'd told the nurse, just as it had when the nurse had checked for evidence and told her she was scratched and torn. "The nurse said even though it was his hands... it was still... he still..." She couldn't get the word out.

"He still raped you." Malcolm stood up and walked to the window.

Glory waited for him to take back his question.

"And because you've been touched, I shouldn't want you? You think I go around looking for virgins? Half the mothers in church throw their virgin daughters at me every Sunday. I don't care about your virginity. I saved you from a monster, and you saved me from a monster. God put us together. You don't get to question that." Malcolm moved closer and leaned over the bed, his brief flash of anger gone. "Glory Bishop, you are my lady. That's not a request."

Glory relaxed and accepted his gentle kiss. He wanted her, and eventually, he'd want all of her, but he didn't expect her to be a virgin. She would let the monster take the blame. *Demon of lies and deceit!* When she could pray again, she would ask God for forgiveness.

Glory blinked. Her vision of Malcolm as a shining angel changed to one of an avenging angel who would kill for her. She would never tell him he'd almost killed for nothing.

Chapter 7

The Wolcott Tech bookstore was almost as old as the school itself. Back in the day, it was an old-fashioned soda shop that filled with students for lunch periods. The big black bell on the wall rang at the same time the bells in the school did, and speakers mounted high on the maroon-and-gold-draped walls cranked out the announcements every day after third period. The shelves on the left were once lined with textbooks, notebooks, and hot-rod and teen magazines, and on the right side, a cute boy used to make sodas and an old man flipped burgers while kids in saddle shoes and poodle skirts spun on the stools and filled the six booths in the back.

But now the dingy place looked as rundown as the neighborhood—maroon and gold had faded to brown and beige. The photos on the walls were streaked with years of dust and grease, the bell and speakers long silent. The glass display case on the left served as the school supply counter where the current owner, Mr. Harris, sat at the old cash register in a greasy apron, smoking a smelly cigar, a permanent leer on his face. The wall behind him was lined with books, Cliff's Notes, and magazines in plain brown wrappers. On the right side of the room, Mrs. Harris, Nita, and students who asked to make a few bucks that period worked the grill and soda fountain, flipping burgers, tossing fries, and filling just the top edges of ice cream cones.

Walking into the crowded little store at fifth period in late November, Glory tried to imagine Malcolm stalking this neighborhood in his wild days. *Did he stand outside and pick on the nerd kids? Did he fight? Did he have a knife?* She waved to Tressa and Christy, who were waiting in their usual booth in the back, then paid for Sunkist Orange pop and slid into the booth next to Tressa.

"So, we've been sitting here talking about you behind your back." Tressa spoke slowly with the soft, elegant voice of an old-time radio star, always sounding like she wasn't really serious. Glory imagined her friend playing the brilliant reporter in the old detective movies she used to watch with her dad. "The stories we're making up sound great, but we think yours might be better." Tressa, who often laughed at her own jokes, might quietly break out in song at any moment.

"Yup," Christy added. "I mean, we could make up our own story about your secret life and all, but it would be like a Jackie Collins novel. Folks are asking about the bodyguard and the limo. Inquiring minds wanna know!" Christy was the most outgoing of their trio. She had friends among the jocks, popular kids, nerds, and even the bad kids. She had a car, and all the teachers loved her.

Glory was still amazed that these two girls were her friends. Tressa sat beside her in art class and once, the previous year, they'd cut first period to sneak downtown for cookies, but Glory was sure a girl like Tressa was only being nice to her out of pity. Short and dark, Tressa was perfectly beautiful, and Glory regularly prayed that God forgive her for jealousy, because all eyes followed Tressa when she walked down the hall. But shy, selfless Tressa was also the most Christian girl Glory knew. Christy, meanwhile, moved through the world like she owned it. She had the necessary light skin, long silky black hair, and dazzling smile, but her large size excluded her from the glamour girls' clubs. It didn't matter. The glamour girls wanted to be her friend because everybody wanted to be Christy's friend. Glory imagined Christy as the voice of godly sarcasm, and people came to bask in her wisdom. Every day, Glory was shocked that Christy noticed and spoke to her.

"I told you," Glory said, "I got mugged. I get a ride to school now."

Her friends looked at each other.

"Tee, where's your list?" Christy asked.

Glory wasn't surprised. Tressa kept lists of everything. She dug through her book bag and handed Glory a yellow notepad covered with doodles and notes. After flipping through a few pages, Glory stopped at a page with her name at the top, embellished with stage lights, drama masks, and question marks. Glory tried to keep a straight face while reading the list of her friends' observations and suspicions.

"Well." Glory pointed to the first thing on the list. "The makeup is only to cover the bruises, and I hafta take it off 'cause I can't wear it home."

"Aha! Add sneaking around..." Christy said.

"And I don't have a bodyguard—"

"Glory, a man in dark glasses walks you to the door every morning and meets you at the door every afternoon—the last door where nobody goes out of. He keeps one hand on your shoulder all the time, and he's always looking around—"

"Not always," Glory said

"Always!" both girls said at once.

"And it's not a black limo—it's a brown Cadillac, and it's not that long—"

"And he's got gangsta white walls just like that song from the seventies," Christy said, and Tressa launched into a song about a Cadillac.

Glory covered her face with her hands. She had to admit the list was funny. Foreign princess, gangster's daughter, secretly rich, in witness protection, illegitimate daughter of a politician—they all shook with laughter as Glory denied item after item.

"But, Glory, we go to a nerd school in Englewood. Everybody here gets mugged. People stand in line to mug us. Nobody else has bodyguards." Tressa marked *Golden Child* and *Next Dali Llama* off her list.

"Yeah," Christy said. "And suddenly, you're walking around, bouncing and happy. Staying late every day and coming to Campus Life every week. Coming *here* for lunch. *Talking* to people. And what's with the hair?"

"Yeah, Glory." Tressa touched Glory's tightly bound hair. "You went from uptight to wild and free... but your hair went from wild and free to uptight."

Glory sighed. "He grabbed my hair. I feel better with it tied up."

"Oh." Tressa softened her tone. "Yeah, I get that."

Glory wondered how much she should tell them and whether they could understand how her world had changed in the past month. When she'd come back to school a week after the attack, Tressa and Christy had carried her books and insisted she come to the bookstore for lunch instead of walking to the fourth-floor lunchroom. Christy showed her how to cover the slowly fading scratches on her face with lotion and beige powder. Tressa drew her into Campus Life, the weekly tenth-period Bible-study club that Glory had always wanted to join.

"Okay. Well... there is kinda something going on." Glory leaned in to the table. "But you've gotta promise you won't tell. I mean really, really promise. It's kinda big."

"Okay. We promise we won't tell," Christy said.

"You're okay, right?" Tressa asked.

"Yeah, I'm fine." Glory took a deep breath. If she was going to tell her best friends, it was now or never. "It wasn't just a mugger—he tried to rape me. But he didn't 'cause a man from church almost killed him. Now I'm the man's girlfriend. He protects me and treats me like a woman and takes me everywhere I wanna go." The words came out in a rush. Glory was surprised at how simple the story sounded when she told it that fast.

"So, Tee..." Christy said, turning to her friend, "is *Damsel in Distress* somewhere on that list?"

Tressa gasped and scowled at Christy. "You were almost raped? Glory, why didn't you say anything? We're sitting here making jokes. Are you really okay? Did they get him?"

"Yes, I'm fine. They got him. He was too messed up to get away after Malcolm got through with him, and he was wanted for other attacks."

"Do you hafta go to court and stuff?" Christy asked.

"Nah, and Malcolm doesn't want me to. The police report says the monster tripped or I beat him up... or something... because they couldn't find a weapon."

"Huh? What?" both girls asked.

"Well, Malcolm's the pastor's son, and I guess they didn't want anybody to know he was involved."

"Wait," Christy said, "*your* pastor's son? Elder Riley Porter's *son* almost killed a rapist and is now going with the victim?"

"You're goin' with Elder Porter's son?" Tressa asked. "Isn't that, like, church royalty or something?"

"Tee." Christy tapped the notepad. "Put *Fairy-Tale Princess* back on that list. Kidnapped by a villain, and Prince Charming rides up on a shining horse with a blazing sword and rescues her and then claims the princess. Like, *totally* gag me."

"Well"—Glory smiled a little—"it's a shining Cadillac, but I did think that steering-wheel lock was a sword." She shuddered at the memory. The brick wall no longer haunted her, but some sounds and images still shook her.

"Glory?" Tressa asked. "How old is Malcolm?"

Glory looked at her friends. Tressa's concern and Christy's suspicion mirrored her own discomfort with their age difference. It wasn't like she was trying to keep it a secret, but the change in her world was amazing. Her mother now let her go anywhere she wanted as long as she was with Malcolm. She could sit with friends after school or spend hours reading in the library, since she waited for a ride home from Malcolm every day. She'd been to the movies and to fancy restaurants. He'd even taken her to an art gallery. He called her a woman and told her she was beautiful.

"He's in his twenties," Glory said. "He's twenty-seven." She watched her friends' faces.

"Glory, that's kinda old," Tressa said. "What do y'all talk about?"

Glory thought for a minute. "Everything, I guess. We go places—mostly church. We just have fun, and he makes me happy."

"Well," Christy said, "you get pregnant, I'm next in line behind yo' mama to kick yo' butt."

The crowd had thinned out, and the girls gathered their bags to go back to school. Passing the school-supply counter, Glory kept her head down, and Tressa folded her arms across her chest.

"Hey, hey, hey." Mr. Harris grunted, chewing on his cigar. "Large, medium, small. You know I likes 'em all."

"Bless you, Mr. Harris," Christy answered.

Glory was positive Christy meant exactly the opposite.

Chapter 8

S ince that awful day in October, Glory had not had a moment outside alone, and she sometimes found herself missing her private walks. Even though dark strangers and shadowed doorways frightened her, and she really was grateful for her constant escort, she missed sitting at the bus stops, watching the sun come up in the mornings or the stars come out at night. But on wintry December afternoons, when the Chicago Hawk swooped down between buildings and threatened to lift her skirts and knock her off her feet with icy blasts, Glory truly appreciated the benefits of being Malcolm Porter's lady.

After a few near misses on the icy front steps, Malcolm agreed that meeting Glory at the little-used side door on Sixty-First Street was a good idea. It had taken Quentin a few days to spread the news that Glory wasn't secretly a gangster's daughter, but she still didn't like for people to see Malcolm acting like a henchman, so she always tried to leave after everybody else.

Glory tried pushing the Sixty-First Street door open, and a gust of wind pushed back. It took all of Glory's strength to get out of the building. As she stepped out into the cold, the wind caught the door, and it slammed shut behind her. Malcolm stood in the narrow covered space created by the door's overhang, shivering in his long black leather coat, gray wool hat, and dark glasses. He leaned down and kissed her with cold lips.

"See, Malcolm. This is silly." Glory pointed at his car a few yards away, down the block. "You should be waiting right there, warm in the car."

The two pats on her face were light and quick—*love taps*, he called them. "Woman, don't call me silly again." He held his cold hand against her cheek. "You know that's not polite." He kissed her again, taking her backpack from her shoulder. "C'mon. Let's go. I've got a surprise for you."

Glory sighed and let him guide her to the car. She hated when he did that, especially when his hands were cold. At the car, opening the passenger door, he slipped but caught himself, dropping her backpack into a slush puddle.

"See," Glory snapped, bending to pick up her bag. "If you'd just waited in the car, you'd be warm and this wouldn'ta happened."

"Glory."

"What?" She stood up, shaking the slush off her bag and tapping it on the side of the car.

The slap stunned her. Fast and hard. Serious. She blinked back tears as Malcolm moved closer and stroked her stinging cheek.

"Woman, don't talk to me like that," he said softly. "I told you, this isn't a good neighborhood. I'm gonna be at that door, waiting for you every day, okay?"

"Okay," Glory whispered, unable to look up at him.

Malcolm pulled her into his arms. "Are we gonna have this conversation again?"

"No." Glory coughed to clear her throat. She would not cry over something as simple as a slap. It *was* rude of her to snap at him when he was only trying to protect her. She tried to relax in his arms as the wind picked up.

"You're shivering," Malcolm said, letting go of her. "Let's get you in the car."

———— ∽❦∽ ————

THE LAST TIME GLORY had seen Christmas at Evergreen Plaza Mall was the last Christmas her daddy had taken her to see Santa. On this snowy weekday afternoon, the mall was fairly quiet, and Malcolm let her spend as much time as she wanted at each of the holiday scenes of Santa's workshop. The animatronic elves making wooden toys were just as magical as she remembered. The whole mall was still amazing, actually. Every store display sparkled and twinkled with red and green ornaments floating everywhere. The mannequins were all decked out in velvet and sequins, and the smell of hot caramel popcorn filled the air. Glory wanted to throw her head back and sing along to the Christmas carols but contented herself with holding Malcolm's hand and wondering where he was taking her.

At Kroch's & Brentano's bookstore, Glory shocked Malcolm with all the books that she'd never been allowed to read. "My mother worries that I'll learn too many worldly ways. I'm surprised she lets me go places with you."

"Mother Bishop knows I'll take good care of you. She's a wise woman," Malcolm said. "'There shall be no whore of the daughters of Israel. Many daughters have done virtuously, but thou excellest them all—'"

"Malcolm, how did you learn the Bible by heart?" After four months, Glory had gotten pretty good at redirecting Malcolm's impromptu sermons. She saved up her questions for times when he talked about her, and she'd gotten good at interrupting him with questions about his past. She felt a little bad doing it, but the mall at Christmas wasn't the time she wanted to hear a sermon about her virtue.

"Well," Malcolm said, "basically, when God was workin' on me, I listened to it on tape a whole lot."

Glory glanced at Malcolm as they walked. He always got quiet when the subject of his old life came up. Glory imagined he might have been a gang member or sold drugs or something. It couldn't have been too bad, though, because he was a youth minister and no-body at church ever looked at him funny.

The gleaming silver and white of Carson's department store was blinding. Wrapped packages sat beneath giant silver Christmas trees, hung with giant pink ornaments. Mannequins sparkled in fuzzy sweaters dotted with tinsel puffs. Pyramids of gift boxes teetered on counters, and a brightly smiling salesgirl offered Malcolm a per-fumed card that she just knew his *little sister* would love.

Glory hoped she didn't look too terrified when they stopped at the jewelry counter. As they moved along the glass display case, she lingered at the watches and hurried past the rings. Finally, they got to the earring counter, and a chipper young lady bounced into view. Her name badge read "Tammy."

"Merry Christmas. Welcome to Carson's," Tammy chirped. "How are you today?"

"We're just fine, Miss Tammy." Malcolm turned to Glory. "I need to talk to Miss Tammy for a minute. Go have a seat on that stool at the end of the counter. I'll be right there."

Glory looked around and then moved slowly to the end of the counter, relieved that Malcolm wasn't looking at rings. Her mind wandered back to the slap, and her hand automatically went to her cheek. It hadn't really hurt her physically. It *had* hurt her feelings, embarrassed her more than anything. *What if somebody saw?* Glory pushed the thought out of her mind. She and Malcolm were having a great time today.

She twirled the display rack, smiling when her eyes landed on a pair of pearl stud earrings just like the ones JT had given her when they were seven years old. She begged Daddy to get her ears pierced so she could wear them. Right after Christmas, he brought her to this very store. Getting the little gold beads had hurt, but her daddy held her hands and told her how pretty she was. They carefully put away the pearls so she could put them on when her ears healed enough to remove the starter studs. Glory sighed at the memory. As soon as her daddy went back on the road, her mother told her that her ears were infected and the gold beads had to come out. Her piercings had soon closed. It was God's punishment for letting the demons of pride get in her.

Glory jumped when she felt Malcolm's hand on her shoulder. "Having fun?" he asked.

"Sure. So I guess the surprise is earrings?"

"Sort of," Malcolm said. "I ordered your Christmas present, so we hafta get your ears pierced."

Glory moved to get down from the stool. "I don't want my ears pierced. It really hurts."

Malcolm's hands on her shoulders held her in place.

Tammy appeared, carrying a silver tray draped with a blue cloth. "You wanted the fourteen-carat gold with diamond, right Malcolm?"

Covering her earlobes, Glory looked away.

"Yes, that's right," Malcolm said, massaging Glory's shoulders. "Would you give us a minute please, Miss Tammy?"

"Sure, Malcolm. I've gotta go get the care kit. I'll be right back."

Glory watched Tammy dance away and briefly hated her for calling him *Malcolm* instead of *Mr. Porter*. Malcolm grabbed her wrists, pulling her hands away from her ears.

"Malcolm, please. Why can't I get clip-ons?" she begged.

He moved her arms down to her lap, the strength in his grip rendering her resistance useless. With his arms around her, holding her close, Glory felt like a little girl waiting for a shot from the doctor.

"Malcolm, please. I don't even wear jewelry, and my mother doesn't want my ears pierced." Glory tried to pull away from him. He pulled her closer. His grip on her wrists tightened until it hurt.

"Stop it," Malcolm said through clenched teeth. "I've already checked with Mother Bishop. You're my lady, and this is my decision.

Yes, it's gonna hurt, but you're gonna sit up straight and take it like a woman. Do you understand me?"

Glory struggled for a second more then stopped fighting. "Yes, Malcolm." She kept her head down and took deep breaths to keep from crying. She hated when he got like this.

Tammy bounced back to the counter, carrying a bright-pink plastic bag. "All set?"

Glory wanted to kick her.

"Yeah," Malcolm said, giving Glory one last squeeze that made her wince. He walked around and placed a hand on Tammy's shoulder. "Be gentle. She's a little nervous, but I know you're great at what you do."

Tammy giggled and blushed. Glory really, really wanted to kick her.

Though Malcolm stood where she could see him, Glory couldn't look at him. As Tammy measured and marked her ears, Glory barely heard her speaking. At that point, it wasn't about the pain. The click, snap, and stabbing was nothing compared to Malcolm forcing this on her—telling her to "take it like a woman." She didn't look in the mirror, and she didn't care how the earrings sparkled. When Malcolm took her in his arms and kissed her forehead and told her she was beautiful, she just wanted him to let her go. He smelled mean and hard, and she hated what he did to her.

Stopping outside of the mall entrance, freezing wind and angry tears still stinging her face, Glory stood still while Malcolm adjusted her hat and scarf. He lifted her chin and looked into her eyes. "As an earring of gold, an ornament of fine gold, so is a wise reprover upon an obedient ear." He smiled and stroked her cheek.

Glory almost shouted that that Bible verse had absolutely nothing to do with actual earrings. "I need to get to work," she said.

GLORY LOOKED AT HERSELF in the car's visor mirror. She hated to admit she liked the earrings. She had never owned anything this beautiful—or expensive—before. But she was still not over how Malcolm had forced them on her. Looking at Malcolm out of the corner of her eye, she didn't want to be happy or grateful, and smiling at him was out of the question. When the car stopped in front of Herschel's salon, she closed the visor and reached for the door handle but paused. Malcolm hated when she let herself out.

"It's okay," Malcolm said gently. "Go on in. I can watch from here, and there's a lot of people out."

Glory looked at him, not hiding her suspicion. He reached out and lightly touched her ear. It still hurt. She leaned away.

"I'm sorry I had to get so rough. I didn't think it would be such a big deal. Forgive me?"

Glory lowered her eyes. "Of course I forgive you, Malcolm. It's just that... I hate it when you force me to do things." She looked him in the eye. "I'm not a little kid."

"No, you're not. You're an incredible woman." He stared until Glory lowered her eyes. "God, I knew those would be nice, but *wow*! I didn't think it was possible for you to look more beautiful."

Glory felt a blush rising. *Why does he always say those things?*

He lifted her chin and kissed her lightly. "You better get inside before I change my mind about letting you go," he joked. "Herschel's taking you home, right?"

"Yeah." Glory opened the door and climbed out of the car. "I'll call the church if anything changes. Malcolm, thank you. I love the earrings."

"I knew you would."

At the door of the salon, Glory turned back to wave at Malcolm and then walked inside.

"Well, look who decided to grace us with her presence this evening. Hello, Glory-Glory!" Herschel called from atop a ladder in a corner, where he stood hanging silver garland. "That pile in the back is pretty big. Ooo, wait! Don't move! Looks like Santa came early!"

As Herschel came down the ladder, Glory looked at the holiday decorations going up. The mirrors were trimmed with red satin bows, iridescent mistletoe hung from the disco ball, and a black-lit Christmas tree glowed in the corner.

"Ooo, Glory-Glory, I am blinded! I don't know what's brighter, your smile or those rocks!" Herschel grabbed Glory's chin and turned her head from side to side. "Those are fresh pokes, too! I coulda did 'em here, you know."

"Yeah." Glory touched her new earrings, frowning a little. "They're not too much?"

"No, darling! They're just perfect. Well..." Herschel frowned a little, too. "For a girl your age, they could be a bit smaller. But why buy small crystals, right? Come on. I'll admire those some more while I help you get started."

"Um, Herschel?" Glory followed Herschel to the back, waving to the customers and stylists, stepping over clutter. "They're not fake."

"Beg pardon?" Herschel turned and folded his arms. "You mean those are real diamonds?" His voice dropped several octaves. "Does your mother know?"

"Um... yes? And I don't know?" Glory thought she should be embarrassed but wasn't sure why. She could feel Herschel's eyes on her as she moved around the room, hanging up her coat and backpack. After what seemed like eons, Glory finally looked at him. "Okay... what?"

"Well," Herschel said, "I'm just wondering who you are? The Glory Bishop I know would never accept such a gift, especially without permission."

Glory started a load of towels and looked around the lounge, noticing it wasn't as messy as usual. She'd been out so often with Malcolm that people had started picking up after themselves. If this kept up, she'd be out of a job soon. Glory joined Herschel at the table piled high with S. H. Herschel holiday products.

"Everything's tagged and labeled," Herschel said, pushing a stack of small boxes out of the way. "The boxes get the whole sets. The bags just get the lotion and soap."

Glory read the labels and laughed. "These are crazy, Herschel. Pound-cake soap?"

"Yes. You'd be surprised how many old ladies like it. Church ladies can't go around smelling like a perfume factory, but they love smelling like vanilla with a hint of spice."

Glory laughed and sat down to start filling the bags. She'd only worked a few days over the past month, and she'd really missed visiting with Herschel. They talked about the Thursday night parties she'd missed and her dates with Malcolm.

"So, what's the story with the earrings? I can't imagine something this extravagant being okay with your mother."

"Well, she hasn't seen 'em yet. We just got 'em today, and I didn't want 'em really. I mean, I love 'em—I really do—but Malcolm made me get 'em." She sniffed a tube labeled Southern Greens and smiled.

"Made you? What do you mean 'made you'?"

"Well, I was scared, and I kept saying no, but he made me sit there, and I was really mad at him, but... huh... what?" Glory couldn't read the look on Herschel's face.

"What are you using for birth control, Glory-Glory?"

"Huh? Birth control? We're not doing it."

"Hmph. Maybe not yet, but that's not gonna be up to you, is it?"

"Herschel, Malcolm respects me. We haven't even talked about it yet. He kisses me, but he knows I don't want to go all the way. He's not gonna rape me."

"No, it won't be rape, and you'll probably think it was a good idea after the fact—"

"But—"

"But nothing! He decides where you go. He orders your food. He decides if you come to work." Herschel ticked off points on his fingers "Did you want your ears pierced today?"

"Well, not really—"

"Did you? Glory-Glory, you have no control in this relationship. When he decides it's time to lay down, you won't be able to say no, and you won't be able to insist he use protection."

Glory hung her head. They had never discussed it, but she knew that she couldn't say no to Malcolm if that was what he wanted.

"You're overwhelmed and intimidated by him. Some women like that. If that's what you like, have fun, but it needs to be because you like it, not because he says so."

"But I like being with him. Doesn't that count? And I—"

"You're an innocent seventeen-year-old *girl*, and he's wining and dining you like a woman."

"I'm not that innocent." Glory pouted, shoving tubes of lotion into sheer bags.

"Girl, you so innocent, yo' boo boo smells like baby powder."

Glory tried to roll her eyes, a skill she'd learned recently.

"Just because you're not a virgin don't mean you're not innocent. You have no idea what's happening, do you? He's spoiling you. Ruining you for anybody else. What boy at school could compete with fancy restaurants and thousand-dollar earrings?"

"Nobody." Glory sighed. "But, Herschel, he spoiled me when he saved me. No boy could do that, either. And I think Malcolm really loves me."

"Well, darling, maybe he does, but it's not all about him. It's about you, too. How do you feel about him?"

Glory got up from the table and walked around. She knew this question was coming, and she didn't have a good answer. "I think I love him? He does so much for me, and it's like I'm free when I'm with him. My mother lets me do anything and go anywhere as long as I'm with him. It's like when he saved me, he also saaaved me... know what I mean?"

"Glory-Glory, darling, I think you're confusing gratitude with love. You love how he makes you feel. You love what he does for you. Anybody would love that."

"But it's more than that—"

"It might be. And when you have sex with him—don't shake your head. That's a grown man treating you like a grown woman. You know I'm right—already pokin' things in you as it is. When you do, you need to take care of yourself. If he really loves you, he'll use a rubber, but just in case, we need to get you on the pill." Herschel started tying the drawstrings on the silky bags of lotion and soap.

"But, Herschel, we haven't even talked about doing it yet—"

"Oh, please, girl. Don't gimme that mess. You're innocent, but you are not stupid. So how 'bout Saturday you get here early. Malcolm will let you work Saturday, right? Go up north to the clinic with me. You chat with the nurse, get a prescription."

"I don't know. He hasn't even tried to touch me, you know, like that."

"Darling, did you plan that evening with JT?"

Glory blushed. She still thought about JT often. Her first time, in this room, on that couch, the Jezebel spirit demanding he make love to her. Twice. And she had waited so long for him. She'd always wanted to, but JT was the one who'd said "wait." The smell of fabric softener still gave her butterflies.

"Glory-Glory! Hellooo! You still here?"

Glory blinked, shaking off the memory. "Okay, I'll be here Saturday morning."

"Um, you know, darling, I never see you get that lost thinking about Malcolm."

Glory tried to roll her eyes again.

IT WAS TEN O'CLOCK that night when Glory got home, and her mother was up, waiting. The teapot simmered on the stove, but Glory's dread turned to pleasant surprise when she saw the box of hot chocolate mix and the bag of marshmallows on the counter. She sat at the kitchen table while her mother made the drinks.

"I got some news today," Mary said. "We're goin' down south a little early this year. Bigma's ailing. So we're leaving the day you get out of school for Christmas break. We'll have Christmas Day down there with the whole family."

"Okay." Glory was only a little disappointed. She'd heard some soldiers came home at Christmas. She didn't really expect anything, but... she pushed the thought away.

"How was your day, baby?" Mary asked.

Glory tried not to sigh. She should have known—another Malcolm conversation. "It was fine. School was good. It was nice to finally be back at work."

"Oh. That's nice." Mary set the cup with two marshmallows in front of Glory. *Two marshmallows.* This was going to be serious. "Anything interesting happen today, baby?"

"Yes, Mama." Glory sighed. "You know exactly what happened today. Malcolm got my ears pierced."

"Don't take that tone with me. Lemme see."

Glory lifted her chin, turning her head so her mother could see her ears. "It really hurt. I don't understand why you let him do it."

"Ooo, baby, those are beautiful. Are they real?"

"Yes, Mama, they're real gold and diamond. Why did you let him do this to me? You took 'em out when Daddy got my ears pierced."

"Baby, you was too young. You spent all day staring at yo'self in the mirror."

"So they weren't infected?"

"You was infected by the demons of pride. 'I'm so pretty. I'm so *glorious*,'" Mary mimicked. "I couldn't let that evil grow in you."

"Mama—"

"But you're 'bout to be a woman now." Mary sat down across from Glory. "And you got a good man guiding you, keeping demons away."

"Daddy was a good man. He—"

"Your daddy wasn't always here. He'd come home and fill yo' head up with stuff then leave and have you open to all kinds of mess. Had to drive the demons outta you all the time."

"But, Mama—"

"Now, Malcolm, he's a good, godly man. You know he is."

"Yes, ma'am," Glory said. Her mother often implied that her father wasn't good or godly, and Glory would rather talk about Malcolm than listen to bad talk about her daddy. "Malcolm is a good man."

"And he's a godly man. That's the most important thing. Even on his bad days, he'll still be godly. And he cares about you, too, you know."

"I know."

"And he takes good care of you, too—protects you, don't he? A man won't put diamonds on a woman he don't care about. Malcolm said he's gon' pick up the bus tickets and get us to the station for our Christmas trip. All to look after you."

"Yes, ma'am, he does take care of me." Glory sipped her hot chocolate. She knew her mother approved of Malcolm, and his age didn't concern Mary at all. *So where is this going?*

"When a good, godly man wants you, you do what he says. You know he cares and won't hurt you. He supplies all your needs, so you do whatever he wants. He says get your ears pierced, that's what you do."

"But, Mama, what if—"

"Now, baby, God sent him to save you. Your place is to do what he says. He's not gon' tell you wrong. God wouldn't send you a man to tell you wrong." Mary rose from her seat and kissed the top of Glory's head. "He saved you from the worst kind of demon. You owe him everything. Give him whatever he asks. Obey him. He won't ask nothing bad. He's a godly man. Don't let demons of rebellion and disobedience get in you. You obey him. I'm goin' to bed now. Clean up the cups before you go to bed."

"Yes, ma'am," Glory said, not looking up, ignoring her mother's slippers scraping down the hall and the creak of her closing bedroom door. Staring into the cup of melted-marshmallow film, Glory felt a knot grow in her stomach. *Did she really just say what I think she said—that God sent Malcolm, and my place is to obey him? Did she really mean that?*

In her room, ready for bed, Glory looked at herself in the tiny mirror in her ballerina jewelry box, trying to picture her seven-year-old self, a glorious little girl with gold beads. She dug around in the box and found the card with the pearl earrings attached. She touched them to her cheek and smiled. They were cold. Her daddy had insisted on meeting JT after discovering the pearls were actually real. *What would he think of Malcolm?* The knot in her stomach tightened. Her daddy would shake Malcolm's hand but would not approve of him at all.

Warm under her covers, listening to the wind whistling around the plastic-covered windows, Glory thought again about her mother's words. *Everything... even sex? Could I?* Of course, when that was what Malcolm wanted, she would. *But do I want him?* She closed her eyes and tried to see herself in diamond earrings, lying beside Malcolm, but when she dreamed, it was pearl earrings, Barbie shoes... and JT.

Chapter 9

"We've got a busy morning, Glory-Glory." Herschel placed a stack of boxes in the back of his dark-blue car. "Put the boxes marked West in first. Stack those marked North on top."

"So, where're we going?" Glory asked. "I thought we were going to the clinic."

"Oh, don't you worry—we are. We've got a few other stops to make, too. There's some shops and a clinic on the North Side and some stores on the West Side I hafta visit. You ready?"

Glory closed the hatch. "Sure."

In early December, Chicago could be ugly and gray with flecks of red and green. Along Lake Shore Drive, the gray sky touched the thickening gray waves of Lake Michigan, and gray clouds smothered the black-and-gray skyline. Driving through downtown, though, they seemed to pass through a barrier, and light broke through. The gray had a hint of blue, and the flecks of red and green became dotted with silver and gold. On Clark Street, Glory could have sworn she felt sunlight.

That chilly morning, Herschel wore a long fur coat Glory suspected was real mink, but she didn't want to think about it. He went on and on about the stops they'd make and how great it was to have company for the Saturday-morning ride. For her part, Glory felt a little guilty enjoying a day practically alone, speaking out of turn, not minding her words, crossing streets all by herself.

"Glory-Glory, what has gotten into you today, darling?" Herschel asked after their third stop. "You were all over that place. That young man flirted with you, and you looked him straight in the eye."

"I don't know." Glory spun, out of breath, bursting with energy. "I don't know. I feel so... so... alive today. This neighborhood is so awesome. People with purple hair and spikes in their faces... and they all know you. And they don't look at me funny." She moved out of the way of a couple pushing a stroller. "And I can talk here. My mother never let me go anywhere, and with Malcolm, I can go places... but he's like my bodyguard. I don't even cross the street by myself, but today, I'm out, and people are treating me like an adult. Can we get a cup of tea somewhere? I hate coffee. Real tea?"

Herschel laughed. "Of course, darling. This is the North Side. I'm sure there's a tea shop somewhere."

By noon, their deliveries were finished, and they walked up a narrow flight of stairs to the North Clark Medical Center. A receptionist behind a big wooden desk buzzed them into a waiting room.

"Hello, Gladys!" Herschel's big voice filled the room. "How are you this fine, freezing day?"

"Totally awesome as always, Hershalicious one. And this must be the little sister of Hershey?" The orange-haired woman in a rainbow tutu and glitter makeup did a perfect pirouette and curtsy. "Welcome, *glorious* little sister."

Glory giggled and did her best imitation of a curtsy then offered her hand. "Hi, I'm Glory."

"Really?" Gladys beamed, pulling Glory into a hug. "Glory? Oh, my God, that is the most bitchin' name ever!"

"She has an appointment with Angie." Herschel pulled Glory away. "Just basics and a prescription. Have a seat, darling," he said to Glory. "I hafta pick up some supplies, too. There should be a box for me in the cabinet."

Glory took a seat and looked around the waiting room. A young couple sat in a corner, and a pregnant woman sat by a window. Walls were covered with posters in several languages, with pictures of needles and condoms. Her eyes landed on an image of a woman with a heart-shaped black eye, with the words underneath: "There's no such thing as a love tap." Glory looked away and pushed the image out of her mind. Malcolm's slap was no big deal.

"Check your earrings and your pockets," Herschel said, taking the seat next to her. "If anything's missing, I'll get it back. Gladys is a recovering klepto, and sometimes she slips."

Glory knew her pockets should be empty, and her earrings couldn't have gone anywhere, but she checked anyway.

"Angie is the nurse," Herschel said. "She's gonna do an exam, kinda like you had at the hospital. No, don't look so scared." He patted Glory's hand. "It's necessary. It'll be quick. Two minutes tops. She'll ask you some questions and give you some options. Tell her you want the pill. Everything else is too complicated. Now, you don't hafta take 'em immediately. You have time to think about it."

"Okay." Touching her earrings, Glory thought of Malcolm. He wouldn't understand this place. He and her mother could never know she'd come to the North Side with Herschel. *Demon of lies and deceit!* She would make this trip every Saturday so she could sit in tea shops and smile at people with purple hair. Following Gladys back to the exam room, Glory avoided looking at the black-eye poster.

The exam went as quickly as Herschel said, and Glory left with a box of condoms, a compact of twenty-eight pills, and a prescription for more. Back in the car, Glory stared into the white plastic bag and felt a knot forming in her stomach. "How much was all of this? Are they gonna send a bill to my house?"

"No, darling. It's a free clinic. They'll send a letter to you at the salon if there's a problem. You hafta pay to get the prescription filled, but don't worry. I've got all kinds of pills at the shop."

"If you had them, why did I need to come here?"

"Because you still need a checkup. The pills are not all the same. What kind did she give you?" Herschel glanced at the pack Glory held up. "Okay, yeah. I've got that one. She told you to start it on the first day of your period?"

"Yeah. Herschel, I'm not sure about this anymore. I don't feel that way about Malcolm. I don't *want* him. You know? I mean, I care about him, but maybe I just really, really like him." Glory felt relieved saying it, even though she knew Malcolm would be guiding her to his car Monday morning and afternoon just like he'd been doing since October. "I don't need these pills."

"Of course you don't, darling," Herschel said in his *I don't believe you* voice. "I see you rolling your eyes. You're not doing it right. I'm a professional—I know. Just keep the pills in your purse. You might change your mind."

"I can't keep these in my purse." Glory held up the condom box.

"Put two in your purse. Does your mother check your purse?"

"No, just my backpack. 'A lady's pocketbook is private.'"

"Then you're fine. Glory-Glory, this isn't that big a deal. You're dealing with a grown man, and you need birth control. But, darling, it's your decision. You get stuck with his baby, and you'll be paying for those earrings for the rest of your life."

Glory sighed and rolled the bag closed. Lately, it felt like everybody was bossing her around—her mother, Malcolm, and now Herschel. Even Tressa and Christy had something to say. And nasty old Mr. Harris had said her stuff had to be good for her to get diamonds. She'd thought about telling Malcolm on him.

Glory knew they were leaving the North Side when the scenery changed back to gray. Hunched people shuffled along unshoveled streets and waited at crowded bus stops. Colorful shops and cafes gave way to boarded-up and burned-out storefronts. This part of Chicago, Glory had never seen. "Where are we?"

"We're nearing Madison and Cicero, on the West Side. Hafta stop at some stores here, then we'll grab a bite."

"West Side? Isn't this a bad area?" Glory looked around, imagining criminals in every doorway. She saw people carrying grocery bags and stepping over snowbanks. A man snatched a lady's bag but then held her hand so she could walk over a broken sidewalk. A woman in a red fur coat waved at cars passing by. Glory raised her hand. She wasn't sure if she should wave back.

"Don't wave back," Herschel said. "It's no different here than the South Side."

"But everybody says bad people live here. JT's dad lives over here somewhere. This is where JT..." Glory hated saying it. "Where he got that girl pregnant."

"No, darling. Poor black people live here. Twenty, thirty years ago, white people lived north and south, and black folks lived on the West Side. When the riots happened, the West Side went up in flames, and the black folks that could leave left and never came back." They stopped in front of a corner store. "We're going in here. It'll only take a minute. Oh, stop looking so scared. Are you kidding me?"

"C'mon. Let's just go." Glory sighed, getting out of the car. This was JT's world, and suddenly, she really missed him.

A bell jingled somewhere as they entered the store. "Hello, hello!" Herschel called out.

"Hershey, is that you?" a scratchy high-pitched voice called from somewhere behind a Plexiglas-enclosed counter.

Behind the counter, the walls were lined floor to ceiling with shelves covered with all manner of canned and boxed goods. A cooler at the end held dairy and lunch meat. On another wall were paper goods and other things. Glory had never seen a glass-enclosed store before. The cashier delivered the customers' purchases through a tall spinning box.

"This is nothing like home," she whispered.

Herschel shrugged. "Yes, Aunt Rosie, it's me."

A full-length door opened in the glass, and Glory followed Herschel through.

"Hello, Allen. How's school?" Herschel said.

The boy was big and tall but obviously still a teenager, with a warm smile and bright eyes. Glory tried not to stare at his deep-brown skin and bulging muscles, but his tight tank top made it hard. His hair was brushed back in waves, and he wore a single gold stud in his left ear. This was one of the dangerous West Side boys they talked about at church, and Glory totally understood the danger. *Demons of lust!*

"It's good, Herk," a deep voice said. "I played in two games. Didn't win, though."

"Only your first year. NFL will be looking for you soon. Allen, this is Glory." Herschel patted Glory's shoulder. "I love her like a baby sister. Look after her while I talk to your grandmother. I won't be a minute."

Glory's eyes went wide as she watched Herschel disappear into the depths of the store.

Allen laughed. "I promise I won't bite. Can I get you a drink?"

"Um, sure. Sunkist?" Glory said, finding her voice.

"Heh. I like that, too. Follow me." He chuckled again as he walked past her.

He smelled like Polo, just like JT, and Glory had to figure out how to follow him through the maze of shelves without looking at his rippling back or tight jeans. She settled on watching his feet. He had heavy, thick basketball shoes just like JT's. She promised herself she'd pinch Herschel hard for leaving her like this.

"So, Glory, what school do you go to?" Allen handed her the orange pop from the cooler.

"Thanks." It took Glory a second to realize why the can looked odd. Malcolm always opened them for her. She shook her head and opened it herself. "Wolcott."

"Oh, South Side. Yeah. I went to Lane Tech. You junior, senior?"

"Senior." Glory wondered what a normal girl would say. Tressa would probably sing something. "Where do you go now?" Glory asked, probably a little too loudly.

"I'm at NIU, in DeKalb." A bell sounded. "C'mon." Allen started off through the maze of shelves again.

Glory followed him and then watched him take care of the customers. A man hung back until after the last customer had left then passed a plastic baggie through the slot. Allen opened a drawer and pulled out a white plastic bag and passed it back through the slot. The customer nodded and left. Allen dropped the customer's baggie into a red pail under the counter. Glory had a feeling she'd just watched something that wasn't good.

"He's a junkie," Allen said, answering Glory's unasked question. "They bring dirty needles, and we give 'em clean ones and rubbers." He drained his can. "AIDS is killing folks, and they think it's only rich fag white boys on the North Side. They won't even look at what's happening down here." He grabbed a bag of chips from a rack and tore it open. "Herk brings us stuff from the North Side every few weeks. They hand it out all over up there."

This West Side boy was so much like JT—rough around the edges but really good inside. Nothing like she'd expected.

"What's it like on the South Side?" Allen asked, offering her the bag of chips.

"The same," Glory lied, embarrassed that she didn't really know.

"I hope she wasn't too much trouble, Allen!" Herschel called from somewhere back in the store.

"We're up front, Herk," Allen answered.

Herschel emerged from between some shelves, followed by an old woman in a flowered duster. "Glory, this is Miz Rosie, the proprietress of this establishment. Miz Rosie, this is Glory. She's like a baby sister to me."

"Nice to meet you, Miss Rosie." Glory offered her hand.

The short heavyset woman pulled Glory into a bear hug. She smelled of pound cake lotion. Glory grinned over at Herschel.

"Shoulda told her Grandma don't shake hands, Herk." Allen coughed on a laugh. "C'mon, Grandma. You'll suffocate her."

"And miss the look on Glory's face?" Herschel laughed. "Never!"

"It's nice to meet you too, Glory," Miss Rosie said. "My, that's such a beautiful name."

Glory extricated herself.

"Glooory," Miss Rosie said. "A beautiful name for a beautiful girl. They don't make pretty girls like this around here, do they, Allen?"

Allen flashed Glory a smile that could have melted her. "No, Grandma, they really don't." He reached out and took Glory's hand. "It was nice meeting you, Miss Glory. I hope you'll come with Herk on his next visit. I'd love to talk more."

"I'll try." Glory prayed her hand wasn't sweating and promised to pinch *and* kick Herschel for this as soon as they got back to the car. *Did he actually just call me Miss Glory?*

"IS HE STILL LOOKING?"

"No, Glory-Glory. You can open your eyes. The big, fine boy is gone."

"Aaah!" Glory screamed. "I can't believe you did that! You left me alone in there with him like that, and he smelled so good. Aaah!"

"I know one thing, little girl," Herschel said. "You finna stop screaming 'fo you be walking. Girl, what is going on with you? This is not like you at all. You've never been this silly."

They rode a few blocks and stopped at an intersection that looked just like her neighborhood. The signs were different, but the buildings were the same, and the people looked the same. At the corner of Madison and Cicero stood O'Reilly's, a restaurant that looked like a brown replica of the Red Apple. Inside, the waitresses wore beige dresses with brown aprons, and the green vinyl seats squeaked when Glory slid across them.

Glory stared into her cup of tea. "I don't know what's going on with me. The lady at the hospital said people would ask me that a lot."

"Ah," Herschel said. "I think I know what's goin' on now. I'm so sorry. I left you there with a strange man—"

"No, Herschel, that's not it. I mean, it's everything." Glory sipped the hot tea and smiled then sighed. "This tea. Malcolm never lets me have tea, but I'm having it 'cause he's not here. I used to be so good, but I'm letting so many new things rule me. It's like after JT left, all sorts of... things... started getting in me."

"Darling, what 'things' are you talking about? You're a normal girl—"

"No. I'm not. I'm not supposed to do what worldly girls do. Did you know I stood up in church and lied? I said me and JT only slept in the car—"

"Y'all did it in the car, too? That was a busy night."

"No, but everybody testified and asked forgiveness, and I didn't. I was lying—"

"What did you lie about if you really only slept in the car?"

"I didn't tell the whole truth. I only said something to hurt Trina. And then Malcolm almost killed somebody to protect my virginity that I already threw away, and I'm lying to him every day—"

"Oh, darling, slow down." Herschel held up a hand as the waitress brought their food. Somewhere, a glass broke, and the old woman at the register clapped and cackled with glee.

"How are you lying to Malcolm every day?" Herschel asked.

"He thinks I'm this good and pure thing that he has to protect. He walks me to the door. He opens pop cans for me. But I sneak and go to the store he told me not to go to. It's bad, but I go anyway. He always gets me coffee, but I'm drinking *tea* right now. He tries to show me the 'world,' and I hafta act like I don't know anything. You know all the books I read? He doesn't know about any of those books. He thinks I've never had alcohol before. I've had wine coolers lots of times."

Herschel wiped his whole face with a napkin and cleared his throat when he put it down. "Well, Glory-Glory, you are certainly more worldly than he knows, but that doesn't make you a liar—"

"But I'm not supposed to be worldly. I'm not supposed to want to be this way. That boy wasn't supposed to get to me just 'cause he looked and smelled nice."

"Oh, darling, yes he was. That's what I've been trying to tell you. You're a normal girl."

"Why do I feel so bad about it?" Glory asked.

"You've been caged up so long, and Malcolm is letting you out, but he's keeping a fancy leash on you."

"Why does it feel like I'm giving in to demons?"

"I don't know anything about demons. I think you're feeling freedom, and it feels good. If all you've known is that the world is evil and bad, you get confused when it makes you feel good. I mean, look around you. We're on the West Side. The *oooh, scary* West Side. Is this anything like what you heard?"

"Well, no—"

"Do you see criminals and police chases and crazy people everywhere—don't look at the register, 'cause that old lady *is* crazy as hell—or hear gunshots?"

"No. Everybody is normal," Glory conceded. "And that boy was so much like JT. Sometimes I miss JT, and this whole place makes me think of him."

"But Malcolm..." Glory touched an earring. She closed her eyes, took a deep breath, and pushed the teacup away. JT was gone and wasn't coming back. "Malcolm is much better for me than JT. I've never wanted to be worldly, and God sent Malcolm when I needed him."

Glory bit into her grilled cheese sandwich and avoided looking at the disappointment in Herschel's eyes.

RIDING BACK HOME, GLORY watched the people on the streets, trying to see the really bad parts, but she finally decided the West Side looked just like the South Side. Herschel drove around and pointed out a few landmark buildings, some covered with layers of signs, still boarded up from the 1960s.

"Allen said you bring them needles and stuff for junkies," Glory said, trying not to stare at a woman in the thin jacket shivering in the doorway of a boarded-up building.

"Yes. Rubbers, too. I can get 'em. They can't," Herschel said.

Glory thought he sounded angry. "He asked me what it was like on the South Side. I said it was the same. I lied 'cause I don't know."

"Yeah. It's the same. People think AIDS is only in Boystown. They don't know. No... they act like they don't know because they don't want to know. Men go to the North Side and get it from other men—don't look so shocked—and then bring it home to their wives. Folks act like it's just a gay thing. Junkies pass it around. Teenagers pass it around."

"Wow," Glory said. "I didn't know. At church—" Glory stopped herself. She wouldn't tell Herschel her church said AIDS was punishment from God for homosexuality, adultery, and addiction. She wouldn't tell her best friend that she let Malcolm think she believed that. *Demon of lies and deceit!*

"I know what your church says, darling. That's not my business. When I lived in New York, I had lots of friends and made a lotta connections. So much that I decided to try Hollywood, and I worked with gods. Gods, I tell you! Superstars asked for me. Those pictures on the walls at the shop are real. But this sickness came up, and my friends in New York were dying. Dying! And then it came to California, and they started dying there, too, and nobody knew what was happening.

"I got scared. I came back home and set up shop here 'cause the disease wasn't here yet. But then it showed up here, too. People knew what it was, but *our* people were acting like it wasn't happening. My cousin Marcella was Allen's mother. She died of it. Mighta been from a needle or her man—who knows." Herschel wiped an angry tear. "Miz Rosie and me started passing out clean stuff and rubbers. All the money on the North Side fills the clinics with more supplies than they know what to do with. The clinics don't care where the stuff goes as long as it gets used. I collect it and give it to all the stores I can. Some try to sell it. I don't care."

Glory placed her hand over Herschel's on the gear shift. She felt so useless seeing her friend this way. "I'm sorry."

"No need to be sorry, darling." Herschel's mood brightened. "Life made me who I am and put me here for a reason. I can get things that people can't get for themselves. Did you know you can get free pills and rubbers on the North Side but not on the South or West Sides where people don't have the money to buy 'em? A black man in a dress can walk into any clinic on the North Side and get anything he wants, so I do what I do for whoever I can."

Glory wanted to hug Herschel. Here her biggest problem was choosing between a man who loved her and a boy who no longer existed, and Herschel had lost people he cared about to AIDS and was trying to save strangers. "This is gonna sound stupid, but I really wanna be you when I grow up."

"I love you too, Glory-Glory."

Chapter 10

"I know it's not what you're used to, *Princess*," Christy said, "but I'll try to keep the ride as smooth as possible."

Glory laughed and poked her tongue out at the girl looking at her in the rearview mirror. Cramped in the back seat of Christy's tiny red car, Glory was thrilled just to be there. It had taken her a week to convince Malcolm that a trip to the mall with friends to finish Christmas shopping was necessary. Once he agreed, he easily convinced her mother. Malcolm would pick her up at six o'clock, so Glory had an entire afternoon of freedom.

Tressa broke into a chorus of "Jingle Bells," and they all joined in. Christy tuned the radio to WGCI, which was in the middle of an extended Christmas block, and Glory rocked while her friends sang along to "This Christmas." When the Temptations started singing "Silent Night," Glory agreed to help kidnap and marry all three singers if she could have the baritone. Christy took the falsetto, and Tressa the gravelly one.

"So, who are we shopping for?" Tressa asked, turning the radio down. "I'm actually done shopping. I just want cookies."

"I need something for my mama and myself," Christy said. "Rest of them folks ain't gettin' nuttin."

"I need a picture frame or a plaque for my mother, something for my boss, and I don't know what to get for Malcolm," Glory said.

"We'll stop at the auto supply," Christy said. "Get him a new lock. Ow! Dammit, Tee, don't pinch me again. Man might need a new one, right, Princess?"

"No, Christy." Glory laughed off the joke. "He already got a new one." She knew her friend meant no harm, but it wasn't funny to her yet.

"Hey, Christy," Tressa said, "remember that time something horrible happened to you, and we kept making jokes about it to make you feel better? Ha ha, heffa. It ain't funny."

"Tee, it's okay, really," Glory said.

"No, Glory, it's not," Christy conceded. "I shouldn't do that. I swear, I'm not trying to be mean. I just say stupid stuff sometimes."

"I know you do," Glory said. "That's why it's okay."

Once again, Glory was amazed that these girls were her friends.

———— ⬥ ————

IN THE MALL, THEIR first stop was Orange Julius for snacks. Glory ordered her nachos with extra peppers, exactly the way Malcolm never let her have them. They discussed the latest rumors, and Glory felt gratified to know she was no longer the subject of any. She wasn't sure she liked Quentin having a girlfriend, but she was glad somebody's boyfriend had punched old Mr. Harris at the bookstore.

"Like, omigod! Gloria! Hi! Remember me? Tammy from Carson's!"

The voice grated on her nerves, and Glory looked up into the smiling face of the chipper young lady who'd pierced her ears. "Hi, Tammy. It's Glory."

"Like, omigod! Those earrings! They're still so totally awesome! I mean, I couldn't believe when Malcolm said he didn't want the starter ones. I mean, they woulda hurt less 'cause we coulda just left the first ones in, but no, Malcolm insisted on the best. Like, omigod!

I won't say how much they were, and you were such a little trooper. Great seeing you, Gloria! Hugs to Malcolm for me!"

Glory sat frozen as Tammy bounced away to the counter.

"Okay," Christy said. "Please tell me why this cow cain't get your name right but calls you a little trooper and sends hugs to your man?" Christy moved to get up from her seat. "Do I need to go shake this heffa?"

"Kumbaya, m'lord," Tressa sang, slipping an arm through Christy's. "Come on, sister, not today. It's Christmastime. Glory, do something!"

"I am," Glory said. "I'm rolling my eyes as hard as I can."

In the greeting-card store, the girls walked through the aisles of knickknacks. Glory found the perfect frame and plaques for her mother. At a glass display case, she stared a long time at a crystal globe with a ship on top. If she were seeing JT this Christmas, it would be perfect. Glory pushed the thought out of her mind. No need to ruin a great day.

"Oh, that's good. You should get him that."

Glory looked to where Christy pointed. On the shelf below the globe stood a statue of a knight in armor raising his crystal sword, slaying a dragon with red eyes. As the cashier gift wrapped the statue, Glory had to admit it was Malcolm in every way: fighting to save her and fighting the hellion she sometimes thought she saw peeking out of him.

"So, what else should I get Malcolm?" she asked her friends as they walked back out into the mall. "I know he got me at least one other thing."

"Something from Frederick's? Ow! What? Not that Frederick's," Christy said. "I'm finna get tired of you whoopin' on me, Tee."

"I think you should get something symbolic," Tessa said.

"He's in Bible college, and he's the youth outreach minister," Glory said. "Maybe a tie or a tie clip or something?"

"So the youth minister is going with one of the youth, and nobody in the church has a problem with this?" Christie asked. "Don't you dare hit me!"

"Well," Glory said, "we're not holding hands or anything in church. It's nobody's business, anyway."

"I think it's beautiful," Tressa said. "She'll be eighteen soon, anyway—July, right? The whole thing is so romantic, and he's like a superhero. Oh, I know just the thing!" She grabbed Glory's arm and dragged her toward Spencer's Gifts.

In Spencer's, Tressa paid for five neckties, and Christy held up adult toys that made Glory blush. Minutes later, Glory left the store with her hands over her face and waited outside while her friends finished shopping. Then they stopped at a jewelry kiosk, where Glory picked silver charms for a bracelet for Herschel and accessories for Malcolm's ties.

The girls relaxed in McDonald's, waiting for the bracelet to be finished, laughing at Glory's embarrassment in Spencer's. A few classmates stopped by to chat, and Glory enjoyed her place beside Christy, who was holding court. In a nearby booth, Quentin sat with his arm draped around Paula, who looked starstruck. Glory considered rolling her eyes at Paula, too.

There was a bit of confusion when a McDonald's employee approached. She placed three milkshakes in front of Glory, Tressa, and Christy then handed Glory a folded napkin. "A gentleman sends his regards," the giggling girl said and ran away.

Glory glanced at her watch. It was almost six o'clock. "They're from Malcolm."

She looked around then read the note: *Looks like you're having a great time. I'll meet you at the popcorn shop at 7:00.* Glory looked around again, suddenly ready to leave.

"My, damn," Christy said, sipping her shake. "That's either awesome or crazy as hell."

Chapter 11

Malcolm told Glory to dress up for the night, so Mary chose a black sheath dress for her daughter. The short-sleeved dress fell just below the knee and had a tiny split in the back and modest square collar that showed only her collar bone. The short jacket had long sleeves and gold buttons. Her mother had considered high heels, but Glory begged her not to, and they settled on black-velvet low heels with gold bows. It wasn't like the dresses she normally wore. It was her size and shape, a dress like the young women at church wore—the women who constantly chased after Malcolm.

Sitting on her bed, fidgeting, waiting for the doorbell to ring, Glory ran her fingers over the compact of pills and the rings of the condoms in the lining of her purse and tried to still the butterflies in her stomach. She really cared about Malcolm and had sometimes thought about making love with him. She knew he wanted her. Sometimes when he kissed her, he would stop and place his forehead against hers and just breathe. Other times, he would wrap his arms around her, and she could feel his heart pounding. At those times, she really wanted to kiss him just a little longer. But it wasn't about him—it was that Jezebel spirit. It felt good to be wanted like that.

In the two months they'd been dating, their alone time had been limited to car rides and saying good night at her front door. This would be their last time together until after the New Year, and Malcolm had said they would be going someplace special. Her mother's words still troubled her, though, and she wondered if Mary knew this was a *special* date.

The doorbell rang. Glory met her mother in the narrow hallway outside her bedroom and stood still while her mother reached up and adjusted her collar.

"You look real pretty," Mary Bishop said. "Just like a beautiful woman."

"Thank you, Mama," Glory said.

"Malcolm always tells me you're a good girl. A good, obedient young lady."

"Yes, ma'am."

"That's what a godly man looks for in a woman. Obedience. Don't give in to demons of rebellion and disobedience, you hear me?"

"Yes, ma'am." Glory searched her mother's face for some other meaning, something that made sense.

The doorbell rang again, and Mary stepped away to press the door buzzer. "Malcolm's a good man. You be sure to be good to him."

Glory checked her face in the hall mirror. The night before, Herschel had blow-dried her hair straight till it hung well below her shoulders. She'd kept it braided all day, and now it fell in soft waves. She pulled it back behind one ear. That day, Christy had spent an entire period teaching her to apply mascara to just her lashes, and in the dim light of their hallway, her mother hadn't noticed. When she heard the door open, Glory reached into her purse and applied the strawberry lip gloss she'd gotten from Tressa.

"Glory! Malcolm's here!"

Glory smoothed her dress and headed to the living room. Malcolm stood holding her coat and the presents she'd wrapped for him. She watched his face as she entered. She could tell he was pleased by the way his eyes lit up and because he bit his lip while trying to keep a straight face.

Glory couldn't help smiling. "Hi, Malcolm."

Malcolm cleared his throat. "Uh, hi, Miss Bishop. Shall we go?"

"Okay." Glory couldn't stop smiling as he helped her with her coat. The look on his face made her feel more beautiful than she'd ever felt before. She wondered if the women at church felt like this every day.

"Y'all have fun. Not too late, now—it's a school night," Mary said as they left the apartment.

Glory kissed her mother's cheek.

"Remember what I said, now," her mother reminded her.

"Yes, ma'am, I will."

In the car, Malcolm placed his hand over Glory's on the seat. "Hi, I'm Malcolm Porter. I don't believe we've met. I came to pick up *Glory*, and I wind up with *Glorious*."

Glory blushed. "My daddy used to call me that. My mother hated it. She said it made me prideful, but that's the only name Daddy ever used."

"Your daddy was a smart man. I guess he'd be trying to kill me right now." Malcolm laughed a little but then got serious. "I really appreciate your mother trusting me with you." He patted Glory's hand. "I won't abuse her trust."

Glory smiled, not sure what to say. "So, where are we going?"

"It's a surprise, but we hafta hurry. I left dinner warming in the oven. Don't want it to dry out."

"We're going to your house?"

"Yes and no." Malcolm stopped the car. "Ta-da! We're here."

Glory looked out at the side of the church where she spent at least three days a week. The sanctuary lights were on, and the organ swells could be heard on the street. The combined choirs' Christmas rehearsal was in full swing.

"We're going to choir rehearsal?" Glory didn't try to hide her disappointment.

"Nope." Malcolm jumped out of the car before she could ask another question.

"So, then, where?" she asked as he opened her door.

"You'll see." His playful smile made Glory laugh. "Right this way, *Glorious*."

She followed him through a steel door she'd seen but never registered as being part of the church building and then through a wood-and-glass door to a dimly lit hallway. The only light came from the red exit signs and the cracks around the doors leading to other parts of the church.

"Guessed where you are yet?" Malcolm asked, opening a closet door and turning on the light inside.

"Yes." Glory laughed. "This is the haunted hallway, where we used to play hide and seek when we were little." She looked up at the polished staircase winding up into darkness. "We used to dare each other to go to the top of the stairs."

"I know. I lived up there." He winked. "Now, watch this. Step into the closet, please."

Glory looked around then stepped into the closet. Malcolm followed and closed the door behind them. The deadbolt clicked in place as he pulled a metal gate over the doorway.

"Malcolm, this is an elevator? I didn't know the church had an elevator."

"Most people don't." Malcolm pushed the up button. "We have stairs and chair lifts for all the rest of the building. This elevator goes only to the fourth floor, where the apartments are."

"Apartments?"

"Yup!" Malcolm laughed. "Shhh. I've been wanting to do this." He pulled her close for a kiss, crushing the bows on the packages she'd held so carefully.

They stepped out of the elevator into a thickly carpeted hallway with wood-paneled walls and gold sconces. The red carpet and warm lighting reminded Glory of the fancy theater Malcolm had taken her to. She caught a glimpse of herself in a tall gold-framed mirror and paused. She'd never seen herself like that before—in a grown-up black dress with her hair down, standing in a luxurious-looking place. She understood why her mother didn't want her to see this image every day.

"Glorious, isn't she?" Malcolm said, looking into her eyes in the mirror.

Glory lowered her eyes. "Malcolm, stop. That's vain and prideful. I can't be like that."

She watched in the mirror as he moved in close behind her and slid an arm around her waist. With his other hand, he pushed her hair back from her face. "No, look." He gently pulled her hair until she raised her chin and lifted her eyes. "You're beautiful, and when somebody tells you you're beautiful, you're gonna stand up straight and take it like a woman." He kissed her neck. "Understand?"

Glory could barely move for the flutter in her stomach. How did he do that? Malcolm Porter freed her, thrilled her, and scared her—all at the same time. "Yes, Malcolm" was all she could get out.

He grabbed her hand. "C'mon. Let me show you around." He led her to an intersecting hallway. "This is where I grew up. Originally, it was a lot of offices up here. When the church got the building, they turned it into four apartments." Malcolm unlocked and pushed open a door onto a darkened foyer with polished hardwood floors. "Welcome to my childhood home. After you."

Glory stepped into a huge room with a giant half-circle window overlooking the bright lights of Seventy-Fifth Street. In a corner on an end table stood a small Christmas tree with a gold star. In the dark, the lights from the tree and the lights from the street reflected off the polished wood floors, giving the room a rich, sophisticated glow. The only other furniture was an overstuffed couch facing the window, a coffee table, and a pair of high-backed chairs.

"I'll turn the lights on and give you the tour. I wanted you to see the view first. Great, huh?"

"Malcolm, this is awesome! You lived here?"

"Yup. Until I was fifteen." He laid their coats on one of the chairs. "This way first." He led her down a hall to the right. "The bedrooms are down here. Mother spent time in the bayou and once met a gator in an outhouse, so every bedroom has a bathroom." As he turned lights on and off in the empty rooms, Glory didn't know whether she was relieved or disappointed that there were no beds. The only furnished rooms were the maid's suite and the common rooms.

"Malcolm, it's like a mansion up here," Glory said, looking around the kitchen.

"Yeah. It is. But Mother didn't like it. She said the neighborhood was bad, so she bought a building on the lake. Nobody lives here. Technically, it's still the parsonage, so the pastor can do whatever he wants with it. Dad still uses the study and sometimes the kitchen and dining room for visiting ministers. The other apartments are empty, too. When we have important guests, they don't go to hotels. They stay up here. Our housekeeper comes in to do the cooking and cleaning."

"This is just so... so... wow," Glory said. "I've never been in a house this big. Well, my grandmother's house has this many rooms, but that's because they just added 'em as they needed 'em. I can't imagine living in this." Glory suddenly wondered if her mother knew about this. "So, um, what's for dinner?"

"Well, dinner is a gourmet picnic in the living room. Watch this." He walked over to a wall panel and flicked a switch. "This was one of my favorite things growing up here. This radio plays music in every room. The buttons can listen and talk in all the rooms, too. There's a panel like this in the master bedroom and the study. The other rooms just have talk and mute buttons. Cool, huh?"

Glory listened as slow jazz filled the house. She didn't think anything could be more impressive. "Um, Malcolm," she said as she watched him pull two Harold's Chicken bags from the warm oven. "You got wings for a picnic, and I'm dressed like this?"

Malcolm stopped and looked from Glory to the food and back to Glory. "Okay, change of plans. Dinner is a gourmet picnic in the kitchen. We'll go to the living room later. Have a seat. Wait, that jacket will probably be in the way—don't wanna mess that up. Want me to take that?" He pulled out a counter stool for her.

"Okay." Glory reached for her collar, but he brushed her hand away. She stood still while Malcolm loosened the gold buttons and then stood behind her to help her remove it. When she folded her arms to hide them, he reached out and pulled her hands down.

"No," he said. "You're beautiful. I'm not gonna see you like this again anytime soon. I'm just gonna look for a second."

Glory tried to hold her head up, but his appreciation embarrassed her. "Please, Malcolm. That makes me feel funny."

He turned her to face him and pulled her into his arms. "Woman, looking at you makes me feel funny, too." He kissed her on the forehead. "C'mon, let's eat."

Glory laughed all through dinner at Malcolm's stories of life in the giant apartment. "You were terrible!"

"Yeah, I was," Malcolm admitted. "I hated being cooped up here. I spent the first five years of my life down south in the fresh air, going wherever I wanted. I never wore shoes down there. Then we come up here, and it's like I'm in prison. I thought my parents were crazy. And school? I used to just get up and leave. It didn't make sense to me at that age."

"What did your parents do?" Glory followed Malcolm into the living room.

"Beat the heck outta me—what else?" He led her over to the couch and placed a plastic container on the coffee table. "It's cheese-cake from Orly's. Remember we went there?"

Glory smiled. It was the first fancy restaurant they'd gone to. "Yup. This is perfect. So what are our plans for the evening?" She hoped the question sounded casual enough. Dinner was almost over, and they still had a lot of time left. She sat back on the couch and tried to look comfortable and grown-up.

"My original plan was to go out someplace really high-class, but then I decided I didn't wanna share you with a restaurant crowd, so we'll finish dessert." He spooned a bit of cheesecake into her mouth. "Then we'll sit back and talk a while, open gifts, and see what comes up."

Glory had shared Twinkies and ice cream with JT many times, but cheesecake in this sophisticated room with Malcolm was the most adult thing she'd ever done. She crossed her legs and tried to look mature.

"So, do your friends still think I'm weird?" Malcolm asked, feed-ing her more dessert.

Glory laughed behind the cheesecake in her mouth. "No, they think you're okay now. They thought having milkshakes delivered was really cool. Of course, the rumors are starting again, but at least they don't think you're a gangster anymore."

After dessert, Glory excused herself and found the powder room. She wished she could call Herschel or Tressa or Christy. She was so confused, all dressed up and alone with Malcolm in a fancy apart-ment with city lights and soft music. He hadn't tried to touch her, but he'd said she was beautiful. *Is this what adults do on dates?* By this point, she and JT would have been cuddling on the couch or even more. *Why am I thinking about a boy now... here?* She dried her hands, freshened her lip gloss, and left the bathroom.

Malcolm stood at the window, his head resting on his forearm, leaning against the windowsill. It was like one of those scenes Glory read about in the romance novels at the salon, with the older man looking serious and the young maiden nervously approaching. She tried to walk quietly, but her heels clicked on the floor. Stopping to kick them off, she prayed she wouldn't slip in her stocking feet.

"Stop."

Glory stood still and looked up. Malcolm was staring at her.

"Don't move. You look good in this light." He folded his arms, a slight smirk on his face. "Please don't wear that dress anywhere else. Nobody else needs to see you like this. I'd hafta hurt somebody." He held out a hand to her. "C'mere."

The butterflies were back, and walking toward him, Glory could hardly breathe. This was it. With no bed in the apartment, he'd probably pick her up and carry her to the couch. She wondered if it was like this for all men and women. How many other women had Malcolm stood there looking at, seducing?

He held her close, swaying to the music. He smelled nothing like the boys she knew. His cologne was warmer, sweeter, deeper. She wrapped her arms around his waist and rested her head against his shoulder. When he kissed her forehead, she looked up, offering her lips like the women on the book covers did. He gently accepted, kissing her in time to the music.

When he broke the kiss and held her close, Glory couldn't help but feel his heart pounding, his excitement, his desire for her. "Malcolm?"

"Yes?" he whispered, his voice hoarse.

"If you wanna seduce me, it's okay. I brought protection." She kept her head pressed against his shoulder, hoping she didn't sound like a whore, or worse.

Malcolm froze, breathed deeply, then slowly released her. "Hey." He stepped back. "Shouldn't we be opening gifts? You go put the gifts on the table. I'll grab us some drinks." He kissed her forehead again and headed for the kitchen before she could respond.

Glory sighed and went to grab the gifts from under the Christmas tree. She'd just offered herself to Malcolm, and he'd run. But she could feel how much he wanted her. But Malcolm was a godly man. Of course, he could resist sinful urges. She placed the gifts on the coffee table and retreated to a corner of the couch, hugging a small throw pillow for cover.

Malcolm returned from the kitchen and handed her a tall glass—ginger ale, of course. He took a seat in the middle of the couch and sipped his drink. Droplets sparkled at his hairline, like he'd splashed his face with water.

"Malcolm, when you were... my age..." Glory cringed when his shoulders slumped. "Did you bring dates here? I mean, a lot?"

He looked over at her and smiled. "Actually, no. None at all. I got really sick when I was fifteen, and by the time I recovered, we'd moved."

"Oh. Since you've been grown, have you brought women here?"

Malcolm put down his drink and sat back on the couch. "Yes."

"From church?" Glory had no idea why she was asking these questions. His past personal life was none of her business.

"No, not from church. Never from church." He sat up and grabbed his drink again. "From school or women I met working at the mission months and months ago." He looked at her, waiting.

"Did you... um...?"

"Yes." Malcolm sighed. "Not often, but yes, I had sex with them." He took another drink.

"Oh." Glory suddenly felt very young, like a little girl playing dress-up, and she didn't know the rules.

Malcolm patted the seat beside him. "C'mon, let's open gifts. You go first. I wanna see what you and your girlfriends came up with."

Glory slid from the couch to the floor and passed him the first gift: a wide, flat box. As Malcolm carefully peeled the tape, she wracked her brain for an explanation. What had seemed like a brilliant idea that day at the mall now felt childish. Glory held her breath when he opened the box.

"Merry Christmas, *Superman*?"

She prayed that he'd at least take it as a joke. Malcolm ran his hand over the five silk ties with color-matched embroidered *S* logos, and the silver *S* tie clip attached to the center tie. A padded card held a pair of *S* cufflinks, and a clear plastic box held an *S* pen, keychain, and money clip. He opened a velvet box with a silver cuff bracelet, stamped with an *S*. Glory watched his face for some clue. He finally wiped his face with both hands and coughed a bit.

"I'm sorry. I know it's silly—" Glory said.

"Oh, woman. Stop, no." Malcolm stood up, pulling Glory to her feet and into his arms. "No, I'm just overwhelmed. And scared. I don't know if I can live up to Superman."

"Malcolm, you already have." Glory wrapped her arms around him and squeezed until she felt his arms around her. "And I made sure you have enough so you never forget you're Superman every day." Glory grabbed the silver bracelet and held it out for him to put on. "There's one other thing. It's for your desk. It's kinda heavy."

Malcolm sat down again, pulling Glory onto his lap. He unwrapped the box and gave it to her to hold while he lifted the lid and moved the tissue. He lifted the sculpture out of the box and placed it on the table.

"It's a knight in shining armor. Slaying a dragon. Protecting, being a hero," Glory said.

Malcolm sniffed and then cleared his throat. "Woman, you know how to get to a brotha, don't you?" Malcolm paused, sniffed, and cleared his throat again. "Okay. My turn. You hafta sit on the end, though."

Glory moved to the end of the couch, and Malcolm stood behind her and pulled her hair back. "First, we take out these. Sorry if it hurts a little." She reached up to help him remove her diamond earrings, but he brushed her hand away, so she just held her hair. When he finished, he handed her a red leather box tied with a gold ribbon. "Go ahead, open it."

Glory pulled the ribbon and opened the box. It held more gold than she'd ever seen in one place. The four bangle bracelets, too small to fit over her hands, were each decorated with small circles and a single diamond. The matching earrings looked like smaller versions of the bracelets. The box also held what looked like a small gold screwdriver on a gold chain.

"They're beautiful, Malcolm," she said, touching the bracelets. "I don't know what to say."

"Don't say anything. Just listen." Malcolm picked up the earrings. "A man was sent to find a woman, a very specific type of woman. She had to do and say certain things for him to be sure it was the right woman, and sure enough, he found her." He placed the earrings in her ears. "'And it came to pass that the man took a golden earring of half a shekel weight'"—Malcolm picked up the bracelets—"'and bracelets for her hands of ten shekels' weight of gold.' See, in the Old Testament, when Rebecca was chosen, she was given gold jewelry. Have you ever read the Song of Solomon, Glory? Never mind." He smirked. "All girls find it eventually. They try to tell you it's about Christ and the church. It's not."

Glory blushed. She knew exactly what he was talking about.

"The bracelets are about two and a half shekels each. That's why there's four of 'em." He handed one to Glory. "Read the inscription."

Glory held the small circle and looked for a clasp but couldn't find one. Then she turned the bracelet until she could see the inscription inside.

"Read it out loud," Malcolm said.

"I am my beloved's, and his desire is toward me," Glory read. She looked up at him. "But it won't fit over my hand."

"You underestimate my desire toward you." Malcolm grinned and held up the gold screwdriver. "Gimme your hand."

Glory watched as Malcolm used the screwdriver to open and then secure the bracelet to her wrist. It moved freely but could not slide off. He kissed her hand and handed her another bracelet. "Read that one."

"It says the same thing."

"Read it."

Glory read aloud three more times as Malcolm secured the bracelets to her wrists. When he finished, she placed her old diamond earrings in the red box while Malcolm attached the screwdriver to his new Superman keychain. Then he held Glory's arms out in front of her, and they watched the bracelets slide down her wrists, hitting her hands with a soft clink.

"What does that sound mean?" he asked.

Glory smiled. "I am my beloved's, and his desire is toward me?"

"Yes." He stepped close to her. "Glory Bishop, you are my lady, and I love you."

"I lov—"

"Shh." He placed a finger to her lips. "No, you don't." He pushed her hair back behind her ear. "Not yet, anyway. But in time, you will."

Glory felt his grip tighten on her hair, and then he was kissing her like he owned her. In that moment, in that kiss, Glory learned the difference between men and boys. Where JT's kiss had been warm and hungry, Malcolm's was cool and powerful. JT's was playful and full of promise—Malcolm's kiss was purposeful and controlled, one hand holding her to him and the other clutching her hair. Glory felt claimed and branded by Malcolm's kiss. Malcolm moved his leg between hers and gently bent her backward, and Glory held on as he expertly laid her down. As Glory fell back onto the couch, the clink of the bracelets reminded her that Malcolm was her God-sent savior and she belonged to him.

"Malcolm?" Glory panted between kisses that threatened to devour her.

"Yes?" His heart pounding, his need pressed between them.

"Should I get my purse?"

Malcolm paused, his breathing slowing, more steady. His kisses softened. "Yes," he said finally. He took a deep breath and moved off of her. "Get your purse."

Glory felt like the world now moved in slow motion. *Will he take me in his arms as he unzips my dress, slowly peeling it from my body? Will he kiss me more before taking off my slip?* At home, she'd practiced sliding the straps off her shoulders and letting the slip fall, hoping she looked okay stepping out of it. She sat up and swung her feet onto the floor, smoothing her dress and enjoying the clink of the bracelets. *Will he lay me down and slide my stockings and panties off?* She looked over at Malcolm, sitting leaned forward, staring at the statue on the table. *Will he be completely naked, too?* She walked on shaky legs over to the armchair and picked up her purse.

"Get your coat, too," Malcolm said slowly.

"Huh?"

"Get your purse and your coat. I need to take you home."

"Oh, but I thought you wanted—"

"I do want you. I want you so much that I need to get you out of here right now, 'cause I'm not really Superman. I'm just a man, and I've never wanted a woman as bad as I want you right now. If you stay much longer, I won't have the strength to stop myself. And you're seventeen."

"Oh." Glory sat down on the edge of the chair. "But I thought... and you told me to dress up..." Her voice trailed off. She was confused and feeling younger and younger.

"You thought that dress would be off by now." Malcolm took a sip from the glass on the table. "Believe me, I'd love nothing better than to see that dress on the floor right now."

"My mother told me—"

"I know what your mother told you. She tells me every time I pick you up how humble and obedient you are." Malcolm sounded a little angry. "Probably told you to be especially obedient tonight, right? She doesn't know you ask the right questions, though, does she? I bet she doesn't know you have protection, does she?"

Glory blushed. Her mother didn't know. She had already rebelled and disobeyed. And she had already shown Malcolm that she knew more than she should. Glory tried not to cry. She tried to sit up straight and take it like a woman.

"Your mother underestimates me, Glory. I'm a man. Of course, I want you, but she doesn't know that I love you." He looked at her. "I can wait." In his eyes, Glory saw that same man she'd seen in the hospital—the one who'd fought to protect her from a monster and stood to shield her from her mother.

"Now, be a good, obedient girl and get your coat. It's a school night."

GLORY SAT QUIETLY ON the short ride home. Parking in front of her building, Malcolm turned in the seat to face her. "Okay, what's on your mind?"

"You think I'm bad, don't you?" Glory kept her head down. "For... you know, having protection. Like I do it all the time."

Malcolm lifted her chin. "Like a woman. No, I don't think you're bad. I think you're smart. I think you knew the possibilities and planned for them. I admit, I was surprised. I've been underestimating you."

"My mother says I have a Jezebel spirit, and a godly man will—"

"Stop. No. She thought I was gonna—what, screw the Jezebel out of you? And you could maybe catch a preacher in the bargain?"

Glory covered her face. "I'm sor—"

"Do you know how many mothers at church throw their 'good, obedient' daughters at me?"

"Malcolm, please," Glory begged. "She's not like that. Some really bad things happened to her. She doesn't want it to happen to me. She's trying to protect me."

"Yeah." Malcolm got out of the car and let the door slam. By the time he opened Glory's door, though, he'd calmed down. The bracelets clinked as he helped her out of the car. "I love that sound."

"Me, too," Glory said.

Malcolm kissed her lightly and held her hand as they walked into her building. "Your mother's still gonna be up."

"I doubt it," Glory said. "She's usually in bed by nine."

"Not tonight. She sent you on a mission. She'll wanna know how it went." His voice was low and harsh. "Can I come in and tell her it was a success? Tell her we did it in every room and that you're full to bursting?"

Glory just looked at him, shocked by his bitter crudeness.

"That's what she wants, right? Pregnant with triplets?"

"Malcolm, that's mean," Glory protested. "And you don't know my mother at all. She doesn't want me to trap you. She says God sent you for me. You even said it, too. She wants me to be obedient to you because that's what God wants. Maybe she is overprotective, but that's to save me." Glory took a deep breath. "I'm okay with that."

"But, Glory, it's not okay." Malcolm held her close. "She acts like you're not the good girl she raised you to be. She's kept you bound and caged and filled your head with nonsense and shame." He stroked her cheek. "I know you love and honor your mother. You're a good girl. You won't make her mistakes. You're a smart, incredible woman. And you're my lady, so nothing can harm you. 'Cause I slay dragons, remember?"

"Malcolm, please don't come in. Please," Glory begged. The idea of Malcolm confronting her mother terrified her. The demons of ingratitude and dishonor her mother would beat out of her...

Malcolm looked at her for a long time. "Okay," he said finally. "I'll see you in the morning." He kissed her forehead. "Good night, Glorious."

It wasn't yet eleven o'clock when Glory entered the apartment. Even though she smelled sage and burnt paper, she tried to tiptoe to her room.

"Baby, I'm in the kitchen. Lemme look at you!" her mother called.

Glory laid her coat and jacket on the couch and walked to the kitchen doorway. "Hi, Mama."

Mary blew out a puff of smoke and squashed out the roll of brown paper. "Wasn't expecting you this early." She wiped her hands on her robe and walked over to Glory. "Well? How was your date?" She reached out and touched Glory's earring. "New earrings? You did what I said, right?"

"Yes, ma'am." Glory held up her wrists to show the bracelets. "Like Rebecca's from the Bible. They don't come off. Malcolm has the screwdriver."

Mary looked at the bracelets and nodded. "Very nice. Well, you get on to bed."

"Yes, ma'am." Glory walked to the couch and grabbed her coat and jacket to hang up. "Mama?"

"Yes, baby?"

"Malcolm really is a good, godly man. He loves me, and he didn't touch me."

"That's nice, baby. Good night."

"Good night, Mama."

Alone in her bedroom, Glory looked at herself in her tiny jewelry-box mirror. The wide gold earrings cuffed her earlobes. Bigger than the diamond studs, these were definitely a woman's earrings. The bracelets clinked when she tied her hair back and let her dress and slip fall to the floor. Every move she made reminded her that she was Malcolm's, and his desire was for her, and he would wait.

Chapter 12

The last day of school before Christmas break, the bookstore was almost empty when Glory placed her backpack in their usual booth. It was still fourth period, and Tressa and Christy wouldn't arrive until fifth, so she ordered three burgers and two large fries, grabbed an orange pop, and opened a book to wait for their order number to be called.

"Hey. What's your name?"

Glory raised her head. Mr. Harris stood by the next booth, chewing his fat cigar, leaning on a push broom. "I see you in here all the time with them other two. I'm Harris. I own this place."

"Hi, Mr. Harris." Glory nodded, returning her attention to her book. *Please go away, please go away, please go away.*

Stubby fingers with gray-haired knuckles covered the page, blocking Glory's view. She looked up again.

"Didn't get your name. Said I'm the owner. Need a job?" Harris moved his hand, leaving a greasy fingerprint on Glory's book. He wiped his hand on his apron.

"My name is Glory, Mr. Harris. I already have a job."

"You a real pretty girl, Glory. Real pretty. Nice hair. Nice earrings."

Despite her flesh crawling, Glory tried to take the compliment *like a woman*, as Malcolm had said. Somebody called her order number, and she moved to get up. "Excuse me, Mr. Harris, my order is ready."

"You sit there. Fine thing like you don't need to lift a finger." Before Glory could protest, the old man laid his broom aside and took off.

Glory covered her face with her hands, prayed for patience and strength, and really wished Malcolm was somewhere watching.

"Look who beat us here!" Christy's voice carried throughout the room.

"Glory, glory, hallelujah!" Tressa sang.

Glory looked up and smiled, greatly relieved that the girls had arrived before Mr. Harris came back. She stood to allow Tressa to slide in and was still standing when Mr. Harris returned wearing a clean white apron, hair net, and plastic gloves. Glory and her friends stared while he placed three burgers with fries, three milkshakes, an order of nachos with peppers, and three candy canes on the table.

"Mr. Harris, I didn't order this," Glory said.

"Oh, well... you can talk to me about it later." He winked at her and pimp-walked away.

"Okay, see, that's just nasty," Christy said.

"That's a great power you have, Glory," Tressa said, digging into the nachos. "Men just line up to bring you goodies. Nice earrings, by the way."

Glory's hands went to her ears as she sat down. Touching them made her smile. As angry as she'd been at the time, she was glad Malcolm made her get her ears pierced.

"Matching shackles?" Christy grabbed Glory's hand. "Looks like Malcolm was here. Lemme see one." She pulled at a bracelet.

"They can't come off." Glory pulled her wrist back.

"What?" both girls asked at once.

"Well, I mean they can come off. Malcolm has the screwdriver—"

"Jesus! He gave you actual shackles for Christmas?" Christy asked.

"No!" Glory said. "Tee, get your Bible. It's in Genesis. When the servant found Rebecca at the well and knew she was the one, he gave her a gold earring and gold bracelets."

Tressa began reading in a voice that wasn't quite appropriate for scriptures, "And it came to pass, as the camels had done drinking, that the man took a golden earring of half a shekel weight and two bracelets for her hands of ten shekels' weight of gold—"

"See," Glory said. "They're two and a half shekels each."

"Mm-hmph," grumbled Christy, starting on her lunch.

"They're engraved on the inside, too. Turn to Song of Solomon."

"I bet I know what verse," Tressa said, turning the pages. "It's 6:3. 'I am my beloved's, and my beloved is mine.' Right?"

"Not quite," Glory said. "Look at 7:10."

"'I am my beloved's, and his desire is toward me.' Aww," Tressa said. "That's so romantic!"

"Wait a minute. Am I the only sane person at this table?" Christy put down her drink. "Not only did he give you shackles—the Rebecca thing is nice, I'll give him that—but instead of the really romantic verse where you both love each other, your shackles say 'I belong to him, and he's got a hard-on for me'... and he has the only key?"

"It's a screwdriver." Glory pouted at her friend. "And he does love me. I mean, for real."

"Well, is he getting the matching chains for Valentine's Day? Tee, don't kick me no more!"

"Hey, did he like his gifts?" Tressa asked.

Glory's mood brightened. "Yeah. I think the statue made him cry. He sniffed and cleared his throat a lot. I didn't look 'cause I didn't wanna embarrass him. But the Superman stuff—he said he was overwhelmed that I thought he was Superman." Glory reached for her burger. The jingle of the bracelets made her smile.

"That happens every time you move?" Christy asked.

"Isn't there a song about every move you make?" Tressa started humming.

"Yeah. It reminds me..." Glory sighed. "Last night on the couch at his house—well, not really his house, the apartment at church. It was where he grew up—"

"At church?" both girls said at once.

"Move away, Tee. Lightning's coming!"

"No, wait!" Glory laughed. "It wasn't like that. There're apartments on the top floor. The first family still uses it sometimes. But anyway... we were on the couch, making out, and I really thought we were gonna, you know...?"

"You were alone with a grown man, and he gave you shackles, and y'all didn't do it?" Christy looked skeptical.

"You know," Glory mused, "he knows I don't love him. I was gonna do it, anyway. He's my hero, and he loves me so much... but he said he can wait till I love him and I'm eighteen."

"Oh my God, Glory, that's the most loving thing I've ever heard of." Tressa dabbed her eyes.

"Naw," Christy said. "This is some mess. The bracelets are okay, I guess, but this is some straight-up—if one of y'all kick me one mo' time, I swear!"

Leaving the store with their exchanged Christmas presents, Glory kept her head down, and Tressa folded her arms across her chest.

"Ho, ho, ho," Mr. Harris grunted. "Hey, Glory, come back and see me later today. I like me some schoolgirls."

Glory froze. *I like me some schoolgirls?*

She held up a hand before Christy could respond. Tressa bumped into her. The bracelets clinked. "Mr. Harris."

The filthy old pig leered at her.

Take it like a woman.

"Mr. Harris, the last time somebody said that to me"—Glory spoke a little louder than she'd intended—"my boyfriend beat him to death, and the police never found the weapon. Don't ever talk to us again."

Stepping out into the cold, Glory hugged herself and trembled. She heard the heavy door bang shut as her friends joined her on the sidewalk.

Christy put an arm around her. "Wow! You did good, girl. I didn't know you had that in you. You okay?"

Glory nodded.

"Glory, you never told us Malcolm killed that guy," Tressa whispered.

"He didn't die," Glory said. "But I don't know how he survived after what Malcolm did to him. Malcolm knows Mr. Harris and doesn't like him."

"Are you gonna tell him?" asked Christy.

"What's to tell? I told off an old pervert. I threatened a harmless old man."

Crossing the street back to school, Glory couldn't decide if she would tell Malcolm about Mr. Harris. She prayed for forgiveness for her anger and for disrespecting an elder and tried to forget the monster's voice that she hadn't thought about in weeks.

THE SEVENTH-PERIOD ending bell rang, and Glory watched her classmates bundle up to go out into the weather that she no longer had to brave. She felt so different now. The couples kissing goodbye reminded her of a boy she once knew. His kisses had been warm, wet, and hungry. But she was getting used to the gentle, serious kisses of a man. Walking to her locker, Glory shook her head at the kids playing, holding hands and giggling, yelling across the hall at each other... she felt so much older than them—mature, powerful, and free. Mr. Harris's attention might have once embarrassed or even scared her, but the bracelets on her wrists reminded her that God had sent Malcolm to protect her, so she had nothing to fear.

"Okay, so who were you?" Quentin asked, stepping up beside her. "I said, 'Gloria' for obvious reasons. Somebody else said, 'Octopussy.' Paula reached way back and said, 'Coffey.'"

"Quentin, what are you talking about?"

"At the bookstore, fifth period. What movie babe were you doing when you told old Mr. Harris you'd cut off his di—"

"I did not say that!" Glory whirled around. "Who's spreading that?"

"Everybody. A lot of people say they heard you." Quentin laughed. "Frankly, I didn't believe it. I also heard you told him you'd beat him to death and nobody would find the weapon."

Glory opened her locker and sat down inside, hiding her face in her hands. *What psycho demon possessed me to think saying anything was a good idea? Why didn't I just let Christy handle it?*

"Quentin." Glory looked up at the goofy boy smiling down at her. "I need a huge favor."

"Okay?" Quentin dropped to one knee. "What's up? Are you okay? Are you in trouble?"

"I'm fine. What was that first thing they think I said?"

"You'd cut his dick off? But I told 'em—"

"Yeah, that." Glory cut him off. "Just agree with it, okay? Just say I told you I said it, okay?"

"So, let me get this straight. You want people to think you said that?"

"Yes. Please do that for me, Quentin?"

"Okay, but why? You're not normally a liar, Glory. Wait. Did you say the other thing? Did you say you'd beat him to death and lose the weapon?"

"Quentin, stop. It's not that serious." Glory stood up, watching the wheels turning in her friend's mind. "Did I show you my Christmas presents?" She held out her arms to show her bracelets.

"And now the woman tries to distract me with shiny things, hmm?" Quentin shook his head. "I'm a nerd. You'll hafta do better than that."

"Really, Quentin. It's nothing. This whole thing is silly."

"First, you get mugged." Quentin mused out loud, pacing back and forth. "So you get a shady-looking escort and change your hair. Then, you get diamonds and start socializing and even going to the mall with the shady guy always lurking around. Now, you've got—what, fifty pounds of gold on your wrists? And you let slip that you're capable of beating somebody to death and losing the weapon. And now you're begging me to lie for you." Quentin folded his arms and leaned against the locker, smiling like Columbo. "So it wasn't a random mugger, was it?"

Glory's eyes went wide.

"I bet your old man is somebody big, huh? Bigger than Stokes or Fort, maybe... yeah... and his enemies tried to get to him through you, but Pops took 'em out, probably with his bare hands, right? That's why there's no weapon. But your mom is done with that life, so she took you and left, and now you get to live it up. Yeah, I bet that's it." Quentin continued pacing. "But your pops insists you have the bodyguard, and he sends the gifts to make up for it, right? And the dirty old man pissed you off so bad today that you slipped, so now you need to cover it up."

Glory sat down in her locker again and buried her face in her hands. She heard Quentin assuring people she was okay. She knew her shaking looked like sobbing, and when she lifted her head, her face was definitely wet with tears. They were tears of laughter, but Quentin didn't need to know that.

"Holy crap, Glory!" Quentin said, dropping to one knee again. "I was right?"

"Can we please just go with the other rumor?"

"Sure. Anything for you. Geez!"

Glory held out a hand for him to help her up. "Thanks. And my dad never hurt anybody, okay?"

"Yeah, whatever you say." He winked at her. "Your secret's safe with me. Merry Christmas, Glory."

"Merry Christmas, Quentin."

❧

GLORY CLOSED HER EYES and laid her head back against the seat, fighting a headache, glad the day was over and grateful again to Malcolm for keeping her out of the freezing weather.

"For the last day of school before Christmas, you don't look too happy," Malcolm said, climbing into the driver's seat. "How was your day?" He brushed Glory's hair back from her face.

"Fine," Glory said.

"Okay. What happened?"

Glory sighed. "I said something bad, and rumors started again, so I had to start an even worse rumor. It's stupid."

"So?" Malcolm asked. "How bad can it be?"

Glory hid her face. "Like, I told somebody I'd cut their stuff off? I didn't actually say it, but people think I did, and I didn't deny it."

"Wow!" Malcolm laughed. "I'm impressed and a little scared. What brought this on?"

"That dirty old man at the bookstore was messing with me, and then he said something, and it wasn't any worse than usual, but it..." Glory paused and took a deep breath. "But I got really mad, and I just... spoke up."

"Did he try to touch you?"

"No, nothing like that. Just nasty looks and what he said."

"What did he say?"

Glory felt the car slow down and looked at Malcolm. He had that same cold look she'd seen in the hospital. He maneuvered into a parking lot and stopped the car.

His head pressed against the steering wheel, Malcolm asked her again, "What did he say to you?"

"It was the same thing the monster said in the gangway," Glory whispered. "Malcolm, please—"

"Glory, don't make me ask again."

"He said 'I like me some schoolgirls.' Please, Malcolm, it's just words," Glory begged.

"What did you say?"

"Malcolm, I'm sorry. I just got mad—"

"Woman, answer me," Malcolm growled. "Now!"

"I told him the last person who said that, you beat 'im to death, and the police never found the weapon. I just wanted him to leave us alone."

Malcolm pulled out of the parking lot and headed back down the block toward the school. When he stopped the car in front of the store, Glory placed a hand on his shoulder. "Malcolm, please don't go in there. We should pray about this. You're a man of God."

Malcolm opened his door. "I wasn't always a man of God." He stayed close behind Glory as he ushered her into the now-empty store.

"Grill is closed! Women all gone!" a gruff voice called. Mr. Harris raised his head from behind the counter. "Well, Glory Hallelujah. Come back to play, huh?"

"Cal Harris, you ain't changed a bit, have you?" Malcolm laughed.

The old man looked around, seeming to notice Malcolm for the first time. He broke into a wide grin. "You almost scared me. I don't remember your name, but I never forget a face."

"I'm Malcolm. Me and some friends used to frequent your back room." Malcolm stepped up to the counter and offered his gloved hand, and the old man shook it. "Wild times, back then."

"Heh, heh, yes, indeed." Mr. Harris reached under the counter and pulled out a tall whiskey bottle and a tiny glass. "Drink?"

"Nah," Malcolm said. "So how's things?"

Glory watched the two men exchange pleasantries: Mr. Harris, a harmless, dirty old man, happy to see a kid he once knew all grown up, and Malcolm, a smiling shade of darkness that terrified her.

"Heh, heh," the old man laughed. "What she said about her boyfriend, I'da believed her if I knew it was you."

All semblance of light left Malcolm, and his fist hit the glass-topped counter, cracking it along its length, sending the whiskey bottle crashing to the floor. Glory and the old man jumped. "The young lady is mine, and she's very important to me." Malcolm spoke just above a whisper. "Don't mess with her or her friends."

"Now, listen here!" Mr. Harris yelled, inching toward the cash register far to his left.

"Don't try it, old man. You're not fast enough, and she didn't exaggerate."

"Boy," the old man growled, "when you stopped coming around, I prayed they'd locked you up or put you down."

Malcolm backed away from the counter. "They couldn't do either. Don't mess with her or her friends ever again. Glory, get the door. It's time to go. Good seeing you, Cal."

A FEW MINUTES INTO the drive home, Malcolm reached over and took Glory's hand. "I'm sorry you had to see that. I swear, I hated doing it. If it means anything, I'm proud of you. The old Glory would've been scared and probably cried, but today, you stood up to him and took it like a woman." Malcolm sighed. "Then you saw a part of my past I hoped you'd never see and one I plan to never show you again."

"Malcolm?"

"Yes?"

"In your wild times, what *were* you?"

"Look at me," he said.

Glory turned to face him.

"I was a very ungodly teenager. I'm no longer that person and will never be that person again."

Glory looked at him and saw the gentle man who had almost made love to her the previous night. The cold and darkness she'd seen in the bookstore were gone. The Malcolm who'd saved her in the gangway was an angel, a God-sent hero. But the Malcolm she'd just seen in that store terrified her. When he brought her hand to his lips and kissed it, the bracelets clinked, reminding her that she belonged to both of them.

Chapter 13

On the forty-five-minute drive from the school to Herschel's salon, the upcoming overnight and all-day bus ride weighed heavily on Glory's mind. She looked forward to the holidays with Bigma, her aunts, and the whole family, but the trip would be horrible. Her mother would pack too much food and not allow Glory to bring a single book except the Bible. Somebody's music would be so loud it bled through the headphones. There would be crying babies, people passing gas, and a single bathroom that always stopped working. Staring out the bus window, watching the bare horizon, the only good thing to see would be the stars.

"Hey," Malcolm said, patting her hand. "Still upset?"

"Not really," Glory answered. "Just thinking about the trip tonight. I love the visits, but the bus is always such a nightmare. I wish we could just fly."

"It won't be so bad. I got your tickets, and I told your mom not to pack any food or extra pillows. I've taken care of everything." He stopped the car in front of the salon. "I'm gonna give you this now." He reached into an inside coat pocket and pulled out his wallet. "It's for emergencies. I don't want your mom to see me give it to you, okay?"

"Malcolm, I have my own money," Glory protested. "I can't take money from you."

"You don't hafta use it. Hide it in the lining of your purse. If you still have it, give it back when you get home." He pressed five twenty-

151

dollar bills into her hand. "You're my lady. I need you to be okay no matter what."

Glory knew better than to argue. She unzipped the torn side pouch of her purse and slid the money into the lining.

"You still have your protection?"

"Um, yeah." Glory tried to sound casual, remembering her embarrassment from the night before.

"Well, you won't be needing it for the trip, right? I'll hold them for you."

"Malcolm! You're embarrassing me." Glory tried not to blush, but his smile made her giggle.

He held out his hand. "C'mon, set 'em out."

Glory felt around in the lining again and paused briefly at the pill compact, before deciding to keep it. She grabbed the two rubbers and placed them into Malcolm's outstretched hand. "Oh my God, this is so embarrassing." Glory hid her face in her hands. "I'm not taking this like a woman at all."

"Only two?" Malcolm laughed. "Woman, you really underestimated me."

Glory peered at him through her fingers.

He winked.

"Or maybe you underestimated me, and two is all you coulda handled. You have no idea what I've been studying." She poked her tongue out at him and laughed as his eyes went wide.

"Nah, see," Malcolm said, "you tryin' to start stuff." He reached out and touched her cheek, his playful smile turning mischievous. "You know I'll wait, but I have ways of speeding up the clock. I'm Superman, remember? Get inside. I'll be back in forty-five minutes. I gotta pick up you and your mom's last presents. They're for the trip."

Walking into the salon, Glory realized some lines had been crossed. She and Malcolm had just joked about sex, and she was carrying a hundred dollars in cash that he'd given her. Expensive gifts were one thing, but she didn't know how she felt about this level of... she didn't even know what to call it. JT had never offered her more than a dollar for a pop and chips. But JT was a boy, and Malcolm was a man who expected womanly things... and she wasn't sure what womanly things were. Since they'd just talked about sex, maybe she was supposed to be enticing now. *Could we flirt?*

Heading into the back room, she nearly crashed into Herschel. "Merry Christmas, Glory-Glory!" said Herschel. "To what do I owe the pleasure?"

Glory looked up and laughed then threw her arms around the tall man in the red velvet Santa shirt. "Merry Christmas, Herschel. I'm delivering your present, and I... well, just wanna see you before I go down south. I've only got about forty minutes, though."

"Oh, goody, presents and chitchat. My favorite! I'll put the kettle on."

Seated at the kitchen table, Glory watched Herschel dab his eyes looking at the charm bracelet. "Glory-Glory, this is so beautiful and so thoughtful. All of the charms are so perfect, but this Wonder Woman charm is just so..." He dabbed his eyes again. "Okay, your turn."

He handed Glory a huge white box taped at the corners and tied with a big red bow. "You fit in so well on our North Side adventures, I thought, *You're so cosmopolitan*, and—"

Glory blushed. "Can I open it?"

"Of course. Open it!"

Removing the lid and peeling back the top layer of tissue, the first thing Glory saw was red. She pulled out three hats of wool, leather, and dyed fur, each with a gold rose pin and matching scarves and gloves. She peeled back more tissue to reveal a gold wool coat with gold roses embroidered down the lapels. She ran her fingers over the stitching then opened the coat to reveal the same stitching in the silk lining. It was a full minute before she realized she couldn't see because she was crying. There was no way her mother would let her keep such a thing.

"Herschel, this is too much. I can't... I don't know... how... why?" She wrapped her arms around the man who was the closest thing she had to a sister.

"You're not a little girl anymore. You're growing into a fascinating lady, and you're so far beyond that ugly old orange parka. Watching you blossom..." Herschel paused. "You know what? How 'bout we not stand here and blubber all over each other like some old movie? Siddown. Tell me about your day."

Minutes later, Glory looked into Herschel's incredulous face.

"So, let me get this straight. A dirty old man said something stupid, and you, a teenager, handled it quite reasonably, but your mature, grown-ass preacher man had a teenage flashback and went full-blown thug?"

"Yeah," Glory said, sipping her tea. "It really scared me."

"Darling, if you wanted a thug, you could find one of those right outside this salon. You could get a boy your own age to beat up every old man on Seventy-Fifth Street any time you want. Oh. I see you're getting better at rolling your eyes. I'm so proud."

"He wasn't like he was in the gangway," Glory said. "That was... I don't know... that time, he was angry and rescuing me. This was different. He was smiling the whole time. He knew the guy and wasn't mad at all—he was just mean."

"Darling, do you know what a red flag is? If something feels wrong, it is." Herschel grabbed Glory's face. "Look at me. Does Malcolm scare you?"

"No, not really," Glory said truthfully. Malcolm didn't actually scare her. Sometimes he bossed her around or held her a little too hard. The slaps were only when she was rude, and the first hard slap had really only hurt her feelings. She knew how to handle him, so he was hardly ever rough with her. "I mean he *is* bossy and grumpy sometimes, but Herschel, Malcolm *does love me* even though he knows I don't really love him. He says I will in time."

"Of course you will. He's brainwashing you. He's not giving you a free minute to think of anything but him, and he's making sure nobody can compete with him." Herschel went to the stove to add more hot water to his cup. "Even today, you took care of yourself, and he came in and made you look helpless. He's making you need him."

"But last night he wouldn't touch me even though I told him I had protection. He wants to wait 'cause he says I'm too young. He even took the rubbers 'cause I won't need 'em."

"Really? A point for Malcolm. I'm truly impressed. He's making you want him even though you don't love him."

Glory found herself uncomfortably realizing that Herschel might be absolutely right.

Herschel carefully closed up the box with Glory's present. "Darling, you *are* too young for him. You should be out getting felt up by boys, not pushed away by men. When you get down south, a big, fine country boy is supposed to come down the road and look you up and down, make sure he ain't your cousin. You blush a little, you hold hands, he kisses your cheek, you giggle, y'all lay back in the hay wagon and look up at the stars—you know, stuff people your age do."

Glory thought about the boys her age—the boys at church who she didn't want... JT, who she needed to forget... Allen, who she'd met just once and who shouldn't be on her mind at all... and Quentin, who would do anything for her. Any one of them might be cuter and funnier and even nicer than Malcolm, but none of them could compete with him, because her mother would never let her see any of them. Malcolm had freed her. She could spend time with friends and have a life outside of church, because her mother went along with anything Malcolm allowed. He made her normal. No boy her age could do that.

"Wait," Herschel said. "He took your rubbers? Did he take the pills, too? Now, Glory-Glory, that is not—"

"No, he doesn't know I have the pills. I didn't tell him." Glory kept her head down, avoiding Herschel's harsh glare.

"Now, listen, little girl. Yes, I just called you little girl." He shook his finger at her, using his deep male voice. "Do not under *any circumstance* let him know about those pills. He's already trying to own your heart and mind. By taking those rubbers, he's trying to own your body. He's saying your stuff belongs to him."

Glory folded her arms, pretending she didn't hear the clink of the bracelets.

Herschel reached into a nearby fishbowl and grabbed a strip of purple rubbers and dropped them on the table. "Here. Put these in your purse, and don't tell him you have 'em until you need to use 'em. Girl, I'm getting scared for you." Herschel started pacing. "Does your mother know about this? What does she say?"

"My mother loves Malcolm because he's a preacher." Glory grudgingly took the rubbers and slid them into the lining of her purse. "He's the reason she lets me go anywhere." There was no way she could tell Herschel what Malcolm suspected and her mother encouraged.

"I need you to promise me something, darling. Promise me you'll do some thinking on this trip. You're gonna be far away from Malcolm with nothing to remind you of him, completely free from his control. Think about what happened today. Promise me!"

"I promise." Glory sighed.

"And promise me that you'll talk to people your age. If a boy on the bus says hi, you'll say hi back. If that country boy comes down the road and ain't your cousin, you'll sit a spell and talk. Promise me?"

"I promise," Glory answered. "But I know everything's gonna be okay. Malcolm's a really good guy, Herschel. Honest, he is." Glory hugged Herschel and ran out to the car. She hated to leave, but she was already five minutes late.

"How was the visit?" Malcolm asked after she closed the door.

"Too short," Glory said, unzipping her parka. "I got the most beautiful new coat."

"Uh... okay?" Malcolm looked confused. "It looks exactly like your old one."

"Huh? Oh, no. I hafta leave it here. We're gonna exchange it when I get back." Glory laughed a little. "There's no way my mother would let me keep it. It's really beautiful gold, and it came with red hats and gloves." Glory looked out of the window and sighed. "My mother says red is for whores."

"Go get it," Malcolm said.

"What?"

"Go back in and get your Christmas present. Right now."

"But Malcolm, she'll—"

"Glory, are you arguing with me?"

"Okay. I'm going." Glory walked back into the salon and returned with the big white box—and a huge knot in her stomach. There was no good outcome for her from this. She would either displease Malcolm or invite demons of vanity and pride and the wrath of her mother and God.

"Malcolm?"

"Do you like the coat?"

"But, Malcolm, you don't know her."

Malcolm reached over and took Glory's hand. "And she don't know me."

OUTSIDE THEIR APARTMENT door, Glory held the box and looked at Malcolm again. He placed a hand on her shoulder and nodded. Glory opened the door and prayed Malcolm's cold look was just the hallway lighting, then she looked around the living room and sighed. On the couch were stacked pillows, folded blankets, and two Bibles. A cloth tote bag overflowed with fruit and foil-wrapped packets. Two large rolling suitcases stood nearby.

Mary Bishop came out of the kitchen, wiping her hands on a dishtowel. "I was getting kinda worried. If we get to the bus station too late, we won't get seats together," she fussed.

"I'm sorry, Mother Bishop. Have I disappointed you in some way?" Malcolm asked.

"No, Malcolm. Why would you think that?" Mary tucked the towel into her apron.

Malcolm motioned around the room. "Looks like you changed your mind about trusting me to take care of things."

Mary waved him off. "Nothing of the sort. I just didn't wanna put you out, that's all. If you're sure you've got everything, we'll leave this stuff here. Can you take the sandwiches to the food pantry tonight?"

"Of course, Mother Bishop. I've taken care of everything. I've made sure you and my lady"—he grabbed Glory's hand and brought it to his chest—"are well cared for."

Glory breathed a sigh of relief and smiled at Malcolm but saw that his smile was still cold.

"We've got a few minutes," Malcolm said, "and I have a present for you, Mother Bishop. It's a little something for the trip." Malcolm handed her a green cloth travel case with a long strap. "Look inside. I think you'll like it."

Mary sat down on the couch, opened the case, and frowned. "Malcolm, this is something for kids. What do I do with something like this?" Mary held up the tape player and a set of headphones. She looked at Malcolm with confusion and little else.

"Anything you want. Look at the tapes."

Mary set aside the tape player and headphones, and when she picked up the tapes, she laughed out loud. "Well, I'll be. James Cleveland, Walter Hawkins, Shirley Caesar, the Bible. Oh, Malcolm, I don't know what to say. This is wonderful! Me and Glory will have a fine time with this on the bus. We can listen to the Bible the whole trip!"

"No, Mother Bishop," Malcolm said. "That's *your* present. I've got other plans for my lady. You've got a power cord and plenty of batteries, so you can enjoy it all the way there and all the way back. Glory has other interests." He turned to Glory. "Don't you?"

"Well, the Bible is fine with me." Glory looked to her mother. "That's what we always—"

Malcolm gently turned Glory's face back to him. "You'll *read* something different on this trip." He handed her a stack of books. "The boxed set is *Chronicles of Narnia*. C. S. Lewis was a Christian author who wrote of the lion, Aslan, the creator of Narnia. In the story, Aslan is like Jesus."

"Um, okay, but isn't this series kind of... childish?" Glory looked at her mother, but Mary averted her eyes.

"Are you arguing with me, Glory? This is a very good series. I know you'll like it. The other book is by Zora Neale Hurston, one of the most famous writers of the Harlem Renaissance."

Glory's heart raced. She looked at Malcolm, begging him with her eyes. *Oh, God, Malcolm. Please don't do this.*

"*Their Eyes Were Watching God* is the story of a young girl forced to marry an old man because her family doesn't think she's smart enough to take care of herself. I really want you to read this. Your mother always tells me how obedient you are." He reached up to push her hair back from her face and wiped the tear that escaped. "Now, go empty your backpack so you can take them with you. I'll put the suitcases in the car."

Glory grabbed her backpack and bent to pick up the white box.

"Leave that," Malcolm ordered, grabbing both suitcases. "We'll look at it in just a second."

Glory waited for him to leave and closed the door behind him. "Mama?"

"Go do as he said, baby."

Alone in her bedroom, Glory wanted to throw something. She wanted to slam the door and kick and scream and punch the wall. He knew she wasn't allowed to read those things, and he'd deliberately challenged her mother's authority, and he used things she'd told him about her mother and tried to hurt her. *How could he be so mean?* She stuffed the books into her backpack, taking satisfaction in the fact that she'd already read all of them and she wasn't going to read them again.

She heard the doorbell buzz and went back to the living room. Malcolm stood holding the big white box. "Before we go, show us what Herschel got you for Christmas."

"Malcolm, can we please look at it when we get back? Please?" Glory begged. "Let's just go?"

"Glory."

Malcolm's tone ended her protests, and she laid the box on the coffee table and lifted the lid. He helped her move the tissue and accessories and lift out the gold coat. "Try it on." Malcolm held it up for her. "With the wool hat. Then go look at yourself."

Glory tied the belt, adjusted the hat, and looked at herself in the hall mirror. Though she could only see her head and shoulders, the coat and hat were as pretty as she expected. She untied the belt as she returned to the living room.

"Oh, no, keep it on. You hafta wear it. Something this beautiful, on a woman as beautiful as you, needs to be seen."

"Please, Malcolm, don't make me wear it. I can't." She looked at her mother for help, but Mary's face was inscrutable.

"And why not?" Malcolm asked innocently.

"Because I don't wanna become vain and prideful, Malcolm." Glory couldn't look at him. This was a game to him, and she hated it.

Malcolm turned to her mother. "Mother Bishop, did you raise your daughter to be vain and prideful?"

"I certainly did not," Mary said, contempt thick in her voice.

"See, Glory? It's okay." He reached out and stroked Glory's cheek. "According to Proverbs 22:6, since she trained you up in the way that you should go, you will not depart from it. Isn't that right, Mother Bishop?"

"Yes, Malcolm, that's right. It says when she's old, she won't depart from it. But since she's still young, she needs guidance."

Glory saw the slightest bit of triumph on her mother's face, but the flash of anger on Malcolm's face scared her. She'd learned not to challenge him on Bible verses, but her mother had no such restrictions.

"Yes, she does," Malcolm said, tying Glory's belt and adjusting the lapels. "Glory, you are beautiful in gold and red. You will wear it because I want you to. Do you understand me?"

"But—"

"And while you're down south, you will hang out with your cousins. You will go out to boogie and watch TV and listen to music and dance. You will have fun and laugh and play. You will go shopping and buy yourself some pretty things. I think you'd be beautiful in sparkles and something red. Okay?"

"Malcolm, it's—"

"Glory, in the book of Esther, Vashti was cast out because she disobeyed."

Glory swallowed the painful lump of protest that rose in her throat.

"It's okay, baby. Just do as he says," Mary said. "It's getting late—we need to go." She pushed past Malcolm and headed toward the hall. "I need to make a stop. Y'all go on to the car. I'll lock up and be right out."

Malcolm picked up the bag of sandwiches and Glory's backpack and ushered her out the door. At the car, he unlocked her door and paused. "Glory, look at me."

She turned to face him, grateful for the broken streetlights that hid his eyes in the shadows. She didn't feel like facing his anger at that moment.

"Don't ever do that again. Don't ever argue with—"

"But, Malcolm, you don't under—"

The force of the slap turned her head and knocked her against the car. As she tried to straighten up, another slap knocked her over again.

"Don't ever argue with me in front of your mother again. Do you understand me?"

Glory pressed her hand to her cheek. *Not stinging—throbbing.* Tears burned behind her eyes and nose.

"Answer me."

"Yes, Malcolm," she whispered, trying her best not to sob.

GLORY SAT AS FAR AWAY from Malcolm as the front seat would allow, facing forward, ignoring his and her mother's chatter. The tears she didn't try to hold back streamed down her face, and she didn't hide her sniffling. She prayed her mother would notice and ask but soon realized her mother *had* noticed and was not going to ask at all.

When Malcolm slid his hand across the seat, Glory pulled hers away. He brought his hand up and wiped her tears, his knuckles scraping her cheek where he'd struck her only minutes ago. He moved his hand to her shoulder and down her arm, pushing up her sleeve and wrapping his hand around the bracelets that... *constantly*... reminded her that she was *his beloved* and his desire was for her.

Chapter 14

Christmas in downtown Chicago could lift even the most burdened spirits, and Glory found herself enchanted by the lights, in spite of her pain. When Malcolm entwined his fingers with hers, she did not resist. Her cheek still ached when she touched it. Malcolm had never before hit her that hard, and his voice... it was calm and cold, the voice of the person he'd been with Mr. Harris—the person he'd told her not three hours earlier he'd never show her again.

"Malcolm, where are we?" Mary asked from the back seat as they entered a tunnel heading down under a large building. "This isn't the bus station."

"No, it is not, Mother Bishop," Malcolm said, smiling into the rearview mirror. "It's the train station. Merry Christmas!"

"I see," Mary said. "Thank you, Malcolm."

Glory just stared at him.

Malcolm stopped the car at a set of glass doors. "I'll be right back, ladies. Wait here." He kissed Glory's hand and stroked her cheek before getting out of the car.

Glory pulled down the visor mirror to look at her mother in the back seat. "Mama?"

"That man will do anything for you, won't he, baby?"

"Yes, ma'am, he will." Glory closed the mirror.

Glory's door opened and Malcolm reappeared, followed by a man in a blue uniform and red cap, pushing a handcart.

"This gentleman is gonna wait with you while I move the car." Malcolm helped Glory out then Mary. "Follow him, and wait inside. I'll be right back."

"Yes, Malcolm," Mary said, turning to follow the redcap and their luggage.

Malcolm placed a hand on Glory's shoulder. "Go on. I'll be in in a minute." He touched the still-sore spot on her cheek. "I'm sorry."

Without a word, Glory turned and followed her mother and the redcap. Moments later, Malcolm joined them inside. Glory could tell Malcolm was enjoying treating them to this trip as he held her hand walking through the station.

Nearing the ticket counter, Mary pointed at the huge crowd. "Are we getting in this line? What time does the train leave?"

"Nope. We've got time—you'll see," Malcolm said. They passed the crowds and stopped at a small podium with one attendant. Malcolm presented their tickets, and the attendant smiled. The redcap disappeared with their luggage through a door on the left, and an automatic door on their right opened to a dark-paneled room staffed by waiters in white coats.

"Mother takes this train all the time," Malcolm said, guiding them through the door.

Mary gasped. "Malcolm, this is really too much."

"Nonsense, Mother Bishop. This is just right." Malcolm turned to Glory. "You like this lounge, Glory?"

Glory looked around. "It's okay." The navy-draped room with silver furniture looked like old-fashioned elegance. She could definitely believe Malcolm's mother traveled this way all the time.

Malcolm removed his gloves and accepted a hot towel from a waiter. Mary declined a cup of coffee. Glory remained silent. A man in a blue uniform approached, speaking low to Malcolm.

Malcolm turned to Glory and Mary. "Ladies, follow me."

He ushered them through another door onto the freezing train platform, and the porter gestured to a waiting electric cart. They rode past a long line of people carrying all manner of baggage, all waiting to board the train. Glory had a feeling this cart ride was more than just a way to bypass the long line. They passed coach after coach, then lounge and dining cars, before finally stopping at a sleeping car.

"Okay, ladies. This is your car." Malcolm shook the cart driver's hand. "Come back in... say, twenty minutes? I just wanna get them settled."

The driver nodded and left.

Stepping onto the train, they were greeted by a smiling attendant in a sharp blue uniform. "Good evening. I'm Wendell. I'll be your attendant this trip. Coach is pretty full, but it's nice and quiet up here. Is everybody traveling?"

"No." Malcolm handed Wendell the tickets. "Only the ladies. I'm just here to see them off." He shook the attendant's hand. "Call me Malcolm. Lead the way."

Still smiling brightly, Wendell led them up a tiny staircase and down a narrow hallway, finally opening a door to a small room with a couch and an armchair. Wendell helped Glory and Mary out of their coats and hung them in a tiny closet then pointed out all the room's features and amenities. Glory pretended not to see him raise an eyebrow when he looked at her. While Mary made herself comfortable in the armchair, Glory sat on the couch, watching Malcolm make friends with the attendant. They seemed about the same age, but Malcolm obviously felt more important, and Glory knew he only pretended to be friendly. When she caught his eye, he smiled and nodded at her. Glory considered rolling her eyes as she turned her head to look out the window, catching a glimpse of her mother's stern glare.

"So," Wendell said, pulling out a small black notebook. "I've got dinnertime tonight for eight o'clock. I'll personally escort them to and from the dining room. What time should I turn down the beds?"

"Mother Bishop, what time would you like?" Malcolm asked.

"I think ten o'clock is good, don't you, Glory?"

"Yes, ma'am. It's fine," Glory said. *Why are they pretending to care what I think?*

"Ten is fine for Mrs. Bishop, Wendell," Malcolm said. "When you do that, escort Miss Bishop to the observation lounge. She has some reading to do, and she likes to watch the stars." He looked at Glory until she lowered her eyes. "Give her all the time she wants."

"Will do, Malcolm. Anything else?"

Glory stared at her folded hands while Malcolm talked. Wendell sounded so happy, promising to do everything Malcolm asked. She'd gotten used to Malcolm giving orders. He made people want to do things for him. *Does he hit everybody who argues with him?* She jumped when Malcolm touched her shoulder.

"Step outside with me for a bit," Malcolm said.

Glory let him help with her coat, accepted her purse when he handed it to her, and followed him down the stairs.

"Ten minutes, Malcolm," Wendell said as they passed him.

Stepping out onto the platform, Malcolm immediately pulled Glory into his arms. She relaxed in spite of herself but did not return his embrace. When he released her and pushed her hair back from her face, letting his finger light on the sore spot he had caused, Glory turned her head.

With two fingers, he turned her face back to him. "Glory, please look at me."

She lifted her eyes, quickly wiping a tear.

"God, you're so beautiful. Even now." He ran his thumb over her cheek again. "'I have wounded thee with the wound of an enemy, with the chastisement of a cruel one.' I'm so sorry."

Glory opened her mouth to speak, but nothing she could say would be good. What did he want her to say? "I know," she said finally. That was the best she could give him.

"Now, therefore forgive, I pray thee, my sin only this once"—Malcolm pulled her into his arms again and kissed her forehead—"that you may take away from me this death."

When Malcolm kissed her, it wasn't possessive or controlling—just loving, reassuring, and begging forgiveness. Glory wanted to be like normal girls and slap him away and scream at him. She wished she could be like the girls who hit back and cussed and embarrassed him in the street. Instead, Glory yielded to Malcolm's kiss and knew she would eventually get over it.

"I've always wanted to kiss a beautiful woman on a train platform," Malcolm said.

The conductor signaled all aboard, and Malcolm gave Glory some last-minute instructions, their return tickets, and an envelope of tip money before helping her back onto the train. Heading for the staircase, Glory caught a glimpse of herself in the mirror over the drinking fountain. The small mirror framed her face and the ugly mark of Malcolm's anger.

"Excuse me, Miss Bishop?"

Glory turned around. "Oh, hi, Wendell."

"Maybe you could use this." He held out a small plastic bag of ice wrapped in a white washcloth. "It'll keep it from being too ugly tomorrow."

Glory looked at him then at the ice pack.

"Go ahead. It'll dull the pain, too."

"Thanks." Glory took the ice pack and pressed it to her cheek. "I'm going upstairs now."

Back in their room, Glory sat down on the couch across from her mother and held the ice to her cheek.

"I see you found an ice pack," Mary's tone was cold. "You don't deserve it. He shoulda took his belt to you, way you was actin'."

"Mama, what did I do?"

"You so headstrong! I tell him I raised you to be a godly, obedient girl, and you act like you got nothin' but rebellion and disobedience in you. You back talk and argue! Godly women don't do that. You should be shamed! Man give you exactly what you want, don't he? Take you everywhere you wanna go, don't he? Ain't tryin' to get in yo' pants, is he? You said it yo'self—he loves you. All you hafta do is let him! I almost took the cord to you myself!"

Mary's words hit Glory like a kick in the stomach—harder than the blows to her face. *My mother not only approves but thinks I deserve worse?*

"But, Mama, can I please explain?" Glory begged. "You don't know the whole story."

"Explain what? How you ungrateful? He standin' there, tryin' to show off how he taking care of you, and you throw it all back up in his face! I'm surprised he waited till y'all got outside. You disrespectful...!"

As her mother spoke, Glory's mind reeled. Malcolm had intended to embarrass her mother. She'd seen it in his face, heard it in his voice. She knew in her heart he'd meant no good, and her mother blew it off like it was nothing. Glory had tried to protect, honor, and respect her mother, but Mary didn't need her protection at all. And now her mother was saying that it was *Glory* who'd humiliated *Malcolm,* when all he'd wanted to do was ensure she could do whatever she wanted and keep the coat she loved...

A knock at the door interrupted Mary's tirade. "Come in!" Mary called. Glory turned her face away from the door.

Wendell stuck his head in. "It's almost eight o'clock. I'll show you to the dining car."

Mary checked her face in the mirror before stepping out into the hall.

"We're going right through there, Mrs. Bishop." Wendell gestured toward the door. "And after you, Miss Bishop," he added to Glory, who had her purse in her lap but hadn't moved from her seat.

"Go on. I'll find it." Glory pulled out her lotion and powder, not caring if her mother saw.

"Should I come back for you?"

"No. I said I'll find it."

"Miss Bishop, Malcolm left specific instructions that you should be escorted everywhere."

Take it like a woman. "Wendell, is Malcolm here now?" Glory snapped, applying the powder to the red marks on her face.

"No, Miss Bishop, he's not. I'll see you in the dining room. Dinner is in ten minutes."

MALCOLM'S DINING ARRANGEMENTS included preordering Glory's meal. She didn't touch a thing, and when the coffee came, Glory pushed it away.

"Ungrateful, wasteful, prideful," her mother hissed.

Glory stared out the window and watched the passing city lights.

"Sittin' here wit' yo' face all painted up, tryin' to hide yo' shame." Hidden behind the coffee cup and piled cloth napkins, Mary reached across the table and grabbed Glory's wrist. "Demon of rebellion, I bind you in the name of Jesus," she whispered.

Glory continued to stare out at the scenery while her mother pinched and twisted the skin on the back of her hand. After a minute or so, Glory pulled her hand back, upsetting a water glass. When the waiter arrived to clean up the mess, she offered neither apology nor thanks. If the demon of rebellion were a puppy, Glory would have cuddled it in her lap.

Back in their room, Glory sat down, and Mary exploded. "I cain't drive the demons outta you in here, but we gon' pray all the way to Canton! You hear me? We gon' beg God to take this ugliness from yo' heart right now. Shameful!"

"Yes, ma'am," Glory said.

"We gon' pray all night!"

"Yes, ma'am. And will you please tell Malcolm why I didn't read like he told me to? I don't want him to hit me again for being disobedient." *Demon of false humility!* Glory kept her head bowed. She didn't want to watch her mother struggle in Malcolm's control game. There was no way for Mary to win. Maybe now she would understand.

"Well, then we gon' pray right now till it's time for you to go." *Nope. She still doesn't understand.*

While her mother laid hands on her head, Glory tried to concentrate and ask God to make her a godly woman, but her prayers kept changing to pleas for peace. While her mother prayed for God to fix her heart, Glory prayed for God to fix Malcolm's. And she prayed to JT's God for a normal life and freedom.

While Mary prayed, Glory let her thoughts wander to Malcolm, and as she'd promised Herschel, she thought about what had happened earlier in the day. Not twenty-four hours before, she'd offered herself to Malcolm, and he'd rejected her. She'd stood up for herself and told off a dirty old man, but then Malcolm had stepped in and made her feel weak and silly. Then he'd taken the rubbers. *Did he think not having them would stop me? Why does he hafta be so bossy?* And he loved her. *How could he be so mean?*

Glory's thoughts and Mary's prayers were interrupted by Wendell, letting them know it was nearly time to prepare the room for bed. Glory quickly grabbed a book and her purse, kissed her mother good night, and stepped out into the hallway.

"I'll find my way," she said to Wendell

"I know you will, Miss Bishop. I noticed you didn't eat. Was something wrong? Malcolm ordered—"

"I didn't want what Malcolm ordered."

"Oh, I see." Wendell motioned for Glory to follow him down the staircase. "The dining car is closed, but Malcolm arranged for you to have—"

"Wendell, can you get me a taffy apple, nachos, and orange pop? None of that's on Malcolm's list, is it?" Glory was surprised at how irritated she felt.

"No, Miss Bishop, it isn't. Is that what you want?"

"Well, if *Malcolm* said—"

"Miss Bishop?" Wendell asked. "Is Malcolm here?" He winked at her. "Can I ask a question, Miss Bishop?"

"Okay?"

"You're what—sixteen, seventeen?"

"Seventeen."

"Does he do that often?" Wendell nodded in her direction.

Glory lightly touched her face. The ice pack had helped—it didn't hurt as much as it had.

"Once they start, they don't stop, you know," he said. "You're too young for that."

Glory didn't have a response.

"I'll bring your snack to the lounge," he said.

"Thanks, Wendell."

Chapter 15

The observation lounge was a large room full of small tables surrounded by deep armchairs and curved couches. With a powder room at one end and a bar at the other, the glass-domed space offered an expansive view of the night sky. In the mostly dark car, the only artificial light came from the bar and tiny lights under the tables and along the floor.

Glory found an empty table near the center of the room and picked up a magazine lying nearby. The low light made reading difficult, so there was no way she could read the book she was refusing to read, anyway. She gritted her teeth in annoyance that her rebellion had been thwarted, even though she actually liked the book and Malcolm had *ordered* her to do exactly what she'd normally want to do. *Argh!*

Sitting in the dark, under the stars, Glory continued her rebellion as best she could by pretending to be a normal girl traveling alone with nobody to tell her what to do. Flipping through an abandoned fashion magazine, Glory imagined herself and Malcolm in the glamorous world of the photos—Malcolm cool and serious in a high-backed leather chair while she leaned against it in a slinky, shimmery dress, or Malcolm dangerous and mysterious in leather and shades while she hung provocatively on his arm. A cologne ad of solid gray smelled just like Malcolm. Every page reminded her of Malcolm—sophisticated and in control. She pushed the magazine away, her bracelets jangling as they brushed the table edge. She pulled her sleeves down to muffle the sound. She didn't want that reminder tonight.

Wendell appeared at her table, carrying a tray. "Pardon me, Miss Bishop. Our chef has been experimenting with some new recipes and hoped you'd consider sampling them." He winked at Glory. "Just play along in case Malcolm *is* here," he whispered.

Glory giggled. "Of course, Wendell. I'd be delighted," she said in her most adult voice.

"First, we have croustilles de maïs avec du fromage." He placed a basket of nachos in front of her. "Next, crisp fall apples with a creamy burnt sugar and peanut dipping sauce, and finally, a custom-blended cocktail of the freshest sparkling orange elixir."

Glory laughed at the fancy cocktail glass of orange pop with an umbrella and sword of fruit sticking out of it. "Thanks, Wendell."

He bowed then left her to her snack, promising to check on her later.

She grabbed another fashion magazine, this one more to her liking—just as flashy as the first but more fun. The faces were smiling, laughing, free—not coolly sophisticated, just warm and alive. The couples faced each other. The boys and girls hugged. *Boys and girls, not men and women.* Glory sighed. *And not men and girls.* She tried to see herself and Malcolm in those pages, and Malcolm didn't fit... anywhere.

But JT did. For the first time in weeks, Glory watched the stars and let herself entertain thoughts of him. He'd be the laughing boy in those pages. The sweaty jock playing basketball and drinking Gatorade. The boy pushing the girl on the swing. The boy holding the girl's hands and kissing her. She wondered what JT was doing now and what had happened to make him abandon her. *Did he hear about what Trina said and think I believed it? Does he sometimes dream about me like I dream about him?* She wondered if he was okay and if he really had forgotten her.

"How's it going?"

Glory looked up into the face of the bartender, who placed another orange-pop cocktail in front of her. "From the young man." He nodded toward the bar.

Glory twisted around, half-expecting Malcolm to be nearby. Most of the tables were empty. The few people left were spread out and talking quietly. Near the bar, though, sat a nervous-looking boy holding a tall glass.

"I can tell him to leave you alone if you want me to," the bartender said. "Wendell said to look out for you."

"No. It's okay. Uh, tell him I said thanks?" Glory said, *taking it like a woman*, though she doubted this was what Malcolm meant. The boy held up a deck of cards. Glory shrugged and beckoned for him to join her. *Okay, Herschel, I'm keeping my promise.*

Glory sat back in the chair and crossed her legs. Stirring her drink with the long red straw, the way people did in the movies, she tried to look cool and sophisticated.

"Hi, I'm James." His words were sung in a thick Southern drawl. "Mind if I sit down?"

The laugh she tried to hold back nearly choked her, and Glory felt the orange pop burning the back of her nose. When James went to pat her on the back, she waved him off. "I'm okay." She coughed. "Went down the wrong pipe." Glory coughed a few more times. "Have a seat."

James took the seat opposite Glory, facing the windows. He tapped the deck of playing cards on the table. "Spades?"

Glory coughed back another giggle. "I'm sorry. I'm so sorry."

"Okay, what's so funny?" James asked.

"I'm really sorry, but it's kinda bad." Glory took deep breaths to stifle her giggles. "Oh my God. I'm so... this is just—hic!" The hiccups swept away any trace of her cool sophistication.

"Um, what's in that drink? He said it was just orange soda and fruit."

Glory's giggles, punctuated with hiccups, proved contagious. Soon James was laughing with her. The bartender appeared with a pitcher of water and plastic cups. Glory gulped down the water and prayed for deliverance from her fit of giggles.

"So now what's so funny?" James asked as Glory finally calmed down.

"I'm sorry. But see..." Glory took a deep breath. "Before I left, my friend made me promise that if a certain type of boy did a certain thing, I'd hafta do something. And I was just thinking about it when you showed up." Glory took a deep breath and swallowed another giggle.

"Okay," James said. "I'll bite. What type of boy and what thing, and what did you promise to do?"

"Oh, please don't ask me that. It's so silly and kinda rude. I only know Go Fish and War. Can we play one of those?"

"You mean to tell me you're the kind of gal that'll laugh in a man's face and then worry about being rude? You must be from Chicago." James started dealing the cards.

"What's that supposed to mean?" Glory picked up and studied her cards.

"I mean, Chicago girls are always being rude and trying to act all innocent. Gimme all your fives."

"Go fish." Glory looked at him for a second. *What would Christy say? The truth, of course.* "I promised my friend that if a country boy—who wasn't my cousin—came down the road, I would sit a spell and talk. Then you came up and said, 'Haa, ah'm James.'" Glory exaggerated his Southern accent. "I don't believe I ever said it wasn't rude. Gimme all your sevens."

"Go fish. Well, I guess you did say it was rude. I stand corrected. What's your name? Got any jacks?"

"Go fish. Aces? I'm Glory. And yes, I'm from Chicago."

"Why do folks from Chicago think everybody from the South lives in the country? Ya know"—James leaned in close—"we's gots two-story skyscrapers in Jackson, and some of us'n keeps our out-houses inside the house."

"Okay, I'm sorry." Glory laughed. "Like I said, it was rude." She breathed a sigh of relief when he straightened back up in his seat. He smelled like Polo cologne, and that dimple... *Stop it!* "I'm sorry, what was that? Queens? Go fish."

Their game continued. Glory easily won. James, a freshman art student at University of Illinois, spoke about the fun and drama of college, while Glory talked about the drama of senior year. He laughed at her tales of her friends, and she laughed at his tales of campus life. He loved to cook and liked Chinese food. Glory admitted she'd only had Chinese food once. He laughed and called her "the country one." James was surprised at the comic books she'd read, and Glory was shocked that he never went to church. As the night wore on, they watched the stars, and James told of the struggles of being away from home for the first time. Glory wondered who he was missing. She dreamed out loud of leaving home and freedom and didn't think of Malcolm at all.

The bartender refilled their drinks before closing the bar for the night, and Glory soon found herself alone with the not-so-country boy from Jackson, Mississippi.

"Okay, new game," James said, shuffling the deck. He placed it in front of Glory. "Cut. This game is pretty simple but can get kinda deep. You scared?"

Glory paused with her hand over the deck. James's devilish grin was challenging but not frightening.

She cut the deck. "Nope. What's the game?"

"Simple. We both draw a card. High card gets to ask any question. Low card draws again, cuts the number in half, and has to answer the question for that long. So, say I win the draw. I ask what's your favorite color. You draw a five. You hafta talk about your favorite color for two and a half minutes. Still wanna play?"

"So, is this a college game? Where's the fun part?"

"That depends on the questions and answers," James said. "Scared?"

"You keep asking me that," Glory answered. "Is there something I should be worried about?" She drew a card. "Seven."

James drew. "Nine. Well, less see... tell me something you like about me."

Glory drew an ace and smiled. "I guess this is a one, so thirty seconds?"

James looked at his watch. "Yup. Go."

"Okay. I really, really, really—and I mean this from the bottom of my heart," Glory said slowly, "I really like your cologne. It reminds me of almost every single boy in my school. Was that thirty seconds? I can keep going?" Glory tried innocently batting her eyelashes.

"I see you ain't gon' make this easy at all, are you?" James drew a card and smiled. "Jack."

Glory drew. "Queen. Ha! What do I want to know?" Christy would be teasing him with cool sarcasm, and Tressa would be making him uncomfortable with doe eyes and her soft voice. Glory had none of those skills. She looked at the no-longer-nervous boy sitting across from her, all confident, as if he knew there was a trick to this game and he couldn't lose.

"Okay," Glory finally said. "What exactly do you expect to get from me out of this game?" *Thank you, Herschel, for teaching me about boys and games.*

She watched James's confidence crack.

He drew a king, and his head slumped in defeat. "Thirteen. That's enough time to force me to spill my whole evil plan."

"Oh, is it?" Glory grinned. "So you had evil plans for me, and I've defeated you by a simple card game? You're not a good villain at all, are you?" She had to admit, this was almost as much fun as playing in the hall with Quentin.

A few seconds passed.

"You're stalling," Glory said.

When James laughed, he showed all his teeth and wrinkled his nose. He brought a hand up and massaged his thick eyebrows then smoothed back his close-cropped hair. "Well, okay. I thought maybe I'd get to know you and maybe get you to ask questions so you could get to know me. Then, I don't know, maybe when you pick a school, you come to U of I and... you know what? This is a silly game, now that I think of it. Let's play something else—how 'bout it?"

"Oh. Your game's too deep?" Glory heard herself and was surprised at how mean she sounded. The game was supposed to be nice and friendly and slow, and she'd sabotaged it and tried to embarrass him. *Just like Malcolm would've done.* "Wait. I'm sorry. Is it too late to change the question?"

James leaned back in the chair and folded his arms, smiling a little, a bit of his confidence back. "Well, technically, it's too late since you already asked, but since you're the asker, you can stop the time. You wanna stop the time?"

"Um, yeah. Let's try again. I'll play nice this round." Glory drew a two.

"Heh!" James gloated. "You had me, and you chickened out. I admit I'm not a good villain, but you're a pretty weak femme fatale." He drew a six. "I first saw you riding on the platform and then again at dinner, but when you left, you didn't go to coach. Then that conductor brought you a tray after the kitchen had closed. Why the special treatment? Who are you, for real?"

Glory drew a three and breathed a sigh of relief. "Isn't that two questions?"

"I'm the asker—my game."

"Cheater." Glory put on her best pretend pout. "Okay. My name is Glory Bishop, and I'm one of the X-Men. My power is that men just like to give me goodies." Glory laughed. "My friend said that to me this morning, and I never thought I'd get a chance to use that line myself. Thanks, James."

"You know, Glory, I actually believe you do have that power." He pointed to the empty glass in front of her. "It worked on me and the bartender. I think I'mma need you in my evil army."

Glory smiled. "The one you'll eventually give to me?"

"Well, yeah. But you'll just give it back, so the world is gonna be pretty safe when we come to power. Anyway, back to the question."

"Okay. Actually, I'm nobody special," Glory admitted. "We're in first class because a guy—a man from church—paid for this trip for my mother and me. The special treatment is because he's trying to prove a point to my mother, you know... impress her with how powerful he is." That was mostly true. Malcolm was from church, and he was trying to prove a point. *Demon of lies and deceit!*

Malcolm had set up this trip just for her, yet Glory had just denied him. She had a purse full of money to meet every need, thanks to him. Every time she moved, the bracelets reminded her that she was his beloved, but she'd just denied the man to hold a boy's attention. *Filthy Jezebel!*

"Wow, your mom has the same power, huh?" James laughed. "You two must be pretty rad together. But I get the feeling she might not be as nice as you. I bet this guy is giving it all he's got, huh? He must really want her." He reached across the table, resting his hand on Glory's. "If she's anything like you, well..."

Glory pulled her hand away. "It's getting late. I'm surprised she's not up here looking for me. I really should be going."

James stood up. "I'll walk you back to your seat."

"No, thanks." Glory stood up. "It's not a seat—it's a room. Not too far. I'll be fine."

"Oh, okay," James said. "It was nice meeting you, Glory."

Glory pretended not to hear his disappointment.

"It was nice meeting you, too, James."

She grabbed her purse and book, avoiding looking at him and instead watching the stars. "Good night." She headed toward the exit.

James grabbed her hand. "Glory. Wait."

Glory turned around and let it happen—the kiss she knew was coming and really wanted. She stood still and didn't resist. Then she let her book and purse drop to the floor and wrapped her arms around the boy, whose kiss was warm and hungry and full of promise.

James pulled back, and Glory found herself peering into eyes that smiled even when they were serious. "I've wanted to do that all night," James whispered. "My evil plan worked."

Glory wished she had a smart answer, but she didn't. She just smiled and waited for him to kiss her again.

He did. His touch, his scent, his warmth—everything about him reminded her of home and a boy she still loved, and Glory wanted nothing more than to stay that way forever, a normal girl kissing a boy and slow dancing under the stars. Feeling him against her body, moving to the rattle and the rhythm of the rails, Glory let the train whistles drown out the sound of the bracelets that mocked her false loyalty and drown out the voices condemning her Jezebel spirit and ungodly rebellion.

GLORY WOKE TO THE SOUND of her mother singing in the shower and the rhythmic chug of the train. It took her a minute to realize where she was, and as the events of the night before came back to her, she couldn't help smiling. She had been a weak femme fatale who kissed a not-so-evil villain. Herschel would be so proud. Christy and Tressa would be shocked and confused, and Malcolm... Glory felt a mixture of guilt and fear when she thought of Malcolm. He'd arranged this trip just for her, and she'd betrayed him with a boy she'd just met. She kind of feared for James if Malcolm ever found out.

She pushed off the covers and climbed down the ladder to the floor. At the small sink, she splashed her face with water and pushed her hair back. In the full light of the vanity mirror, the mark where Malcolm had hit her the previous day was almost gone. He'd apologized, she'd forgiven him, and she knew it wouldn't happen again. Before Malcolm, her world had been church, the salon, and JT. She had been a church girl with a secret life of books. Then Malcolm had saved her life and treated her like a queen. He protected her, and he would kill for her. He freed her to see and do all the things she wanted, and he loved her. With Malcolm, she had the life she'd dreamed about, and when he was happy, even though she wasn't in love with him, she loved being Malcolm's lady.

But the night before, Glory got to be exactly who she wanted to be: something Malcolm and her mother would never allow. And this morning, with the mark of Malcolm's anger fading from her face and the warmth of James's kiss still on her lips, Glory knew she was too young to be Malcolm's lady.

Glory splashed her face again. It felt good to complete that thought. Malcolm wanted an obedient, godly woman, and Glory was a girl just learning how to argue. Malcolm couldn't be questioned, but Glory needed answers. Maybe when she was older, she could be what he wanted, but she wasn't ready for that yet. Herschel was right. Malcolm gave her everything but choices. She looked at the bracelets locked onto her wrists, her constant reminder that she was *his beloved*. The bracelets made her feel special, but they said she belonged to him, and she couldn't take them off.

Her thoughts were interrupted by light tapping at the door. "Just a minute, please!" Glory called. She grabbed a blanket to cover herself and cracked the door a bit. "Good morning, Wendell."

"Good morning, Miss Bishop. Is your mother around?"

"She's indisposed right now," Glory said. "Is everything okay?"

"Yes," Wendell whispered, "but this message is just for you. A boy in coach is waiting to meet you for breakfast. I told him I'd ask you, but I didn't think you would."

Glory smiled then tried to look serious but couldn't help smiling again. "Tell him I can't but that I'll be in the lounge after breakfast."

"Glory, is that the door?" Mary called from the bathroom.

"Yes, ma'am!" Glory answered. "It's Wendell. It's almost time for breakfast." She turned back to the door. "What time did Malcolm schedule breakfast?"

"Eight thirty, but you get to sleep in and have room service if you want. Wanna know what you're having?"

Glory sighed. "It doesn't matter. Can we at least pretend there's tea instead of coffee?"

Wendell looked at his notebook. "Well, what do you know? We're out of coffee. I'll come back for Mrs. Bishop at 8:20. You coming, too?"

"Yes, Wendell. I'll be ready at 8:20." Glory giggled. "Don't look so surprised—it's a new day."

Glory closed the door and turned to face her mother's shocked and angry glare. "Jesus! Child, what is wrong with you? Standing there half-naked, giggling with that man like you ain't spoken for. Like you some common whore!"

"Mama, I didn't do anything. I just told him I was going to breakfast. The door wasn't open."

"Malcolm got you up in here like a queen, and you out paintin' yo' face all up, whisperin' and laughin' with that Wendell. I saw how he looked at you yesterday."

"Mama, no... it's not like that at all—"

"Soon as we get home, I'mma tell Malcolm he needa take the hand of God to you 'cause spoilin' you ain't workin'!"

"You want Malcolm to beat me for talking to Wendell?"

"I raised you to be good. Godly women don't go to the door like that. And yesterday, you was just crazy. I didn't know you. You just let demons rule you all day and all night!"

Glory stumbled through the tight space to get to her mother. "Mama, look." Glory held out her arms to show her wrists. "On the side that touches my skin, these say 'I am my beloved's.' These are Malcolm's. I can't take them off. Why do you think I would cheat on him? I was laughing because Wendell was surprised that I'm going to breakfast this morning. He looked at me yesterday because he saw the mark on my face. That's all." Glory looked into her mother's eyes. "Mama, why do you think I'm bad?"

"Girl, there's been evil tryin' to get in you since the day you was born, and the older you get, the more I hafta fight to keep it outta you. And since that monster touched you, you been changed. You have! You actin' all worldly and loud. Paintin' yo' face. Acting like somethin' got in you. Changing your heart."

Pulled into Mary's anxious arms, Glory was amazed at how right her mother was. Something *had* gotten into her, and something *was* changing her heart. And the night before, yes, she *had been* wild, and this morning, she *had* been plotting to disobey Malcolm. Her mother was right about everything.

"Please, Mama, you hafta know—you have poured the love and fear of God into me my whole life. You fight demons all the time. All I wanna be is the godly woman you raised me to be." *Demon of lies and deceit!* Even as she squeezed her mother, Glory silently begged forgiveness for the lie because she wanted so much more.

"I pray that every day, baby, and I do the best I can," Mary said. "You the last miracle I got, and all the evil in you is my fault. But I swear, I'll give you back to God 'fo I let the devil have you."

Despite the chilling words she'd heard all her life, Glory hugged her mother even tighter and planned a morning visit with James for her last few hours on the train.

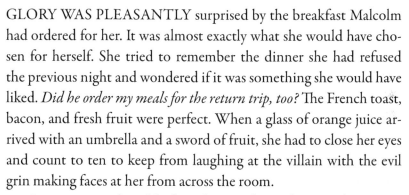

GLORY WAS PLEASANTLY surprised by the breakfast Malcolm had ordered for her. It was almost exactly what she would have chosen for herself. She tried to remember the dinner she had refused the previous night and wondered if it was something she would have liked. *Did he order my meals for the return trip, too?* The French toast, bacon, and fresh fruit were perfect. When a glass of orange juice arrived with an umbrella and a sword of fruit, she had to close her eyes and count to ten to keep from laughing at the villain with the evil grin making faces at her from across the room.

Sitting across the table from her mother, Glory tried to sit up straight and keep her head down. She tried to remember her posture from before she'd learned how to sit back and relax in a restaurant booth or casually stir a drink with a straw. When the waiter came to clear her plates, she whispered thanks but barely looked at him and didn't smile. *Would breaking up with Malcolm mean returning to living this way—silent and subdued? Could I go back?*

THE DIFFERENCE BETWEEN night and day in the observation lounge was jarring. The room looked a lot bigger, and nearly every table and space was occupied. A group of old people laughed out loud, a baby cried, and a toddler screamed about fairness. The sounds of dice rolling and blocks falling blended with the sounds of the train moving through the open fields.

Glory found James at a corner table at the far end of the car. Even in the same shirt that he'd worn the previous night, he seemed different in the daylight. He sat hunched over a notebook with a box of crayons in front of him. "Hi. Have a seat," he said, not looking up from his drawing.

"Okaay...?" Glory sat down and tried to steal a glimpse of his artwork. All she saw was red, orange, and brown before he moved his arm, hiding it from her view. "What is it?"

"I'll show you in just a minute. It's almost done. I've kinda been working on it all night." He looked up at her and smiled. "Hi."

"Good morning. Thanks for the drink. My mother doesn't know about my secret identity. You almost blew my cover."

"I noticed." He looked up at her again. "Who are you during the day?"

Glory laughed. "By day, I'm Church Girl. Mild-mannered teenager dressed as a frumpy old lady who folds her hands and sits up straight..." She leaned in close to him and lowered her voice to a whisper. "And who definitely doesn't talk to boys."

James cocked his head to the side and stared at her.

"What?" Glory asked.

He leaned closer. "Your disguise is terrible."

"Thanks, I think. So, what're you drawing?"

"Not yet. Almost. Talk to me. Tell me some more about Weak Femme Fatale." James's hand flew over the page, switching colors and scratching with bits of straws and napkins.

"Well," Glory said, "she's a loner. And she works for a mad scientist who makes love potions. Maybe that's how she got her power. She fell into a vat of love potion, and now men just give her stuff, so she's not really bad, because she feels guilty and tries to give it back."

"She feels guilty, but she enjoys it, right?" James looked up and winked at her.

Glory blushed. "Well... she tries not to enjoy it too much."

"Okay," James said. "I'm done, but I can't show it in here. Let's go back to my seat—less noise and crowd."

"Um, okay," Glory said, "I guess." She looked around the crowded car. A baby screamed again, and more loud laughter convinced her that leaving wasn't a bad idea. Taking James's hand, she ignored the clink of the bracelets as they slid down her wrist.

She followed him down a tight staircase and into the next car, through a long hallway and into another lounge car with just as many people and, finally, into coach. What struck Glory first was the dank and musty smell of the crowded car. The seats on either side of the narrow aisle were piled with blankets and pillows. Parts of the floor were sticky. Passing the bathrooms, Glory realized that sixty people shared four bathrooms. Coach on the train was still much better than the bus, but Malcolm had her in first class. *Have I become so spoiled that this could make me change my mind about breaking up with him?*

Halfway down the aisle, in the second coach, they got to James's seat. He stepped aside to let her in first. She was surprised that the seat actually felt more comfortable than the couch in her compartment.

"I know it's not first class, but you're the first girl I've ever brought to my mobile lair." He held up his left hand. "Villain's honor."

"I can't complain. I share my lair with my mother."

James sat down and handed her the notebook.

Glory gasped. "Oh my God, James! You did this last night?" She stared at a comic book drawing of Weak Femme Fatale, a supervillainess in a tight red costume, reclining on an orange cushion, holding an orange drink with an umbrella. The cushion sat atop a pile of goodies—candy, cookies, and toys. At the bottom of the pile, boys in college shirts struggled to climb, bringing her teddy bears and more fruity drinks. James had drawn everything she'd mentioned to him.

In the upper left corner was the face of a laughing mad scientist surrounded by vats of love potion, and on the right was a coat hook with a nun's habit hanging on it. The character was Glory, down to her earrings and bracelets. And the face... it was a cartoon, but it was definitely her face. Glory wanted to touch it but drew her hand back. The clink of the bracelets suddenly sounded like thunder, and ten shekels' weight felt like a thousand pounds.

"James, I don't know what to say. This is the most awesome thing I've ever seen."

"Thanks. It really wasn't that hard. I mean, all female heroes are drawn the same really—"

Glory placed the notebook on the seat beside her. "James, you should stop talking and kiss me now."

"Yeah. I guess I should." James leaned in and kissed her, and Glory knew that she would be going back to her old life as Church Girl, because she was definitely breaking up with Malcolm.

When they'd parted, Glory stared at the drawing. "James, I can't tell you how much I love this, but I can't keep it. I'd hafta fold it up really small and hide it. This needs to be in a frame somewhere. Church Girl can't have things like this. My mother wouldn't understand it was a joke." *She would burn it for being demonic and drive the demons out of me.* Glory handed the notebook back to him, not surprised that she felt like crying. "I should be getting back. We're getting off in Canton."

"Okay." James sighed. "I understand. If you ever see her in a real comic book, find me. I promise, I'll remember you."

"You're a villain. I bet you say that to all the villainesses." Glory laughed, accepting his help up from the seat.

"Naw, girl, you special." He raised his left hand again. "Villain's honor."

Walking through the long corridor back to the lounge, James slowed and then stopped. "Okay. I think I really like you, and I think you like me a little, too. So can I call you over the holidays? Maybe write when I get back to school?"

Glory leaned against the wall and folded her arms, surprised at how loud the bracelets sounded. "I wasn't joking about Church Girl. You can't call me. But I can write to you. I really wanna know how Weak Femme Fatale turns out."

James sighed. "I guess I'll take what I can get. It was really nice meeting you, Glory."

"It was nice meeting you too, James." Hugging him, Glory was reminded of saying goodbye to another boy and surprised at how bad it felt. So bad, in fact, that she held on probably longer than was reasonable and wouldn't have cared if her mother *and* Malcolm had come through the doors at both ends of the car.

"Yup," Glory said, regaining her composure. "Same cologne as every boy in school."

"Well, your perfume is like—I don't know. What is that?"

Glory laughed. "Gimme just a second, I'll show you." She felt around in her purse until she found the small tube of lotion. "I wasn't joking about working for the mad scientist." She handed the tube of S. H. Herschel body lotion to James and watched his eyes go wide.

"Holy shit! This *is* a love potion. Pound-cake body lotion?" He pulled Glory into his arms again, burying his face in her neck and inhaling loudly. "I thought I was going crazy. Girl, you smell good enough to eat. Pound cake? You've gotta be kidding me!"

"Nope," Glory said. "My boss invented it. He's really a genius and the best friend I ever had. He makes it at his salon. It's in a few shops on the North Side, but the best place to get it is right at the salon and only at Christmas. He's got other flavors, too."

"Oh, my Lord, girl," James said, sniffing her again. Glory giggled. "This is pure evil. Do you know what you've done to me?"

"Made you hungry?"

"Worse. I'm going home for Christmas. Everywhere I go, somebody's gonna be trying to feed me pound cake, and all I'm gonna think about is you. If I don't hear from you, I'll never enjoy pound cake again."

Glory did her best evil laugh but then felt a little guilty and hoped James wasn't serious.

In the observation lounge, Glory slid a folded slip of paper into the lining of her purse next to Malcolm's emergency money and smiled while the bartender took a picture of her and James with James's camera. Just past the bar, Weak Femme Fatale and the Not-So-Evil Villain hugged goodbye, then Church Girl made her way back to the compartment. Passing by Wendell in the hall, she blushed when he flashed her a huge smile and gave her a thumbs-up. Back in the compartment, Glory leaned against the window, staring at the bracelets she'd soon be free of, and tried to remember how Church Girl was supposed to act.

She honestly didn't know if she'd ever write to James. Maybe this was just one of those brief romantic encounters she'd read about so many times—ships passing in the night or something like that. But his manner and attention, his warmth and easy laugh were so much like... *him*. It had been six months since *he* had left, but surrounded by the luxury Malcolm provided, and glowing with romance and adventure courtesy of James, Glory still missed JT.

By the time Wendell knocked and announced their arrival in Canton, Glory had made some decisions. She would spend her last ten days as Malcolm's lady, honoring his wishes like a proper, obedient, and godly young woman. Then, when she got home, she would break up with him and go back to living like Church Girl if necessary. Finally, she would love JT forever and probably be with him if he came back, but she would try to move on for real. She would always be grateful to Malcolm for saving her and freeing her, but she wasn't ready for him, and she didn't want to be the person he wanted her to be.

Chapter 16

Stepping out onto the platform, Glory was waving goodbye to Wendell and scanning the tinted windows toward the back of the train, hoping to catch a last glimpse of James, when she felt her mother pat her arm. Two neatly dressed men approached. The older man, in a sharp black suit and dark-gray overcoat, had a slight limp and a delighted expression on his face. Looking at his carefully trimmed silver beard and mustache, Glory imagined he must have been the finest man in town forty years before.

"Good morning, ladies. I'm Lee Espy," the dark-skinned man said in a genteel Southern drawl. "Are you Mrs. and Miss Bishop?"

"Yes, sir. I'm Mary Bishop, and this is my daughter, Glory."

"Pleased to meet you, ladies," Mr. Espy said, shaking hands and holding onto Mary's long enough to make her smile. "Malcolm Porter sent me to take you on to Flora." He reached into his coat and handed Glory a sealed envelope. "This arrived for you yesterday, Miss Bishop. I believe it's an assurance from Mr. Porter."

Glory opened the envelope and pulled out a simple note:

Glory, Mr. Lee Espy is from Espy Funeral Services. He has the only limo in town, and I want you traveling comfortably. He'll ride in back with you and Mother Bishop while his son drives. When you get to your grandmother's, tip Mr. Espy $50 and his son $20. They will pick you up next week for your return trip. Love, Malcolm.

Glory sighed and nodded at her mother. "It's okay. Malcolm sent him."

The younger man, dressed in black pants, a black polo shirt, and a black Members Only jacket, didn't say a word—he just nodded quietly—but while Mary and Mr. Espy talked, Glory saw him peering over his dark shades at her. When he winked and licked his lips, Glory turned her head and smiled, not because she appreciated the attention but because she'd already kept her promise to Herschel, so she wouldn't have to talk to this one.

"Ladies, the car is this way," Mr. Espy said, holding his arm out toward the station-lobby doors. "Darnell will get your luggage."

Glory shook her head and smiled when her mother took Mr. Espy's arm and allowed him to escort her to the car. Something tugged on her backpack. Glory whirled around, preparing to scream.

"I need to put your backpack on this here buggy." The deep nasal voice came from Darnell, who was standing a little too close.

"No. I can carry it," she said, backing away. "It's not heavy."

"I don't know, Ponytails," Darnell said. "Yo' sugar daddy say you ain't supposed to lift a finger. Don't see why, though." He looked Glory up and down. "You ain't that fancy. Nails ain't done, no makeup. Oh, I guess he like you clean and natural, huh?"

Glory walked away, quickly catching up with her mother and Mr. Espy. Seated in the back of the limo, Glory watched with amusement as her mother went from "Mrs. Bishop" to "Oh, call me Mary." Glory had to admit Mr. Espy was charming, and seeing her mother enjoying the attention was nice.

She spent much of the ride watching the scenery but occasionally caught Darnell in the rear-view mirror watching her and not the road. Darnell, she decided, was worse than nasty old Mr. Harris. He actually made her feel dirty, and she found herself wishing Malcolm was there to hurt him and make him stop looking at her like that. It slowly dawned on her that since the attack in the gangway, she'd not spent a full day without Malcolm by her side. Breaking up with him would mean losing that protection.

Driving through Flora, Mississippi, Glory recognized every corner, because nothing had changed since she was a little girl. Gray streets, gray buildings—even the lighted signs seemed to be only tinted shades of gray. They turned down a paved road and after another mile turned onto a gravel driveway lined with pecan trees. From the front, the red house looked like any other small wood frame house, but looking along the side, the years of additions made for a ramshackle hodgepodge of wood and aluminum siding.

A tall, heavyset man in faded jeans and a white button-down shirt came out to the porch and watched the car come to a stop in front of the house. Glory couldn't help smiling. Uncle Bobby was using his mean face. He could look so scary, but really, he was a teddy bear. She was ready to call out to him as soon as Darnell opened her door, but he walked all the way around to the other side and opened her mother's door first. Before she could scoot to that side of the back seat, he closed the door. Glory sat back and took a deep breath, praying for patience and sorely tempted to call Malcolm.

Darnell opened the door again. "Oh, I'm sorry, Ponytails. I thought you wanted to go with me." He looked over his shades and sucked his teeth.

It took all Glory had not to spit on him.

"Mary, Mary, quite contrary!" Uncle Bobby yelled. "Gal, why you always gotta make a scene?"

"Now, Bobby," Mary yelled back, "you know this ain't none of my doin'. I don't need no mess like this, but Glory's fella don't let her feet touch the ground with common folk!"

"You don't say?" Bobby came down from the porch, looking around. "Where's Mr. Moneybags at?" He pointed at Darnell. "You Glory's fella?"

"No, sir," Darnell said. "At least not yet."

Glory pushed past her mother and Mr. Espy and flung herself at her uncle, burying herself in the big man's embrace. She didn't dare say anything because her only words would have been to beg Uncle Bobby to make the nasty buzzard stop looking at her, and she didn't want to cause an even bigger scene. She just smiled up at him and hugged him even tighter.

Uncle Bobby shook his finger at her. "We're gonna hafta talk about this fella of yours, missy." He used his stern voice.

"Don't worry, Uncle. You're much bigger than him." Glory held on to her uncle's arm while her mother introduced Mr. Espy like an old friend, and Darnell unloaded their luggage.

"Maaaryyy!" A round, screaming woman came running out of the house and down the stairs, barreling into Mary, nearly knocking her over. Glory tried not to laugh when Mr. Espy grabbed her mother's waist to keep her upright while her baby sister hugged her.

"Dang it, Bobby. Why is Ellie screaming out where folks can see?" Glory's grandmother, Bigma, came out to the porch. "I told y'all about that mess!" The rail-thin woman leaned on a neon-green-painted cane and made her way to the edge of the porch.

"Uh-uh, Ma." Bobby pulled his arm from Glory and rushed to help his mother-in-law down the stairs. "This ain't got nothin' to do with me this time."

"Well, I see." Bigma looked at Glory with a smirk. "I guess it don't." Coming off the bottom step, she straightened up to her full height, all five feet of it. Her seventy-eight years in the sun showed on her face, and Bigma carried herself like a queen. Her coarse hair, jet black with a few streaks of silver, hung in a thick braid over her shoulder.

"Come 'ere, girl. Lemme look at you. Lawd, Glory, yo' granddaddy would be so proud. We got a lot to talk about, baby girl. A whole lot." Bigma looked past Glory. "Mary. I said I was ailing, not dying. I see you brought the funeral car, anyway."

"Hey, Ma." Mary hugged her mother. "You know this ain't my style at all. Your baby girl over there is well loved."

Glory moved to sit on the steps while the adults laughed and talked. Her mother looked so happy holding Mr. Espy's arm and talking about the train ride.

"Sugar Daddy make you scream like that, Ponytails?"

Glory jumped. She'd forgotten Darnell was there, and he'd snuck up on her.

"How old is he? Thirty, forty, fifty? You don't know nuttin' 'bout a young stud, do you, baby girl?"

His gritty nasal voice made Glory's stomach churn.

"You need to lemme show you something while you here. Just me and you, Ponytails. Money ain't everything, ya know." He sucked his teeth again.

Glory closed her eyes and took a deep breath, imagining Malcolm in his long black leather coat and black gloves, swooping down and swinging his steering wheel lock... *No!* Glory opened her eyes. She was not about to let this nasty buzzard give her a nightmare with her family a few yards away.

"Yeah, Ponytails, five minutes, I'll have you purring like a kitten."

The nasty buzzard won, and Glory ran into the house, chased by Darnell's ugly laughter and the happy sounds of her family out in the front yard. Hiding in the shadows of the front hallway, Glory stood at the screen door listening in horror as Mr. Espy and Darnell accepted Bigma's invitation to stay for lunch. Glory ran through the living room, nearly tripping over a giant box with her name on it then barely avoiding knocking over a huge vase of flowers. Taking refuge in her grandmother's bedroom, she tossed her coat on the bed, grabbed the phone from the nightstand, and sat on the floor between the bed and the wall, safely hidden from anybody casually opening the door. Her hand shook as she dialed the number.

"Hello?"

"Hi, Malcolm." Glory breathed a sigh of relief.

"Hi, Glory." His voice was soft and gentle. Glory guessed he thought she might still be mad at him. "How are you?"

"I'm fine," she said. *Except I'm gonna break up with you next week, but right now, I need you to come hurt somebody for making me feel dirty and scared.*

"You don't sound fine. What's wrong?"

"Everything's okay, honest. I just wanted to hear your voice." *Because there's a demon trying to give me nightmares, and I want you to kill him.*

"Glory," Malcolm said in the voice that always got her attention. "If something's wrong, I can't fix it if you don't tell me what it is. I hear it in your voice. Do I need to come down there?"

"No, Malcolm." Glory breathed deeply and felt better, just knowing he would be there that night if she wanted him to. "I'm just tired, and the limo attracted a lot of attention. I'm not used to that kind of stuff. My uncle wants to talk to me about you."

"Oh, okay. I hadn't thought about that. Mother always goes that way. I didn't consider anything else. I'm sorry if it made you uncomfortable."

"It's okay. We're here now. How was your night?" She didn't want to keep talking about the limo, or she might be tempted to mention the nasty buzzard.

"I was at the mission. It was good. I sent you a tape of the service from last night. You'll get it tomorrow. How was the train ride? Did you like it? Sleep okay?"

"It was nice." Glory could hear people coming into the house, Aunt Ellie being as loud as ever. "I really liked being in the lounge under the stars." *Especially the part when I kissed a boy, so I hafta break up with you, but please keep saving me.* "The food was good. You ordered exactly what I like."

"I know I did. That was the plan."

Glory could hear the smile in his voice. She decided not to tell him about refusing dinner or that she traded the coffee for tea. "Tell me about the night ministry. What's it like?"

"Now? Shouldn't you be visiting with your family? We can talk tonight."

"No, it's okay now. They're having lunch. Mr. Espy is making my mother laugh—kinda weird. Please? I just wanna talk to you right now." Glory heard the pleading in her voice and cleared her throat. She didn't want to sound like there was a problem, but she needed to hear him right then.

"O-kaay," Malcolm said slowly. "Gimme a second to grab a drink. I'll be right back."

"Sure. Thanks."

Somebody opened the bedroom door but didn't seem to notice she was there. Glory let out a breath. Huddled on the floor, hugging the phone, she chided herself for being such a baby. *Why is my stomach so in knots over that nasty buzzard? Is he really any worse than dirty old Mr. Harris?* Even though she knew that Uncle Bobby could crush Darnell, Glory didn't breathe easily until Malcolm came back to the phone.

"Hey. I'm back. What do you wanna know about the night ministry?"

"I don't know," Glory said. "What is it?"

"Well, it's a different kinda church. Service is usually at ten at night. It's for people who don't feel comfortable in regular church or the daylight."

"Why do you go there? You work at a regular church."

"Yeah, I do," Malcolm said. "But when the Lord was working on me, that's where he led me. I told you, I wasn't always a man of God, and people at the night ministry need somebody who knows what it's like to be where they are. Sometimes we cuss. We've had a few fistfights. Nothing like any church you know, but it's still a church. Not the kind of people you know, but still good people."

"So what exactly do you do there?"

"Mostly, I lead the services on Monday and Thursday nights. Sometimes I get calls for other stuff—counseling and..." Malcolm's voice trailed off. "Glory, why are you trying to keep me on the phone? This is long distance. What's going on with you?"

"I just wanted to know about the night ministry."

"Glory. Answer me. Now."

"Malcolm, I don't know." Glory tried to keep her voice steady. "I'm being stupid. I haven't been away from you since... you know... and I just... I don't know."

How can one jerk make me this crazy? Maybe Herschel was right that Malcolm made me need him. And if I need him this much, how will I break up with him?

"Oh, woman, I'm sorry," Malcolm said. "I miss you, too. It's not gonna be that long. I promise. You have my pager number, right?"

"Yeah." Glory knew she sounded pouty.

"You can page me anytime, and I'll call you right back."

"I know." The door opened again. This time, Aunt Ellie walked around the bed and stood in front of Glory, scowling and tapping her foot.

"I want you to go visit with your family. Okay?" Malcolm said. "I'll talk to you tonight. I love you."

"I lo—I know. I'll page you tonight. Bye, Malcolm." Glory hung up the phone and looked up at her aunt.

"Young lady, we have guests." Ellie held out her hand to help Glory up. "You are being rude, and you're missing your mother trying to remember how to flirt."

"Ugh," Glory groaned. "Do I really need to see that?"

"Yes, you really do." Ellie laughed. "It's hilarious."

"Auntie, I really don't wanna be around that nasty—"

"You mean the one that keeps lookin' at you? Your uncle can rip him in half if you want."

"Nah. I don't wanna ruin Mama's fun. I just wanna stay away from him. Talking to Malcolm helped."

"Um, baby... doesn't Malcolm do really bad things to people who mess with you?"

Glory tried on her best evil grin. "Yes. Yes, he does."

———————⟨◦⟩———————

IN THE FRONT YARD, beside the limo, Glory shook hands with Mr. Espy just like Malcolm had taught her. Mr. Espy laughed out loud and pressed the money back into her hand. "Oh, no, Miss Bishop. I should be paying you for the pleasure of meeting your lovely mother. Mary!" he called out to Mary, who was standing on the front porch. "I'll see you tomorrow at ten a.m.!" He waved goodbye to everybody before going around to the passenger side.

Darnell leaned out of the driver's-side window. "So, no tip for me, Ponytails?"

"Bless you, Darnell." Glory stepped back from the car. The look on his face told her he knew exactly what she meant. She promised herself she would sic Malcolm on him if he came near her again.

Following her family back into the house, Glory stopped at the huge bouquet of flowers on the front room table. The colors overwhelmed everything in the museum that was Bigma's living room. The brightly colored spray looked like a mix of holiday candy pretending to be flowers. The card simply said: *To Glorious, from Superman.* She had to smile. She'd just freaked out and almost asked him to come and rescue her. So much for spending ten days with no reminders of Malcolm.

The big box on the floor said Do Not Open Until Christmas. Since they'd already exchanged gifts, she couldn't imagine what was in it. She briefly entertained the thought that it might not even be from Malcolm. Maybe somebody else had sent it—someone she'd been anxiously waiting to hear from, who knew where she went every Christmas. But of course, it could only be from Malcolm, who was making sure she had no room for thoughts of anybody other than him.

Bigma kept the heavy drapes drawn in the living room to protect her photos from the sun. The photos near the top of the wood-paneled walls hung in gilded frames, some sagging or tilted, having come unstuck from their backing. Farther down, the frames were plain wood or metal, then cardboard or plastic, until the ones from the late seventies, when Bigma had given up on frames and just taped pictures directly to the wall.

The wall—Glory's wall—hadn't changed since 1976. It was one of many places in the house that seemed frozen in time. Glory stared at the photos, some yellowing, some cracking, and some torn and taped. In her baby pictures, she was a tiny bundle of scrawny arms and legs small enough to be cradled in the pair of rough-looking hands that held her. That same baby a little older, her hair an unruly mess, smiled at the camera from inside a giant work boot. The one from her first birthday showed her concentrating on the mutilated cake in front of her, a huge hand resting on the corner of her high-chair tray.

There it was: the first picture she actually remembered being taken. She was four years old, sitting on her daddy's knee while he taught her to tie her shoe. Glory remembered the day like it was yesterday. She'd been angry because she couldn't get the shoe tied, and Daddy bounced her on his knee until she laughed, but then she slipped off and bumped her head. He'd bought her ice cream *and* candy that day. It still made her smile, because she hadn't really been *that* hurt.

The picture from her sixth birthday made her sad. Daddy had taken her to buy new clothes, including a pink sundress with the back out. When he saw her scars, she'd had to tell him how bad she'd been and that she'd gotten a lot of whoopings. She was so scared, but when he hugged her and told her she wasn't bad, he was crying and telling her how glorious she was.

When Mama came home, he was so angry, his normally quiet voice so loud. "Woman, I love you, and I'll never do you wrong!" he yelled. "But if you ever mark my child again, I'll whoop you like a man. Ya hear me? I'll whoop you like a man!" Glory hadn't gotten another whooping until after he died. Her mother said that was why the demons got to her so easily now.

There was the picture of Daddy meeting JT after he gave her the pearl earrings. "You the one tryin' to marry my Glorious? Givin' her expensive gifts? Didn't even ask me."

JT stood up to Daddy without flinching. "Too late. I already married her!"

Daddy said that the little boy was either very brave or very stupid, but they'd shaken hands, and JT's mother had taken the picture.

In a picture of the couples—Mama and Daddy, Aunt Ellie and Uncle Bobby, Aunt Ruth and her dog, and Aunt Martha and her boyfriend of that year—they all looked so young and happy. Even Mama was smiling. There were pictures of Daddy and Uncle Bobby sleeping when they were supposed to be watching the meat on the grill and of Glory swinging from Daddy's giant muscle. Another one had Daddy carrying Mama and Mama not liking it at all.

The Christmas after Daddy died, Mama had tried to take down the pictures on Glory's wall. Bigma threw a shoe at her. "You leave that baby's pictures alone!" Bigma had hollered. "That's all she got left of her daddy! This ain't about you and yo' mess. Just 'cause he gone from your heart don't mean you get to rip 'im outta hers. You move one thing, I'll never let you back in this house. I swear!"

Mama had never forgiven Daddy for dying. She'd taken almost every trace of him out of their apartment, as if he'd done it to on purpose.

Glory touched her parents' wedding picture. At the bottom, it said: *Mary and Paul Bishop, December 22, 1965.* Mama looked so pretty in her light-blue dress, and Daddy towered over her and Grandda, who did the ceremony. Daddy was so big. So strong. So powerful. Her first love. Her first hero. Her first savior. Every Christmas, Glory stood at this wall and cried... and wondered why she did this to herself every single year.

She dried her eyes and went to join the others.

"You hungry, baby?" Bigma asked when Glory entered the kitchen. "There's a little somethin' left. Want me to get you a plate?"

"Nah, I got it," Glory said. She knew her grandmother had no actual intention of getting her a plate but was always polite enough to offer.

Bigma's kitchen looked exactly the same as it always had. The whitish metal cabinets hung at slightly off angles, so the doors didn't quite close. The shallow whitish sink took up an entire wall and was propped up in front by wooden posts. Legend said that when Grandda couldn't get the right part for it, he took the two-hundred-pound steel sink off the wall and out the back door all the way to the hardware store to get what he needed to fix it. The old Frigidaire had a handle with a latch, and you had to slam the door to close it properly. The only new thing was the stove, because Aunt Ellie refused to cook on a death trap.

The flowered wallpaper had long faded from pink to beige, and the curtains sagged and frayed at the edges. Uncle Bobby had nailed a piece of metal over the built-in ironing board to keep it from falling out and killing people, and a single chain attached to a wobbly ceiling fan twirled over the four people seated at the kitchen table.

Glory put a bit of Aunt Ellie's chicken and noodles on her plate and took a seat at the table. She tried to pretend everybody wasn't waiting expectantly, but after the second bite, she put down her fork. "Okay. What? I figured Mama told you everything by now."

"Well, actually, your mama was kinda busy tryin' to remember how to talk to a man." Ellie laughed. "Girl, you shoulda seen her! Mary, Imma teach you how to bat your eyelashes before your date in the morning."

"It's not a date," Mary protested. "It's just brunch and a quick run to the grocery store."

Glory loved seeing her mother blush. Mr. Espy wasn't the first man to look at Mary Bishop, and she would enjoy his company while she was here, but Glory knew this would be as far as it went. She wondered if her mother ever kissed anyone good night but quickly pushed the image out of her mind.

"So, the box got here yesterday, and the flowers got here this morning," Bigma said. "Anything coming tomorrow? This boy gon' clutter my whole house up?"

"Yes, ma'am. He's sending a tape of the service he did last night. He works for two churches." Glory watched her mother's expression. "The night ministry is for people who don't go on Sunday. He goes to where they are to minister to them."

Mary raised an eyebrow but didn't say anything.

"Your granddaddy had two churches. Worked his fool self to death," Bigma mumbled.

Uncle Bobby leaned forward, placing his elbows on the table. "Let me get this straight. Your *boyfriend* is a minister at two churches, got you drippin' in gold, and sends you and your mama on fancy trips." He looked at her mother. "Mary, what the devil is goin' on?"

"Oh, Bobby, calm down." Mary got up and took her plate to the sink. "He's one of many ministers at our church. It's one of the biggest on the South Side, you know. I don't know nothing about

that night-ministry thing. I'm sure it's good, because Malcolm is Elder Porter's son." She poured herself a glass of iced tea. "And this is
the only trip. He doesn't want Glory on the bus since... you know.
He's real protective. And I'll let her tell you about the bracelets, but
I promise you, she ain't 'drippin'' in gold.'"

"Dripping, sparkling—same thing," Ellie said.

Uncle Bobby scowled at his wife then turned to Glory. "Well,
missy?"

"Malcolm gave them to me for Christmas." Glory held out her
arms to show her uncle the bracelets. "It's like in Genesis. When the
servant knew Rebecca was the one he was looking for, he gave her a
gold earring of one shekel weight and bracelets of ten shekels. These
are two and a half shekels each."

"Oh, that's so romantic," Ellie said.

"They're even engraved on the inside. From the Song of
Solomon—"

"Oo, lemme see one." Ellie grabbed Glory's wrist and pulled.

"Ow, wait," Glory said, drawing her arm back. "I can't take 'em
off. Malcolm has a special screwdriver."

Aunt Ellie's eyes went wide. Bigma looked away, and Uncle Bobby exploded.

"Dammit, Mary! You done let some jackleg preacher put shackles on this child? What the hell she mean she cain't take 'em off?"
He stood up from the table, nearly pulling the tablecloth and all the
dishes with him. "'Bout to put a stop to this mess right now. Ellie!
Where's my hacksaw? Don't make no goddamn sense. None at all,
Mary. Not one bit. Paul is turnin' in his grave. Ellie, woman, I said
get the hacksaw!"

"You just sit down and mind yo' own children, Bobby." Mary
stood toe to toe with the big man, poking him in his chest. "You not
touchin' her or those bracelets. Malcolm Porter is a good, godly man,

and in her time of need, God sent him to save her! Not even you can deny that, *Deacon* Ellis!"

"So what? Give him a medal!"

While the adults continued their argument, Glory stayed low and made her way out through the kitchen door to the dining room. There, the drapes were open, and burgundy-flocked wallpaper was hidden behind plaques and awards for gratitude, distinguished service, citizenship, and all sorts of things. Rev. Charles A. Johnson Sr. had been an important minister in this part of Mississippi, and this dining room was a shrine to him. Though he'd been gone since 1970, people still visited on Sundays to sit in the dining room and reminisce with Widow Johnson about the old days.

The noise from the kitchen drove Glory out to the front porch. Uncle Bobby had gotten out his Bible, and Mama was defending Malcolm like he was her own son. Glory shook her head. *If she only knew how Malcolm really felt, would she be so quick to defend him?* Glory sighed. *Probably.*

"Thought you went to hide again." Bigma came out to the porch. "Come sit up here with me. Tell me about Malcolm and why you let him put them things on you. They in there acting like you ain't almost grown. Ain't tryin' to ask you nuttin. Lemme see yo' arm."

Glory sat down on the stack of plastic crates next to her grandmother's rocker and held out her arm.

"My, my, my. They are pretty—jingly, too. Bet every time you move, you think about him, right?"

Glory nodded.

"You know, that's why the priests in the Bible had to wear tassels. Things was probably worrisome as heck, but every step they took, they knew they belonged to God. I think your Malcolm is a smart man, makin' you think about him all the time like that. How old is he?"

"He's twenty-seven," Glory said, waiting for Bigma to be shocked.

"Hmm. Is that all? Those bracelets show a lot more wisdom than that. I'd have thought he was older."

"Well, he kinda knows the Bible by heart."

"Really? Is that a fact? Which one?" Bigma asked. "Not the *Readers' Digest* one, I hope?"

"All of 'em, maybe?" Glory said, trying—unsuccessfully—not to sound like her mother bragging about Malcolm. "He mostly uses King James, but sometimes he uses RSV, too."

"So, what do they say on the inside?"

"'I am my beloved's, and his desire is toward me.'"

"And how you feel about that?" Bigma asked.

"I don't know, Bigma," Glory admitted. "At first, it made me feel really good, but sometimes, he's so bossy. And he can be mean sometimes, too. But he lets me do everything I've ever wanted to do, even things Mama said I can't. And he saved me."

"Well, I can see how that would turn your head. 'Cept the mean and bossy part—ain't nobody got time for that. Bet he treats you like you grown—shows you stuff you never seen, huh?"

"Yes, ma'am."

"Yeah, that's how yo' granddaddy caught me. He needed a first lady if he was gon' start a church, and he treated me like a good and proper lady. I heard how Malcolm saved you. A man that'll kill for you? Make you feel like you owe him."

"I know. Mama says I do owe him."

"Well, yo' mama got a lotta funny ideas."

"Bigma, he does so much for me," Glory said, "and Mama lets me do anything as long as he says it's okay. It's like God really did send him to free me. But he has to control everything. He won't even let me cross the street by myself. Like I'm this dumb little girl—"

"Ah... I see your problem. Those things do feel like shackles sometimes, don't they?"

"Yes, ma'am. They do, and I only got 'em two days ago. It's like he let me out of prison, and I can go anywhere I want as long as I'm exactly what he wants me to be. But then he tells me to be what I wanna be. Ugh! Like these books he's making me read—"

"Making you read books?"

"Yeah. He knows Mama doesn't want me to read any books except the Bible, so he stood in front of her and told me to read these books that would make her mad. And I really wanna read 'em, but not just 'cause he told me to. But then these things"—Glory shook her wrists—"say I belong to him. I let him put them on me, so I hafta do what he says."

"Baby girl, is you crazy?" Bigma's green-gray eyes narrowed. "Is you out yo' ever-lovin' mind? Has yo' mama knocked all the sense outta you?"

"No, Bigma. I'm not crazy—"

"Them ain't no doggone weddin' rings! You ain't gotta do nothin'. Yo' uncle in there ready to cut yo' hands off to get them things offa you. What year you think this is?"

"I know I don't have to," Glory said. "It just feels like I hafta do what he says so I can still get to do things, but I think I hafta break up with him so I can just be myself. But then Mama won't let me do anything or go anywhere anymore." Glory buried her face in her hands. Saying everything out loud didn't help at all.

"How do you feel about him?"

Glory looked up at her grandmother. "I know he loves me."

"That ain't what I asked you. It's pretty obvious how *he* feels. How do *you* feel?"

"I love him, too." Glory heard herself say the words without thinking, and she wanted to cry. She cared about Malcolm, and she was grateful to him, and she couldn't imagine spending the next ten days without him, but she didn't want to love him. She was breaking up with him because she wasn't ready.

"No, I don't love him. I *need* him. Mr. Espy's son made me feel so icky, and talkin' to Malcolm made me feel better. I'm scared to be without him."

"You lay down with him yet? Don't blush—I won't tell on you."

"No, ma'am. He wants to wait till I'm older. He thinks Mama is trying to get me to trap him. I kinda think he's right."

"Lawd, yo' mama... what I'mma do with that girl?"

"Bigma, she keeps telling me I hafta obey him and give him whatever he wants. That's how I know he loves me—'cause he doesn't want anything from me."

"Baby, time was only thing a po' colored girl could be was a maid or a mammy. Yo' grandaddy wanted more for his girls. If they could get to college, they could be teachers, maybe find a man with his own land. Next best thing was a preacher's wife. See, he was thinkin' ahead. Get 'em married to old men, they'd inherit land or money while they were young and not hafta do hard, lowly work. He found a nice old preacher for yo' mama, but she ran off with a boy and came back five years later hurt and broken. What happened when she was up north hurt her so bad she think God still punishing her. Even after she married that old preacher, anyway, she still hurt. I didn't know she was doin' that to you, too."

"She thinks God punished her for being ungodly," Glory said. "She's trying to save me from her pain and thinks keeping me from the world and making me be with Malcolm will do that.

"But, Bigma, Malcolm is making me ungodly—making me wanna sneak and do things. I disobey him all the time. It's like he let out this hellion in me, and I don't wanna be good anymore."

"Hellion?" Bigma leaned back in her rocker and laughed out loud. "Baby girl, ain't a bad bone in yo' body. You a teenage girl just wantin' to cut loose. Ain't nuttin wrong with that."

Glory put her head down. She hated being laughed at, and her grandmother was underestimating her like everybody did except, it seemed, her mother. "You know how Mama doesn't let me go anywhere when we're here?"

Bigma nodded.

"Malcolm stood right in front of her and told me to go out with my cousins and watch TV and dance and buy sparkly clothes. Everything Mama says I can't do. And he knows that."

"And Mary didn't say anything?"

"No, she told me to just do what he said. It's like she's just giving me to him, and I don't have any say at all. Even though it's what I wanna do, it's like she and Malcolm decided for me. What if I change my mind? What if I want somebody else?"

"Oh, I see now." Bigma smiled a little. "Mama promised you to a nice old preacher, and you wanna run off with a boy. Now, don't that beat all?"

Glory leaned against her grandmother's shoulder, wishing she was smaller so she could curl up in her lap. She hated that her mother probably knew exactly what she was feeling, and she hated that she needed Malcolm so much.

"Oh, Lord, here she comes," Bigma said.

Glory looked up. She could feel the vibrations of something loud coming. Looking out, she saw a red car speeding up the road. It made a sudden turn into the driveway then headed straight for the porch, braking at the last second and turning completely around, sending gravel flying in every direction. The pounding and screaming of Prince singing "Little Red Corvette" shook the house for a full minute before the driver cut the engine and hopped out of her little red Chevette.

The skinny young woman with half-cropped spiky glittered hair bounded up the stairs. Glory couldn't figure out how she moved so fast in her tight miniskirt and combat boots or how the giant cut-up sweatshirt managed to stay attached to her body.

"Hey, Bigma! Hey, Glory!" the young woman yelled as she ran into the house.

"Hi, Jillian," Glory and Bigma said to the slamming screen door.

At twenty-three, Jillian was Glory's closest first cousin and the woman Glory always wanted to be. She lit up whatever room she entered. An artist and actress, she was beautiful, funny, and brilliant. Ever since Glory could remember, when Jillian was around, there was bound to be fun. From making baby food for dolls using flour and water to making a party with real cake mix in the Easy Bake Oven, Jillian always had the best ideas, and everything she touched turned out great.

From the front porch, Glory would watch her twirling her baton, practicing mime, or even just painting her toenails and braiding her hair. Whatever Jillian did, Glory wanted to do, and Jillian would sit patiently and teach her "cousin baby" whatever she wanted to know. It was Jillian who gave Glory a hand mirror when she turned twelve and told her to see what was *down there*, "'cause God didn't make anything nasty about you." She taught Glory how to use a tampon at fourteen, how to put a condom on a broomstick at fifteen, and at sixteen, bought her sexy stockings. Her mother always said Jillian was too wild and never left Glory alone with her too long for fear that her wildness was contagious. That made Glory want to be like her even more.

Jillian came running back out of the house. "Bye, Bigma! Glory, run. Don't look back!" She jumped down the stairs.

"What? Why?" Glory yelled at the back of her cousin's sweatshirt.

"I got your purse! Your mama's smokin' something and just told me to take you out to buy something sparkly. Come on before the drugs wear off." Jillian hopped in her car and revved the engine.

Glory yelled goodbye to Bigma and ran down the stairs, almost bursting with joy.

———————————⟋⟍⟍⟍———————————

"WHAT?" GLORY YELLED, trying to be heard over the music.

Jillian turned down the radio. "I said, what is your mother smoking, and why is my daddy yelling about selling you into bondage like Joseph?"

Glory laid her head back against the seat. "My mom's smoking rolled-up brown paper... don't ask. Uncle Bobby's talking about these." She held out her wrists. "Ten shekels. More like Rebecca, not Joseph."

Jillian glanced over at Glory's outstretched arms then looked back at the road. "Nice. Who's Rebecca?"

"All the Bibles in that house, and you haven't read a single one? She was Isaac's wife. When she was picked, she got ten shekels' weight in gold bracelets."

"Oh. You mean the one who helped her scheming youngest son trick his father, a favorite of God, and cheat her hardworking oldest son out of his birthright?" Jillian said. "The one who helped betray her own husband whose name means laughter—that Rebecca?"

"Yeah," Glory said, folding her arms. "I'm rolling my eyes at you."

"Ha!" Jillian laughed. "Don't mess with me, Cousin Baby. I know everything you know, but you only know half of what I know. So, why are they trippin'?"

"I'll tell you if you promise to stay calm."

"Oh, Lord. Did your mother really sell you into bondage?"

"No. They were a gift from somebody who likes me, and you need a special screwdriver to take 'em off—"

"Holy shit, Glory! Superman got you in shackles? Yeah, I read the card on your flowers."

"Why does everybody keep saying that? No! It's not like that—"

"Where's the screwdriver?"

Glory sank down in the seat. "Malcolm has it."

"Mm-hmph."

"Jill, it's really not like that. Bigma understands. Malcolm loves me, and he wants me to remember it all the time. They're engraved and everything. I sort of got him the same thing. That's why he signed the card, Superman."

"Glory, I'm sorry." Jillian patted Glory's knee. "It's just kinda weird, that's all. Especially... that you can't take 'em off. Tell me about Malcolm. He goes to your school?"

"No, we go to the same church. He's the pastor's son."

"Okay. He's in college?"

"Yeah. He goes to Mayfield Bible Institute. He graduates in June."

"Okay. So, that's not so bad." Jill frowned. "C'mon... what's the bad part?"

"There's really no bad part, Jill. Honest. He's a minister at our church and at another church—"

"Um, Cousin Baby, how old is this guy?"

Glory covered her face with her hands. "He'll be twenty-eight soon."

"Damn. I see why Daddy is trippin'. Your mother is okay with this?"

"Jill, he saved me from a monster. My mother thinks Malcolm is Jesus Christ."

The trip from Flora to the Canton Shopping Center was the best car ride of Glory's life. They bounced to the music and waved at truckers, and Glory impressed Jillian with her new freedom and stories of her times with Malcolm.

"So, um, Cousin Baby, how's he hangin'?"

"I guess he's okay. I talked to him earlier—"

Jillian laughed. "You don't know what that means, do you? His stuff, you know…" She made a gesture with her hand. "How is it?"

Glory cringed and covered her face.

"You mean, after all that, you haven't had sex yet?"

"Not with Malcolm, no—"

"Hold up! Wait a minute. What do you mean, 'not with Malcolm'? You screwing somebody else?"

"Oh my God, Jill! When you say it like that—"

"Glory? You are!"

"No, I'm not. Honest! I mean, I did once—well, twice—before Malcolm ever spoke to me—"

"Oh my God, Cousin Baby, you're not my cousin baby anymore! Hand me a tissue outta the glove box."

"Really, it's no big deal." Glory sighed. "I get what you mean now, and I think… um… it might be scary."

"What might be scary?"

Glory covered her face again. "How he's hangin'."

Jillian's laugh was a combination of sobbing and coughing with an occasional hiccup. She threw in howling screams for good measure. "Okay… okay…" Jillian panted. "What's scary? How do you know?"

"Well, okay. The other boy, I've been knowing him for a long time, and we kinda touched sometimes with clothes on, and when he was, you know"—Glory lowered her voice—"excited…"

"Yeah?"

"Well, I could feel it, and it was, I guess, normal. And when we did it, it was exactly like I thought it would be. But boys can keep growing until their twenties… and Malcolm is almost thirty."

"But, Glory, that doesn't mean he's any bigger than—"

"Jill, we were on the couch, and I could feel it through his clothes *and* my clothes, and it was like… giant."

"Well, damn. Superman, huh?"

"Yeah, Jill. Superman."

There were more screams of laughter and loud music. Glory en-joyed ungodly freedom with her favorite cousin all the way to Can-ton.

· ⟨∿⟩ ·

GLORY FOUND THAT SHOPPING with Jillian was nothing like shopping with her own mother. Mary would head straight for anything made for old women who wanted to blend in with the floor, while Jillian went straight to lingerie and accessories, then shoes, and finally, tops and bottoms.

"Never pick a complete outfit off the rack. It's lazy, and every-body will know where you got it. You'll look like an amateur." Jillian flipped through the rack of sweaters, tossing several into the cart. "See this tag? It says acrylic. Wool is better, but it's expensive. Don't let anybody get too close, and they'll never know."

Glory just nodded and followed her through Marshall's, catching whatever Jillian threw.

"Show me your legs. Pull up your skirt just a bit. Great! You've got awesome legs. We won't do zippers, just elastic. That way, you can wear it long for Auntie and roll it up as short as Malcolm likes. Does he like 'em short?"

"I never asked," Glory said, catching a blue denim skirt with a black leather ruffle attached. It was hideous, but she dropped it into the cart anyway.

Later, Glory stared at herself in the fitting-room mirror. Jillian's picks were great, she had to admit. The fluffy off-white cardigan with flecks of holiday sparkles in red, gold, and green went beautifully with her bracelets, but Jillian had the idea of wearing it backward with the gold belt. She was a genius. Glory could wear it like a regu-lar sweater or turn it around when she dressed up. The red knit skirt and black velvet flats completed the look. The only problem left was opening the door and stepping out of the fitting room.

"C'mon, Glory. Lemme see you. It can't be that bad."

"It's not bad at all. I just feel funny."

"Do I hafta come in and get you?"

"How 'bout I just open the door a little so just you can see?" Glory cracked open the door and watched Jillian's jaw drop.

"Wow, girl. That is awesome on you! Turn around."

Glory spun.

"Yes," Jillian said. "You're getting that outfit. Malcolm will love it. We'll get a couple more sweaters, too. You can't have too many. Oh my God, girl! You are so beautiful! I'm so glad Aunt Mary is finally letting you grow up."

Jillian insisted Glory put a new outfit on in the car, and Glory had to admit she felt pretty. The royal-blue sweatshirt and blue denim skirt were just like what normal girls in school wore. The skirt went below her knees, but the split went well above, and the slouchy sweatshirt with the torn collar was perfect. She wouldn't let Jillian loosen her hair, but Glory liked the sparkly gold clips.

The parking lot at KK's drive-in was packed, but Jillian insisted the burgers were to die for, so Glory relented. It was one thing to dress like a normal girl inside but another thing to be seen in public that way. Walking past cars of people with thumping music and clouds of smoke, Glory focused only on getting to the front door. Inside, she grabbed a table while Jillian placed their order at the counter. The red-white-and-yellow-decorated room with a No Smoking sign on every table was surprisingly not as crowded as the parking lot. Over the murmurs, Glory could pick out the sounds of old-fashioned blues, and she understood why. The music and no-smoking policy kept most of the young people in the parking lot. She found herself swaying a little to the music, because the moaning organs sounded exactly like church.

"Hey, Ponytails, Sugar Daddy know you out here, shakin' it like that?" Darnell scooted into the booth next to Glory, trapping her inside. "Girl, you really need to ditch that wild thing and take a ride on the D train." He slid his arm around her, brushing his fingers against her back. "I'll make sure you get home."

Glory could hardly breathe, and the nasty buzzard was touching her. Fighting her rising panic, she tried to concentrate on the scribbles on the table in front of her. Jillian would be back any second.

"Cain't even say hi, Ponytails?"

She tried to shrug his arm away.

"Sugar Daddy ain't teach you no manners?" Darnell asked.

Glory couldn't speak. The knots in her stomach felt like they were crushing her insides. She held her breath to stop the tears.

Jillian dropped a tray on the table. She plucked a fry from a basket then sat down across from Darnell. "Glory, he doesn't know, does he?"

"Well, ain't you a wild ride." Darnell moved his arm from around Glory and offered his hand to Jillian. "I'm Darnell. Mr. Porter hired me to drive Miss Bishop around while she's here. I was just saying hello."

"No, you weren't," Jillian said, not shaking his hand. "I heard you. Glory, you really should've told him. I mean, he's a jackass, but he deserves a fair warning, right?"

"Now, listen here—"

Glory kept her head down, praying Jillian would stab him with a spork.

Jillian sighed. "Please don't make it worse. Her sugar daddy can buy and sell your whole family."

"Now, wait a minute. All I said—"

"I guess you're not smart at all, are you?" Jillian leaned in close to Darnell. "Look at her. "She's upset. I'm pissed. Now you're in danger."

"Ain't nobody scared—"

"Sugar Daddy kills people for upsetting her. You should be backing the fuck off right now. In fact, you should run. Don't talk—you'll only make it worse." Jillian sat back in the seat.

Glory felt Darnell slide out of the booth and heard him mumble something about *siddity bitches* as he walked away.

"So, Cousin Baby, how was I?" Jillian stuffed a french fry into her mouth.

"Can we go, please?" Glory pushed herself up from the booth, not waiting for an answer.

On the dark highway back to Bigma's, Glory watched the stars. Without the light pollution of the big city, the sky looked almost silver. The cool night was still much warmer than a December night in Chicago. Glory rolled the window down and let her hand surf on the wind. The damp, heavy air smelled of decomposing cotton stalks, and the tires on the road sounded like static. And Glory heard the nasty buzzard's voice over and over, and she needed a bath because he'd touched her, and as soon as she got to Bigma's, she could call Malcolm, and Malcolm could offer to come and kill him, and she would be able to go to sleep that night.

Chapter 17

"Hello?"

"Hi, Malcolm." Hearing his voice, Glory breathed a sigh of relief.

"Hi, Glory. Having a good time?"

"Yeah. I went shopping. I bought a lot of sparkly stuff."

"Oh, really? I can't wait to see what you got. I bet you're glorious."

"My cousin Jillian picked them. She likes 'em. I'm not really sure."

"I'm sure I'll love it all. We'll have a fashion show when you get back. What else did you do today? You had fun, right?"

"Malcolm." Glory took a deep breath. "Something scared me today. I don't know why I was scared. We were in a restaurant, and he was just being a jerk, and Jillian—"

"Glory, slow down. Somebody messed with you?"

"Sort of, but it's no big deal... Jillian made him stop, but I was so stupid. I just sat there trying not to cry. I couldn't even say anything. I just wanted you to come and—"

"You know I will, right?"

"But that doesn't make sense. Everybody who looks at me isn't dangerous, and you can't come after everybody who's a jerk."

"Woman, understand: I *will* come after everybody who's a jerk to you. I'm Superman, remember? You are my lady, and I love you, and it's my job to protect you. No matter where you are, even in the middle of nowhere in Flora, Mississippi, I will always come to you. There's nowhere you can go that I can't get to you, nowhere that I won't come for you, okay?"

"Malcolm, you're not that way anymore, remember?"

"I'm not saying I'll hurt everybody." Glory heard the smirk in his voice. "I'll just come to see about you. Make sure you're okay. If I hafta slay some dragons, well..."

"I just hate freaking out over some jerk. Jillian scared him, though. He kept saying stupid stuff about you again, and Jillian told him you killed people for touching me."

"Wait... what? He touched you? And what do you mean *again*?"

"No, I mean this morning when—"

"Glory..." Malcolm's voice had gone cold. "Start from the beginning, and tell me everything."

"But Malcolm, it's not—"

"Glory, start talking or I'll be there to get you tomorrow."

This wasn't what she wanted. She wanted him to tell her not to worry and make her feel better, maybe promise to threaten somebody. She wanted warm, protective Malcolm, not cold, vengeful Malcolm. Telling him about Darnell, Glory felt like she was talking into a dead phone. The only sound she heard was the music Malcolm had playing in the background.

"Malcolm?"

"Yeah."

"Please don't do anything. In the bookstore yesterday, you scared me. I don't like that side of you. And Mr. Espy is making Mama really happy. Please don't mess that up."

"Okay. I promise I'll try not to ruin your mother's fun. I said I didn't plan to show you that side again, and I won't this time."

Glory pretended he hadn't showed her that side again only a few hours after the bookstore incident. She touched her cheek—it was still sore. It wasn't important.

"I had to do something about Cal Harris," Malcolm continued. "He's an old pimp who messes up young girls—"

"Wow," Glory said with no enthusiasm whatsoever. "You really thought a pimp could get to me? How stupid do you think I am?"

"I'm sorry, Glory. I don't think you're stupid. I didn't think he could get to you." Malcolm sighed. "I just got mad. I needed to make sure he knew you and your friends were off-limits. But this Darnell kid, he's just got bad manners. *Sugar daddy,* huh?"

"Yeah. And he kept looking at me, all nasty. Worse than Mr. Harris. It made me think of..."

"I know," Malcolm said quietly. "And I promise he won't bother you again."

"What are you gonna do? Please don't—"

"Calm down. I won't come after him. I *will* tell his father to talk to him, though. Is that okay?"

"I guess," Glory said, relieved that Malcolm sounded normal again.

"So, your cousin is pretty cool. I like her."

"Yeah, Jillian is my hero. Well, she was before you came along."

"Hey, take Darnell's tip money and the money Mr. Espy gave you back, and buy her something from me. Tell her Sugar Daddy said, 'Thanks for being my backup,' and to holla if I need to come show some leg."

"Uh, okay..."

"Yeah, she can be Supergirl." Malcolm laughed. "We'll tear the place up if somebody else messes with you."

Glory listened to Malcolm talk about his day and the Christmas plans for the night ministry. He had never talked about it much before, and she felt like he was sharing something important—like he was telling her his secrets. Before saying good night, he reminded her that he loved her and that he could be there the next day if she wanted him to. She knew she would soon be breaking up with him, and that thought made the bracelets feel heavy... and Glory felt unworthy.

AT TEN O'CLOCK, THE house was mostly quiet. Bigma was in bed, Uncle Bobby sat snoring in front of the TV in the back bedroom he and Ellie shared, and Mary and Ellie whispered in the kitchen. Glory kissed her mother and aunt good night then followed the sound of the wailing blues through the house, out the front door, and down the steps to the front yard, where Jillian's car sat idling. The night was a little chilly. Jillian reclined against the windshield on a blanket laid over the warm hood. Glory climbed up next to her, accepted the wine cooler her cousin offered, and pretended she knew how to open it. Jillian chuckled and opened it for her.

The tangy citrus drink wasn't really cold, but when Glory took a swallow, it was refreshing. She leaned back against the windshield and looked up at the stars. For some reason, her thoughts went to JT. This would be a perfect night and a perfect spot to be next to him. None of Malcolm's seriousness or even James's silliness, just she and JT quietly watching the stars. She closed her eyes to push the image away because it felt like her heart would burst.

"So, did you tell him?" Jillian asked.

"Yeah. I told him," Glory said. She took a long swallow.

"What did he say?"

"He said for me to buy you a present and to tell you Sugar Daddy says thanks for being his backup and to holla if he needs to come show some leg."

Jillian's guffaw sent wine cooler spraying everywhere. Glory watched her laugh and choke for a full minute until she caught her breath and took another swallow. "Woo!" Jillian hooted. "Girl, I think I love your man!"

"Um, okay. What am I missing?"

"Okay, okay, okay." Jillian laughed again. "Okay. You didn't miss a thing. You're the one who said he had a third leg. Aha ha ha!" Jillian howled some more. "He wants me to call him if he needs to come slap somebody with his—"

"Oh my God! Is that really all you people think about. For real? Is everything a dirty joke to people your age?" Glory drained the bottle and snatched another one from the six-pack next to her. "Open this," she snapped.

Jillian opened the bottle and handed it back to Glory. "Yeah, pretty much. We like dirty jokes. You'll understand one day."

"I hope not. It's stupid."

"I'm sorry," Jillian said, taking deep breaths. "I guess that wouldn't be funny to you today, would it? What else did Malcolm say?"

"I wasn't gonna tell him, but I slipped and said it happened this morning, too. Nasty buzzard was bothering me when they picked us up. Didn't expect to see him again. Malcolm was gonna come and get me if I didn't tell him everything. He's not coming, but he is gonna talk to Mr. Espy. I hope he doesn't ruin Mama's fun. She's gonna say it's my fault Darnell looked at me, 'cause I've got a Jezebel spirit."

"No offense, but yo' mama is crazy. So, he was gonna drive all the way down here to do what—take you back home?"

"Yup." Glory sipped her drink. "He would've left as soon as we hung up. Mama would've made me go home with him. I don't get a choice when it comes to Malcolm." She looked over at her cousin's confused face. "Notice I didn't disagree when you said my mother was crazy."

"Glory, that's nuts," Jillian whispered. "Why is Aunt Mary okay with this?"

"I told you, he saved my life. A monster had one hand on my neck and one hand in my—" She choked on the words and took another swallow of wine cooler. "And God sent Malcolm to save me.

Malcolm beat him unconscious, kept on beating him until I begged him not to kill." She drained the bottle and took the half-empty one from Jillian's hand. "He saved her last baby. He can do whatever he wants with me as far as she's concerned. He's a *good, godly man* who's earned me." She drained Jillian's bottle, too, and reached for another one.

"Slow down, Cousin Baby. I know it's a cooler, but you're not used to—"

Glory looked at Jillian. "I'm not a baby, Jill. It's wine cooler." She took another bottle and used the edge of her sweatshirt to twist the cap open. Taking a long swallow, Glory realized she didn't actually like the taste, but she was going to do whatever she wanted that night. Period. Even drinking yucky wine coolers.

"Glory, you don't seem okay with any of this. How do you feel about him?"

"Malcolm will kill for me. He loves me so much... sometimes too much." Sipping her drink, Glory felt her tongue loosening. "In the hospital, he went off on my mother when she said the attack was my fault. He was so mean. It was like he was slapping her with the worst words he could say. And he was so powerful. I loved him that day."

"Damn, that's terrible."

"Yesterday, before we left Chicago, a dirty old man in a store said something that really bothered me. Turns out Malcolm knew the guy from his 'wild times.'" Glory looked at Jillian. "Old man used to be a pimp, and Malcolm got really mad. Not like when he beat up the monster. This time he was smiling when he smashed the counter and dared the old man to do something. He was enjoying it. I was scared of him.

"And then later, he went on this power trip to prove to Mama I was his." Glory shook her wrist as if to fling the bracelets across the yard. Of course, they wouldn't budge. "He tried to embarrass her by telling me to do things he knows she's against, and when I tried to ar-

gue, he—" Glory caught herself and took a drink. She was feeling relaxed but not relaxed enough to tell Jillian that Malcolm had hit her.
"I hated him yesterday. I hated him so much last night that I kissed
a boy I met on the train. Kissed him again this morning, too." Glory took another swallow and looked out across the yard. *James.* He'd
been so nice.

"Glory! You tramp!" Jillian laughed. "I'm so proud."

"Not tramp, Jill. Jezebel," Glory said. "Or Weak Femme Fatale,
depending on the victim."

"Huh?"

"She's my alter ego. You'll like her. She's a supervillain. Her power
is that men give her goodies, but she feels guilty so she gives it all
back." Glory sipped quietly for a minute, aware that her cousin was
watching her and probably worried. She laughed a little. "It's a heck-
uva power. I get gold, diamonds, drinks, you name it."

"Okay, kid." Jillian reached for Glory's wine cooler. "You're
done."

Glory blocked Jillian's reach and took another long, loud swallow, exaggerating wiping her mouth on her sleeve. "This morning, I
decided to break up with Malcolm. I'm too young for this." Again,
she tried to fling the bracelets from her arm. "He keeps calling me
'woman.' I don't wanna be a woman. I'm a girl. I just wanna hold
hands and make out and do normal teenage stuff. I just wanna be a
girl, and they're making me be this church lady, except when Malcolm wants me to be this princess woman thing that can't talk or ask
questions and just waits for him to open and close her cage."

Glory drained the bottle and threw it across the yard, where it
landed somewhere in the dark with a soft thud. "This morning, I
was so done with him. I was gonna give back everything and go back
to being Church Girl and sitting quietly and sneaking and reading
books and not letting Mama just give me away to some old preacher
man. Then that nasty buzzard started messing with me... and I need-

ed Malcolm. I needed him *so bad* I wanted to die. If I coulda run all the way back to Chicago, I woulda." Glory felt herself crying and wondered if she was drunk. She'd seen drunk people crying on Seventy-Fifth Street all the time and hoped she didn't look like that.

Jillian tossed the empty box, and Glory felt her cousin wrap her arms around her.

"Jill, he does everything for me. He won't let me do anything by myself, and he wasn't joking about coming to get me. Malcolm won't ever let anything bad happen to me again. I don't know if I wanna be with him, but I need him. I'm scared without him. Jill, I hate my life so much." Glory laid her head on her cousin's shoulder and cried like she hadn't cried since the attack. "Why am I so messed up? Why do I have demons in me making me wanna do things? Why can't I be normal?"

Jillian held and rocked Glory until she stopped crying.

"Jill? I'm drunk, right?"

"Yes, Cousin Baby, I think you are."

"Okay, good. Forget everything I just said, okay?"

"Nope. Not a chance. I plan to laugh at you tomorrow morning. We're gonna have a serious talk later, but I'm gonna laugh my ass off at you."

"You know what Malcolm does to people who mess with me, right?"

"Not me. I'm his backup, remember? Superman won't bother Wonder Woman."

"You're Supergirl. My sister is Wonder Woman. His real name is Herschel. Don't ask."

Chapter 18

Glory always imagined waking up in heaven would be like waking up at Bigma's. Sunlight coming in, and morning birds singing no matter what time of year... bed not too hard and not too soft, always just right... sheets smelling like fabric softener and fresh air... music from the kitchen floating out the back door and coming in through the slightly open bedroom window... and the smell of fresh coffee and homemade biscuits and bacon or ham, hot sausage or corned beef hash frying in Bigma's giant skillet.

But this Christmas Eve morning, as demons burned her eyes and pounded her head, music and birds screamed of her sinful drunkenness, and the smells caused her stomach to boil, Glory prayed for forgiveness and vowed to never drink alcohol again.

And then Jillian threw open the bedroom door. "Good morning, Cousin Baby."

Glory hadn't even noticed her get out of bed.

"Oh, wait. You're not a baby anymore, are you? You're Princess Woman Thing now, right?"

Glory didn't actually remember going *to* bed.

"Oh, no—I remember. You're the Weak Femme Fatale supervillainess who gets goodies!"

"I'm gonna have Malcolm fire you." Glory pulled more covers over her head.

Jillian pulled the covers back. "I tried to stop you, but I believe your exact words were, 'I'm not a baby, Jill. It's a wine cooler.' What was I supposed to do?"

"You're the adult. I'm just a kid. You're supposed to be protecting me. I'm the cousin baby, remember?"

"Oh, so this is my fault?" Jillian sat down on the edge of the bed and hugged the lump of covers where Glory lay. "Oh, Cousin Baby. You're a drunk, a tramp, and you're blaming other people for your screwups. You're a perfectly normal teenager. I'm so proud!"

"Jezebel, Jill. The proper term is Jezebel."

"Well, whatever. It's time to get up. Breakfast is ready. I brought you something for a headache." Jillian picked up a glass of water and a bottle of pills from the nightstand.

"Will that help?"

"A little. But you probably don't have a real hangover. It was only wine coolers. You're just dehydrated and haven't eaten anything. When you move around, you'll feel better." Jillian stood up. "You got a package this morning. Your mother's trying to open it. Bigma's guarding it, and my mother's gonna hide it in her bra. You should hurry."

Glory pulled the covers back over her head.

"Now, Cousin Baby, do I need to call Malcolm to come show some leg?"

Glory sat up and threw a pillow at the closing bedroom door.

"Good morning, baby!" Mary sang when Glory entered the kitchen. "Did you sleep well? You and Jillian were up real late."

"Good morning," Glory said, keeping her head down. "I'm still tired. *Some* people don't understand *vacation*." She made a face at her giggling cousin, hugged her grandmother, aunt, and uncle, and kissed her mother. "You look pretty, Ma. You sure it's not a date?"

"Now, you hush, girl." Mary giggled. "We're just having brunch and gettin' groceries—"

"Yeah," Uncle Bobby said, "because my car and your aunt's car and your cousin's car need to sit there in the yard and rest. I think yo' mama's kinda spoiled. She needs a fancy ride to the Piggly Wiggly to get greens and chitlins."

Bigma pulled a large envelope from under the table and handed it to Glory. "This came for you. Some folks"—she rolled her eyes at Mary—"got no respect for other people's privacy."

"Hmph," Mary grumbled. "My child ain't got no privacy from me."

"Hush!" Bigma turned back to Glory. "That's from him, right? G'on—open it."

"Privacy, my eye," Mary grumbled again.

"Ellie." Bigma turned to her youngest daughter. "In a minute, I'mma need you to go cut me a switch fo' yo' sister. This child think I'm playin'." She turned to her oldest daughter. "Enough!"

Glory and Jillian looked away while Mary went to the stove to pour more hot water into her cup of fresh sage leaves. Glory opened the envelope and poured its contents on the kitchen table: a brochure, a few tracts, a video cassette, and a small envelope with her name on it. She put the envelope in her pocket to open later and passed everything else to Uncle Bobby.

"Well, c'mon. Let's go take a look." Bobby pushed back from the table. "I wanna see what this boyfriend of yours got to say." He picked up the tape and brochure and headed out of the kitchen. "Y'all coming? Ain't got all day."

Glory hung back as her family filed out. Malcolm's preaching was one of her least favorite things about him, and she didn't think she could bear seeing her family watch the spectacle. Her mother and aunt would, of course, love it because Malcolm could get loud and passionate, but Bigma, Uncle Bobby, and Jillian wouldn't be distracted from his Biblical gibberish by theatrics. She slipped into the dining room and found a corner where she could see the living room TV but not be seen by the others. On the screen, a man played "Amazing Grace" on the saxophone while the camera panned over the small chapel with about thirty people in it. The room had chairs instead of pews and looked more like a meeting room than a church. It had no real pulpit, just a podium on a table. Glory couldn't see any reason Malcolm would want to be there, let alone call it a church. She could just imagine what her mother was thinking.

After the music, a man led a prayer, and a woman read announcements. So far, it was just like any other church service. Another woman came up to sing a capella. Her waitress uniform too tight around the middle, the greatly pregnant woman soon had the congregation on its feet. Glory found herself smiling when the camera landed on Malcolm standing in the back. He looked happier than she'd ever seen him at their church. She waited for her mother to point him out, but Mary didn't say a word.

By the time the song ended, Malcolm had moved to the front. Instead of standing behind the podium, he stood beside it, leaning against the table, his collar open, sleeves rolled up, ankles crossed, and arms folded. He looked more relaxed than he did at their home church, too.

"Well, well, well. Nice catch, Cousin Baby," Jillian said. "Very nice catch."

Glory couldn't help smiling. Malcolm did look very nice.

"Hey, everybody. How y'all doin' tonight? Let's all bow our heads for a minute." *Malcolm is using his normal voice, not his preacher voice?* The prayer was in plain English, simply asking for wisdom, guidance, and forgiveness. Not loud or bombastic, it was humble and nothing like the Malcolm Porter she heard every Sunday.

"I had a message all prepared, verses picked out a few days ago, everything in place, but today has been kinda weird for me, and God put some things on my heart, so I'mma talk about that instead. Is that okay? See, what's been on my heart is a part from Jeremiah, chapter thirty, verse fourteen: '... for I have wounded thee with the wound of an enemy, with the chastisement of a cruel one, for the multitude of thine iniquity...' In context, the prophet, speaking for God, is telling the people that they have acted like such fools, and God is so pissed he will whoop them like they stole something, make it hurt on purpose. This is the verse that's been on my heart today. We're gonna come back to it in a minute. Right now, let's look at Numbers 31:19–24."

Glory's hand went to her cheek. There was no more pain, but the memory still stung. Those were the words he'd used to apologize and... and beg for her forgiveness. Now he stood in front of a congregation looking thoughtful as he talked about it. This was a Malcolm she'd never seen before. Glory moved closer to the living room. Her mother looked confused, while everybody else looked interested.

On the screen, Malcolm moved around like a teacher, even grabbing a chair and turning it backward to straddle it and sit while talking. He recited the full text from memory while some in the congregation followed along in their Bibles. Uncle Bobby looked mildly impressed.

"So, you see, the Israelite soldiers are out fighting for months. They're out there crushing, killing, destroying. They're out there doing their God-given jobs but effectively being monstrously violent agents of destruction—so much so that when the work is done, they're not allowed back in the camp for seven days, and they hafta purify themselves on the third and seventh day. Not only that, but they also hafta purify everything they use, with fire if possible. If fire isn't available, they at least have to wash it. How many military veterans do we have in here tonight?"

Hands rose.

"Okay, a few. How many veterans of the street do we have?"

More hands went up.

"Ah, a lot more. Tell me, at the end of a day of fighting or hustling, is it easy to stop being a soldier or a hustler?"

This Malcolm was not yelling or scolding, not shouting or stringing together unrelated verses because they sounded good. He was not performing—he was teaching. He was making a King James Bible passage make sense and relate to normal people. The congregation all agreed that a person couldn't just stop being a soldier or a hustler. He was reaching them.

"See, the soldiers had to take some time to come down. They had to wash off the sweat and blood. They had to purify their minds and spirits. Can you imagine them trying to go in to their wives with blood on their shoes? Or worse—that rage of war still in their hearts? Myrna, at the club, you get grabbed at all the time, right? You spend the whole night slappin' dudes off you. And then you hafta go home, and your man wants to hold you... what happens? Yeah... you hafta remember that he's not the enemy. 'For I have wounded thee with the wound of an enemy, with the chastisement of a cruel one...' The soldiers could not go home with the blood of the enemy on their hands or the heat of battle in their hearts. They had to purify themselves, let go of the ugliness first.

"I've been working with a guy for a while. A veteran of the street. A fighter, a hustler, a brotha' who once 'embraced the dark side,' but the Lord did some work on him, a whole lotta work, and he's been on the straight and narrow for quite some time. Well, not too long ago, he was called into battle again. It was a good and righteous battle, and he fought a tough enemy. And when he defeated that enemy, you know what? My man kinda liked it... started feelin' like his old self again. Walkin' around like Billy Badass..."

Glory's mind reeled as she watched Malcolm spend fifteen minutes telling the story of a man so caught up in fighting that he started enjoying it, started looking for enemies, seeing everything as a battle... the thinly veiled story of his actions the night he'd hurt her.

"And in the grip of this pride—'cause it wasn't even real anger but just pride—he struck her. He 'wounded her with the wound of an enemy.' He hit her like she had attacked him, 'with the chastisement of a cruel one.' He did it twice to make sure it hurt. He marked her face like he would've marked an enemy on the street. Think about that... her questions were so great an iniquity to him that he treated the woman he loved like an enemy. What the hell kinda madness is that?"

On the screen, some in the congregation stood clapping. Others waved their arms and nodded in agreement. Malcolm didn't seem to notice them at all, though. He just kind of looked toward the back of the room while he talked, sometimes pacing with his arms folded, sometimes highly animated. Glory watched her mother's face for a sign that she recognized the story. Mary actually looked disappointed, like she was expecting more. Glory was relieved. With her mother's silence, she wouldn't have to explain who or what Malcolm was talking about.

Bigma sat on the couch nodding and smiling, while Aunt Ellie kept poking her big sister, and Jillian kept giving Glory the thumbs-up. Uncle Bobby took notes.

"'I have wounded thee with the wound of an enemy, with the chastisement of a cruel one, for the multitude of thine iniquity...' What could your loved one do that would make you treat them like an enemy off the street? What could they do to make you want to beat them like they stole something, like they attacked you? How could you let that darkness own you so much that you can't shake it off when you go home?

"The Israelite soldiers were elite, the best and the baddest in the world. God was on their side, and nobody could beat 'em. They could and would be ready at the drop of a hat, but they couldn't be soldiers all the time. They had to stop fighting sometimes. They had to, by God's law, cleanse themselves of the darkness, purge themselves of the ugliness of battle before they could face their loved ones.

"Yes, you hafta be ready to protect and defend yours when you need to, but what we do out here on the streets, every day? We cain't take this mess home. 'I have wounded thee with the wound of an enemy, with the chastisement of a cruel one, for the multitude of thine iniquity...' What iniquity? Your man wants some lovin'? Your woman wants to talk? Your kids want attention? They are not your enemies! You let the devil win, and they become your victims. Let's pray."

On screen, the congregation bowed their heads, and in Bigma's living room, Glory's family bowed theirs. Again, Malcolm's prayer was humble, praising and thanking God, but when he begged for purity, patience, and forgiveness, he wiped his eyes with the back of his hand.

Glory stared at the screen. This man in shirtsleeves, praying in a makeshift chapel, shedding tears in front of a crowd, was not the Malcolm Porter she knew, not the man girls laughed at and women swooned over, not the man her church knew. This was the Malcolm who'd saved her in the gangway and shielded her in the hospital, the one who would fight for her and kill for her, the one who scared and thrilled her, the one she loved that one day and needed every day, the one who kissed her like he owned her... and the one she was breaking up with next week.

The tape ended with the saxophone playing "Precious Lord" and the congregation crowding around Malcolm.

"Well," Mary said, getting up from the couch. "He's usually a lot more interesting. I guess this night-ministry thing is charity work or something. It's not even a real church. Our church is so much better."

"Hush, Mary," Bigma said. "That young man gave a brilliant message. He preached to the people he was trying to reach. You saw how they reacted. He reached them. That's what a good preacher does."

"I think it was great, and he's so handsome, Glory," Ellie gushed. "I see why you like him, but isn't he a bit older than you, sweetie?"

Uncle Bobby leaned forward in the big chair, his elbows on the armrests, fingers steepled. "Come round where I can see you, girl."

Glory walked around and sat on the floor beside Jillian, facing her uncle.

"So, that's him, huh?" Uncle Bobby asked.

"Yes, sir."

"That's not a boyfriend. That's a real grown man. Pretty good preacher, but what's a man that age want with a girl like you?"

"You let her alone, Bobby," Mary snapped. "Malcolm is a good, godly man, and he takes care of her—"

"Dammit, Mary! You the one supposed to be takin' care of her, not some—"

"I am takin' care of her. I found her a good husband, just like my daddy found for—"

"This child is seventeen. She don't need no damn husband!"

To Glory's great relief, the doorbell rang, silencing the discussion. The clock on the VCR showed ten o'clock in the morning.

Ellie jumped up and ran to the door. "I know who this is," she sang. "Mary, stop fidgeting. You look fine."

Ellie opened the front door and invited Mr. Espy in. Bobby stood to shake hands, and Glory and Jillian got up from the floor.

"Can I get you a cup of coffee, Lee?" Bigma asked, not moving from her seat.

"No, thank you, Mrs. Johnson. I'm much obliged, but I'm saving space for brunch with your lovely daughter."

Glory and Jillian pinched each other to keep from giggling, and Glory felt a small knot forming in her stomach, wondering if Malcolm had called him yet.

"Um, Miss Bishop..." Mr. Espy turned to Glory. *Yup, Malcolm called.*

"Yes, sir?"

"My son sends his apologies for his behavior yesterday. He was showing off for his friends. Of course, that's no excuse, but it won't happen again. He apologizes to you also, Miss...?"

"Ellis," Jillian said "But I'm just Jillian."

"Boys." Mr. Espy shrugged, nodding to Bobby. "Sometimes they're just plain stupid. Ready, Mary?"

"Of course, Lee," Mary gushed, heading for the door.

"Good seeing everybody." Mr. Espy helped Mary on with her coat. "I won't keep her too late."

"Oh, keep her as long as you want," Ellie yelled out the door behind them. "Her train don't leave till next week!"

"Ellie, you hush!" Bigma said.

Jillian laughed, and Glory noticed Uncle Bobby still scowling at the TV screen. She sighed. The conversation wasn't over.

THE PILLS HADN'T HELPED, but after food, water, and moving around, Glory felt a lot better. Working in the kitchen with her aunt, cousin, and grandmother, Glory was glad her mother wasn't around. She could freely answer their questions about Malcolm and laugh at Jillian's *leg* jokes, which were getting kind of funny.

"So, Cousin Baby, why were you hiding in the dining room? You don't like Malcolm's preaching?"

"Honestly, I don't." Glory sat across the table from Bigma, cleaning the pecans as Bigma peeled the paper shells. "He knows the whole Bible by heart. I mean the whole book... and a lotta different versions. He usually just strings together verses that don't really go together. He gets loud and dramatic. It's all a big, silly show, but our church eats it up."

"Well, baby," Bigma said. "I don't know what you was lookin' at, but I didn't see nothin' like that. It was a good message. Right to the point. Looked at those verses in a new way. Learned something, and I'm seventy-eight. Preacher teach me something at this age, that's a good preacher."

"Yeah, Glory." Aunt Ellie stood at the sink, peeling the mound of sweet potatoes. "He was really good. I'd love to hear him again. When you talk to him tonight, tell him to send us another tape. And, baby, he is fine! Ooo wee!"

"Mama, please," Jillian said. "He's young enough to be your son-in-law. Seriously, though, Glory, what was wrong?"

"Well," Glory confessed, "I stayed in the dining room 'cause I thought it was gonna be embarrassing. I knew Mama would like it 'cause she loves anything he does, but that wasn't the Malcolm I know. I've never seen him preach like that. He was actually good."

"Yes, he was," Ellie said.

"And he looked so natural," Jillian added. "Maybe what we saw on the tape is his normal style, and what he does on Sundays is just performing."

"I don't know." Glory sighed, again grateful that her mother wasn't there. "I'm thinking that, too. In church on Sundays, he's so uptight and nice and sweet—kinda soft, even. But when... when he saved me, and when I was in the hospital, I saw that he's not really nice and sweet at all. And seeing this, I think *this* is the real Malcolm, and Church Malcolm is just an act. Does that make sense?"

"Girl, I remember when I found out yo' uncle Bobby wasn't nice and sweet either. Lawd ha' mercy, chile."

"Mama, please!"

"Heh, heh, heh. Yo' granddaddy wasn't so nice and sweet either, mm, mm, mm."

"Aw, Bigma. Not you, too?" Jillian said.

"Okay, Jill. I get it now," Glory said. "It's all right for Malcolm to show some leg, but your daddy and granddaddy can't?"

Jillian looked around the kitchen. "Oh, no. This little girl did not just go there! Y'all hear this child? Bigma, you need me to go cut a switch?"

Glory loved being in the kitchen with her family. Christmas Eve cooking had started just after breakfast. They made pies, cobblers, cakes, and a banana pudding from scratch. All the desserts would be done by midday. Then Aunt Ruth would arrive with the wine, the music would come on, and the real work would begin. Glory and Jillian would sit back and watch while Bigma and her daughters created Christmas dinner: styrofoam coolers with ice and meat marinating overnight to go on the grills first thing in the morning... Mary at the counter, cleaning buckets of chitlins under Bigma's close supervision... Ellie at the sink, up to her armpits in greens... and Ruth making cornbread and dicing vegetables for the dressing.

When Aunt Martha and her clan arrived on Christmas Day, there would be homemade rolls, macaroni and cheese, potato salad, and whatever else she and her boyfriend of the season felt like bringing. One year, a guy named Bruce had brought a giant smoked turkey. Everybody wondered what had happened to Bruce.

GLORY MADE HER WAY out to the front porch. It was nearly two o'clock, and much of the baking was done. She'd spent the last several hours entertaining her aunt and grandmother with stories of Malcolm. Then Jillian had reminded her about the letter.

Glory was grateful for the opportunity to escape the kitchen. Seated on the top step, Glory unfolded the note. Even his handwriting on the South Gardens Mission stationery looked different.

Dear Glory,

If you haven't watched the video, do that before reading this so this letter will make sense.

*I told you that I'd never show you that person again and then at-
tacked you for questioning me. I can give you a lot of reasons—but no
excuses. I let pride rule me, and I hurt you. I understand if you can't forgive me. It wasn't until we were on the train and I saw you in the full
light that I saw what I did to you. I can't forgive myself. I love you more
than life, and I will do anything for you. I swear I will never touch you
that way again.*

*After seeing the tape, I guess you're pretty confused right now. The
night ministry isn't like our church at all. People are actually seeking in-
formation and understanding. They come here for help, and I do what I
can, but they come as they are. When I speak here, I get to loosen up and
tell the truth—the real truth, with no fancy words—because the people
here actually listen to what I say. I can't tell you how good it is to serve a
church like this.*

*If you're still speaking to me when you get home, I'll bring you down
for a visit. I know I sound prideful, but it's because I feel so good about
the work we do here.*

*I'm hoping I've talked on the phone to you a couple of times by the
time you read this. If not, call me when you get this and at least let me
know you're okay. I need to hear your voice. It gets me through the day.*

I love you, Glorious.
*Begging your forgiveness. I swear I will never hurt you
again,*
Malcolm

Glory folded the letter and put it back in the envelope. She
wiped away a tear that she didn't understand, and she wanted to
scream, but she didn't know why. She shouldn't be feeling sorry for
him. She shouldn't want to comfort him. He'd hurt her. He even
admitted it! And he'd publicly confessed in front of his church. Jillian was right. This *was* his true self, and he'd showed it to her and

her family just to prove himself to her—just to tell her he knew how wrong he was and to beg her forgiveness.

And Herschel was right. Malcolm *was* brainwashing her. He *was* making her love him. All she wanted to do at the moment was be with him and tell him everything was okay. No boy could compete with Malcolm, not even JT. Malcolm wanted to pull her into his secret life, and she wanted to see it just as much as she wanted to be free from him. That hard edge that he showed only to her was more exciting than anything. What the girls at church laughed at would scare them if they only knew—and what the grown women wished for. *Ha!* They couldn't handle him. He could crush the stupid boys who made fun of him. Even though her mother had watched the whole tape, Mary would never tell because she didn't get it. It was like he really was this dark hero pretending to be a mild-mannered youth minister. Malcolm had shown himself only to Glory, and she hated that she loved him for it.

Glory wiped away another tear and willed her thoughts to simpler things. Worldly and blasphemous things. Boys who liked her. New clothes. Valentine's Day dances. Senior Prom. Graduation. College. A life free of complications and other people's control. Normal girl things. Except she really wanted to talk to Malcolm.

Seated in Bigma's room, twisting the telephone cord around her fingers, Glory waited for Malcolm to pick up.

"Hello?"

"Hi, Malcolm."

"Hi, Glory. I was just thinking about you. Did you watch the tape?"

Glory lay back on Bigma's bed. "Yeah. Everybody did. Mama said it was boring. My uncle said you're a pretty good preacher, but he still doesn't trust you. Everybody else liked it."

"Well, I figured it wouldn't be what Mother Bishop was used to. Um... did anybody ask...?"

"Oh, no. Nobody knew. I got an ice pack on the train, and I put makeup on it. I'm not gonna tell anybody."

"Oh, God, woman. I don't need you to cover for my sin. If anybody asks, don't you dare lie—"

"Malcolm, it's gone. It's not even sore. I don't want anybody to know." *I don't want anybody to know that you sometimes hurt me and that I take it because I need you.* Glory took a deep breath. "I just wanna forget about it. Please?" *Because it's never gonna happen again.*

"Okay, fine. And I swear I'll never do that again, Glory."

"I know you won't, Malcolm."

"So, you told me what everybody else thought. What did *you* think?"

"Honestly, I didn't know what to think." Glory hesitated. "Jillian helped me work it out a little, and now... I'm still a little confused, but I'll sort it out."

"Okay... go on." Malcolm sounded guarded.

"I mean, when you're at our church, you're a completely different person than I saw on that tape. You're kinda goofy. I'm sorry, but you are. You always talk in Bible verses, and sometimes it's just weird."

"I see. Goofy."

"I'm sorry. Should I just shut up now?" Glory asked.

"Not on your life, woman. You're gonna finish this one. Keep talking."

Glory was surprised that he actually sounded amused.

"But in the hospital, you were different, and in the store, too. It's like Church Malcolm is Clark Kent, but Night Ministry Malcolm is Superman. In the letter, you said at the night ministry, you get to loosen up and tell the truth, but I think it's more than that. I think the person you are at our church is fake." *There. I said it.*

Glory listened to silence for a minute. She could hear the choir rehearsal in the background, so she knew he was still there.

"Jillian told you that?" he asked finally.

"No," Glory said. "She said you looked completely comfortable—like, natural—on the tape. That's when I started thinking that I saw you like that more than I saw you like you are at church. I mean, at first, I saw Church Malcolm all the time, but after you saved me, I only saw Church Malcolm at church. You even stopped speaking in Bible verses so much. It's like the real Malcolm came out."

"Glory, who I am at our church is *not* fake. I do hafta be a bit more uptight here, but I'm not faking anything."

"Okay, maybe *fake* wasn't the right word. I think who you are on that tape is who you really wanna be all the time, but on Sundays, it's your job to be Church Malcolm."

"Wow. Woman, I think I underestimated you again," Malcolm said. "You're right. I *do* wish I could be at the mission full-time. And what I said in the sermon was true. I'd been away from the mission for a while, but after the day you were attacked, I went back 'cause I was suddenly ready to fight everybody. I feel peace there. I started counseling and ministering again—preaching for real"—he laughed a little—"not just speaking in verses. And until I actually hurt you, I thought I was in control. Yeah, *Church Malcolm* is my job, and I owe Lakeshore my life. The church is putting me through school. So, yeah, I hafta be there, but I promise you it's not fake. I bet you can't imagine not being able to choose what to do with your life. It makes you try to control everything else."

Glory looked at the bracelets on her wrist and almost laughed. *He really doesn't know, does he?* They talked a while longer, until Jillian knocked on the door and announced Aunt Ruth had arrived and Mary was back.

"Sounds like you gotta go," Malcolm said. "Wanna hear something funny?"

"What?"

"I'm seriously thinking about coming to get you tomorrow. I haven't been away from you this long since... you know. That's crazy, huh?"

Glory realized she wanted to reach out and wrap her arms around him. "Nah, it's not crazy. I miss you, too. Hey, I almost forgot. My aunt said to send another tape. She really liked your sermon, and... um... she thinks you're cute."

"Oh, really?" he said. Glory could hear the smile in his voice. "Well, I guess I can strut my stuff one more time. Is your aunt cute?"

"Depends on what you call cute. She looks just like a short, round version of my mother."

"Well, see, here's the thing..." Malcolm laughed. "You forget where I work. I hear things. I know for a fact there's a whole lotta men just waiting for a chance at your mother. If your aunt looks anything like her, well—"

"You know what, Malcolm?" Glory interrupted. "I hope it's six feet of snow in Chicago, and I'm rolling my eyes at you."

"Well, if it gets too bad here, you know I'll just come keep warm with you, right?"

"Yeah, Uncle Bobby and his shotgun'll love that."

"I ain't scared. I'm Superman! Hey," Malcolm said quietly, "get going. Tell everybody I said hi. I'll send a tape of the Christmas service, okay?"

"Okay."

"Merry Christmas, Glory. I love you."

"Merry Christmas, Malcolm. I lo... I'll talk to you tomorrow."

Stop making me need you. I'm too young for this. I don't want to love you. I don't want to... I don't want to... I don't want to!

Chapter 19

Glory had been nine years old the last time she saw her mother cook Christmas dinner with her family, and on this Christmas Eve night, Glory sat quietly in a corner watching her mother sway to the blues with a piece of rolled brown paper smoldering in the corner of her mouth. She tried to picture her mother as how Malcolm described her—somebody who men at church wanted. Glory had to admit her Mary did look great for sixty-three, and she wondered, not for the first time, if her mother would ever love again.

Of all Glory's aunts, Ruth was the coolest. She had been all around the world and could do anything. Her current job was a truck driver, but she'd been a cook, a writer, an artist, a photographer, a model, and a teacher. She was also the last daughter Grandda tried to marry to a preacher—it had lasted one day. In the kitchen, she always wore her chef's outfit, complete with the hat and a sweat rag around her head. Bigma said she looked silly, but Aunt Ruth took her cooking very seriously. She carried a rolled-up set of knives too sharp for normal people to touch and a bag of special spices. Once, Aunt Martha said the green stuff was reefa, and that started a big fight.

Aunt Ellie, the baby sister, clearly considered herself Bigma's favorite. The only advanced college graduate of all her sisters and the only one still married, she was usually the cause of much eye rolling in the kitchen. With her sisters around, she became extra wifely—so much so that Bigma usually told her to shut up at some point. "Y'all live in my house. I know what goes on. Don't have me start tellin' yo' business up in here." That quickly quieted Aunt Ellie right down.

Ruth's knives were flying and Mary's pretend cigarette bobbing. Ellie was being scolded for leaving stems in the greens, everybody was drinking cheap wine and swaying to the music, and Glory and Jillian sat in a corner, watching the women's antics. Jillian nursed a wine cooler, and Glory held a teacup. Aunt Ruth walked by and discreetly poured red wine into it, winked, and walked back to her cutting board. Glory looked into the cup, then at Jillian—who was doubled over with silent laughter—then back into the cup before finally tasting it. The sweet red wine mixed with wine cooler was actually pretty good.

"So, Glory," Aunt Ruth said, "if yo' mama tries to make you marry that old preacher, you just kick 'im in the nuts on yo' weddin' night. I got some bolt cutters out in the truck—cut them shackles right off."

"Ruthie, I'm telling you, you need to see that tape," Ellie said. "That is not an old preacher. Lawdy, no he ain't."

"Yeah, Aunt Ruth," Jillian chimed in. "And Glory calls him Superman. Maybe kicking is a bad idea!"

The women in the kitchen howled with laughter. Glory hid her face in the teacup, quickly draining its contents, kind of wishing she was somewhere else. She tapped Jillian with her empty cup and held it still while her cousin refilled it with wine cooler.

"Ruthie, you need to get you some business." Mary took a deep drag on the roll of brown paper. "Malcolm is a good man. He saved my baby's life, and he loves her. He gives her the world and ain't tryin' to get in her pants. He's gon' make her a good, godly wife, and ain't nothin' wrong with being a good, godly wife, right, Ellie? Mama?"

Glory silently drained her cup again and felt her cousin's hand squeezing her knee. Glory just sighed and held her cup out for a refill.

"Of course not. Right, Mama?" said Ellie. "When a *grown woman* is ready to become a wife, she accepts a marriage proposal from a godly man *of her own choosing*—"

"Her own choosing!" echoed Ruth, walking over and adding more wine to Glory's cup.

"One she chooses with the *guidance of her parents*," added Mary.

Bigma leaned over toward Glory and Jillian. "Y'all notice ain't nobody asking you a doggone thing, right? You might be just havin' a little fun, but they already pickin' out big hats. Baby girl, I'm surprised yo' mama let you sit in here listenin' to your aunt Ruth cuss."

Glory giggled. Wine definitely made her feel different than wine cooler. "That's 'cause Malcolm said I hafta hang out with my cousin." She wiggled her wrist, making the bracelets clink. "I'm his, remember?"

Bigma smirked and shook her head.

"Okay," Jillian whispered to Glory. "I'm protecting you, starting now. No more for you after this."

"Well," Mary said, "all I know is when my daddy found a good husband for me, I was a little nervous—"

"Mary," Ruth interrupted.

"But I eventually came around—" Mary continued.

"Mary," Ruth interrupted again.

"And married a God-fearing minister who saved me from—"

"*Mary*! You can tell that lie if you want to, but *I was there*!"

"Calm down, Ruthie," Mary said, turning back to the counter, continuing her work on the chitlins. "I was there, too."

"Mary, the night before you was supposed to marry that old man, you ran like hell," Ruth said, chopping furiously at a pile of already diced onions. "I helped you pack a bag, and I took food the church ladies had made for the wedding, even some of the sweet potato pies, and stuffed 'em in a sack. You climbed out the window, and then you ran like hell, Mary. You ran like yo' ass was on fire. You didn't wanna be stuck with no old-ass man, so you ran like hell!"

"Oo wee, it's getting warm in here. Baby, don't you and Glory wanna go outside?" Ellie asked, motioning toward the kitchen door.

"No, we're fine," Jillian said. "Just waiting to see if y'all need any help."

"Maybe y'all need to talk about something else?" Bigma suggested.

"Okay, I ran," Mary snapped, still not facing her sister. "And I told you I was sorry. I told everybody I was sorry, and he forgave me and still married me. That preacher still wanted to marry me, even after I shamed him and—"

"And then that sick, twisted, evil muthafucka spent the next fifteen years beatin' the shit outta you!"

"Mama, make Ruthie stop cussing." Ellie threw a handful of green stems into the wrong section of the sink and cussed under *her* breath.

"Ruthie, you are *so* dramatic. We fought sometimes. Every couple does. I had a bad attitude, and I wasn't the good wife at all when we first got married. I talked back—"

"Mary, that's bullshit. I was there. I saw it. He whooped yo' ass till the day he died! You got beat for burning dinner. You got kicked if dinner was late. You got choked unconscious for being too tired to fuck."

Glory stared at her mother's back. The cloud of smoke from Mary's paper cigarette rose over her head as she pulled another one from her bra and lit it before crushing out the first one. She then picked at the membrane attached to the slippery beige piece of pork intestine and pulled, separating the two pieces cleanly, discarding the sheer membrane into a bucket.

"I didn't do like I shoulda," Mary said. "He was the man. Bible say the woman should be in submission, learn from her husband in silence—"

"Mary, he beat babies outta you," Ruthie whispered. "I cain't understand why you stayed with him. I swear I woulda helped you get away. I woulda killed him for you."

"Jillian, get Glory outta here," Ellie hissed. "That child don't need to listen to this mess!"

Glory sat dumbfounded, wishing for more wine. She'd heard that the old preacher was harsh, but this was all new to her—a horror her mother had lived that she couldn't imagine.

"I'm not a baby, Auntie. I'm staying right here," Glory said.

"Leave her be, Ellie," Bigma said. "She ain't been a baby in a long time."

"I stayed because God gave me strength to stay"—Mary turned to face her sister—"and Daddy got elevated to Elder Johnson. And you got to college, and Martha got to college, and Ellie got to college. I stayed because I am a strong, godly woman, and godly women don't just leave. You would know that if you was something other than a selfish, ungodly whatever the devil you are!"

"Mary, when that preacher came to marry me, and Daddy nailed the windows shut, you told me God would give me strength. You told me it was time I took my place and became a good wife." Ruthie pounded her cleaver through a bunch of celery stalks. "God gave me strength, all right. When I got to his house, I kicked that old fucka in the balls. Said he was gon' beat me till I learned. I told him he betta kill me 'cause when he went to sleep, I was gon' cut him into a woman." She chopped through the celery again. "I wish a muthafucka would." Ruth started dicing the celery into tiny pieces. "I stepped over that son of a bitch and went straight to my big sister's house... and you told me I was wrong for leaving my husband. You sittin' there with yo' eyes swollen shut 'cause the coffee wasn't hot enough or some bullshit... but you a strong, godly woman—"

"Ruthie, Malcolm loves Glory, and he would never hurt her. My daughter knows how to be a good wife. She ain't gon' have no trouble doing what she's supposed to do. Just 'cause you—"

"Now yo' crazy ass done let this muthafucka put irons on yo' child, talkin' 'bout she gon' be a 'godly wife.' Know what, Mary? Somethin' happen to Glory, I'mma see how strong and godly you are, 'cause Imma kick yo' ass. I'mma kill that muthafucka, but I'mma kick yo' ass worse than four old preachers!"

Ruth slammed the cleaver into the cutting board and stormed out the back door. Moments later, the sweet, earthy smell of burning herbs drifted in through the open window. Bigma followed Ruth out the back door, Jillian moved to the abandoned cutting board and started working on the celery, and Glory went to her mother.

Mary had turned back to her work on the chitlins and jumped when Glory touched her shoulder, a bit of ash falling from her paper cigarette. "Oh, hey, baby. Why you come over here? You know you just gon' start gaggin' at the smell, makin' me mad."

"Just checkin' on you, Ma, that's all."

"Oh, I'm fine. Your auntie just a little high-strung!" she yelled loud enough for her sister to hear from outside. "You know how she is. Now she out there, smokin' that stuff, like it's gon' make her feel better about her life! She need Jesus—that's what she need! Comin' in here and startin' this mess on Christmas Eve. Did I tell you Lee and his boys are coming to dinner tomorrow afternoon?"

GLORY WENT TO BED IMAGINING her mother as a young wife, not much older than herself, trying to be good—trying and failing to please an evil man. Glory prayed that the old preacher was burning in hell for what he'd done to her mother and thanked God that her daddy had come along and loved her. She promised God she would tolerate Darnell if Mr. Espy would keep her mother happy for the rest of their visit, and she prayed for Aunt Ruth to stop being angry and find peace and somebody to love.

Chapter 20

After the pillow hit her face the second time, Glory raised her arm to block a third blow, silently vowing to sic Malcolm on her favorite cousin before she broke up with him.

"C'mon." Jillian raised the pillow a third time. "We've gotta cook breakfast. Daddy's got the grills started. He's gonna put the meat on in a minute."

"Jill, I'm calling Malcolm if you hit me again." Glory snatched the pillow and threw it across the room. "Why do we need to get up now?"

"'Cause... um... Santa Claus came." Jillian winked at Glory.

Glory raised an eyebrow, and Jillian nodded. Glory jumped out of bed and dressed in less than a minute. In the living room, near the couch, sat two boxes: their presents from Aunt Ruth that they always opened in private.

Jillian's box had tiny bottles of what must have been every liquor ever made. She opened a bottle of peppermint schnapps and took a sip. "Ooo... mouthwash!"

Glory opened her box and gasped. What looked like a pile of fluff and lace was actually a lot of silky slips and underwear, stockings, and a garter belt. A handwritten note said: *I know your mother makes you dress like an old lady, but whatever touches your skin should make you feel beautiful, even if nobody but you knows it's there.*

Glory closed the box with a sigh. There was no way she'd get that home without her mother noticing. "Hey, Jill, can you do me a favor?"

"Want me to mail this to your job? What did you do with last year's stuff?"

"I read every one of 'em twice." Glory laughed. "They're still on the shelf at the salon. I'll figure something out with these. Maybe I'll wear 'em here and say Malcolm said I had to."

"Well, you could, but it's not like your mother's gonna lift your skirt and check your underwear."

"Jill, you have met my mother, right?"

Pretending to try to be quiet, the girls quickly got breakfast on the table while Uncle Bobby put the meat on the grills. Aunt Ruth came in from sleeping in her truck and hugged her sisters, the drama of the previous night forgotten. Uncle Bobby blessed the meal, and Aunt Ellie turned on the Christmas music. Seated at the crowded table, Glory couldn't help smiling. She hadn't been to Bigma's for Christmas Day in a long time, and it just felt so right.

———— ✦ ————

"OKAY, GIRL, THAT BOX is big as a car," Bigma said, settling into her rocker. "Been takin' up space for three days. C'mon, open it."

"Yeah, Glory," Aunt Ruth said, taking a seat on the couch. "Show us what your Superman sent."

Uncle Bobby took his seat in the big chair and patted his knee. Aunt Ellie curled up in his lap and giggled. Jillian rolled her eyes and shook her head.

"Y'all leave her alone. Maybe it's *personal.*" Mary moved to the couch, careful not to spill her tea.

Glory tore open the envelope attached to the top and read the card. "Um, Bigma, this is for you. It says, 'To Mrs. Johnson and Family. Merry Christmas from Malcolm Porter.'"

"Well, does it, now?" A wide grin spread over Bigma's face. "So, c'mon. Open it. Let's see what that nice young man sent me."

Glory and Jillian cut the straps on the box and lifted out a Swiss Imports deluxe gift basket. The basket was easily three feet tall, overflowing with holiday goodies: cakes, cookies, cheeses, sausages, and candies.

"Wow," Jillian whispered to Glory. "Bigma has the power to get goodies, too."

"Well, well, well." Bigma smiled. "I'm liking your Malcolm a little more every day."

Glory looked up at Uncle Bobby. Aunt Ellie was poking his cheek because he was refusing to smile.

"Woman, would you quit?" he said. "Yeah, it looks nice—all that shiny paper. But you know that's all sittin' on top of balled-up newspaper. That basket ain't filled to the bottom."

"Daddy, it's a nice little gift he sent to the family," Jillian said. "But I guess it's not as nice as the gift *you* gave Bigma when you started dating Mommy, huh? How big was Daddy's gift, Bigma?"

"Well, I don't quite recall," Bigma said, diplomatically. Mary and Ruth rocked with laughter. Ellie looked at Bobby and batted her eyelashes innocently.

"Yeah," grumbled Uncle Bobby. "Y'all think it's funny gettin' sucked in by this big shot. I, for one, think my niece is worth a lot more than a basket of sausage and cheese and that nasty strawberry candy. Ain't other stuff under that tree? C'mon. Ain't got all day!"

Glory and Jillian passed out the rest of the gifts, and the morning was filled with love and laughter except for a few minutes when Ruth unwrapped the box with two Bibles from Mary, and Mary unwrapped the three packs of C-sized batteries from Ruth, sending Ellie and Bobby into fits of hysterical laughter and spurring Bigma to threaten to send Jillian outside for a switch.

"Okaaay, there's one more gift under here." Glory choked back the last of her giggles as she took a little longer than necessary to pull out the shiny purple gift bag she'd placed under the tree the night before. "This is kind of an experiment we did at work... so these are presents from my boss."

She emptied the bag onto the carpet and held up two small tubes. "These are just lotion, but the boxes are full sets with soap and body spray, too. They're for... um... mature people... who don't wanna smell like perfume stores."

"Oh, so you mean stuff for old people?" Jillian asked, grabbing a tube, opening it and sniffing. "What the hell... I mean, heck? Pound cake lotion?"

"Actually, it's for church people who don't wanna smell like heathens." Glory rolled her eyes at her cousin. "That's the most popular one." Glory handed two tubes to Aunt Ellie. "The green one is a men's scent. It's herbal with a touch of earth and smoke. See if you can guess what it is. The other one is gonna be easy."

Ellie opened the green tube and sniffed. She rubbed a little on Bobby's neck and sniffed again then started giggling. Bobby smelled the orange tube and laughed. "Girl, you come in the room smellin' like sweet potato pie, the neighbors gon' think you lost me 'cause they gon' hear you callin' my name!"

"Well, if you come in smelling like southern greens, it's gon' sound like we both lost!"

"Ellieee!"

"Bo-bbyyy!"

Jillian covered her face. "Oh my *God.* Y'all are too old for this! Cousin Baby, how could you give them this mess?" She looked through her fingers at Glory. "Gimme that pound cake set, though."

Glory laughed while her aunts bickered over the gift sets and which one to leave for Aunt Martha. Mary, of course, said everything was ungodly and wanted no part of any of it.

"Yeah." Ruth laughed. "Five dollars say she be smellin' like peach cobbler when that man gets here." Bigma and Bobby quietly passed her five-dollar bills.

MARTHA JOHNSON WILSON Barnes Smith, etcetera, the often-married third sister, came through the door like a loud, bright, colorful, sparkling whirlwind. She flitted around the house, kissing and hugging everybody, finally throwing her arms around Glory and sobbing, "Oh, baby girl—oh sweet, glorious baby girl, how awful that must've been." She straightened up and sniffed loudly. "But you're safe now. You're here among your loving family, and we will help you heal from this ordeal. Oh, you poor, sweet baby." Glory staggered under the weight as Aunt Martha fell on her sobbing again. "I can't believe we almost lost this glorious ray of light!"

"Aunt Martha, please, I'm okay." Glory looked around at her family for help and glared as her mother and aunts all averted their eyes. Even Bigma had her hand over her mouth, shaking her head.

"Aw, Martha, would you quit? The girl is just fine," Uncle Bobby said finally. "Only healing she need is for you to get off her."

Martha sniffed and stood up straight again. "Of course, you're right, Bobby. Just look at her. Her fire is burning brighter than ever." She placed a hand against Glory's belly and raised an eyebrow. "I'd say she's practically... glowing?"

"Aw, hell... here we go." Ruth pulled Glory away. "Martha, where's the macaroni and the bread? Quit tryin' to make everybody pregnant. Just 'cause you and yo' kids breed like rabbits don't mean everybody else do! Where's this year's man?"

Glory retreated to Bigma's room as the house began to fill with family. She tried calling Malcolm but got no answer. Thanks to him, she would be the center of attention that day. Everybody knew about the attack and rescue, and Aunt Ellie had told everybody about the bracelets. And with the *giant basket of everything* overflowing in the living room, Glory found herself wishing Christmas Day was over.

"I found her!" a child's voice on the other side of the bedroom door yelled. "She's in here, but the door is locked. I can see her through the keyhole. She just picked up the phone. Now she put it down again."

Glory put down the phone and sighed. As she headed out to see her family, she guessed she'd be sighing a lot over the course of the day.

With the exception of Jillian, Glory's first cousins were at least fifteen years older than her, and their kids were her age and younger. Having never been allowed to hang out with her cousins, Glory barely knew their names, but that day, they all seemed to know her. She got hugs and congratulations, and somebody was always tugging on the bracelets. By the time dinner was over, she'd worked her way through the crowd and made it out to the back porch. The air was cooling, and Uncle Bobby, Aunt Ruth, Mr. Espy, Aunt Martha's date, and her three sons stood near the grills, talking, drinking, and keeping warm.

Glory took a seat on the top step and watched the men around the fires, sorely missing her daddy and wondering how Malcolm or JT might fit in here. JT would no doubt be in the house, playing cards or out front playing football, but Malcolm might be over by the grills with her uncle and older cousins. From somewhere in the house, she could hear Malcolm's voice. Somebody was playing the tape again, and the points of the sermon were being hotly debated.

"Merry Christmas, Ponytails."

Glory hung her head as Darnell sat down beside her on the step.

"Don't worry, I ain't gon' mess wit' you. Just wanted to say I'm sorry. For real. I was just messin' around, ya know? Tryin' to be friendly, ya know?"

"Yeah." Glory raised her head a little, glancing at him. "Real friendly."

"Oh, you do talk, huh? Yo' kin in there saying yo' man really did kill somebody for messin' with you. I was like, damn! And I'm tryin' to push up on you, playin' wit' fire. Since he only told my pops, I guess I should count myself lucky, huh? I probably owe you my life."

Glory laughed a little. He had no idea. "Malcolm didn't kill anybody. He gave it a good try, though."

"Is that a smile I see?" Darnell asked. "Yeah, it is. You real pretty, Ponytails. That's a smile to kill for, all right. Um... you know, my pops is kinda into yo' moms."

"Yeah, I noticed. She's been smiling since we got here. She likes him, too."

"Well, don't tell him I told you his weakness... but if she can make a peach cobbler, he might just follow y'all home. Women always bringin' cakes and pies, but he say he'a marry whoever bring him a good peach cobbler. You shakin' yo' head, but I'm serious. I'm just tryin' to help yo' mom out. Next year this time, you might be my sister."

"We'll see." Glory enjoyed the thought of her mother being happy. "We'll see."

"So, tell me about Cousin Wild Thang. Now, that's a ride I'd like'ta try, and I saw how she was lookin' at me, too."

Glory laughed until she started coughing, and Darnell had to pat her on the back. She waved him off and looked up to see her cousin Ricky walking toward them, arms spread wide, a big smile on his face.

"Baby Girl, Baby Girl. Oo wee, Baby Girl!" If Aunt Martha was a whirlwind, her oldest son, Ricky, was thunder and lightning. His large size and deep voice made him seem scary, but everybody knew he was harmless... mostly.

Glory came down the steps to hug him, and he picked her up and spun her around, not putting her down until she was good and dizzy.

"Look at you, Baby Girl. Look at you! Growin' up all fine as hell!" He turned to Darnell, offering his hand. "Hey, I'm Rick, the oldest cousin."

"I'm Darnell." He nodded toward the men at the grills. "Lee Espy is my pops."

"Oh, yeah." Ricky shook Darnell's hand. "He's a good man. Real good man." He wrapped an arm around Glory's waist. "Baby Girl, here..." He kissed her cheek with a loud smack. "Most powerful woman in the world. Powerful stuff. Mighty powerful stuff. Turned the man of God into a killer. Preacher took a crazy, ragin' muh'fucka down with his bare hands for messin' wit' this. Oo wee! That's some powerful stuff."

"That's what I heard." Darnell laughed, holding up both hands. "She got a smile to kill for—no man in his right mind gon' play with fire like that. No way!" He stood up and headed back into the house. "I'mma go in, get a drink. Don't forget what I said, now, Ponytails. Let your moms know."

"I will," Glory said. "But I bet she knows already!"

Ricky hugged her again. "Sit down, talk to me for a minute, Baby Girl." He settled on the top step, patting the space beside him.

Glory sat down, and he draped an arm over her shoulder. He smelled like liquor and cigars.

"You know, Baby Girl," Ricky said, "when we heard what happened, you know me and the boys was about to hit the road... comin' to tear shit up, right?" He laughed a little. "But then we heard your man handled the business. I mean, brotha handled the business! Johnny on the spot, he handled it. I couldn'ta done any better myself."

Glory knew her cousin was a little drunk but was still surprised to see him wipe away a tear.

"What he drink?" Ricky asked. "I'mma send a case of liquor back wit' you."

"He doesn't drink," Glory said, trying to keep the amusement out of her voice.

"Smoke? I got a box of Cubans I been savin' for—"

"He doesn't smoke, either."

"Oh... clean living. A true man of God. I guess it's just as well. Ain't nothing this family got can pay him back for what he did. He handled the business!" Ricky reached into his jacket and pulled out a bottle. He took a swallow, started to offer it to Glory, but pulled it back and returned it to his inside pocket. "Yeah, Baby Girl. He handled the business. I looked at that tape. Smart man. Good message. He knows some shit. He ain't always been a man of God, though, has he?"

"Well, he's only twenty-seven—"

"Naw... that ain't what I mean. He ain't no church boy. I know a soldier when I see one."

"Oh." Glory understood what her cousin meant but didn't know what to say.

"I know that story he told. I been there. I can see it in his eyes he been there, too."

Glory didn't say anything.

"Look at me, Baby Girl."

Glory looked at her cousin, whose hazel eyes were bloodshot from too much smoke and liquor.

"I ain't gon' ask no questions this time. But if he cain't stop bein' a soldier, you cain't be wit' him." He grabbed Glory's wrist. The bracelets jingled. "Yo' mama act like you gotta marry him. He saved you, but he don't own you. And you don't *owe* him. Hear me? He ever forgets you ain't his enemy, call me. I'll come get you. Understand? You leave his ass in the dust. Don't make me hafta come kill a preacher." Ricky pulled out the bottle again and took another drink.

"Yeah. I understand. Ricky?"

"Yeah, Baby Girl?"

"Malcolm really is good to me. Everything's okay." She hugged her cousin and rested her head on his shoulder. In a while, she would go in and call Malcolm and *not* tell him how much her family loved him.

Chapter 21

The day after Christmas, Aunt Ruth accepted a load to Miami and prepared to head out, promising to be back for New Year's Eve. Glory and Jillian filled her cooler with leftovers and held back tears when they hugged their coolest aunt goodbye. Mary got up and dressed early, too, ready to spend the day with Mr. Espy. Glory pretended not to notice the scent of peach cobbler body spray on her mother, and apparently, Mary pretended not to notice everybody giggling. Aunt Ellie and Bigma packed up baskets of leftovers to deliver to the senior center, police, and fire departments. Uncle Bobby worked on cleaning the grills and collecting cans and bottles from the backyard. And Jillian sat Glory down for some worldly education.

"Jill, you're wasting your time," Glory protested. "I've read a lot of books. Church Girl is my public identity." Sitting on the living room couch, ignoring the soap operas, Glory wished for a wine cooler and briefly wondered if she had become an alcoholic in the last three days. "There's nothing you can tell me that I don't already know."

"Well, I promised Aunt Ruth I'd have the talk with you, so you're gonna listen," Jillian said. "Malcolm is your first real boyfriend, and he's a grown man—"

"No, he's not my first, and I'm breaking up with him, so it doesn't matter."

"Well, you said the other boy wasn't a big deal—"

"I lied. JT was my boyfriend since I was twelve. Real boyfriend. We almost did it lots of times before we actually—"

"JT? The little boy in the picture? Oh my God, Cousin Baby, that's so adorable!"

Glory rolled her eyes. "Jillian, JT isn't a little boy."

"Well, it's still adorable. Did you use protection?"

"No," Glory admitted. "But I wasn't thinking right back then."

"Well, while you're here, we can go to Jackson and get you some—"

"Hold that thought." Glory ran and grabbed her purse. She felt around inside the lining and pulled out the beige compact. "Got 'em. Next?"

"Oh, I see." Jillian smirked. "Well, there're worse things you can get than pregnant—"

Glory reached in again and pulled out the strip of purple condoms. "Grape flavored."

"Well, damn," Jillian said, smiling and shaking her head. "I guess my work here is done."

Glory nodded. "Jill, I'm not a baby. I'm almost a woman. I can take care of myself."

"Okay, Cousin Woman," Jillian said. "Why do you freak out when you're away from Malcolm for three hours if you're breaking up with him? How are you gonna take care of yourself if you can't breathe without him?"

"I'll get used to it," Glory said defensively. "I lived without him just fine up until two months ago. I'll be all right." She didn't like to think about being without Malcolm. She wished there was a way to break up with him without entirely losing him.

"How are you gonna break the news to the whole family that you're dumping their new favorite relative? Even Ricky likes him. My dad is still skeptical, but that's just him."

"Aunt Martha does it all the time. They'll get over it."

"What's your mom gonna say?"

"I don't know," Glory admitted. "She won't be happy." *She'll beat demons out of me. I'll never see the sun again.* "I'm gonna wait a week or two after we get home. I think it'll look bad to break up with him as soon as we get back, like right after he paid for all of this. I'm not gonna call him today. I'm gonna get used to not talking to him or thinking about him all day, every day."

"Gonna practice being without him, huh?"

"Yup. By the time I get home, I won't need him anymore."

Right on cue, Uncle Bobby came in through the front door, carrying a tall white paper bag. "This man don't let up, do he? This just came for you, girl."

Glory stood and took the bag. "No, I guess he don't."

She tore it open. The vase of red roses and white daisies and little green flowers was much smaller than the other bouquet, whose colors still overwhelmed the living room—a simple reminder that he loved her. A short note came with it: *I'll be downtown at eight tonight. Call me there before ten. I love you. Malcolm.*

"Okay," Glory said. "I guess I *will* be calling him tonight."

Jillian smirked.

"I'll start practicing being without him tomorrow."

THE NEXT DAY, A BOX of chocolate mints from Marshall Field's arrived. The day after that came the tape of the night-ministry Christmas service. Glory and her family watched as Malcolm told a story of shepherds cooling out in the fields, watching the stars. She laughed a little when he mentioned a girl he knew who loved nothing better than to watch the stars.

"And think about it. This news of the birth of the king, the birth of the savior, was delivered to the shepherds first. Not to the high priests, who had probably been waiting all their lives for the sky to open up and the angels to appear, but to people who probably didn't care at all: the servants. Folks who didn't have time to think about saviors and angels, who didn't have the luxury of hopes and dreams. That's who got the news first..."

Glory watched Malcolm take a lighted candle and pass the flame to someone, who then passed the flame on. The small chapel was packed. Some people dressed up. Some kids wore Christmas pajamas. Each person passed the flame. Finally, Malcolm lifted his candle.

"Then spake Jesus again unto them, saying, I am the light of the world—he that followeth me shall not walk in darkness but shall have the light of life."

As everyone raised their candles, somewhere in the chapel, a man started singing "O Holy Night," and a horn played softly. The camera moved around the room, stopping on a few faces and finally landing on Malcolm.

"Cousin Baby," Jillian whispered. "Maybe it's the candlelight, but that just might be the finest man in the world."

"Why is he not married?" Ellie whispered. "You'd think somebody woulda caught 'im by now."

"'Cause he needs a special woman for a ministry like his," Bigma said. "His first lady gon' hafta work hard to support him."

"He's single," Mary said, "'cause he's waitin' on that girl right over there—"

"Yeah, and she still got baby teeth," Uncle Bobby grumbled.

Glory watched as long as she could then slipped into the kitchen and out through the back door. If she was going to break up with Malcolm, she couldn't stand another minute of watching him be perfect or listening to her family worship him. Yes, it was the most moving Christmas candlelight service she'd ever seen, and yes, Jillian was right—the light did make him the finest man in the world. Glory laughed. It seemed the closer it came to their breakup, the better Malcolm Porter got.

"YOU KNOW YOU'RE FRETTIN'" over nothing, right?" Jillian said. "My dad can't shoot him through the phone."

"I know." Glory pressed her ear to the bedroom door and heard her uncle's muffled voice but could understand nothing. "I just wanna know what they're talking about for so long."

"My guess is, I don't know. Maybe you? But hey, this might be your way out. Maybe Dad'll break up with him for you. That way, he's the bad guy, and you're just a poor, innocent church girl, doing as you're told."

"Jill, if Uncle Bobby did that, Malcolm would be on his way here." Glory laughed, but in truth, she was nervous.

After noticing Uncle Bobby watching the Christmas tape twice the day before, Glory had woken up the next morning to him watching the first tape again. When he was interrupted by another package delivery, this time a bag of her favorite popcorn from Evergreen Plaza, Uncle Bobby just shook his head. "Ya know, missy, yo' daddy was like a brother to me, and this man comin' at you like this—he wouldn't like it one bit. Time I had a talk with Malcolm. Get 'im on the phone."

Now Glory paced in front of her aunt and uncle's bedroom door, wishing the call was over.

"Why didn't you just tell Daddy you were breaking up with him?" Jillian poured a tiny bottle of liquor into a tall glass of iced tea, took a sip, and made an ugly face. "Yuck! Let's go for a ride," she said, pouring the drink into the sink. "We've been stuck in this house for days. Go put on your silk undies, and let's go out and be fascinating."

"But what if he gets off the phone—"

"I'm off the phone now," Uncle Bobby said, coming into the kitchen. "C'mon, girl. Let's talk." He took a seat at the kitchen table and nodded toward the empty chair across from him. "Jilly, what's good in that box Ruth gave you? Thought I didn't know, huh?"

"Um... well..." Jillian stuttered. "I don't know. Uh..."

"Put me a shot of rum in a tall glass of iced tea. Don't tell yo' mama." Uncle Bobby winked at the confused girls. "And you need to let up on them wine coolers, little girl. You ain't grown yet. Have a seat."

Her uncle had on his serious face, but to Glory's relief, he didn't look angry.

"Malcolm's a nice fella," Uncle Bobby began. "Different circumstances, I might even like 'im. Smart. Knows the Word. Got a lot to learn on some things, but he ain't thickheaded." He tasted the drink Jillian handed him. "Aaah! That's nice. Yeah, don't tell yo' mama."

"So, what did Malcolm say?" Glory asked. "Y'all talked for a long time."

"Well, I asked him what his intentions were. He said, and I quote, 'I intend for your niece to be my wife and the mother of my children.'" Bobby took another drink. "I almost cut the call right there, but I wanted to see what else he had to say."

Glory looked at Jillian and then down at the table. She kind of knew that was what Malcolm wanted, but hearing that he'd actually said it out loud to Uncle Bobby made it realer than she was ready to deal with.

"Don't look so scared," Uncle Bobby continued. "He knows how old you are. He said he's gonna wait as long as you want. After college, even. But he's not gon' let up. Gon' make sure you know how much you mean to him." Uncle Bobby laughed a little. "Ya' know, when I met Ellie, she was in college and I was in the army, 'bout to go to Korea. I didn't want her to forget about me, so I sent her five dollars a week. That was good money back then. I wasn't where I could send her presents and stuff. All I had was cash, so that's what I sent.

"She said she spent the first, maybe, twenty dollars, but then started saving it in case she didn't want me when I came back." He laughed a little. "She used that money to buy her wedding dress."

"I love that story," Jillian said.

"Anyway," Uncle Bobby continued, "Malcolm says he loves you, and he's gon' make sure you know it every day. Cain't say I blame 'im. Johnson women are mighty fine women. Make a man wanna give you everything in the world." He drained his glass.

When her uncle wasn't looking, Glory shrugged and batted her eyelashes at Jillian, who hid her laugh behind her own drink.

"I cain't say I'm okay with this, but I'm trusting you to be smart, missy. Understand?"

"Yes, Uncle Bobby, but—"

"Jilly, you make sure she know how to take care of business, 'cause you know her mama ain't tellin' her nothin.'"

"Don't worry, Daddy," Jillian said. "I made sure Cousin Baby has everything she—"

"Uncle Bobby, I'm breaking up with Malcolm when I get home," Glory blurted.

"Oh, really?" Uncle Bobby's eyebrows went up.

"Yeah," Glory said. "Please don't tell anybody. It's just that I'm too young for all of this." She held out her arms, jingling the bracelets. "I mean, I do love him, but I don't wanna be anybody's fiancée right now. I'm only seventeen, and I just—"

"Hey, slow down. You don't hafta explain it to me. I think you too young for this, too. I won't say nothin'. I'm just glad you making your own decision. Between Malcolm and yo' mama, don't seem like you get much say in what goes on. He don't give you no trouble, does he?"

"Nah, he's the best thing that ever happened to me," Glory said, "but I'm just not ready. And all this stuff... it's just too much."

"Yeah, that's what I tried to tell 'im. Funny, he said you the best thing that ever happened to him, too. Well, you go on and cut him loose. In a few years, when you ready, if he's who the Lord means for you, he'll still be there. C'mon, gimme a hug, and y'all go on out to play. Only got a couple more days till it's time to go. I'mma go see what's on TV. Oh... Malcolm said call him tonight, but I know you was gon' do that, anyway."

Glory hugged her uncle while Jillian headed for the car. Saying it out loud made the coming breakup feel real. She would call Malcolm that night, but she was definitely not calling him the next day. When she got home, she would start going back to work every day and even start taking the bus again. She would go back to living without Malcolm, and her mother would just have to understand.

———— ❧ ————

"HELLO?"

"Hi, Malcolm."

"Where were you?" Malcolm demanded.

"Huh? What do you mean?"

"Woman, there's a plane leaving from Jackson in two hours. I will have a ticket waiting at the airport and have you home before dark if you don't stop playin' dumb. Where were you, and why didn't I hear from you last night?"

"Malcolm, this is crazy. I was doing exactly what you told me to do," Glory snapped. "I was out having fun with my cousin. Exactly like you said!"

"Glory, who do you think you're talking to? Know what? You need to start packing, 'cause you coming home—"

"Malcolm, wait. Please." Glory took a deep breath. "I'm sorry for snapping. I was out with Jillian, and when we got in, I thought it was too late to call."

"Out where? Where were you that you couldn't find a phone?"

"A place in Jackson called New Edition. It had music and dancing and stuff."

"Jillian took you to a night club." It wasn't a question. At first he'd sounded cold and angry, but now Malcolm's voice had dropped to a terrible whisper.

"I guess," Glory said. "I've never been to one. And you said—"

"You were drinking?"

"No, of course not!"

"Watch your tone, and don't lie to me."

"Malcolm, I didn't do anything wrong. I was with Jillian all the time." Glory shifted the receiver to her other ear. "I only had orange pop, and she told me not to take my hand off my drinks. She didn't even let me go to the bathroom by myself. All I did was talk with her and her friends from school. I didn't even dance or anything."

"And you couldn't find a pay phone?"

"I'm sorry, Malcolm. I wanted to call, but... I was with college kids, and I thought I would look like a little kid, calling to check in." *Demon of lies and deceit!* Glory easily told the lies she'd rehearsed in her mind all morning.

The truth was, she hadn't wanted to call him. The dim lights and the smells of smoke and liquor in the lounge nearly panicked her enough to look for a pay phone, but Glory steeled herself to practice being without Malcolm. She'd sat in the club surrounded by strangers, drinking wine coolers and pretending to be worldly but reminded of Malcolm by the sound of the bracelets that clinked every time she moved.

After her fourth drink, though, she started feeling the blues, and after the fifth, she felt a revelation. She felt the pounding rhythm of the drums, and the twang of the steel guitar calling to her. The groaning organ and wailing horn stirred her soul, and suddenly, she understood the secret to catching the Holy Ghost. When the singer started moaning, she wanted to moan, too. And she knew now what made the church ladies dance and shout, and she raised toast after toast to hot sweat, cold drinks, and sweet, sinful blasphemy until her cousin declared she was done drinking for the night. And on the drive home, she prayed the bugs were all asleep, because she kept her face out of the window to keep the nausea down.

When Uncle Bobby told her that morning that Malcolm called three times while she and Jillian were out, she knew he'd be angry, and she was glad they were seven hundred miles apart. She'd actually thought of calling him when they'd gotten home from Jackson, but Jillian told her drunk calling was unladylike and the night would have to be their little secret.

"Malcolm, I'm sorry." Glory listened to silence for a long time before she heard Malcolm sigh and clear his throat.

"Glory, I almost lost you once," he said finally, his voice gentler. "After I talked to Bobby this morning, I was about to get in the car and come get you. When you're away from Chicago, I need to hear from you. Do you understand me?"

"Yes, Malcolm." Glory didn't try to argue. She was just glad he didn't sound angry anymore.

"Are we gonna have this discussion again?"

"No."

"Glory, I love you, and I couldn't take it if something happened to you. When you're not with me, I need to know where you are, okay?"

How does he always make me feel like I'm wrong? She'd only done exactly what he'd told her to do.

"Okay, Malcolm. I'm sorry I worried you." Glory sighed. *No chance of practicing being without him for the rest of this visit.*

"I'm sorry I was so rough," Malcolm said. "So, what all did you do yesterday?"

Glory tried to sound nonchalant, talking about the previous day's visit to Jackson State University. She tried not to gush about the dorm that looked like a fancy apartment building or the elegant brick courtyard, and she pretended the tree-lined paths through the quad were no big deal. She tried to sound like she had no interest in life as a college student. She failed.

"So you really liked the campus, huh?" Malcolm asked.

"Well, it was okay, I guess. My whole family went there, but I'm not. It's no big deal," Glory said. "What did you do yesterday?"

"I worried about you, remember? Um, we've never talked about it, but what schools do you wanna go to? Nothing outta state, right?"

"Malcolm, I don't waste time thinking about real college. I hafta go to junior college."

"Waste time? What do you mean 'hafta go to junior college'? Glory, talk to me. This is important."

Glory tried not to blame her mother, telling Malcolm that a university wasn't something she wanted and that her mother couldn't sign the financial aid forms or permission for the SAT or ACT tests because college was "full of demons and worldly temptations to devilment."

"She says godly women shouldn't want that type of life."

"Wow," Malcolm said. "I can't believe you're just now telling me this."

"I don't like to think about it. I got in trouble 'cause my guidance counselor called her at work about the tests and some other college forms. But, hey, I have a plan, and it'll be fine. I'm goin' to college. I'll just wait a year to start."

"So, your mother is protecting you from demons at college, but you get to party all night at adult clubs—"

"Malcolm, if you didn't say so, there's no way she woulda let me go anywhere with Jillian. Hey, guess what my Aunt Ruth gave me?"

Malcolm laughed a little. "Okay. What did Aunt Ruth give you?" Glory knew he was indulging her, allowing her to change the subject.

"A big box of silky things. Oh, wait, I'm just a kid. Never mind. Forget I mentioned it."

Malcolm's loud, long laughter surprised her. "So, now you're gonna try to distract me?"

"Is it working? Are you distracted?"

"Nope, I'm Superman, remember? I'll let it go for now, but we'll talk about school when you get home. And, yeah... we hafta do something different next year. Ten days without you is too long. I'll call you after watch service tonight. It'll be about twelve thirty, okay?"

"Okay. I'll talk to you tonight. Ten days does seem like forever, but you'll see me in two days." *And next year, it won't matter.*

Chapter 22

A little more than a week before, she would not have imagined it possible, but on this brisk Mississippi New Year's Day, Glory sat laughing beside Darnell in the front seat of the limo so her mother and Mr. Espy could spend one last hour together.

"So, Ponytails, when y'all comin' back?" Darnell asked as they rolled through the gray streets of Flora. "Pops gon' be mean as hell till he sees her again. Yo' mom's peach cobbler was the bomb."

"I wanna come back for spring break, but I don't know..." Glory said. "I'm sure we'll be back this summer."

"Why cain't you come back for spring break? Yo' man ain't gon' give you up for a full week no time soon, huh? Ya know, I really coulda showed you a good time. Nah, don't be rollin' yo' eyes. I mean fun stuff. I swear, I ain't tryin' to mess with you. Between yo' man and yo' cousin, Rick, I don't want no parts of you. There's plenty women out here that won't get me killed."

Glory laughed. "You know, you're not so bad when you have manners. I'm glad I didn't ask Malcolm to kill you."

"Yeah, me, too."

When the train arrived, Glory looked away while her mother and Mr. Espy said goodbye. He refused his tip again, but Darnell accepted his and declined a hug. "Naw, Ponytails. I ain't taking no chances. I ain't gon' try to hug you till you my sister. Maybe next year."

Glory laughed and accepted his handshake. "Nice meeting you, Darnell."

Just as Malcolm had in Chicago, Mr. Espy shook hands with the attendant and gave specific instructions for their care. Glory wasn't surprised to learn that Malcolm had arranged meal times and everything, including personal escorts everywhere, and that their attendant, Luke, was expecting them. When the ladies were settled into their compartment, Luke returned with a fancy snack tray and drinks.

"Mm-hm," Mary said. "See, Malcolm will give you anything. More than any man I ever married. More than even your daddy did."

"Thank you, Luke," Glory said as he placed the tray on the small table between them.

Luke handed a rose to Mary. "The tray is compliments of Mr. Espy. I'll be back at eight to take you to dinner."

Glory laughed at her mother's consternation. "Feels good, doesn't it?" She nibbled on a carrot stick. "Don't go gettin' spoiled."

"Well..." Mary reached for a celery stalk. "I guess it is kinda nice to have somebody thinkin' about you, but Lee just wants to get the last word 'cause I wouldn't let him spend no money on me."

"Really, Ma? You went out with him almost every day, and you paid for everything?"

"I certainly did," Mary said. "I'm not tryin' to get used to another man. I'm done with that mess. No, no, no. I'll enjoy the company, but I'm paying my own way."

"But, Ma, what if God sends somebody for you?"

"Baby, you know I trust God, but it's gon' take more than a week of dates to convince me it's God's plan."

"Mm-hm." Glory smirked. "But you made two peach cobblers, didn't you? And I love your new perfume."

"Little girl, you just hush." Mary giggled. "Stay outta grown folks' business."

They rode in silence for a while, Mary wearing her headphones and Glory watching the darkening sky. In the morning, they'd arrive in Chicago, and Malcolm would be waiting for her. He would hug her, push her hair back from her face, and look into her eyes. He wouldn't kiss her in public, but he'd say how much he wanted to. He'd drive her mother straight home and unload the car and maybe give her time to freshen up. Then for the rest of the day, he'd be at her side. When he finally took her home, the good-night kiss would weaken her... but she'd have to remember that she was still too young for him.

"You know, baby." Mary removed her headphones. "Malcolm's probably gon' ask for you when we get home."

"Ask for me?" Glory pretended to misunderstand the statement.

"He told your uncle he wants to marry you. I think he's gon' ask you soon."

Glory stared out of the window, unable to face her mother's excitement.

"What's the matter?" Mary frowned. "Ain't that what you want?"

"Mama, I can't marry Malcolm," Glory said finally. "I'm too young. I don't know any—"

"Oh, girl, don't be silly." Mary waved off Glory's concern. "You know everything you need to know. You can take care of a house as good as me. Raising babies comes naturally. And believe me, he'll teach you anything else you need to know."

"Mama, I don't wanna be with Malcolm anymore. That wasn't the first time he hit me. I don't wanna be with somebody—"

"Then you need to learn your place," Mary chided. "You watch your mouth and mind your tone, and he won't hafta do that. A man can only take so much disrespect, and baby, sometimes you just let these demons rule you."

"Mama, JT—Josiah—never hit me. No matter how mad he got, he didn't—"

"*No!* Josiah Jackson is a boy, and he did what boys do. He left! Things wasn't goin' his way, and he got hisself in trouble, so he left. That's what *boys* do. He left you and never looked back. A *man* won't do that. No matter what's happening, a man won't just up and leave. When you needed him, Malcolm was there, wasn't he? That's what a *man* does. That boy couldn'ta done that."

"But, Ma—"

"When you with a *man*, you take 'em how they come. If that means you get a lickin' till you learn, then you better learn faster. A godly woman don't throw away a good man over a few licks!"

"Ma," Glory asked, "why would God want that for anybody?"

"The Bible say a wife should be in submission to her husband. If she ain't, what's he supposed to do?"

"But Malcolm isn't my husband—"

"Baby, he's gonna be. We both know it, and you need to start acting like it."

Glory stifled an exasperated sigh. "Ma, I've been reading the Bible my whole life, and I know—"

"Little girl, you don't know nothin'," Mary snapped. "When I ran off with that boy at fifteen, I thought I knew everything. I was pregnant with my second child by the time we got to New York. And that boy said he love me, and you know what he did? He left! All the time he left, but I waited like a good, godly woman, and he come home again and again, 'cept I talked back and cussed him, and instead of puttin' me in my place, he just kept leaving. That weak boy left me to nurse four sick babies and then bury all of 'em. Then he was so weak he let the dope take him, and I had to bury him, too. That's what *boys* do. Malcolm is a good, godly man, and if he hafta knock the demons of rebellion and disrespect outta you, so be it. It's better than an ungodly boy leaving you with four dead babies!"

The force of her mother's words pressed Glory back in the seat. She'd heard the story of her mother's first husband and the death of her older siblings but never like this, with such venom. Glory watched her mother take deep breaths and whisper prayers. She recognized the ritual. It was her mother's way of calming herself when she felt the devil was attacking her.

"Mama," Glory finally asked, "why did you marry the old preacher? Was Aunt Ruth right? Why did you stay with him?"

Mary sighed. "Baby, God showed me the price of my rebellion. Before I run off, he would come to court me, but I didn't care. He'd be on the porch with Daddy, and I'd be in the barn with Mason. I was shameful. When I ran off, I paid the price of Job for being headstrong and spittin' on what God had for me. When I came back, and he still wanted me, I knew God gave me another chance. I was back for a month when he married me. But I didn't know nothin'. I talked to him like I talked to Mason. He tried to set me straight, but I was hardheaded, and he was still smartin' from how I shamed him when I left.

"I got pregnant right away, but he said it wasn't his 'cause it was too soon. Made me take cotton root and get rid of it. I didn't want to." Mary paused, looking down at her hands. "But he changed my mind straight away. I knew I would have another one, anyway."

"Oh, God, Mama," Glory whispered. "Why didn't you ever tell me I coulda had another brother or sister? Why did you stay with him?"

"'Cause, baby, that was my husband!" Mary insisted. "That's who God sent for me. When I was hurt and broken, he was waiting for me. He was harsh sometimes, but he knew the Word, and the Bible say the wife is supposed to learn from her husband and not shame him. I admit I shamed him a few times. He thought he was too old to make babies, so if a baby was comin', he say I shamed him and make me take cotton root. Got to where I'd just not tell 'im and take cotton root, anyway. Times I didn't know till too late, he just... one he couldn't knock loose... but... she didn't... never even cried..."

Mary's words trailed off, her voice breaking. She turned to face the window. "Girl, you don't need to care 'bout none of this old stuff. You ain't gon' shame Malcolm. You ain't got the demons I had. I make sure of it."

"Mama," Glory whispered, her voice choked with rage that could only come out as tears. "That old preacher is burning in hell."

"I wasn't a good wife, baby," Mary said, her voice again steady and sure. "But he made me a godly woman. When yo' daddy came along, I knew how to be in submission to my husband. I was the good wife for your daddy. When you marry Malcolm, you'll be the good wife, 'cause I made sure you know how."

Glory stared at her mother—a strong, badly wounded woman who deserved so much better. *What kind of God allows this? What did God prove by forcing Mama to endure this... to kill her own? What kind of God does she believe in?*

They took their dinner in their room, and Glory didn't leave her mother's side for the rest of the trip.

Chapter 23

As morning broke on January 2nd, Glory looked out at the passing scenery of the waking city. In a few minutes, their attendant would tap on their door, announcing their arrival in Union Station. Glory glanced over at her mother sitting with her eyes closed, wearing headphones and a peaceful smile, obviously enjoying one of the tapes from Malcolm. Glory looked around the small but comfortable room. If they'd taken this trip by bus, by now they'd be cramped, sweaty, and dirty. Thanks to Malcolm, they'd traveled in luxury. The compartment went dark as they pulled into the station. Moments later, the lights flickered back on, and Luke lightly tapped on the door.

"Come in!" Glory called as she and her mother gathered their belongings.

"There's no rush, ladies." Luke motioned for them to slow down. "Your ride is right outside. I'll take these and meet you at the stairs."

"Thank you, Luke," Mary said as the attendant grabbed their overnight bags. "You're so sweet."

They followed Luke out to the waiting electric cart, and Glory shook his hand the way Malcolm had taught her. At the entrance to the first-class lounge, Glory shook the cart driver's hand as well and said a last goodbye to the trappings of luxury. There would not be another trip like this, but that was okay. She was Church Girl, and she didn't need this stuff anyway.

"HI, MALCOLM." GLORY slipped her hand into Malcolm's, rolling her eyes at the painted-up blonde with the over-teased hair who was trying to slide her business card into his shirt pocket. Glory might be breaking up with him soon, but that day, he still belonged to her—blondie had to go. The tall thin woman in the fluffy mink coat fit perfectly in the fancy world of the first-class lounge. With her sparkly hair and makeup, licking her thin lips and leaning too close to Malcolm like she was about to bite him, smelling of smoke and perfume, this flashy woman was definitely not Malcolm's type. Glory wanted to laugh in her face.

"Hi, Glory." Malcolm's mouth turned up in an amused smirk. He handed the woman back the business card and dismissed her with a wave then pulled Glory into his arms. "God, I missed you so much. You're never leaving me again." Breaking all protocol, he held her close and kissed her forehead right there in the crowded lounge.

"I missed you, too," Glory said. She really had missed him, and it was good to feel his arms around her. She closed her eyes and breathed in his scent, his cologne, and the warm, rich leather of his long black coat. She would really miss that.

"How 'bout we get me home, and y'all can spend the rest of the day together?" Mary said, not hiding the amusement in her voice. "I'm getting weary of all this fancy livin'."

"Oh, you didn't enjoy the limo or train rides, Mother Bishop?" Malcolm asked, taking the bag Mary carried and leading them to the baggage claim area.

"I liked it just fine," Mary said. "I just wanna get home to my own normal stuff, that's all."

Malcolm kept a hand on Glory's shoulder, guiding them through the train station, even taking her with him to get the car, while Mary and a redcap waited with their luggage.

"I saw that look back there with the blonde woman," Malcolm said as they walked to the car. "You're cute when you're jealous."

"Why should I be jealous?" Glory held her head high, with feigned innocence. "I'm Glorious, remember?"

"There's no way I could ever forget." Malcolm squeezed her hand. "You're my *beloved*, and who is my desire toward?"

"Me." Glory giggled. *I'm so gonna miss you!*

"So, what's in the boxes?" Malcolm asked, looking down at the two white boxes he carried for her.

"Pies for you and Herschel. Pecan from my grandmother and sweet potato from my aunt."

Malcolm smiled. "Make sure you tell them I said thanks."

At the car, he unlocked the door, waited for Glory to get in, and handed her the boxes. Before closing the door, he leaned in and kissed her. "I've been waiting for too long to do that. Maybe next year, I'll hop on a plane right after Christmas Day service, and then we'll fly back for New Year's Eve." He kissed her again. "Yeah... you're never leaving me this long again."

Glory felt her resolve wavering as he started the car. He loved her and never wanted to be without her. He gave her everything she wanted and the freedom to enjoy it—as long as she didn't question him or argue.

No! Sometimes, she couldn't help but argue... because sometimes Malcolm was wrong. Glory was not her mother, and she would not have her mother's life. As they pulled up to Mary and the redcap, Glory fingered the bracelets that she'd grown accustomed to. Riding out of the train station tunnel into the gray Chicago morning, Glory lowered the visor, shielding her eyes from the late-morning sun. As much as she'd enjoyed her time down south, it was good to come home, and thanks to Malcolm and the comfort of the first-class train ride, she felt wide awake and refreshed. She glanced over at him. His mirrored shades made him look like a cool TV cop: serious, tough, and really cute. *Am I crazy for breaking up with him, giving up the benefits of his love and protection?*

But Glory couldn't shake the vision of what her mother had suffered under the *love and protection* of the old preacher, the torture she'd endured at the hands of her own husband, and the lessons her mother had learned for shaming that *godly* man. She returned her gaze to the front as they pulled onto Lake Shore Drive. In a week or so, she would break up with Malcolm, and that would be that.

"So, have you decided what schools you're applying to?" Malcolm asked a little louder than Glory thought necessary.

"I'm going to Kennedy King or Loop, downtown," Glory answered. *Please, Malcolm, don't do this right now!*

"I mean *real* college," Malcolm pushed. "It's time to get your financial aid forms in, and you hafta sign up for the ACT and SAT—"

"But, Malcolm," Glory said carefully, "I told you I'd work for a year and—"

"Wait for a year? Why?"

"I really just don't think it's that important," Glory said quietly. *Please stop! Please stop!*

"How could you think education isn't important? If we're at an event with Dr. Hargraves or Dr. Langdon, how could you talk to their wives with only a junior college education?" Malcolm looked up at the rearview mirror. "I mean, 'The heart of the prudent getteth knowledge, and the ear of the wise seeketh knowledge,' right, Mother Bishop?"

"Absolutely," Mary agreed from the back seat. "And—"

"So," Malcolm interrupted, talking to Glory, "tomorrow, you're gonna see your school counselor and get financial aid forms and whatever paperwork you need to start applying to schools, understand?"

"Yes, Malcolm, but—" Glory started, glancing at him.

"Mother Bishop, what's wrong with your daughter?" Malcolm asked, again a little too loudly. "Is she trying to argue with me again?"

"Lord, I hope not," Mary said. "She should know better by now."

"But we've already talked about—" Glory tried again.

"Mother Bishop, your daughter seems to keep forgetting herself. I need an educated woman by my side. You understand, right?"

"Of course, Malcolm," Mary said.

"Then, I trust you to see that she gets her paperwork completed this week, and I'll take her to look at schools on the weekends, okay?"

"I'll see to it, Malcolm," Mary said. "Don't you worry."

Even though this was exactly what she wanted, Glory's stomach churned as she listened to her mother going against everything she believed in, bending her own will to suit this *godly man*.

Please, Malcolm, you don't understand. You don't need to do this. Glory listened in silence as Malcolm listed the schools she could choose from, all colleges and universities in the city and nearby suburbs. She couldn't get excited at the prospect of touring the University of Chicago or the possibility of going to Loyola, because she understood that her mother's broken spirit was the only thing allowing this to happen.

When Malcolm reached across the seat and gave her hand a gentle, triumphant squeeze, Glory returned it, even though accepting his manipulation felt like she was lying *and* selling her soul to the devil.

MALCOLM STOPPED THE car in front of Herschel's salon, and Glory was happy to see the security gate open. Even though the sign said Closed and the blinds were drawn, Herschel was probably working inside, maybe cleaning up from the New Year's Eve's spa party.

"I'll only be a minute," Glory said. "I'm just gonna drop off the pies and—"

"Tell you what," Malcolm interrupted. "I'll get Mother Bishop home and come back for you in a half hour." He looked up into the rearview mirror. "No need to keep you waiting, right, Mother Bishop?"

"That's fine with me, Malcolm," Mary said. Glory could tell her mother was anxious to get home. Though always agreeable to whatever Malcolm said, her tone was not as warm as it had been earlier.

Glory got out of the car and went to the door. She pressed the doorbell and laughed at the look on Herschel's face when he peered through the blinds.

"Happy New Year!" she said when he opened the door. She held up the pie box. "Want some company? I have goodies for you."

"Of course, Glory-Glory! I always want your company! Come in, darling!"

Glory turned and waved to Malcolm before going inside and locking the door.

The salon had seen better days, but it wasn't a total wreck. Confetti and streamers had been swept into piles, large black trash bags bulged with the telltale shapes of bottles and cans, and the chill in the room meant Herschel had the fans going to blow out whatever smoke had filled the air. Glory felt kind of glad she'd missed the party. Herschel's work clothes that day were denim overalls and a lavender dress shirt. Glory was surprised to see his cornrowed hair tied under a plain red-and-white bandana.

"Are you okay?" she asked. "What's with the bandana? It doesn't match."

"Well, darling," Herschel said, "if I knew you were coming, I'd have put on a wig. Got too much to do to be pretty today, but you brought goodies, so it's break time!"

Glory followed Herschel to the kitchen, stepping over piles and around bags. "I brought you sweet potato and pecan pies from my aunt and grandmother." She placed the box on the table while Herschel turned on the kettle and grabbed two mugs.

"So, did they like the products?" Herschel asked, adding tea bags to the mugs.

"Oh, wow, yeah. They really liked your stuff. My aunt and uncle *really, really* loved it. And my mother met a man and spent the whole trip smelling like peach cobbler."

"Oh, really?" Herschel laughed. "Ms. Mary had a good time, huh?"

"Herschel, I haven't seen my mother that happy in years. She was so giggly." Glory placed two small slices of each pie on a paper plate.

"Well, good for her! Is she gonna keep seeing him?"

"I doubt it," Glory said. "I mean, he is in Mississippi. Maybe they'll write."

"So... did you have fun, Glory-Glory?" Herschel asked, taking a seat at the table and grabbing a slice of sweet potato pie. "Did you do what I said—talk to the country boy and not think about Malcolm?"

Glory laughed. "I thought you'd never ask."

"Uh-oh. What did you do?"

Glory's tale of her holiday trip was punctuated by Herschel's gasps and howls of laughter. He roared to hear himself described as a mad scientist making love potions, and he cheered when Glory told of kissing James and deciding to break up with Malcolm.

"Girl," Herschel said, catching his breath, "I'm glad you didn't tell me about those bracelets before you left. I can see why your uncle went off. I can't imagine any man being okay with Malcolm pursuing his little girl like this. Aw, quit rollin' your eyes. You know what I mean!"

"Well, I'm not a little girl. And I couldn't avoid thinking about Malcolm, but I'm just not ready for him." Glory looked at her watch. "I've gotta go in about ten minutes—"

"Okay, listen. I hafta tell you something." Herschel stood and walked to the stove to add more hot water to his cup. "JT stopped by."

Glory sipped her tea. "Who?"

Herschel looked over his glasses. "I'm sure you remember JT," he said dryly. "Cute little boy, thought he was your husband. Snagged yo' cherry right over there—"

"Okay, okay," Glory said, nearly dropping her mug. "I know who you're talking about!"

"You sure? I could tell you more... like the time you tried yo' best to be pregnant with his—"

"I said, okay! I know who he is. What did he want?" *I don't care.*

Herschel returned to his seat and cut another slice of pecan pie. "Lord, this pie is good! He was looking for you, of course."

"Oh? What for?" *I don't care.* Glory kept her tone casual. She would not be charmed by JT again, no matter what he had to say.

"He was home for a couple of days. Asked how you were and said to tell you hi." Herschel looked over his glasses again. "Oh, girl, don't give me that look. You been pining for him for months. I know you mad, and rightly so, but it's okay to miss him."

Glory looked again at her watch. Malcolm would be outside any minute. "No, Herschel, it's not okay to miss him, and besides, I don't. Know who I miss? I miss James, the nice boy I met on the train. And I even miss Darnell, since I learned he's not so icky. And I'll really miss Malcolm in a few weeks. But I *do not* miss Josiah Jackson."

"Wow," Herschel said. "Feels like there should be some kinda flag waving behind you after that speech. Maybe crowds cheering—"

"I hate when you act like I'm being silly," Glory whispered, not up looking at him. "Herschel, my life is almost like a normal girl's life. I don't need JT anymore. Okay?"

"Who said you need him?" Herschel stood to clear the plates. "All I said is you still miss him. He was your first love. It's not like you can just forget him."

"Well, I need to forget him." Glory pulled on her coat. Malcolm was probably outside waiting. "I need to forget JT just like he forgot me." She headed out of the kitchen and back into the salon with Herschel close behind.

"Well, darling," Herschel said, "I don't know what happened, but I don't think he forgot about you. That young man didn't look like—"

Glory stopped at the door, her hand on the doorknob. "Please, let it go. I'm over JT. For real." She peeked through the blinds at Malcolm's long brown Cadillac idling out front. She glanced at her watch. There was still a minute left.

"Herschel, is it bad for me to break up with Malcolm *after* I get my college stuff set up?" Glory asked. She was done talking about JT.

"Hmph. Is it bad for you to use a man to get what you want? Are you *really* asking me that, Glory-Glory? Is it bad to walk away from somebody *after* you finally get some—"

Glory hung her head. "Sorry I asked." She hugged her best friend and promised to be at work at least two days that week. She could always count on Herschel to tell her the truth, even when she didn't want to hear it.

"SO, HOW DID YOU LIKE the tape of the Christmas service?" Malcolm asked as he pulled away from the salon and headed back downtown. "Not what you expected, huh?"

"No," Glory answered. "It was so quiet. Soft—"

"Soft? You think I'm soft?" Malcolm laughed. "How you just gon' call Superman soft?"

"No, Malcolm. *You're* not soft. You're the toughest man in the world," Glory gushed, batting her eyelashes at him. "There's nobody tougher than you."

Malcolm reached out and stroked her cheek. "That's cute. When did you learn to do that?"

Glory giggled. "Aunt Ellie tried to teach my mother. You shoulda seen her—"

"Well, you picked it up pretty good." Malcolm laughed again. "Just make sure you don't bat those glorious eyes at nobody but me, okay?"

"So, where are we going?" Glory looked around. The late-morning traffic moved slowly, giving her a chance to watch the waves rolling in on Lake Michigan. A few diehard runners braved the freezing January air out along the path, bending and stretching in the patches of sunlight that completed the typical scene of morning on Lake Shore Drive.

"We're going to the mission. You up for a long day and a late night?" Malcolm asked. "I told your mom you'd be home around midnight."

"That's pretty late, Malcolm, and I wanted—"

"I know... but you probably stay up later than that sometimes, right? And it's not like tomorrow is a big day at school. It'll be fine." Malcolm reached across the seat and patted Glory's hand. The discussion was over. After she'd been allowed ten days of freedom down south, Glory once again belonged to Malcolm, and her plans would be whatever he said they were... *for now.*

THE SOUTH GARDEN MISSION looked like any other old Michigan Avenue office building on Chicago's South Side. Six stories of gray concrete and greenish-black windows, a metal plaque near the double glass doors announcing that the mission had been established in 1922 and moved to this building in 1972, and a white neon cross beckoning them to "Come Unto Jesus."

Approaching the building, Glory was grateful for Malcolm's hand on her shoulder as the group of men in front of the building cheerfully greeted them. Malcolm shook hands or bumped fists and chests all around and even handed out a few dollars, keeping a firm hand on Glory yet not introducing her to these men who obviously knew him well. She kept silent and avoided eye contact with the bundled-up men in dirty coats and mismatched gloves.

Inside the building, the marble reception desk was staffed by an old man. The nameplate on the desk simply said Tutu. The old man's skin looked like ancient tree bark, his frayed brown suit hung loose on his thin frame, and his pinned name tag was slightly askew. When Tutu smiled, it looked to Glory like every other tooth in his mouth was missing, but when he came out from behind the desk and embraced Malcolm, he laughed and moved with the strength of a very young man.

"Brother Malcolm, my son," Tutu said, "you bless me every time I see you."

"Pops, I see you almost every day." Malcolm laughed as they hugged.

"And I am reminded of how great God is almost every day, my son." Tutu's red-yellow eyes landed on Glory, and his face lit up. "And who is this vision? She is like the Queen of Sheba herself."

Glory felt herself blushing and lowered her head. Malcolm reached out and lifted her chin. "Pops, this is my lady, Glory. She's an angel and the light of my life. Glory, this is Tutu. He's been like a father to me."

When Tutu took both of Glory's hands in his, she realized that of all the people they'd spoken to, this was the first person Malcolm had allowed to touch her. Up close, the old man's smile showed brown stumps in some of the gaps that had once held teeth. His dark eyes shone as bright as his smile. He squeezed her small hands in his rough knobby ones.

"I will call her *daughter* soon?" Tutu asked. He looked at Glory but directed his question to Malcolm. "Has this beauty actually tamed the beast?"

Glory blushed and lowered her head again. Tutu's musical accent reminded her of the wise old oracle in a fairy tale. He made everything sound magical.

Malcolm squeezed Glory's shoulder. "Maybe one day, Pops, but let's not rush it. You know the Lord tamed me a long time ago."

"No, son. The almighty subdued you. But the princess..." Tutu squeezed Glory's hands again. "Only the princess tames. You know Adam lived wild with the beasts until Eve—"

"Okay," Malcolm conceded, holding up his hands. "I get it. But let's not spook the princess, okay?"

Glory looked around the reception area while the two men talked as if she weren't there. Giant photos of nature scenes, with Bible verses, covered most of the walls from floor to ceiling. The off-white tile floor had randomly placed black tiles inscribed with more Bible verses. A six-foot wooden cross hanging on the wall behind the reception desk, lit from behind, glowed against a photo mural of a partly cloudy sky. And from somewhere, soft Christian music filled the air, making Glory feel like she was in God's office building.

Following Malcolm through the building, Glory understood why he loved the mission. There was warmth and peace here. Every man he passed greeted him as a friend and a brother—more true respect than he got from the boys at church. The women looked him in the eye when they spoke to him and then went about their business, not fussing or fawning, giving no extra smiles or flirting. Everybody was just so good and open. There was no sign of her mother's angry God here. Glory found herself smiling. JT would have liked the mission.

On the first floor, beyond the lobby, they toured the grand sanctuary, dining room, and kitchens. Glory laughed when Malcolm was tackled by a group of toddlers in the nursery and challenged to a Biblical duel by an old man in the library. Most of the second-floor rooms featured everything from classes to clinics, and the third through fifth floors housed the men's, women's, and family shelters. On the sixth floor, Malcolm led Glory through a maze of hallways hung with family portraits, stopping to introduce her to a few people and pointing out the apartments and lounges of the residential staff. Finally, he opened a heavy security door marked Staff Only, leading to a metal staircase with an emergency elevator to the roof.

"In the summer, we come up to the roof to kick back," Malcolm said as they reached the top landing. "This is where I spent a lotta time when I first came here. C'mon."

He opened the door, and Glory followed him out into the freezing January air. In spite of the cold, the perfectly clear day allowed the sun to create warm spots on the tar roof.

"I was born again on a cold day just like this," Malcolm said. "I'd actually snuck up here that day to jump. I was feeling that lost."

"That's hard to believe," Glory said. "You're not like that."

"Not now. But back then, I was a mess."

"You always say God worked on you. What did he do?"

Malcolm sighed and took a couple of steps away then turned back and shoved his hands in his pockets. "You know the story of Paul?"

"Yeah. He was a bad guy who was changed and wrote most of the New Testament."

"Well, I'm not gonna add anything to the Bible." Malcolm laughed. "But I was struck down and blinded and wandered up here. It was Tutu who washed the scales from my eyes."

"Okay..."

Malcolm smiled. "You don't understand, do you?"

"Not even a little," Glory admitted.

"Okay." Malcolm sighed. "In my wild times, I was pretty bad. You name it, I did it. At first it was to get sent back to Louisiana, 'cause people sent their bad kids to live down south to get straightened out. I cut up in school till I got kicked out. I fought. I stole stuff, and you know I had plenty of money." Malcolm hung his head. "And I hurt people because I could.

"But my dad knew too many of the right people, so the police always just brought me home. I never got in any real trouble, and I started liking it." He began pacing slowly. "And see, my mother, she's got her own power thing going on. She's got these society clubs and things outside of the church with all these rich people with connections. And all these society kids wanted some of the wild life that I had, so they started coming to me like their parents came to Mother. I did some pretty bad things and messed up a lot of 'em."

Glory tried to imagine Malcolm as a tough teenager surrounded by rich kids in preppy sweaters, looking for a good time. She fought back the urge to laugh when the image of the Fonz, Richie, Ralph, and Potsie appeared in her mind.

"Then, when I was fifteen," Malcolm continued, "God said, 'Enough!' I still don't know exactly what happened. Somebody found me on the Dan Ryan Expressway, bleeding through my ears. Drugs. Maybe I fell. Mighta got beat up and dumped. Mighta got hit by a car. Maybe I jumped from the overpass. Don't know."

"Oh my God, Malcolm."

"It wasn't that bad. I was asleep. It was more messed up for my parents." Malcolm shook his head. "But they got back at me for it. After I was in a coma for a couple of weeks and the doctors told them I was gonna be a vegetable forever, my parents decided to let me go. Dad wanted to make sure the last thing I heard was the Word of God, so he stood by my bed and read the Bible while they pulled the plug. Yeah." Malcolm spat on a dark patch of the roof. "My parents pulled the plug."

Glory just stared. Another *Oh my God* didn't seem appropriate.

"But see, apparently, God wasn't done. Dad says I talked—that I said, 'Not yet.' He got the idea that it was the Word of God keeping me alive, so he pulled up a chair and kept reading. He read the whole Bible, and then he read it again."

This time, Malcolm wiped away a tear. Glory moved closer to him.

"So now," Malcolm continued, "the whole church is getting involved 'cause the pastor's voice is gone. They're reading in shifts, and then other churches start coming, and then donations start coming. So, I'm fifteen years old, in a coma, and churches all over the South Side are getting together to come read the Bible to a thug who turned out a lotta their kids."

"Is that why you know the Bible by heart?" Glory asked.

"Basically." Malcolm smiled thinly. "See, it turns out miracles take longer than people think, and God's time ain't our time. Eventually, somebody figured out getting a good boom box and a few tapes of every version of the Bible and just lettin' it play would do the same thing. When they figured out I would probably be that way forever, Mother took me back down south."

Glory hugged Malcolm. "At least you got to go back home. How long were you in a coma?"

"More than three years. I started waking up when I was nineteen."

"Oh my God. You heard the Bible nonstop for that long?"

"Honestly, I don't know. Maybe longer." Malcolm shrugged. "They don't really know how much I could hear or when I started hearing. What I do know is that I could hear and respond for a long time before I could actually tell anybody to turn that crap off. But by then, it was already deep in here." He tapped his temple. "When I finally woke up, I couldn't talk straight—my words came out all King James-ish. Speech therapists thought I was delusional because I talked like Jesus. They thought I'd snapped for real. Took me two years to get back to *almost* right. Had to learn to walk again, too. Hmph. Everything.

"Well, then," Malcolm continued, "folks from up here started making pilgrimages to look at me. I was a living miracle." He spat on the roof again. "Proof of the power of the Word... I knew all the Bibles by heart... I hated that so much. And then when I was close to normal, I started working on catching up on school, and Mother started with the tutors—society girls wanting to see if there was any bad boy left in me."

"Your mother was just trying to help—"

"But those girls weren't. Some actually came from up here to see if I remembered them. One day, I just left. I was twenty-two and had a bunch of money. I wound up coming right back here to Chicago." Malcolm looked out to the horizon. "Turns out the lakes and swamps down south scared the hell outta me. Too dark. Too many trees. I was used to this lake right here. Only thing scary is the water. And over there..." He pointed west. "The West Side, nothing but the lowest scum in the city. Even on my worst days, I didn't go there."

Glory decided not to tell him how wrong he was about the West Side.

"North Side?" Malcolm pointed north toward the downtown Chicago skyline. "Kids from up there used to come looking for me. But the South Side..." Malcolm turned back south and smiled. "That was my stomping ground. All of it, from Beverly Hills to Pill Hill to the projects. When I came back to Chicago, I tried to come back to that old life. And a lot of people wanted me back. They thought I'd been locked up or something and wanted to run with me again."

Glory pictured Malcolm in his wild times, not as a tough-talking teenager but something much worse: the *hellion* he'd told her about.

Malcolm sighed and hugged Glory closer. "But I couldn't do it. As bad as I wanted to be who I once was, the Word was stuck in my head. When you trying to cuss at somebody, and the words of Christ come out, or when a woman is throwin' it on you and your actual thought is *Thou hast made thy beauty to be abhorred and hast opened thy feet to everyone that passed by and multiplied thy whore-doms,* there's no way you can stay in that life. The Word was in my head twenty-four seven. I wanted to blow my brains out."

He looked down at Glory. "Do you remember when I came back to church, 'bout five years ago? Everybody wanted to lay hands on me and stuff? You had to be about eleven or twelve, right?"

"Yeah, I remember," Glory said. "I didn't think much about it. There was a commotion about you coming home and it being a miracle."

"Yeah. It was a lotta noise, and I left. I left the church and my parents' house. I lived on the money I had till it ran out, then I tried to hustle, but my hustle had always been dirty, and the Lord wouldn't let me do that anymore, so I was on the street and then wound up here... and somebody recognized me."

Glory tried to look up at Malcolm, but he held her too tightly, trembling. She could feel his heart pounding.

"Somebody who hit rock bottom because of me and was glad that I was finally there, too, told me how his parents died while he was in jail." Malcolm's voice broke, and he took a deep breath. "When I snuck up here to this roof, Tutu was up here, smoking. Asked me what I was doing. Asked me to stop and talk for a minute. Started telling me the story of Paul... pissed me off, 'cause I knew it already inside and out. But then he put his hand over my face and said, 'Son, I'm taking the scales from yo' eyes. Ya know these streets and these people, and they wanna listen to ya. God gave ya life an' 'is Word to minister to them.'" Malcolm sniffed and cleared his throat. "Old man broke me all the way down."

Glory held on to Malcolm until he stopped shaking.

"So, by the time my parents found me"—Malcolm was cool again as he led Glory down the staircase, back to the first floor—"I'd been here a few months, giving testimony and teaching. Mother tried to drag me back, saying I was still sick, but Dad actually listened to me. He liked what I was doing and agreed to build a real chapel here for the night ministry if I came back to church sometimes. That's why it's called the Porter Chapel. Then the church, after I came back, paid for me to go to school as long as I come back and work there for seven years when I finished."

"Seven years? Like Jacob? Malcolm, that's a long time."

"Yeah," Malcolm admitted, "but I was asleep and useless for almost that long. It'll go by fast. Anyway... so then Mother had to go one better and remodeled the Devereaux-St. Jacques women's center on the fifth floor. Yes, she bought and paid for the whole fifth floor."

"Wow. I didn't know Mother Porter was like that," Glory said.

"Oh, Mother is somebody you definitely want on your side." Malcolm chuckled. "She thinks being first lady at Lakeshore Church is the same as being queen. She always makes things happen. All the donations that came in when I was sick... she set up a trust fund with investments and stuff. It'll take care of me forever as long as I don't make her mad."

"Malcolm, that's not nice. Mother Porter is awesome," Glory chided. "She's nice to everybody."

Malcolm smiled and shook his head. "No. She's polite to everybody. There's a difference."

Glory spent the rest of the day watching Malcolm in his world. This Malcolm was nothing like he was at church, and she honestly wished she could stay with him. The way he talked and moved, she even wished the other girls could see him... a little. She did notice a couple of the women standing closer than coworkers, touching his arm a little too long. Maybe those were the ones who'd visited the parsonage.

Glory pushed down her flash of jealousy. It wasn't her business. It wasn't like she planned to keep him. But she could if she wanted to.

SEATED IN THE FRONT row of the nearly full Porter Chapel, waiting for the night ministry service to end, Glory thanked God she hadn't dozed off. It had been an exhausting day. She glanced at her watch—it was nearly eleven o'clock—then looked up just in time to catch the baby handed to her by a smiling woman in a waitress uniform rushing to the front to sing.

Malcolm paced casually as he spoke, just like on the tape, like he was in a room with just a few friends. Glory made a mental note to suggest he speak this way to youth services at the regular church.

"Have you ever had God just hand you heaven on a platter?" Malcolm asked the congregation. "I mean, something so good that you look around and think, 'God made a mistake, 'cause there's no way this is for me'?"

The crowd smiled and nodded.

"I mean, have you felt *so* blessed—I'm not talking about 'woke me up this morning' blessings. I mean a job you didn't apply for, unexpected check in the mail—for kids, an A on a test you didn't study for..."

There was more laughter. Children in pajamas clapped.

"What do you do with those blessings?" Malcolm asked. "I bet I know. You might say, 'Thank you, Lord,' and keep on stepping. Or you convince yourself that you really did something to deserve it, and it was about time God came through for you." He looked around the room. "Uh-huh. Y'all know what I'm talking about. But how many of us will make ourselves worthy of those blessings?"

Glory found herself smiling, watching Malcolm work the congregation.

"Who in here will bust their butt working that job they accidentally got? Which one of y'all will invest that unexpected check in something other than new clothes... in something that will last? Kids, how many of y'all are gonna start studying and actually earn that next A? Who's gonna take care of the gifts God gives them this year?"

People raised their hands and clapped. Malcolm wiped away a little sweat.

"A lot of y'all know my story," he continued. "Lord knows I'm not perfect and don't deserve to be alive, let alone get a true blessing from the Lord. But last year, God handed me heaven on a silver platter. If y'all haven't had a chance yet, look here toward the front... but not too hard. Wave to my lady—Glory."

Glory squeezed her eyes shut for a second then turned around and waved to everybody behind her. She'd be sure to pinch Malcolm for this later.

"I've been knowing her for a while actually, but this year, she arose like light in the darkness. 'She is gracious and full of compassion and righteous.'"

Glory lowered her head and sighed, glad Malcolm wasn't close enough to lift her chin.

Malcolm leaned against the podium with his hands in his pockets, looking thoughtful. "In Hosea, the prophet writes: 'And I will betroth thee unto me forever. Yea, I will betroth thee unto me in righteousness and in judgment and in lovingkindness and in mercies.'"

The congregation gasped.

Glory's eyes went wide. *No!*

"And the author of Proverbs," Malcolm continued, "writes: 'Whoso findeth a wife findeth a good thing and obtaineth favour of the Lord.'"

From his pocket, he withdrew a small red box. The singing waitress rushed forward and grabbed her baby from Glory.

Glory covered her face and prayed. *Please, Malcolm, don't do this. Oh, God, please don't let him be doing this. Not here in front of these people.*

Somewhere in the back of the room, a woman sobbed loudly. Glory peered through her fingers to see Malcolm in front of her on one knee, an open ring box in his outstretched hand. It matched her bracelets and earrings. *How long has he been planning this?*

"Glory? Will you be my wife?" Malcolm asked.

She took a deep breath and lowered her hands. There was no way she could say no to Malcolm in his world surrounded by his people. "Yes," she whispered.

Malcolm's hands trembled, and there were tears in his eyes when he put the ring on her finger. The congregation went wild, the saxophone started up, and Glory and Malcolm were crushed in a throng of hugs. For the time being, she would stand here accepting hugs and compliments, taking it like a woman. *Demons of lies and deceit!*

After all, she was breaking up with him, anyway. What did it really matter?

———— ❦ ————

GLORY JUMPED WHEN MALCOLM reached across the seat and laid his hand on hers. "What's the matter?" he asked

She twisted the ring on her finger. "You told my uncle you weren't gonna do this now, but you had it planned all along."

Malcolm sighed. "I said I wouldn't *marry* you now. You coulda said no."

Glory rolled her eyes. "Yeah, right. In there in front of all your people? I couldn't do that to you."

"So, what are you saying?"

"I don't know," Glory said. But the truth was she did know. She just didn't know how to say it. "I'm too young to get married now."

"We're not getting married *now*." Malcolm turned a corner a little too hard then slowed down.

"And I don't want babies for a long time, at least till I'm almost thirty," Glory pressed on. Maybe he would reconsider the engagement but keep dating her.

"Woman, calm down," Malcolm groaned. "I love you, but I'm not rushing you to get married next week." He reached over and squeezed her hand again. "After you start college, we'll think about setting a date, okay?"

"Okay." Glory twisted the ring again.

STANDING IN THE HALLWAY outside her apartment, Glory accepted her *fiancé's* good-night kiss.

"Happy New Year, Glory."

"Happy New Year, Malcolm."

"Hey..." He pushed her hair aside, wiping a tear away with his thumb. "What's the matter?"

"I don't know." Glory choked back a sob. "I'm think I'm just tired. It's been a long day, and I'm just feeling all mushy right now."

"Okay," Malcolm said, kissing her again. "Go on in. I'll see you in the morning. Good night, Glorious."

"Good night."

After a long and emotional day, Glory cried herself to sleep, trying not to think of kissing Malcolm good night in the hallway littered with Barbie shoes.

Chapter 24

Gloria:
 I am quite excited that you have accepted our dear Malcolm's proposal. Please call at our home for luncheon on Saturday next at half past noon. Do include your parents.
 Best Regards,
 Mrs. Anita Porter
 First Lady
 Lake Shore Christian Fellowship Church

"Hmph." Herschel dropped the fancy notecard on the table and turned back to stirring the pot on the stove. "That first lady is a piece of work, and you 'bout to be stuck with her for the rest of your life."

"Why?" Glory reached for the delicate ivory paper with the frayed edge. "What's wrong?" She turned the card over in her hands, tracing the monogramed *A. D. S. P.* with her index finger.

"What's wrong, darling, is that the bougie heffa knows good and damn well your father died a long time ago, and furthermore"—Herschel slammed the wooden spoon on the pot—"she's sitting back, waiting for you to look stupid 'cause you have no idea what anything in that note means! Ooo! I wanna shake her—"

"Herschel! Calm down. I *can* read. I'm gonna call her about lunch Saturday—"

"*Buzz!* Wrooong!"

"But—"

"That *invitation* is uppity talk for, 'Come to lunch at my house next Saturday at twelve thirty. Not this Saturday—next Saturday. And don't call—come. Ring the doorbell at exactly twelve thirty, not one second before or after.'"

Glory looked at the note again, silently reading it in Mrs. Porter's Southern accent. The woman could be uptight, but she was the first lady of a huge church, married to a famous minister, and younger than all the church mothers. She was director of the Sunday school and chairwoman of the Eves Women's Auxilliary. She always looked so pretty and elegant. All the girls wanted to look like her. There was no way she was trying to be mean or embarrass Glory.

"Look down there, over in that first cabinet by the door. Pull out that big brown box marked Stuff." Herschel pointed over his shoulder with the wooden spoon.

Glory went to the cabinet and pulled out the box filled with zipped plastic bags of different sizes. She carried the box over to the table and set it down with a loud thud.

"Careful with my goodies, darling." Herschel glanced back at her. "Look around in there and find something in a box—not perfume or anything."

Glory rifled through bags of scarves and hats and perfumes. "Herschel, why do you have all this stuff?"

"Because, darling, people love me! I am constantly showered with gifts. Suitors come from miles around to give me cheap copies of designer originals. See if there's some gloves or hankies in there."

Glory found two boxes of white gloves and a box of white handkerchiefs with an *H* monogram. "So, um, boyfriends gave you all of this, and you keep it in a box in the cabinet?"

Herschel laughed. He tapped the spoon on the pot, set it down on the stove, and moved to help Glory dig through the box.

"Well, no, Glory-Glory. You caught me. I catch them on markdown at the beauty supply. You'd be amazed how many women think they have time to stop at the store after they leave here. I keep all the Sunday-morning essentials." He pulled more items out, sorting some to the left and some to the right. "Ribbons and stockings and gloves, and I can whip up the biggest Mother's Day hat you ever seen with all the feathers and flowers back here. *Voila!* This is perfect." Herschel handed Glory a boxed set of white gloves and a handkerchief with lace trim and black-and-red-ribbon accents.

"Okay..." She turned the box over in her hands. "I hafta wear these?"

"No, silly. This is your hostess gift. You wrap this in white or brown paper—there's white packing paper on the counter—and if you can't tuck it properly, tie it with string. No tape. It has to be easy for her to open in the foyer and then hand off to the maid—"

"But aren't gifts supposed to be personal and thoughtful? I mean this is nice and all, but..." Glory shrugged.

"Of course they are, but this isn't just a gift—it is an answer to her challenge. At some point, she's going to give it back to you as a gift, like she just bought it, and say, 'A lady can never have too many white gloves and hankies.' She thinks you're unsophisticated, common. She's gonna try to prove that you're in way over your head, which you are, but"—Herschel held up a hand, stopping Glory's interruption—"I'm going to equip you as best I can so you won't look like a total... now, don't look at me like that. It wasn't even a year ago you was trying to be pregnant, talking about trapping a teenage boy. Now you trying to marry a preacher man ten years older than you."

Glory hung her head, not bothering to stifle the sigh. Of course, Herschel was right about Malcolm, but she hadn't been trying to trap JT. She placed a hand on her belly and sighed again. As desperately as she'd wanted Barbie Shoes, she'd resigned herself to moving on... as, apparently, JT had done.

Herschel continued, "This gift says, 'I am meeting my social obligations and nothing more. I don't care if you like it, since I will have no way of knowing if you ever use it because it's plain white gloves and hankies—'"

"But it's not plain white. It's got black and red, and isn't black and red together kind of, you know, trampy?"

"'—it's plain white gloves and hankies, you bougie, uppity tramp.'"

Glory tried not to giggle. It wasn't right to joke about the first lady like that, even if Herschel thought she was an enemy. "Herschel, she's not like that. She's always nice to me and all the girls. She used to be a teacher, and she tries to uplift the girls, even Trina. She passes out scholarship stuff and—"

"But now, Glory-Glory, you're messin' with her baby boy. You are no longer a little girl for her to mentor. She thinks you're trying to be the wife of her son and mother of her grandchildren and, one day, first lady of her church. She needs to see if you're good enough." Herschel went back over to the pot and stirred. He took the spoon out and tapped it on the rim.

Whoa... wait... first lady? Glory had forgotten about that. She tried to think of what exactly Mrs. Porter did at the church. She always sat in the third pew on the right side. She wasn't in the choir and didn't play the piano. Somebody said she could play the saxophone, but nobody ever saw her do it. She sometimes worked with the Mary and Martha Young Ladies Circle on being proper Christian young ladies, even though she mostly talked about education and stewardship. She had a powerful voice. She never needed a microphone when she spoke. She dressed like a fashion model, and Glory couldn't remember ever seeing her in the same outfit twice. She carried herself like a queen.

There was no way Glory could ever be a Mrs. Porter. *I'm only seventeen!* JT had once told her all he knew at seventeen was basketball and *Ms. Pac-Man*. All Glory knew was reading and cleaning up. She wasn't trying to be first lady—not even first lady in training. Maybe Herschel was right. Maybe she was in over her head.

"Glory-Glory, am I wasting my breath?" Herschel's voice broke through Glory's thoughts.

"I'm sorry, Herschel. I was just thinking about what you said about being first lady. I never thought about that part. But that's not gonna happen, anyway. It's not like we're getting married for real. I'm still probably gonna break up with him."

"Well, frankly, darling, I think it's too soon for you to be engaged. He's got yo' stuff locked up tight at the time when you should be trying it out." He looked at Glory over his goggles. "Oh, stop blushing. You know what I mean. You're turning eighteen soon. You should be out learning what you like, trying new things, and seeing the world. Heh... here I go, lecturing you again."

He tapped the spoon on the pot again. "You about to spend the next four years acting like you trying to be a wife and limiting your options when you should be exploring them. What if you meet Prince Charming in one of your college classes?"

"Oh." Glory didn't try to hide the smirk. "You mean the guy who rides in on his white horse and rescues me from the bad guy trying to steal my virtue?"

"Okay, fine. A point for Malcolm. Heh, heh, heh. He did take care of you, didn't he?"

"Yeah." Glory shuddered at the memory. "Malcolm probably saved my life. I owe him—"

"Hold up! Please don't tell me you're doing this just because he saved you. Sweetie, bake him a cake. Hell, give him all yo' coochie if you think he earned it. But, honey, you don't owe him the rest of your life." Herschel turned back to the stove. "I'm serious, Glory-Glory. You know I love you like my own, and I will support you, but please take some time and see if your world don't open up. Clear that table and get the molds ready. It's almost time to pour the soap."

GLORY TRIED NOT TO fidget. The high-collared white blouse had too much starch, the light-blue sweater vest was itchy, and the light-blue pleated wool skirt fit just loosely enough that it scraped whenever she moved. Standing in the foyer of the ornate Hyde Park building, Glory was already wishing that the ordeal was over. Though it had not been the worst ten days of her life, the week and a half since the arrival of Anita Porter's invitation had been trying. In explaining the invitation date and the meaning of *call*, her mother had yelled at her only once for talking back and once for being uppity.

Watching the gilded clock high on the wall, Glory didn't dare mention that it was past twelve thirty. Her mother had insisted that 12:35—*fashionably late*—was the correct time, and mentioning the time again or pressing the bell a second earlier would have gained her a slap, and she didn't want to sit across the table from Malcolm's mother with a handprint on her face.

In her mind, Glory went over Herschel's instructions: *Expect strange food. Follow the hostess. Use the outside silverware first. Don't be ashamed to ask.* Such easy instructions, but she was terrified, mostly because Mary was so confident, and Glory was sure her mother was wrong about everything.

Mary Bishop pressed the bell at exactly 12:35. It was immediately answered by a buzzer, allowing them to enter the lobby. The reception desk was unattended, but an open guest book stood propped beside a large feathered pen. Glory paused to sign it, but her mother grabbed her arm and pulled her into the elevator, where black bars on the left and right walls had only names, no numbers. Glory pressed the top bar marked Porter.

Dials over the front and back doors indicated they were going up to the ninth floor. When the car stopped, the back doors opened onto a rich wood-paneled lobby not as large but just as grand as the first floor. Glory imagined it was as big as her whole apartment.

Before them was a set of double doors. Mary Bishop marched forward and rapped on the door with the lion-headed brass knocker. She turned and gave what she probably thought was a reassuring nod. The left door was immediately opened by a tall dark woman in a light-blue maid's uniform—the same shade of blue as Glory's outfit.

Glory sighed. *Strike one.*

"Mrs. Beyers, is that our guests?" a voice called from somewhere inside.

"I don't know, ma'am," the woman answered. "Weren't our guests due to arrive some time ago?"

Strike two.

The right door was thrown open, and Mrs. Porter appeared. Even in her embarrassment, Glory couldn't help but smile. The petite woman glowed in the gauzy white dress with wide black straps and a black ribbon belt with tiny red rosettes. Her long brown hair fell loosely around her shoulders. *She looks just like a light-brown white lady.*

"Now, Mrs. Beyers, don't be so harsh. They're fashionably late, a forgivable sin of modern times. Ladies, do come in."

They followed her into the wide foyer, the first lady's heels clicking on the white marble floor.

"Mrs. Beyers, this is Mary Bishop and her daughter, Gloria. Mary, Gloria, this is our housekeeper, Mrs. Beyers." Anita Porter's accent reminded Glory of a perfect Southern belle, her voice like a song, even if she did get Glory's name wrong. Glory sensed her mother about to correct their hostess, but Mrs. Porter continued speaking while walking away.

"I'll try to save the artichokes while you seat our guests. Mrs. Beyers, little Gloria here is affianced to our dear Malcolm. Isn't that wonderful?"

"Is that a fact?" The older woman smiled at Glory.

"Yes, ma'am," Glory said to the smile that seemed to hold only amusement at her expense.

"Well, just bless yo' heart, Gloria. Bless yo' little heart. Mary, Gloria, follow me."

Glory felt her mother's hand on her shoulder, holding her in place. "The child's name is Glory."

"Of course it is. Right this way." The housekeeper didn't look back, and after a moment's hesitation, Glory and her mother followed.

Walking from the foyer, Glory wished Mrs. Beyers would describe the rooms. She guessed one was the living room, but then they passed a smaller living room and walked right past what was obviously the dining room. They stopped in a sunny room with a grand piano. A small table had been set for three, with what Glory assumed were artichokes. There was no silverware. Mrs. Porter stood waiting beside the table.

"We're going to lunch here in the conservatory, and then we'll take dessert in the library." Mrs. Porter belonged in this room. The tall windows with flowing curtains matched her dress. The pecan floors matched her hair, and the tan wallpaper matched her skin. Even the green in the plants offset her eyes. But now Glory was on guard. Even if Mrs. Porter seemed like an angel, she wasn't so sure about Mrs. Beyers.

"I bought you something, Mrs. Porter." Glory held out the package and took a step forward. "Thank you for inviting us." She said it exactly as Herschel told her, keeping her head up, looking Malcolm's mother in the eye, and remembering to smile.

"Why, thank you, dear. How thoughtful. Your mother helped you?" Mrs. Porter unfolded the wrapper, obviously impressed. "So neatly wrapped."

"No, ma'am. I just know a lady can never have too many nice gloves and hankies." Glory smiled again. She felt her mother's hand lightly pat her shoulder. *Thank you, Herschel!*

Mrs. Porter nodded and handed the box to Mrs. Beyers. "Please put this on my vanity. Shall we dine, ladies?"

Seated in front of the strange food, Glory bowed her head while the first lady said grace. She looked at the greenish thing on her small plate and the three tiny bowls. One obviously held butter, but she didn't recognize the contents of the other two—a fourth, slightly larger, empty bowl, and finally, what she knew was a finger bowl with a lemon slice for cleaning her hands. *Watch the hostess.*

"Is there a problem, Mary?" Mrs. Porter tore off a bottom petal from the artichoke and dipped it into one of the sauces. "The beauty of artichokes is that you can enjoy them hot or cold." She placed the petal between her teeth and pulled. "Mmm. Delicious!"

Glory mimicked everything Mrs. Porter did. The hard outer petal felt weird against her teeth, but then a smooth, warm, soft, buttery goodness inside made Glory wonder what other foods she was missing in her life.

"Nita, you know we don't eat no mess like this." Mary tapped the hard vegetable on her plate.

"Well, Gloria seems to be an old hand at it."

"Her name—"

"Please try it, Ma. You'll love it. I promise." Glory averted her eyes from her mother's glare, silently begging forgiveness. She knew there would be trouble for interrupting, but a slip of the tongue wasn't important enough to fight about. She was sure it wasn't deliberate. She met Mrs. Porter's eyes. *Is that pity?*

"So, where did you learn to eat artichokes, dear?"

Glory blushed. *What would Herschel do?* "From watching you just now, ma'am. At church, you always tell us to pay attention and learn from the world around us, so I just did what you did."

Glory relaxed. Mrs. Porter's smile and nod were just a little warmer this time. Mary, however, scowled at Glory and pushed her plate away. Glory prayed her mother wouldn't see a demon in her.

Mrs. Beyers appeared and took away the artichoke plates, replacing them with small bowls covered with cheese and a small plate of bread and butter with herbs. Glory touched the bowl and was surprised to find it ice-cold. She glanced over at her mother to see her watching their hostess for instruction.

"I decided to go with cold and spicy. It's one of Malcolm's favorites."

Glory pressed her spoon through the blanket of shredded cheese into the bowl of tomatoes and vegetables. It looked like regular vegetable soup, but Mrs. Porter's expectant smile and Mrs. Beyers's smirk made Glory pause. She stopped and buttered a piece of bread as her hostess had done and took a bite. Mrs. Porter nodded in approval. The spoonful of soup was cold, like a delicious spicy mouthful of the best Cajun vegetable she'd ever tasted. Then came the burn. It made her eyes water, but the cold and the cheese soothed... but the burn... but it was delicious... but it hurt...

Glory heard a voice telling her to swallow and eat the bread. After catching her breath, she used her napkin to wipe her brow and dab her tears and then dug in for another bite. She looked up to see Mrs. Porter nodding approval and Mrs. Beyers placing a sandwich in front of her mother.

THE LIBRARY WAS ALMOST the exact opposite of the conservatory. High bookshelves of deep mahogany covered three walls, and the floor-to-ceiling windows on the fourth wall were hung with heavy burgundy drapes. A ladder on a brass rail ran along the bookshelves to allow access to the highest books. A large old Bible lay open on a podium in a corner. On a marble stand in another corner stood a globe. A table off to the side was covered with several maps, and more were rolled up in a stand beside the table. Looking around, Glory decided this was the most beautiful room she'd ever seen. She wandered away from her mother and her hostess, entranced by all the books.

"Glory! Get over here and sit down! Stop being rude."

"Mary, leave her alone. Let the child explore. It's just books. Children need knowledge of the world. So, how are things in the choir?"

Glory let their voices fade away and wandered. She expected to find religious texts from all over the world, and she wasn't disappointed. There were entire shelves of Islam and Hinduism and Buddhism as well as Sikh and Zoroastrianism and religions she'd never heard of. She was shocked at some of the books in the fiction section, and looking up, she guessed what she might find if she climbed that ladder. She glanced over at the two women sitting, sipping iced tea: one who loved books and education and one who feared both of those things. What would her mother say if she knew what was in these books? Glory moved to join them so as not to draw their attention, lest Mrs. Porter misspeak her name again.

"So, Gloria," Mrs Porter began, pouring her a glass of tea. Her mother cleared her throat but said nothing. "What are your plans for the future? To what schools have you applied?"

Glory took a deep breath. She and Herschel had rehearsed this. *Tell the truth. No shame in not knowing. The plan is to learn.* "Well, ma'am, I haven't really made plans yet. I'm thinking of going to Loop for my first two years while I see what really interests me."

"Loop Junior College? Downtown? I see." Mrs. Porter sipped quietly. Her eyes moved between Glory and her mother. "So you haven't applied to any universities? Did you apply for any scholarships through the church?"

"No, ma'am," Glory said.

Mrs. Porter was looking at her mother, and Mary was looking at Glory. "I only just now started looking at universities, but I don't really know about the scholarships, especially since I haven't decided on a major. I'm leaning toward something that will help people or maybe lead to missionary work."

Mary nodded approval and sipped her tea. Glory pretended not to see Mrs. Porter roll her eyes.

"Well, *Gloria*," Mrs. Porter said while looking at Mary, and Glory realized, this time, that Mrs. Porter had not misspoken. "My son is quite taken with you, but I know so little about you. You're still in high school. What's your favorite subject?"

This is the "piece of work" Herschel was talking about. Glory didn't know what was going on, but she knew it was about more than her and Malcolm. Her mother stiffened in her chair and put down her glass.

"My favorite class is gym," Glory said a little faster and a little louder than she'd intended. Both women turned and looked at her. Glory dropped her eyes. Though she actually hated gym, it had seemed the only safe answer. If she'd said math, Mrs. Porter might have asked her a math question, and there'd be no way she could answer correctly. If she'd said science, social studies, or literature, there'd be no way she could answer a question in front of her mother.

"Did you like your language classes? What language did you take? *Hablas español? Sprechen Sie Deutsch? Parlez-vous français?*"

Glory shook her head.

"I see. Of all the classes you could take, of all the subjects you could explore, what you enjoy most is *gym*."

Glory tried to keep her head up. There was no need to answer because it wasn't a question. It was a statement directed at her mother. Glory wondered if tornados ever struck in January.

"Well, tell me... *Gloria*... what do you like to read? You seem very interested in our library. I'll have Malcolm give you a key so you can visit as often as you like. The classics? What have you read?"

And just like that, Glory understood being caught between the devil and the deep blue sea. This woman challenging her only wanted the person who was best for her son, and Glory knew that so far, she didn't measure up. Answering honestly might change that, but it would also show her mother that she was possessed by the demons of worldly knowledge.

Glory prayed the few books her mother knew about would be enough. "I like Zora Neale Hurston," she finally answered.

"Really?" Mrs. Porter asked, clearly impressed. "Which of her works have you read?"

And then Mary chimed in. "She's only read that one Malcolm gave her for Christmas. And he gave her something else about a lion. Those the only books I let her read. I want to keep her mind pure and clean for the Lord."

"So you haven't read any books before this year?" Mrs. Porter asked.

"I mostly read the Bible, ma'am," Glory answered. "That's really about all." She tried to sip her tea but put the glass down. She couldn't look at Mrs. Porter or at her mother's satisfied smirk.

"Oh, come now! In four years of high school, the only book you've read is the Bible and a couple of books Malcolm just gave you? How did you pass your English classes?"

"I got excused or just used different versions of the Bible." Glory struggled to keep her voice above a whisper. She turned to face her mother as she spoke, knowing Mary would see her humiliation only as godly humility.

"Mary, is this true?"

Glory cringed at the shock in Mrs. Porter's voice.

"This child has gone years without reading a book other than the Bible? Through school without reading a book?" Mrs. Porter was now on her feet. The polite Southern belle with the sing-song voice was gone. "Gloria, when did you last read a real book? Eighth grade, seventh grade? Did you read then? Mark Twain? Judy Blume? Laura Ingalls Wilder? Dr. Seuss? The encyclopedia?"

Glory kept her head down, not caring that tears were falling. Then she felt a soft hand on her shoulder and a compassionate voice in her ear. "Sweetie, did your daddy at least read to you? Did anybody care about your education?"

"This child goes to the best school in the city and does just fine without all that worldly mess!" Mary Bishop's voice dripped with righteous indignation. "She's gon' make a good, godly wife and mother using what she learned from the Bible. She don't get that from those books you talking about. Pushing all that worldly stuff just opens kids up to evil. Satan is not gon' have this child."

Mrs. Porter stared at Mary for a moment then shook her head and handed Glory a tissue. "Well, have you and Malcolm set a wedding date?"

"No, ma'am." Glory sniffled, dabbing at her eyes and nose. "We want to wait until after I finish college."

She heard her mother's triumphant "harrumph" but didn't look up.

"Well, thank God. At least you're not pregnant." Mrs. Porter leaned back in her chair, fanning herself with a napkin.

"Anita Porter, I don't care if you are first lady." Mary Bishop was on her feet now. "You will not sit here and call my child a whore! I raised this child to be a good, God-fearing young lady—"

"But what you got is a dumb, mama-fearing little girl who hasn't read *The Cat in the Hat* and is not woman enough for my son." Mrs. Porter stomped around the room. "Hell, she can't even stand up and say her own name!"

"I raised her to be humble and in godly submission!"

"You raised her weak and dependent!" She turned again to Glory. "Gloria, do you have a bank account?"

Glory shook her head. *Herschel, how did this happen?*

Mrs. Porter whirled on Mary. "See? How can she run my son's house if she can't balance a checkbook?"

"The man is the head! He runs the house. A woman's place is—"

"Helpmeet! Have you ever actually read the Bible? The wife helps and advises. How can an uneducated woman advise her husband? My son loves your daughter, and you've made her a burden to him. You have deprived her of an education and told her being stupid is good enough. Does she even know what a checkbook is?"

Glory sat quietly, listening to the women argue. She could allay Mrs. Porter's fears and admit to loving the fruit of the tree of knowledge and communing with the devil... proving herself deceptive and ungodly. Or she could stay silent, and maybe Mrs. Porter would convince Malcolm to move on to somebody more worthy.

Glory didn't know how long the women argued. They were an immovable object and an irrational force. Both absolutely certain they were right. They went back and forth as if she wasn't even in the room.

"And when my daughter is first lady, we'll show you—"

"We? Oh, I get it. Well, I guess... forcing your child into marriage to somebody ten years older than her while she's still practically in diapers is as close to first lady as you'll ever get!"

"Mama, can we go, please?" Glory knew she'd hear about the rude interruption, but this needed to stop. She stood up and stepped between the two women, facing Mrs. Porter, praying she would understand. "Mrs. Porter." Glory quickly glanced around the room. "*Ego multos codices legi. Nominis mei Gloria.*"

Mrs. Porter froze. Her eyebrow twitched, and then she gave a subtle nod.

"What did you just say?" Mary demanded. "What was that?"

"It was Latin, Mama. I had to take a language sophomore year, remember? You said Latin was okay because it was spoken in the time of the Bible." *Please understand, Mrs. Porter. Please understand... please, please, please!*

"Ye-es." Mrs. Porter's sing-song drawl was back. "She said, 'I enjoyed the cold soup. My name is Glory.'"

"See," Mary said. "My child is smart, and she learned it from the Bible. Ha!"

Chapter 25

February 1984

"Have you heard anything I said, Glory-Glory?"

"Not really," Glory answered, turning her attention back to her friend and stirring her lukewarm tea. "I was looking at the hotel across the street. It looks like something from an old movie."

"The Toledo?" Herschel snorted. "Back in the day, it was a gangster hotel. Now it's just a flophouse for junkies and hookers."

"Oh." Glory looked up as the waitress brought their food.

Somewhere, a glass broke, and the old lady at the cash register laughed. O'Reilly's restaurant was not busy this freezing February afternoon as Glory and Herschel relaxed after their Saturday morning deliveries. Glory smiled at Jimmy, the cute busboy wiping a nearby table. As she passed him back by the restrooms, he'd winked at her and said, "Smile, chica." She didn't know what it meant, but it felt like a compliment. A few months before, Glory had been surprised and terrified to find herself on the West Side, the part of town where bad people came from, but now she spoke to strangers and smiled at busboys, and the West Side felt like anywhere else in the city.

"You know, darling," Herschel said, digging into his french fries, "running away to Sodom and Gomorrah might not be a bad idea. I mean, leaving your family and friends and moving in with a bunch of junkies and hookers has to be easier than just taking off the ring and

317

giving it back, right? Probably getting tired of that whole Michael Jackson look anyway, too, huh?"

Glory glanced down at the slightly dingy white glove she wore on her left hand to hide her engagement ring. After almost losing the ring down the bathroom drain and convincing her mother she'd taken it off to protect it from soap, she didn't dare take it off again. At school, only Tressa and Christy knew why she wore the glove. She allowed Quentin to feed the high school rumor mills with whatever wild stories he liked. She'd been engaged to Malcolm Porter for more than a month and still hadn't been able to break up with him or even call off the engagement. She was preparing to go to a real college, and life was almost perfect, except that she was expected to get married in a few years.

"I'm not running away." Glory sighed. "I was just wondering about the hotel. It looks like it should be in a black-and-white movie, with the little lightbulbs and the neon on the sign. And I'm sure it's not Sodom and Gomorrah. It can't be any worse than the places up and down Stony Island Avenue." Glory started on her usual grilled cheese sandwich.

She didn't feel like hearing another lecture from Herschel—or anybody else—about Malcolm. Her mother had, so far, kept her promise to keep the engagement a secret but talked about her future son-in-law constantly, often reminding Glory of her impending position as first lady of the biggest church on the South Side. And at school, Tressa and Christy never let up about the fairy-tale-princess thing. Glory took her annoyance out on her french fries, smashing them into the puddle of ketchup on her plate.

She was grateful for her short schedule at school, because the three free periods after her last class let her get all of her homework done early, which was good since Malcolm had made himself the center of her universe. On Sundays, Mary made big, old-fashioned dinners and insisted Glory wait on Malcolm like a proper, godly woman. Mondays, Malcolm had her at the mission, helping kids with homework, serving dinner in the dining room, or corralling toddlers in the nursery and then sitting in the front row during church service, usually holding Stella's newborn or one of the other babies. Tuesdays and Wednesdays, Malcolm arrived at school early with a hot meal, and they visited colleges up to an hour away. On Thursdays, Fridays, and Saturdays, he let her go to work at the salon because his church and mission duties kept him out too late, but he was at her door every weekday morning at five forty-five to drive her to school, and the waitresses at the Red Apple restaurant always had their order ready within minutes. If Glory had actually been ready to be a godly wife, her life would have been perfect.

But Sunday dinners were too much for three people, and Glory felt that the small TV Malcolm sometimes brought with him was extremely disrespectful to her mother's home. On Mondays at the mission, while she appreciated that Tutu called her "daughter," his reminders to everyone that "she belongs to Brother Malcolm" made her uncomfortable.

She once stood in stunned silence when he interrupted a conversation by shooing away a couple of young volunteers. "Listen carefully, daughter," Tutu hissed, the usual magic gone from his voice. "You belong to Malcolm. You will not humiliate him by involving yourself with this riffraff. He is a great man, and you will stand properly by his side, daughter, or you will go away!" Glory wasn't sure whether it was a threat or an invitation to leave. She never mentioned the incident to Malcolm, but when she told her friends, Tressa sang a prayer, and Christy offered to come and shake the old man silly.

Glory smiled at the busboy as he cleared their dishes and winked at her again.

"Hey, chica. That apple pie looks too hot."

Glory giggled as he moved away after placing a small dish of ice cream in front of her.

Herschel laughed and shook his head. "You know, Miss Femme Fatale, you're not weak at all. If you used that power for evil, you'd be rich! Ah, ha, ha, ha!"

Glory couldn't help but laugh, too, when Herschel threw his head back and laughed just like the man in the 7-Up commercials.

LEAVING THE WEST SIDE, Glory watched the people on the now-familiar streets. What Malcolm had told her on the roof that day—the crime and filth on the West Side, no love and no peace, nothing good—was wrong. Glory saw people holding hands and walking, stores decorated in red and white for Valentine's Day, and couples cuddled against the cold at bus stops. Too bad Malcolm only saw evil when he visited this part of Chicago. Glory knew he only wanted to protect her, but she decided to keep these trips secret a little longer.

Heading south on Halsted Street, they passed through University of Illinois Circle Campus, one of the schools she'd toured with Malcolm. On their college visits, she tried to focus on the campuses, but the people always caught her attention, especially the groups of students rushing around, laughing and talking. Months before, Glory wouldn't have believed she belonged among the smiling coeds, couldn't have imagined she'd even have a chance, but now she saw herself strolling with friends, waiting for a bus, maybe even holding the arm of a boy. She tried to push away thoughts of other boys when she was with Malcolm... sometimes.

But on Thursday nights, Glory no longer mostly avoided the girly party at the salon. She still read books, but sometimes she had wine coolers and danced around the shop and sang worldly songs and even let Herschel's clients give her makeovers. She tried on wigs and sparkly makeup and stood still while they draped her in gold lamé to be Glorious or draped her in red velour to be Femme Fatale, but at the end of the night, Glory would scrub her face clean and bind her hair and go back to being Church Girl again.

LATE SATURDAY AFTERNOONS, the salon was always over-booked. Following Herschel in through the back door, Glory always found it ironic that the gospel music and howling church ladies getting ready for the Lord's day sounded exactly like the worldly music and howling men getting ready for the weekend on Thursday nights. Getting right to work, Glory would move a load of wet towels to a dryer, started another load, and looked around the back room. With the overflowing crowd out in the shop and no time for courtesy, the hairdressers just tossed things into the back room—towels, bottles, clothes, anything—and Glory's job was to sort it and clean it up. Saturday was the only day Glory felt she truly worked. After starting the laundry, she'd check the bathrooms and clean the mess that was always there, never understanding how church ladies could be so nasty. Then she'd start clearing the mess in the back room: chip bags, pop cans, lunch trays, and coffee cups. Sometimes she worked around sleeping babies or wrestling children. Once, somebody's great-grandmother napped in a corner. But still, Glory loved her time at the salon.

"SO, Y'ALL THINK I SHOULD make the first move? I know he likes me. I think he's just shy."

"Girl, if a man wants you, he'll ask you, especially on Valentine's Day. Amen?"

"Honey, he's a preacher. He is not shy!"

Carefully stacking warm towels at the wash bowls, Glory tried to ignore the ladies' conversation. The late-Saturday-afternoon crowd was mostly older women and sometimes included her mother. The young lady asking advice was Cheryl Cannon from church, and Glory knew exactly who she was asking about. Glory finished stacking the towels and scurried into the back rooms just as another familiar voice began speaking of the endless virtues of Malcolm Porter. This was going to be a long day.

"You've got a package," Herschel said, looking up from the pile of mail in front of him at his desk.

"Open it for me, please," Glory answered. "It's probably something from Malcolm's mother—something she wants me to wear tomorrow." Nearly every Sunday at church, since that eventful lunch, Glory had received small gifts and notes from the first lady—notes written in Latin that only she and Mother Porter understood. The first had been a pair of lace gloves with yellow rosebuds that perfectly matched her sweater, and a note: "*Inicienda est quod ridiculum.*" Glory had gone into the ladies' room, removed the gauze bandage from her left ring finger that she didn't think at all ridiculous, and slipped on the gloves. Other times, Mother Porter had sent gold pins, hair clips, and a small string of pearls.

"I almost opened it before I saw your name on it," Herschel said, tearing into the envelope. "It just says, 'Miss Glory, Care of Herschel's Salon.'"

Glory froze midstride, nearly dropping the trash bags she carried. *Miss Glory? After more than six months, has JT finally written? And why send it here?* "Oh? That doesn't sound like Mother Porter. Who's it from?"

Glory walked to the large trash can near the door, careful to remain calm. He'd made her wait this long. She was not about to rush for him now.

"Well, I'll be damned, Glory-Glory! Who is James Mattley?"

"Who?" Glory asked, surprised at the stabbing disappointment. "I don't know." She put down the trash and moved to Herschel's desk.

"Well, darling, he certainly knows you!" Herschel laughed, holding up a plastic-covered sheet of paper.

Glory gaped at the smiling image of Weak Femme Fatale reclining on the bright-orange cushion atop the pile of goodies.

"Is this supposed to be me up here?" Herschel tapped a scowling face in the corner of the page. "I might consider a wearing a goatee this Halloween! Girl, this is beautiful!"

Herschel carefully opened the plastic sleeve and removed three folded sheets of paper.

"Looks like he sent you a few copies. Can I keep one?" Herschel asked, opening a sheet and laying it out on his desk. "Girl, this is amazing! Your superpower making men give you stuff..." He moved his finger over the two inside pages then turned to the back page. "And here you are defeating the villain on the train with a giant pound cake. He's got your cheeks and your big, pretty eyes just right. Even those bracelets..."

"It's the boy I met on the train to Mississippi," Glory said, slowly finding her voice. "I don't know how he found me. Is there a note?" She dug into the cardboard envelope and pulled out a smaller white envelope decorated with cartoon hearts on the flap, her first real valentine in years. Not even JT had sent her a real valentine since they were kids.

Glory smiled and practiced her quietest evil laugh when she saw the black-and-white greeting card with the shiny color photo of an orange drink with a fruity umbrella.

Dear Glory,

I really hope this gets to you. I'm not a crazy stalker or anything like that. I forgot to give you back your lotion, and there's an address on the tube. You said the mad scientist was your best friend, so I took a chance. It was great meeting you on the train. I saw the limo waiting for you when you got off. Whoever that church guy is, he must be rich. I hope he and your mom work out.

I really did spend the holidays eating pound cake and thinking about you. When I got back to school, I did a few more sketches. My roommate thinks I should sell 'em. What do you think? Are you ready to be a superstar, Church Girl? I sent a few copies in case you want to give one to your mad-scientist friend.

When we were on the train, I didn't ask if you had a boyfriend because I didn't want to know. When I think about kissing you, I really hope you don't have a boyfriend and give me a chance. If you do have one, he's a lucky man. Either way, happy Valentine's Day. Hope to hear from you.

Your not-so-evil villain,
James

"Wow!" Glory handed the card to Herschel. "He wants to be my boyfriend. For real. Like a normal girl!"

"My goodness, he sounds nice." Herschel slipped two of the sheets back into the plastic sleeve. "And he seems to really like you. What are you gonna do? You should ask Malcolm if you can have a boyfriend... at least until the wedding. Oh, your eye rolling is almost perfect now!"

"You know I'm breaking up with Malcolm." Glory placed everything back into the envelope. "After I get accepted somewhere, I'll do it. But, Herschel, I could apply to U of I and go to school with James!" Glory spun around, hugging the envelope to her chest. "I could have a college boyfriend who's an artist."

"Slow down, girl, you've met him once—"

"Twice. At night on the train, then again in the morning, but—"

"You know exactly what I mean. Don't get me wrong. I think you definitely should go away to school... but not just for a boy you barely know. If you get the money, I'll drive you there myself. I'll drive you all the way to Alaska—I promise I will."

"Oh my God! This is what normal girls have. And he's so cute! I'm gonna write him back today!"

"Slow down, darling. You're still engaged," Herschel cautioned. "Don't be messy. You need to clean up this first thing before you think about another one."

Glory returned to her work, feeling a little deflated.

"I know. But Malcolm is so... much." There was no way she'd tell Herschel she couldn't break up with Malcolm because she was still a little scared to be without him or that she would stay with him until she went to college so she could keep the life she'd come to enjoy. Yes, she'd write to James and be his girlfriend and apply to his school and get accepted, and if she could get a trip to U of I, she'd visit him... but she'd *also* stay with Malcolm just a little while longer.

"HEY, GLORY."

Glory looked up from the letter she was almost finished writing and sighed as gray-haired fingers placed a can of orange pop on the table in front of her.

"Don't worry. I ain't gon' mess wit' you." The old man leaned on the push broom. "I be just playing anyway." He nodded toward the pop can.

"Hi, Mr. Harris," Glory mumbled. It was her first time in the bookstore since Christmas, and she tried to remember why she thought it was a good idea to come back.

"You and them other two, y'all seem like good girls. Why you wit' him?"

Glory scowled. "I don't know what you mean. Malcolm goes to my church—"

"Hmph. You ain't dumb, girl. He ain't nice, an' you know it." Mr. Harris quickly held up both hands. "I ain't tryin' to start nothin'. I just don't get it. You ain't gotta go tellin' him I'm messin' wit' you." He grabbed his broom and went back to his sweeping.

"Mr. Harris, wait!" Glory called out to him. "When you knew him... when he was younger... what did he do?"

The old man in the dingy white apron stopped and turned back to face her. "Ain't my place to say. Maybe he changed. Maybe he take good care of you. You just watch yourself." He turned back to his work as Tressa and Christy approached. "Afternoon, ladies." He tipped an invisible hat and headed back toward the front of the store.

"Malcolm really did a number on him, huh?" Tressa said, taking her seat in the booth. "He was actually polite."

"Quentin's started a rumor that you're wearing the one glove because you broke that counter and cut your hand," Christy said. "I'm telling everybody I was there and saw you do it."

The girls looked up again as Mr. Harris appeared at their table, carrying a tray. "This yo' order, right? Three burgers, no onions, two fries, mild sauce?"

"Um, yes, sir," Glory said.

"Here ya go." He placed the cardboard trays on the table. "Y'all good girls. Don't forget what I said. Hear?" He pulled three chocolate bars from his apron pocket and dropped them on the table. "Early Valentine present. Don't mean nothin' bad. Y'all be good."

Glory and her friends stared as he walked away.

"Glory?"

"Yes, Tee?"

"What exactly did Malcolm do to him?"

"He only talked to him. Honest. I was right there. But anyway"—Glory reached for her french fries—"remember that boy I met on the train?"

WALKING THROUGH THE crowded hallway, Glory smiled back at the people who smiled at her. When somebody bumped her, she said, "Oops," and kept on walking. When the sophomore with the three hairs on his chin tried to return the pen he'd borrowed, she squeezed his arm and told him to keep it.

Nearing her locker, Glory slowed down and tried not to see Quentin and Paula kissing goodbye. She cleared her throat, opening her locker as Paula giggled and skipped away. Glory pretended not to notice that Quentin's adorable blush was as red as his hair and wondered why she felt so annoyed when she saw him and Paula together like that.

"So people really think you beat up the dirty old man. They said today he was kissing your—"

"Hey, Quentin, are you giving Paula carnations for Valentine's Day tomorrow?" Glory didn't feel like hearing the latest rumors.

"Oh, I got her a bunch of stuff. A giant stuffed kitten—hmmm, maybe it's a cat 'cause it's really big—and a chocolate heart filled with chocolate hearts..."

Glory listened to Quentin's list as she sorted through her backpack. She wasn't really *that* bothered about Quentin and Paula because she knew Malcolm had something special planned, and she would have a normal boyfriend soon anyway—secret, but still normal.

"Hey, wanna see something cool?" She pulled the plastic sleeve from her backpack and handed it to Quentin. "It's an uncirculated first issue."

"Yeah, right," he scoffed. "First issue of what?"

Glory watched Quentin's face as he looked at the packet in his hand then back up at her. He carefully opened the sleeve and pulled out a folded sheet of the first issue of *Weak Femme Fatale*. He flipped through it, looking back and forth between Glory and the pages before slowly returning it to the sleeve, a bemused smile on his face.

"Well?" Glory said. "Say something. Is it that bad?"

"Um... where'd you get it?" he asked, turning his attention back to things in his locker. "It's cool."

"That's all?" Glory didn't hide her disappointment. "I thought you'd like it. I was gonna let you have this one."

"That's cool." Quentin held out his hand but kept looking into his locker. "I'll add it to my collection. It might be worth something one day."

"Uh, yeah," Glory said, handing it back to him and closing her locker. That was disappointing. At least her girlfriends had liked it.

"Okay, okay, okay! Oh my God! *Okay!*"

Glory looked around.

Quentin's head was buried deep inside his locker, his voice muffled. "Damn! I always knew you were hiding special powers, but this is..."

Glory tapped her friend's back. "Quentin, your nerd is showing. Please come out."

"I can't. I'm hyperventilating... or having an asthma attack... or something."

"No, you're not. I can hear you talking and breathing just fine."

Quentin pulled his head out of his locker. "Glory, this is awesome." He balanced the packet in his open palms. "Who did it? Who is this guy?"

"Somebody I met over Christmas." Glory smiled. "He's pretty good, huh?"

"Yeah, and he knows your secret identity. Wow. You're just so... wow." Quentin lowered his voice, looked in Glory's eyes, blushed, and looked away. "Uh, you know, me and Paula... I mean, we really aren't that... I always kinda—"

"C'mon, man!" Glory slapped her friend's arm, causing him to fumble and nearly drop the packet. She ignored his annoyed glare. "It's not *that* great. I just thought you might like it."

The bell rang, and the crowd started thinning. Glory watched Quentin's face switch from an almost-serious look back to the smile of her playful old friend. He carefully placed the packet in his notebook and softly punched her in the shoulder.

"Weak Femme Fatale, huh?"

Glory turned dramatically away, wishing her gold coat was longer and made a swishing sound. "Shhh... don't tell anybody, or I'll steal all your goodies."

"Ya' know what?" Quentin called after her. "I'm gonna leave that one alone!"

Heading up the stairs to the school library, Glory couldn't help smiling. She was normal. Well, okay, being engaged to Malcolm wasn't quite normal, but she had friends and a job and would soon go to college and would have a boyfriend in college and even had a sort of normal boy who kind of liked her but was too scared to say it. She did feel a twinge of guilt about Quentin. *Is the Jezebel spirit making me so happy to have all this attention? Am I really letting the devil cloud my mind and convince me to use Malcolm to get what I want?* Glory smiled again. No. God wanted her to be happy, and she was grateful. Glory said a prayer of thanksgiving for the blessings of a normal life.

Chapter 26

Pulling the blanket tighter around herself, Glory felt the sting and burn of her tattered T-shirt rubbing against thick, open welts. She tried not to move lest the deep cuts on her arm, legs, and back bleed again.

Demons of doubt had made her question God's will.

What if God sent somebody else for me?

Demons of disrespect had loosened her tongue and caused her to speak against Malcolm.

Mama, he's too old for me! I don't wanna marry him!

Demons of worldliness had made her forget her place, made her ungrateful, made her argue.

Why can't I be normal? I hate this!

Demons of rebellion had made her run and resist the purging, but the Lord had tripped her, and she fell. When her head hit the metal bed frame, there was so, so much blood. She'd called out to Jesus, screamed and cried for Jesus, but demons of confusion clouded her mind, and the room swayed, and she couldn't focus... couldn't look straight into her mother's eyes... and the purging went on and on and on.

And then she drifted off to sleep while her mother pressed the pillow over her face and watched to see if God would take her this time.

PULLED FROM DREAMLESS sleep, gasping, pushing the pillow away from her face, Glory stretched and felt the splitting and stinging of welts. Sitting up, her whole body hurt, and a headache thundered and burned in her skull. Moving her feet to the floor, she felt the dried blood on her back and left side crack. Her bedside clock showed 8:34 p.m. When she stood, the room swayed. She steadied herself against her dresser, then the door frame, and then the wall, and lurched painfully down the hall to the bathroom. *I need aspirin.* Holding the sink, Glory turned on the light and faced the mirror.

There was no time for screaming, no time to waste on tears or prideful vanity. With shaking hands, Glory splashed her face and used a warm washcloth to carefully clean the dried blood from the matted spot at the front of her hair where she'd hit her head. She applied ointment and bandages to the open welts and bleeding cuts she could reach.

Her mother wasn't home. No doubt, she was at church for Bible study, praying for Glory's soul.

"But, I swear, I'll give you back to God fo' I let the devil have you."

Glory made her way to the kitchen, each footstep jarring her whole body. Though she hated the taste, sage was supposed to be good for headaches. Glory used the tea to wash down three aspirin tablets, the honey soothing her burning throat.

Her mother's words resounded in her head. "Whore of Babylon!"

How could I have been so careless, leaving that stuff in my book bag?
"Filthy Jezebel!"
How could I be so ungrateful, shaming Malcolm and plotting against him after all he did for me?
"Demons of lies and deceit! I bind you in the name of Jesus!"
How could I sin against Malcolm and God?
"I'll give you back to God fo' I let the devil have you."
How could I think I was a normal girl?

She looked up at the sunburst-shaped clock on the wall above the long-dead television set. The motion made her head and neck hurt. It was a little after nine o'clock. Mary would be home by ten. Glory slowly made her way over to a plastic-covered window. Peeling back a corner of the plastic, she looked out onto Seventy-Fifth Street.

"I'll give you back to God..."

The evening traffic was dying down, headlights shining on the slush-covered street. She laid her forehead and then cheek against the cold glass triangle, careful not to let her hair touch the tape. *Is this really how demons get in, creeping in through uncovered window corners on dark February nights? Is this why there is so much evil in me? Is this what makes me want to turn my back on Malcolm and God?*

"Acting like somethin' got in you. Changing your heart!"

She smoothed the plastic back in place, shutting out the light from the street. Glory pressed her hands over her ears, but her mother's words only grew louder.

"I'll give you back to God... back to God... back to God."

She'd heard those words all of her life. She was tired of those words. Tired of the purgings. Tired of pretending to have demons to satisfy her mother. Tired of calling on Jesus. Tired of gasping for air all the times God didn't take her back. Tired of wondering when he would.

She squeezed her eyes shut, forcing tears at the corners.

Tired of being Church Girl.

Back in her bedroom, Glory pulled on a long brown skirt and a light-green blouse and sweater. Careful not to brush the bandages too much, she tied on a headscarf to hold the gauze near her hairline in place. Herschel always laughed at her in this outfit, saying she looked like a nun. He was always on her side. The mad scientist had been her best friend, big sister, confidant, and hero since she was eleven years old. His salon was her refuge, her sanctuary, her peace. There, it was easy to make plans for a normal life with college and a boyfriend her own age—easy to imagine a life of making her own decisions. She put on her gold coat and paused to look in the hall mirror.

"Don't ever argue with me in front of your mother again. Do you understand me?"

She touched her hand to her cheek. Even though those blows had happened well over a month before, the memory of them still stung.

"God put us together. You don't get to question that."

He had been there when she needed someone.

"There's nowhere you can go that I can't get to you, nowhere that I won't come for you."

Could she imagine life without Malcolm's protection?

SEATED ON THE TELEPHONE bench in the living room, twisting the bracelets on her left arm, Glory willed her thoughts to the immediate issue. Mary would be home in fifteen minutes and would act like nothing happened. She'd talk about Bible study like she hadn't just left her unconscious daughter bleeding with a pillow over her face. She'd want to pray. But when she found Glory gone, Mary would just figure she'd gone to the salon.

Glory stepped out into the hallway. Obviously, the hall had been swept since Christmas, but in a few places, neon-colored Barbie shoes lay wedged between the baseboards and the floorboards, crushed under the feet of the building's residents, including Glory. Down in the foyer, she pushed open the heavy door, fighting the wind.

Outside, the wind was cold, but the sky was clear, and she could see the stars. Just breathing in the crisp night air made Glory feel free. She turned up her collar and headed up Seventy-Fifth Street toward the store with the pay phone.

Acknowledgements

A whole lotta people had a lot to do with helping me tell Glory's story.

My husband Chris, whose love and support and listening and analyzing and encouragement and reminders and cooking and music and much, much more kept me going when I felt like giving up.

Red Adept Publishing, especially Lynn, Jessica, and Sarah for their faith, time, and infinite patience.

Carol DaLuga and Geraldine Cunningham, my sixth- and seventh-grade teachers respectively—the only teachers who actually let me open my imagination and write whatever I wanted.

My "sisters," cousins, and friends: Angela, Cheryl, Jennifer, Rae, Miranda, Jilon, Nicole, Della, and Simone, whose beta reading, critiques, editing, and genuine love and support helped me make sense of Glory's life and get the story told.

My Facebook friends and family who indulged my many questions, especially Rick, Rodney S., Andre, Brandi, Bobby, Joe, Erica, Mike, and Rodney E.

Lindblom Technical High School alumni—especially the class of 1984— for all the references and all the memories.

The creative writing department at UW Madison for guidance and encouragement, especially Christine, Kristin, Laurie, Chris, and Laura.

Hanover Place in Tinley Park: the best writer's hideaway ever!

And last but not least, Jovanda, Joseph, Jeremy, Marcus, and James. The lights of my life and my reasons for living. Thank you for your patience with me. I love you.

About the Author

Growing up, Deborah L. King always wanted to be an author. She published her first short story when she was seven years old. When she's not writing, she can be found enjoying cooking, photography, and watching cartoons and *Star Trek*.

Born and raised in Chicago, Deborah has managed to achieve all her childhood dreams and still lives in the area with her husband and two youngest children. According to her daughter, she has "literally aced her life"!

Read more at deborahlking.com.

About the Publisher

Dear Reader,

We hope you enjoyed this book. Please consider leaving a review on your favorite book site.

Visit https://RedAdeptPublishing.com to see our entire catalogue.

Don't forget to subscribe to our monthly newsletter to be notified of future releases and special sales.